THE
COMMODORE

Books by
Jan de Hartog

The Commodore
Star of Peace
The Trail of the Serpent
The Lamb's War
The Peaceable Kingdom
The Children
The Captain
The Call of the Sea
   including
     The Lost Sea
     The Distant Shore
     A Sailor's Life
The Hospital
The Artist
Waters of the New World
The Inspector
The Spiral Road
A Sailor's Life
The Little Ark
The Distant Shore
The Lost Sea

PLAYS:

William and Mary
The Fourposter
Skipper Next to God
This Time Tomorrow

JAN DE HARTOG

THE COMMODORE

A Novel of the Sea

A Cornelia & Michael Bessie Book

HARPER & ROW, PUBLISHERS, New York
Cambridge, Philadelphia, San Francisco, Washington
London, Mexico City, São Paulo, Singapore, Sydney

Fiction
De Hartog

FIRST EDITION

Designed by Ruth Bornschlegel

Copyedited by Paul Hirschman

This book was set in 11/13 Zapf Book Light by Tapsco, Inc. and
printed and bound by R. R. Donnelley & Sons Company.

Library of Congress Cataloging in Publication Data

De Hartog, Jan, 1914–
  The Commodore.

  "A Cornelia & Michael Bessie book."
  I. Title.
PR6015.A674C6   1986   823'.914   84-48591
ISBN 0-06-039041-7

86 87 88 89 90 RRD 10 9 8 7 6 5 4 3 2 1

RWB

Author's Note

As was *The Captain, The Commodore* is a work of fiction. The international ocean-going tugboat business is a small world; because of my intimate relationship with it over a good many years, some characters, ships and events in this story may appear to have been taken from life.

I wish to state that all persons in this book, all events and all ships are my own invention. Any similarity to existing ships, historical events and real people, alive or dead, is unintentional and accidental.

I am indebted to E. F. Count van Randwijck D.Sc. for his invaluable advice on the stability of ships, to the directors of Smit International Ocean Towage and Salvage Company for their generous hospitality, and to Captains van der Poel and Slotboom of the ocean tugboats *Smit London* and *Zwarte Zee* for the happy hours spent with them on the high seas.

Jan de Hartog

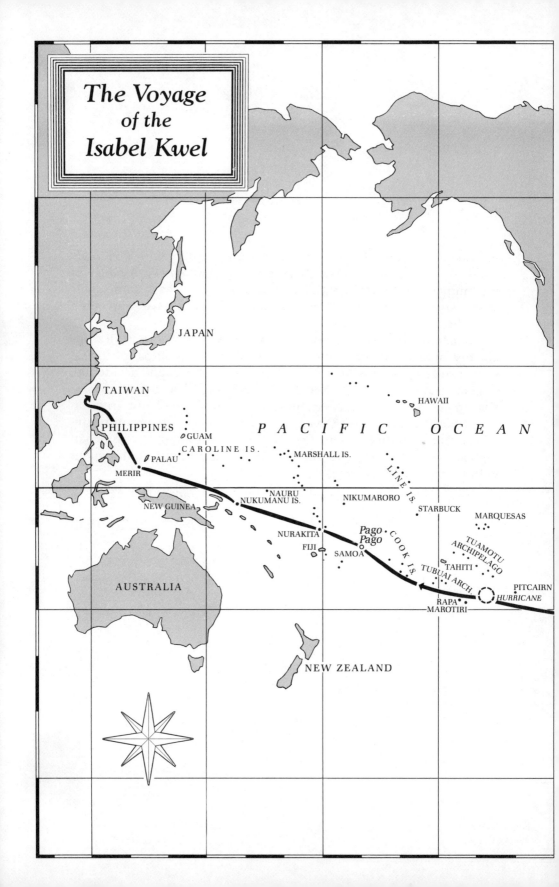

The Voyage
of the
Isabel Kwel

JAPAN

TAIWAN

PHILIPPINES

GUAM

CAROLINE IS.

PALAU

MERIR

NEW GUINEA

NUKUMANU IS.

NAURU

NURAKITA

FIJI

SAMOA

Pago Pago

AUSTRALIA

PACIFIC   OCEAN

HAWAII

MARSHALL IS.

NIKUMARORO

LINE IS.

STARBUCK

MARQUESAS

TUAMOTU ARCHIPELAGO

COOK IS.

TAHITI

TUBUAI ARCH.

RAPA

MAROTIRI

PITCAIRN

HURRICANE

NEW ZEALAND

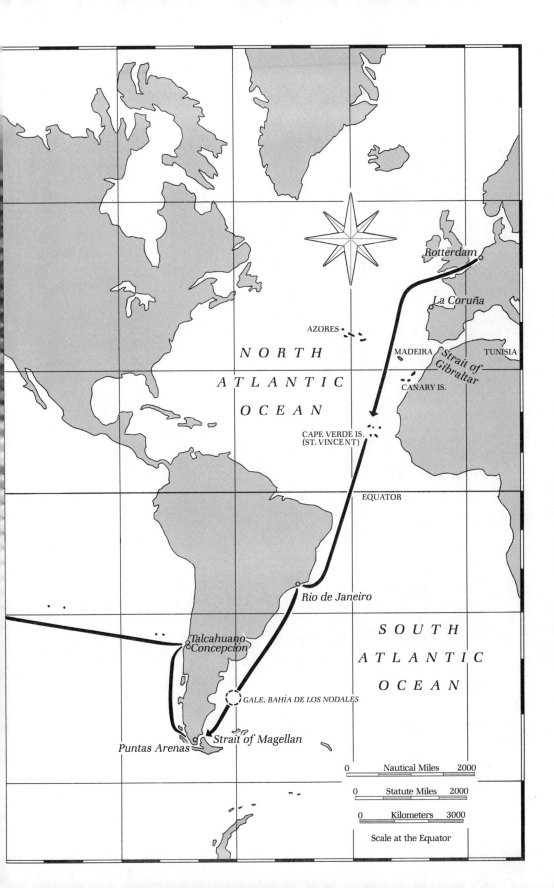

NORTH

ATLANTIC

OCEAN

Rotterdam

La Coruña

AZORES ·

MADEIRA

Strait of
Gibraltar

TUNISIA

CANARY IS.

CAPE VERDE IS.
(ST. VINCENT)

EQUATOR

Rio de Janeiro

SOUTH

ATLANTIC

OCEAN

Talcahuano
Concepción

GALE, BAHÍA DE LOS NODALES

Puntas Arenas   *Strait of Magellan*

0	Nautical Miles	2000
0	Statute Miles	2000
0	Kilometers	3000

Scale at the Equator

Chapter One

1

The call came a few days before Christmas, while my wife, Sylvia, and I were having one of our Darby-and-Joan tiffs, the usual result of our being under pressure. I was decorating the kitchen of our retirement bungalow in the South of France with holly and angel's hair, the radio was bellowing carols, she had sausage rolls and mince pies in the oven and looked apple-cheeked like a Russian doll. We were expecting two sons, one divorced daughter, one daughter-in-law and six grandchildren for the holidays; the tiny house was going to burst at the seams. I was not looking forward to noisy six-year-olds racing around, moody teenagers sprawled on the floor in front of the television, nor to pies, sausage rolls, fruitcake and, God help us, English plum pudding cooked six months beforehand, the stone the builders rejected.

I stood teetering on a wobbly chair, putting up a paper garland and plastic gnomes; Sylvia was running around, flushed and flustered; the radio, turned up to enough decibels for a stadium, bullhorned "Hallelujah!" from Handel's *Messiah*. "If I hear one more 'Hallelujah,' " I said, "I'm going to kick the set."

She said, "Don't talk nonsense," opened the oven door and the smell of Christmas hit me like a blast. "You're turning into a cantankerous old cuss in your old age, Martinus. Why don't you go for a walk with the dog?"

"But you don't *listen* to the damn radio! To you it's just a background noise, like a ship's engine!"

"Go on." She tipped the baking sheet and dumped a load of mince pies onto the rack on the counter. "Take Héloïse. It'll do you both good."

"The last thing I want right now is to go for a walk with that hysterical bitch. She'll hang herself in the junipers with that ridiculous Christmas ribbon."

"See what I mean?" She turned back to the oven. "Ever since you left the sea, you have become very irritable."

"Crap," I said. "I left the sea nine years ago. I'm only irritable at Christmas."

"Out!" She opened the door with her mitt. "And don't use that word in front of your grandchildren."

"Which word? Christmas? I'll be delighted to forget it forever! It's hell. Sheer, unadulterated hell! Whoever invented it deserves to—"

The phone rang.

She gave hard starboard rudder and headed for it. That would be one of her many women friends; the telephone was a perpetual source of excitement to her, of girlish cries and breathless code words like: "No!" . . . "When?" . . . "You don't *mean* it!" Maybe it was not a bad idea to take off for a bit.

I put on my outdoor jacket and approached the bitch under the holly-laden table with the insincere invitation, "Come on, walkie." Then I heard Sylvia say behind me, "It's for you."

It had to be someone from The Cheerleaders, calling an extra carol rehearsal. I was ready to have laryngitis. "Who is it?"

"KITCO," she said, with a steely look in her eye. "Mr. Kwel."

He had called me only once since the day I retired, and that was to invite me to an old captains' reunion eight years ago. "What does he want?"

"Here. Ask him yourself."

I took the phone; the dog crept from under the table and started to whine and wag her rump in front of me.

"Commodore Harinxma?" a girl's voice asked.

"This is he."

"One moment, please; Mr. Arnold for you."

The poodle crouched for a leap onto my lap. "Bugger off," I said.

"Harinxma?" I recognized the imperious voice at the first word.

"Oh, sorry, sir. How are you, sir?"

"Harinxma, how would you like to take one of our ships to Rio de Janeiro as an advisor to the new captain?"

"Excuse me?"

"It's the *Isabel Kwel*. She has been sold to Taiwan and is about to leave with a crew of Chinese. We've been contracted by the new owners to provide a skeleton staff as far as Rio de Janeiro to show the captain and the other officers the ropes. What do you say?"

"But, sir, I've been out of the service for nine years!"

"Come, Harinxma," the imperious voice said with a hint of

impatience, "don't question my competence. When I say you are the right man, that means you *are* the right man. Can you be in my office tomorrow, ten a.m., to talk it over?"

"Tomorrow?"

"No, dammit!" my wife whispered. "Tell him it's Christmas! That we're expecting the family, the grandchildren—"

"Hush!"

"That you are retired! That your wife—"

"*Please* . . . ! Sorry, sir, would you run that past me again?"

"It's simple, Harinxma." The impatience was audible now. "I'm offering you an assignment and asking you to come tomorrow to talk it over. It's for six weeks. You'll be well paid." He mentioned a figure; it was generous indeed.

"I'm flattered, sir, but it's Christmas, we're expecting the family from Holland, it's the only time of year when we're all together—"

"If you're a normal human male, Harinxma, you'll welcome this opportunity. In my time, if anyone had offered me an escape hatch at Christmastime, I would have jumped at it. Diplomacy, man! My God, how long have you been married? Twenty years?"

"Forty . . ."

"Well, there you go. Get yourself to the airport; your plane leaves at five thirty. You'll have a room on arrival at the Schiphol Hilton. Tomorrow morning at nine hundred hours you'll be picked up by limousine, we meet at ten in my office. Don't bring any gear, we'll provide that."

"Don't let him seduce you, the wily bastard!" my wife whispered hotly, as if she had heard every word; she sounded ready to explode. Hallelujah.

"Well? What do you say?"

"I'd like to talk it over with my wife, sir."

"Never mind your wife, man! Make up your own mind for once!" No one had spoken to me like that for a long time. Come to think of it, no one ever had except this old man.

"I'll call you back within the hour, sir."

"Harinxma, you're a fool. You always were, even though it's been a well-kept secret between us. You have ten minutes."

"But I've been gone nine years! I need more than ten minutes to decide to go back to sea!"

Sylvia said bitterly, "So it's back to sea, is it?"

"Hush! . . . What was that, sir?"

"I said nothing, Harinxma," the imperious voice answered. "But if you'd rather rot in the hills in your cottage for two with your wife's dog, I'll have to look elsewhere. Good day." He hung up.

"Well, let's have it," Sylvia said.

I told her what old Kwel had told me, or most of it.

"All right, let's talk about it."

"No, Syl." I went to get my jacket. "I have to think this over first, alone." I opened the door. "Come on, creep."

"The animal's name is Héloïse!" she cried after me.

Once out of the settlement of retirement bungalows and in the open, the dog sprinted off into the heather and I plowed my way to the top of the first hill, where I always sat down to catch my breath after climbing the slope. I gazed at the haze on the distant hills, the blue brushstroke of the Mediterranean on the horizon. Despite the season, it was hot out here; the hills quivered with heat. Birds swooped and planed, following the undulating curves of the land. The air was perfumed with the scent of lavender.

Kwel's offer came as a total surprise. I had put the sea behind me nine years before and never looked back, except for that reunion of old captains, which had cured me entirely after I saw old Manders, one of the great captains of his day, surreptitiously stuff a handful of cigars into his coat pocket. That had done it for me; no lingering over the past, no old man's nostalgia for the sea. I had deliberately started a new life which had nothing to do with ships. I had moved out of Holland and bought a charming little house in the South of France, in a new development especially geared to the needs of retired executives and their wives. I began by taking up carpentry as a hobby, but it bored me; then I stumbled onto a fascinating subject; the third Roman invasion of Britain, after the barbarian conspiracy of A.D. 367. The Romans had taken five Numeri across the Channel from France in barges especially built for the occasion, towed by galleys of three hundred oars each, the first deep-sea towing job in recorded history. The general who had executed the conquest with too few men, too little money and too few ships, purely by guile, wisdom, experience and the un-Roman practice of pardoning everybody, had been sixty-five years old. I read up on him, collected every fact I could find; Sylvia and I made expeditions into the English countryside to trace forts he had built and roads he had constructed; I became so involved with General Theodosius that I

[4]

enrolled in an evening course in Latin at the Lycée in Cannes. The final fifty years of the Roman Empire became my overriding interest, but at Sylvia's urging I also joined a male quartet, made up of husbands of her friends, called The Cheerleaders. The men were congenial, one English, one German, two Dutch; our settlement was an international community, a small island of exiles in these perfumed hills. I created an entirely new life for myself that had nothing to do with tugboats or the sea; my wife was happy among the English housewives and the German *Hausfraus,* all of them empty-nesters, as we are called by the realtors. And now here was that old man again, whom I had thought I'd shaken after almost half a century in his employ.

The whole of my old life suddenly faced me once more, as if he had opened the door to a busy room: the telephone calls, the hasty packing, the rushing off to some port on the other side of the globe to take on a convoy of six, eight or a dozen tugboats and tow some incongruous floating structure across the ocean. An exciting life; but enough was enough. I was happy now, I was fulfilled; the hell with old Kwel and his imperial stance, his devious ways, his unshakable cool; the man was a maniac, all shipowners in the towage business were maniacs. I was astounded he was still alive; he must be in his eighties.

I stood up and turned for home. The dog was disappointed; but then, she was always disappointed by something. I love dogs, but this one put my hackles up. When I had finally rounded her up and dragged her back to the bungalow, I let her go in first, with surreptitious help from my open-weave tropical shoe.

Sylvia sat sipping a glass of sherry at the dining table, which resembled a display in a pastry shop. She looked up in an absent-minded way when she saw me come in; she was smoking a cigarette, something she had not done for some time.

I hung my jacket on the hook. "Well, I've thought it over. I'll be damned if I'll go! Let him find another sucker. How about some coffee? Or are you into the strong stuff already?"

"Martinus," she said, "I have thought it over too. I think you should go and find out what all this is about."

I couldn't believe my ears. Nine years ago she had reacted to my retirement with utter delight. She had given herself over with abandon to the Indian summer of our marriage crippled by so many absences, so much loneliness on her part, so much unshared responsibility for the children in their most fractious years.

"Why? You don't think I *want* to, do you? I've been gone nine years! Time hasn't stood still, the new tugboats are very different from the ones I was used to. I don't feel competent to act as an advisor or instructor or whatever it is on a type of ship I don't know and have no experience of."

She gave me an absent-minded look and puffed at her cigarette with touching unfamiliarity. I realized she was overcome by a resurgence of her bleak and lonely past as a sailor's wife. I also realized how fragile our new life was, how easy it would be to destroy it all.

"How long did he say it would be?"

"Six weeks."

"And what is he paying you, if anything?"

I told her.

"Then I want you to do it," she said firmly, stubbing out her cigarette. "Go and find out what it involves."

I squatted beside her chair, put my arm around her and looked at her loyal brown eyes, her kind face full of courage. "You don't mean that. You just think it's what *I* want. Well, believe me, I don't. When I said to you nine years ago that I was done with the sea, I meant what I said. And one thing you must have found out after forty years: I may be a bastard at times, but I never break my word. I'm not about to break it now. So let's forget about it. Tipple your sherry; I'll fiddle with those damn tree lights and see if I can stop them flashing like a neon sign."

She gave me a look that I could not interpret. "I would believe you, Martinus, if you had ever talked about your life at sea. If you had accepted just one of the many invitations you've received over the years to go boating. If you carried a photograph of your wife or your grandchildren in your wallet, instead of one of your last ship."

"Love, you don't understand. I'm like an alcoholic: one glass, and I would be hooked again."

"Don't be silly," she said. "You've been perfectly happy for nine years. But a change would do you good. Go and find out what life at sea is like nowadays. What the ships are like. Six weeks on a modern ship, to Rio de Janeiro! You'd be silly not to take it."

[6]

"But what would *you* do all that time? I can't leave you now, at Christmas, with all the children coming . . ."

She waved it away. "Don't worry. I've done it all my life. Once Christmas is over, I'll go and stay with Ella and Tim and wait for the new baby. It's perfect timing. Also the money is very good. Maybe now we can build that new guestroom; the grandchildren are growing. Come, call him and tell him you'll go and look it over."

I rose, with a kink in my knee, and limped to the buffet, where I poured myself a stiff one. "Love," I said, heading for the icebox with my glass, "I'm not competent anymore. That ship'll be as alien to me as a space rocket. I'm seventy years old. The whole thing is ridiculous."

"Well," she said with a smile which meant that she had won the argument and was being nice about it, "if, after you've seen the ship and talked to whoever it is, you still think that you're too old or incompetent, come home. They're paying your fare and your hotel, aren't they? Go ahead. Call them."

I gave in and called the head office in The Hague. The telephonist, when I finally reached her via the cranky French trunk system, asked tartly, "Mr. Kwel Junior or Senior?"

"Senior."

"Hold on."

After a while I heard another female voice: "Miss Bastiaans. Can I help you?"

"This is Commodore Harinxma. I'm calling from the South of France."

"Oh, yes, sir! One second, I'll give you Mr. Arnold." There was some switching and a snatch of someone else's conversation, then the voice of the old emperor asked, "Well, did you talk to your wife?"

"I did. We agreed that I should talk it over with you, have a look at the ship and then decide. So I'll come, but I reserve the right to turn it down if I find I can't hack it. What do you say?"

There was a silence. To my surprise, I felt the same reaction I had felt in the past when I had him on the phone and he went in for one of those silences: a sinking feeling. Ridiculous.

Finally he said, "Tomorrow at ten. My chauffeur will be at the hotel. I now give you to Miss Bastiaans. She has the details." Before I had been able to put in another word, he was off the line.

"Commodore," the woman's voice said, "here are your flight times. Swiss Air flight seven five one from Nice-Cannes at seventeen thirty this evening to Zürich. Change there to Swiss Air seven nine six to Amsterdam, arriving at twenty fifty-five tonight. In Amsterdam, a room has been booked in your name in the Schiphol Hilton . . ."

Only after I had written it all down and put the phone back did I realize how cunningly the old man had manipulated me. It had been a vintage performance: the flattery, the uncanny insight into the workings of a sailor's mind. That bit about my wife's dog sounded as if he had had me researched before calling, but it probably had been just one of his shots in the dark. He had a higher score of hitting bull's-eyes in the dark than any other man I knew.

2

Outwardly, the head office of the Kwel International Towing Company in The Hague had not changed: a patrician brownstone in the heart of the city, looking to the uninitiated like a government office. It seemed incongruous that this should be the nerve center of the largest tugboat company in the world, which had held a monopoly of deep-sea towing for over a century. Only the faint glitter of antennas and electronic receiving equipment against the stormy sky indicated that it was the communication center for a fleet of two hundred ships, ninety of which were ocean-going tugboats dispersed all over the globe, some on salvage stations in places like the Firth of Forth, the Gulf of Oman, Trinidad, Tierra del Fuego, South Africa, others towing, alone or in convoy, colossal floating objects for thousands of miles: "Sea Tank III" from Halifax to Aberdeen, semi-submersible drilling rig "ANCO-K" from Ardyne Point to Stavanger, pontoon "Mulus 15" from Setúbal to La Guaira, three nameless barges from Rotterdam to Salala. Once upon a time I had been part of that fleet, crawling at a snail's pace across the oceans on voyages of up to six months, all the while telling myself it was the only life for me.

I stepped from the windy, rain-swept street into the silence of the marble hall with the old-fashioned porter's booth and the ancient elevator I remembered so well. There was a different hall porter, all of twenty if he was a day, and I did not recognize any of the people hurrying from door to door carrying folders with an air of secrecy. At KITCO the first commandment was never to let the competition know where any of our ships were located at any given time. Of course KITCO knew exactly where each ship of the competition was, and I presumed that the competition knew the same about KITCO, but anyone who disclosed that information was out on his ear. The result was an atmosphere of secrecy and furtiveness.

The porter, who gave me the kind of look immortals under thirty reserve for the elderly, pressed a button on a communication board and muttered, "Someone to see the old man, a commodore somebody. Okay." He turned to me and said, "Someone will meet you here in a few minutes. Please wait over there— Commodore." He said it as if it were a joke.

I suppressed a feeling of irritation. The title of commodore had been discontinued after I left the service. I had been boosted to the lofty rank during World War II, when Arnold Kwel had sent me, looking ludicrously young, to take on the old *Isabel Kwel*. The only way he could give me some weight to throw around in my dealings with the British Navy, which had chartered the ship, had been by giving me the nonsensical title and advising me to grow a mustache. I had lost the *Isabel*, but the title had stuck.

"Commodore Harinxma?"

A strikingly elegant woman in her early forties was standing before me. I rose.

"I've come to take you to Mr. Arnold. The elevator is this way."

In the rattling cage of the old elevator she made polite conversation. Had I had a nice trip? I told her all this had come rather unexpectedly. "Yes, Mr. Arnold is still a man of snap decisions." She said it with a smile. "This way, please."

We went down a hallway with doors behind which I heard the rattle of Telex machines. She opened a door at the end and said to someone, "Commodore Harinxma," then she stood back and I entered.

I had expected a sumptuous office overlooking the boulevard, as in the past; my reaction was one of shocked surprise. The room was dingy and dark, with a window opening onto an air shaft. The walls were bare, the carpet shabby; old Kwel was sitting behind a desk topped with a cracked glass plate. I barely recognized him, he seemed to have aged twenty years. His hands, resting on the cracked desktop, were like claws, his face looked ravaged and ancient like that of a mummy. But his eyes were unchanged: bright blue, unflinching, sizing me up. "So there you are," he said. "Sit down."

I sat down. I might have retired from a life of commanding convoys, but the moment I found myself in front of his desk I felt ludicrously young again, needing to grow a mustache.

"Cigar?"

The ritual had not changed. "Thank you," I said, although the only cigars I had ever smoked were the ones he had forced on me during the rare audiences he had granted me over a lifetime.

He opened a box—the same one—and turned it to face me. It contained the same unappetizing stogies. I went through the motions of selecting one. Now he would ask me to hand it to him so he could snip the tip off with the little surgical instrument dangling from his watch chain, before lighting it for me with his gold lighter. But a woman's hand entered my field of vision and broke the spell of the past. "Excuse me, Commodore." She took the cigar from me for the surgical procedure; it was she who proffered the flame. Was he too feeble now to lift his own lighter?

"Let's get down to brass tacks, Harinxma," he said with a hint of impatience.

"Yes, sir."

The blue eyes observed me with the old unnerving look; they certainly were not the eyes of an octogenarian. But then, his father had looked at me with the same eyes before saying, 'So you are the young bungler who lost my ship?'

"I told you the gist of it on the phone. The *Isabel* is a new ship, built especially for work in the North Sea oil fields, pushing and pulling rigs about. As you may have noticed even in your golden ghetto on the Riviera, the bottom has dropped out of the oil market, so we decided to take an offer we received from a ship-breaking yard in Taiwan who want to use her in their line of work. Miss Bastiaans has prepared a folder which will give you all the pertinent information on the *Isabel*. Captain Fransen, our head of operations, will furnish more details if you need them. The ship is now in Flushing, and I have arranged for you to make a test run with her tomorrow morning. Captain Bron, one of her previous masters, is available but due to sail on the *Fiona* for

Indonesia later tomorrow, so I suggest you go to your hotel now and study the material Miss Bastiaans will give you. After lunch Captain Fransen will visit you at your hotel to answer any questions you may have; after that you go for your medical, get your shots and sign the Articles."

"I'd rather postpone that until after the test run, if you don't mind."

His blue eyes snapped at me. "What's that?"

"We agreed on the phone that I'd have a look at the ship and generally mosey around a bit to get an idea of the assignment, before making a decision."

He sighed. "Harinxma, it's time you recognized your own idiosyncrasies. When I first promoted you to captain, you spent half an hour protesting you were unsuitable. When I promoted you to commodore, you reacted as if I had made an indecent proposal. When I sent you—" The telephone rang. "Take it, Miss Bastiaans!"

"Yes, sir," the woman's voice answered from what appeared to be a storage cupboard.

"So, don't start the old routine. You wouldn't be here if you didn't want the job. All we need now is my grandson's blessing. He's officially in the driver's seat these days, so let's call him in. Miss Bastiaans! Are you off the phone?"

"One moment, sir . . ."

"Get me Mr. Jim, would you?"

"Yes, sir."

He sat watching the telephone on his desk as if he were steeling himself for something. It was just a fleeting impression; but then, as a captain I had learned not to ignore fleeting impressions.

The telephone rang; he picked it up. "Jim? Good morning, Jim." A change of tone: taut, wary. "Could you drop by for a moment?" The telephone mumbled. "All right, in that case we'll come by and see *you*." Mumble. "Indeed, now." He put down the phone. "All right, Harinxma. Let's go."

He wanted to rise from his chair, but had barely moved before Miss Bastiaans was by his side to help him. Once he was standing upright, he was quite mobile. He walked with a quick, shuffling gait to the door; Miss Bastiaans moved to open it for him. She accompanied us to the elevator and helped him step inside, which he did like an old heron. We went down one floor, out again, and headed for a door in a hallway much more impressive than the one upstairs. In the past his own office had been here somewhere.

It was the same one; I recognized it the moment we entered. First there was an anteroom, in which a secretary and a typist sat behind desks; the secretary, half Miss Bastiaans' age and half as courteous, announced us via the telephone. "Your grandfather and a gentleman, Mr. Jim . . . Very well. You remember you have Mr. Raschid coming in five minutes?" She put the phone down. "He'll see you," she said and continued what she had been doing when we came in.

Miss Bastiaans opened the door of the main office for us. To enter it was a strange experience. This was where the old man had ruled the largest tugboat fleet in the world for over forty years, undisputed master of the international trade; now a nondescript young man was sitting behind the ornate desk. He did not bother to rise, but gestured at a couple of chairs in front of the desk. "Good morning. I gather you're the one who's taking our *Isabel* to Talcahuano."

"Rio," the old man snapped. "And mind your manners." Miss Bastiaans helped him sit down, gently, and left the room.

The young man rose and held out his hand. "I'm Jim Kwel. You are Captain—?"

"This is Commodore Martinus Harinxma," the old man said. "He has been with the company for fifty years. I thought you'd done your homework."

The young man smiled at me. "Commodore, how do you do?" His hand was firm and cold; he sat down again. "I presume you've been advised of the delicate nature of the assignment?"

"I'll thank you to leave the handling of this matter to me," the old man said, with such authority that I felt it in the nape of my neck. "Commodore Harinxma and I have worked together for a long time, we're used to each other. This is just a formal introduction."

The young man's reaction to the rebuke was interesting. It was all there: the old ancestor who had to be honored but was a pain in the neck, the way of handling him by humoring him. "I appreciate your help, Commodore. I gather you'll be arranging the details with my grandfather, so all there's left for me to do is wish you Godspeed and happy sailing." He gave me a thin smile.

"Thank you," I said.

The old man rose. As if she were a cat who could locate a

moving mouse through a brick wall, Miss Bastiaans came in before he had been able to move. He did so more nimbly than before; it was obvious that he had had a basinful of his grandson. He shuffled to the elevator with the speed of a roadrunner.

As we stood waiting, he said, out of the blue, "Well, see you at dinner."

I looked at Miss Bastiaans; she smiled seraphically.

"Excuse me, sir?"

"Dinner! I expect you for dinner! To meet the Chinese owner! The car will be at your hotel at six thirty. Don't keep it waiting." The elevator arrived. "We're going up," he said. "Are you coming or going?"

"I think Miss Bastiaans has something for me, sir."

"Ah, yes."

The gate slammed shut. As the shaking old cage slowly made its way back to the top floor, I wondered what the delicate nature of the assignment was that young Kwel had mentioned, causing his grandfather to slap him down.

3

Miss Bastiaans knew how to keep elderly men functioning efficiently. She had the folder on the *Isabel Kwel* ready for me in a plastic briefcase and had booked me into a hotel in the port of Rotterdam, where I would find the water bailiff, the doctor, the outfitters, and from where the *Isabel* would leave three days from now. The limousine was waiting for me; she supposed I would want a quiet hour at the hotel to study the contents of the folder, then a light lunch for which she had booked a table in the restaurant of the hotel; Captain Fransen, head of operations, would be at the hotel at fourteen hundred hours. He would arrange transportation for the test run with the *Isabel* tomorrow morning and give me the program for the rest of that day—supposing I were to accept the assignment. She gave me a ravishing smile; I was quite smitten with her. But then, young women, if they were nice and old-fashioned, smote me easily.

"Now, Commodore, is there any medication you want me to order for you, either in the Cape Verdes or Rio de Janeiro?"

I looked at her with a sinking feeling. "No, thank you," I said. "My wife saw to that before I left. Kind of you to remember."

"My pleasure, Commodore. Now, are there any questions you wish to ask me at this point?"

"Just one thing: has the insurance company been advised of my age, and have they given their okay?"

She dazzled me with her smile again. "Ah, yes, Commodore, that has been taken care of. All emergencies of whatever nature during your assignment will be paid for by the company." Despite her smile, I suspected she had even calculated the cost of the transport of my frozen corpse from the Cape Verdes or Brazil to the South of France. I should stop being charmed by anyone of the opposite sex under fifty.

She took me to the limousine waiting at the curbside. The wind had freshened; the chauffeur had to hold on to his cap as he opened the door. She made sure I was safely seated before handing me the briefcase with the folder; then she said, again with that ravishing smile, "There you are, Commodore. See you this evening." She shut the door, gave the driver a curt signal and we drove off.

In the limousine, on my way to Rotterdam on whispering tires, I opened the folder and glanced at its contents. But weariness won out; I slumped back in the cushions while the car, buffeted by gusts and lashed by rain, drove through the flat countryside between the cities.

In the hotel everyone seemed to have been advised of my arrival. KITCO must have had some clout here; I was treated like a VIP. I decided to follow Miss Bastiaans' advice and have a quiet hour in my room before going down to the restaurant for the light lunch she had ordered for me.

I lay down on the bed and on the spur of the moment called Sylvia. I had the connection within seconds, but there was no reply. She must be off on some Christmas business. I put the phone back and looked at the material on the *Isabel* from Miss Bastiaans' folder.

There were a lot of press clippings; the ship must have made quite a splash when she was launched. The newspaper articles went into raptures about the *Vessel from the Space Age: The age of futuristic ships is here, graceful herald of the twenty-first century.* There were photographs from the publicity department of a squat, ugly vessel snorting toward the viewer with a bow wave

[14]

like a snowplow. After the hyperbole by hacks who clearly had no idea what they were talking about, I happened upon the brochure meant for potential customers. It still sounded breathless: *mightiest tugboat in the world . . . marvel of modern technology . . .* but at least it gave facts and figures.

Judging from her specifications, I thought she was less a marvel than a monster. Maybe I still lived in the world of ten years ago and a decade in the business nowadays was a generation, but even if one allowed for this, she represented an ungraceful leap into the future. Her dimensions were massive: length 270 feet, width 62 and a draft of 30. Her bridge, in a break with tradition, was midships rather than on the forward quarter. Instead of a mainmast, she carried what the brochure referred to as *the Paradise tree.* It looked indeed like a tree full of electronic whiskers, globes, reflectors and dish antennas. It was placed on a walkway between her two squat stacks. Her superstructure, four floors above the main deck, looked top-heavy; when I turned the page, I came upon a photograph of the futuristic vessel seen broadside, on which she looked like a pontoon carrying esoteric spying equipment, the kind of vessel that when spotted by coastal patrols instantly sets bells ringing and Telexes clattering in the naval nerve centers of the world. One thing was obvious: if any ship in distress were to give as much as a rabbit squeak within a thousand-mile radius of this monster, she would come pounding toward it at the speed of an express train within minutes. Her equipment could pick up SOS and Mayday signals with the accuracy of a condor spotting a rabbit a thousand feet below in the Andes.

I lowered the brochure as the meaning of this penetrated to me: the *Isabel Kwel* was not designed for work with oil rigs in the North Sea, as the old man had made me believe. She was a full-fledged ocean-going vessel for long-distance towing and salvage work. Why had he presented her to me as something she patently was not?

His grandson's casual remark about 'the delicate nature of the assignment' came back to me. Maybe I had been too starry-eyed about going back to sea; I should go easy on the romance. Something did not smell right. It would be a blow, but I should seriously consider the possibility of going home. In any case, I decided, I would not sign on the dotted line in a state of senile euphoria before I had located the source of the smell.

4

After Miss Bastiaans' 'light lunch,' which turned out to be a poached egg on toast, I returned to my room to study the material on the *Isabel* again, in preparation for some judicious grilling of Captain Fransen, head of operations.

In my time I had known a number of his predecessors, usually ex-captains who stayed on after their retirement and instead of slowing down found themselves caught in a man-killing job which not only made them the target of everybody's gripes but sent them all over the world on a succession of emergency missions which, in my experience, had turned even the most laid-back, sleepy-time character into a nervous wreck. However, they knew everything that went on on board each of the ninety-odd ships under their management; Captain Fransen was likely to know more about the *Isabel Kwel* and the men who sailed her than the owners did. But because of the paranoid passion for secrecy that pervaded the company, he was likely to play his cards close to his vest.

I must have dropped off, for it seemed only minutes later that the telephone rang. A smoke-hoarsened voice asked, "Harinxma?"

"Yes."

"This is Fransen. Do you want me to come up, or are you coming down?"

"Oh, hello," I said, gathering my wits. "If it's all the same to you, I'd rather you came up, it's more private. We can order anything we want from Room Service."

"Okeydoke." He put the phone down.

I straightened my bed and combed my hair; then there was a knock on the door and Captain Fransen came in. At first sight he ran close to type, only he seemed younger than the ones I had known: a tall man in his fifties, as thin as a rake, with a sallow face and bags under his eyes. He wore an old-fashioned fedora on the back of his head; a cigarette drooped from a corner of his mouth; his wet raincoat had tar and grease marks on it. "Hello there," he said, coughing.

We shook hands; he sized me up with tired blue eyes and said, "You don't remember me, but we've met before. Do you mind if I take this rag off and order something to chase the chill?

[16]

I've just been to Flushing to put the pig back in operation for the test run you asked for." He took off his raincoat, threw it onto the bed, tossed his hat after it, slumped in the only armchair in the room, legs spread, stretched and yawned, which caused a coughing fit. "Sorry," he said, coughing. "I missed out on a night's sleep. Came in from Hong Kong this morning at four o'clock. Mind if I take a leak while you order?"

"Go right ahead. What would you like?"

"What are you into? Whiskey or gin?"

"You name it."

"Let's make it whiskey and order a bottle. You can always keep it in your bedside table. I'll sign for it."

So I ordered a bottle of whiskey and two glasses while he rummaged and hummed in the bathroom and flushed the toilet. When he came back, yawning, and slumped into the chair again, I asked, "Where was it?"

"Where was what?"

"You said we met before."

"Oh, I was Number One on board the old *Clara* when you took those two lock doors from the Clyde to Valparaíso in '66. We were tailholder of the second tow."

"Ah, yes." I remembered the occasion, but not that the old *Clara* had been part of the convoy. "Well, you've come a long way since then."

"Don't let's talk about *that*." He coughed. "The worst thing I ever did to my stomach and my marriage was to take on this job. Did you order?"

"Yes, I did. It should be here any minute."

He lit another cigarette with the butt of the old one. His hand shook. His forehead had a sickly pallor and his hair was slick with perspiration. "It's high time I got out of this rat race," he said, grinding out the stub in the ashtray. "One day Hong Kong, the next Newfoundland, then you sweat your guts out in New Guinea, and when you come home your wife says in a strangled voice, 'While you were gallivanting with the boys, Liza died and I cried my eyes out.' Liza, for your information, was the cat. Well, another two years and it's retirement for me. What's it like?"

"It's okay, as long as you make sure you turn your back on anything to do with the sea or ships. I said it to my wife the other day: a retired tug-driver is like an alcoholic on the wagon. One glass and you're hooked again."

[17]

He gave me a tired look. "Then what made you fall off the wagon, friend?"

I shrugged. "I haven't really. I'm just sniffing the wind."

He said nothing. There was a knock on the door; a waiter came in with a bottle and two glasses. "Where's the ice?" Fransen asked.

"At the end of the passage is an ice machine," the waiter replied. "Want me to get some for you?"

"Yes."

The man collected the plastic bucket off the desk and headed down the corridor, while Fransen unwrapped the neck of the bottle, unscrewed the cap and poured himself half a tumbler, which he downed without waiting for the ice. "Yuck," he said with a grimace, scowling at the empty glass. "Tastes like Aussie booze, panther piss." He looked at the label. "Ever heard of Loch Damn, in Scotland?"

"Can't say I have."

"Sounds like the lake district of South Australia. You know? Mount Hopeless." It didn't stop him from pouring another glass, forgetting about the ice, and me.

The waiter came with the ice, Fransen signed the bill, plunked a couple of cubes into his tumbler and said, "About tomorrow." He pulled a dog-eared notebook from his inside pocket and flicked the pages. "Tonight, I gather, you're living it up with the old man and the Chink."

"That's right."

"Tomorrow morning early, I can't say how early but it's going to be early, you'll be picked up by taxi and taken to Flushing, where the pig will be waiting to carry you off into the great blue yonder, oinking away."

"I gather you don't care for the ship?"

I must have touched a sore spot, for suddenly he lost his cool, or so it seemed. "Hell! Who does? For nine months we've all been yodeling about her being a marvel of technology and so on, but the trouble is she's not a ship, she's a pig. You'll see for yourself tomorrow; the pig has everything, does everything, knows everything, except one thing: how to behave like a ship. She rolls like a barrel, vibrates something terrible—a mechanical sow, that's what she is, dreamed up by a student fraternity of architects who took over after old Nadorst was put out to pasture. She was meant to tow drilling platforms out of Norwegian fjords and set them down on Boyle Field or Dogger Bank, but before she was even finished, the oil market went kerplunk, they stopped drilling and there she was: redundant before she was launched. '*Super tugboat of the 21st century,*' the PR brochure says—"

"Well, that's what she is, isn't she?" I asked innocently. "According to the description I read, she could do a lot more than push and pull oil rigs about. If ever a ship was designed for salvage work on the high seas, it would be this one, I'd say."

He shot me a blue glance like the lunge of a kingfisher, then he took a slug, put his tinkling glass on the bedside table and said, "Don't ask *me*. I'm about to resign. I've had it, and the business is dying anyhow. No objects left to tow, too much competition. All there is for us to do is ferry hulks to the Far East for scrap—"

"Why was she sold?" I asked.

But he wasn't listening, or chose not to. "You know, I did that once," he said with a smile of reminiscence. "Two dead cruisers around the Horn, for Taiwan. My last voyage before I was given this job. Those damn hulks ran into each other in the Forties, piled up, slammed together. Crazy to send one boat through that weather with that bunch of junk. I should have cut the damn things loose, but no one was going to catch *me* losing a tow, not on my last trip; so I risked my neck and those of the runners—"

"How many captains has she had, so far?"

He gave me another of those looks. He was a nimble bird, all right; the whole show of anger, exasperation and nostalgia was well under control; the cards were close to the vest indeed. "Three in all. First Bartels, an egghead with tinted glasses who resigned after her maiden voyage and became a teacher at Amsterdam Naval College. Then mad Bron, otherwise known as 'Beast Rufus,' who could handle the pig all right, but who's a job-hunter born and bred and used to treating tugs like stock cars. They put him on station in Durban, where he started to abuse her on salvage operations—at least, that's what Jim Kwel and the architects called it. So they slapped restrictions on the use of the ship, and Beast Rufus got mad and walked off. They flew 'Spooks' Haversma down to take over—you may have known him: sixtyish, short, bald, little melon belly; he had the *Cornelia* for fifteen years."

"I know of him, but we never met."

"Well, he brought the ship home, was given a string of barges for the Gulf, but he died in Aden—shot by a mugger in the streets.

By that time the Kwels had already decided to sell her to Taiwan. At a loss, of course. The worst of it is that they have a second one exactly like her under contract, almost on the stocks."

"What kind of restrictions?"

He took another slug, lit himself another cigarette with the remaining half of the previous one, drew the first smoke down to his navel, glanced at his wristwatch and said, with rings, "Oh-oh! I've got to go. Let me give you the rest of the program for tomorrow. I'll pick you up here at the hotel around four hundred, four thirty, so take it easy tonight. I've had meals with the old man myself; make sure you have a seeing-eye dog to take you home, like the Bastiaans woman. I must say, with a well-stacked, perfect all-rounder like her, I wouldn't mind being blind myself."

"What do you mean?" I asked, startled.

He stopped on his way to his raincoat. "What?"

"Are you telling me the old man is *blind?*"

"Didn't you know?" He looked amazed. "Blind as a bat, man! If it wasn't for her, he'd run into the doorpost. Well, see you tomorrow bright and early, for my sins. Man! What I need is a second honeymoon. With Miss Bastiaans, or similar. See you." He slammed the door on his way out.

Old Kwel blind? I couldn't believe it. Those blue eyes had stared at me exactly as I remembered from way back when we were both young. But then, there was the way Miss Bastiaans had guided him, which I had attributed to his age. And the cigar-snipping and lighting ritual which she had taken over. It filled me with an odd personal sorrow, much more so than when the same thing had happened to a good friend in our retirement village. I felt so affected by old Kwel's blindness that I had to force my attention away from him to run through the things Fransen had told me. It was obvious that something was being kept from me, something about the ship.

There was one way of finding out. I called the hotel switchboard and asked the girl to connect me with the Naval College in Amsterdam. It took a while before anyone answered; finally a surly male voice informed me that the school was closed for the Christmas vacation. I asked for the private number of Captain Bartels, one of their teachers, and was told to hold the line. I held the line for about five minutes; then the surly voice gave me a number in Leiden.

I could dial it myself. The phone was answered at once, by a woman. "Mrs. Bartels."

"Mrs. Bartels, my name is Harinxma. I'm an ex-colleague of your husband. Is he home?"

There was a silence. "Could you tell me what this is about?"

Something made me reply, "Oh, it's just that I'm in Rotterdam for a couple of days and wanted to find out how he is. Chew the fat, that sort of thing."

"Oh . . ." She sounded doubtful. "All right, I'll tell him. One moment, please."

While waiting, I wondered why a tugboat captain who had left the service to become a teacher should have his calls screened. Then a man's voice came on the phone: reticent, cagey. "Yes? Who is this?"

"I'm Commodore Martinus Harinxma, Retired. I wonder if I could come by and have a word with you."

"About what?"

"About an assignment that's been offered to me."

"What assignment?"

"I've been asked to act as an advisor to the new captain of one of the company's ships that's been sold to Taiwan. I gather you commanded her at one time."

"What ship?"

"The *Isabel Kwel.*"

There was a click, and then the dial tone. He had hung up on me. I sat staring at the phone for a few moments; then I called the hall porter to inquire about trains to Leiden.

5

The weather seemed wilder in the city of Leiden, a mere twenty miles north of Rotterdam. When I came out of the station, the wind pushed me off the curb; the taxi that swerved across in response to my call had to brake or I would have ended up on the bonnet. "Good weather for surfing," the driver said.

I gave him the address I had found in the telephone guide in the hall of the station.

The house turned out to be at the far end of a cul-de-sac on the outskirts of the city, a suburban semi-detached villa with a small front garden. A lawn dwarf and a weathered cement flamingo guarded a birdbath emptied for the winter; the garage didn't seem to be in use, as the driveway was blocked by a stack of garden furniture covered with a sheet of plastic wildly flapping in the wind. The window overlooking the desolate little garden had looped curtains; a few Christmas angels hung suspended in the center. The front door was decorated with sprigs of holly; the rubber mat said WELCOME. I rang the bell.

Despite the promise of the mat, the door was opened at a crack barred by a chain. A woman's voice asked, "Who is it?"

"I'm Commodore Harinxma. I'd like to have a word with Captain Bartels, please."

The face that had been faintly visible through the crack disappeared; the door was closed. I stood and waited. It had not occurred to me that I might be refused entrance when I turned up in person; there came a moment when reticence turned into paranoia. I should have tried to find out more about Captain Bartels and his reasons for resigning before I came on this wild-goose chase.

I was about to turn around and walk down the street to find a taxi when the door was opened at a crack again and a man's voice asked, "What do you want?"

"Sorry to disturb you, Bartels, but I thought you might be willing to give me some information, to help me decide whether to accept that assignment or not."

There was a silence, during which I was being observed through the crack. The whole thing was becoming ludicrous. I added, "As you can see, I'm not a youngster. I'm too old to be drawn into a controversial situation."

"What makes you think it might be?"

I'd had enough. "Look, friend," I said, "the way you carry on tells me enough. I'm sorry I bothered you."

I was halfway down the garden path when the voice called after me, "Harinxma!" I turned around. In the doorway stood a bald, stoop-shouldered man in a business suit, with glasses.

"Come on in! When I tell you the story, you'll understand why I have to be cautious. I thought you were another of those characters that have been pestering me for information under false pretenses."

[22]

"What characters?"

"You don't expect me to holler that in the street, do you?" He stepped back into the house. "Come inside. I'm sorry if all this seems weird. You'll understand the moment I explain."

I stepped into a little hall which smelled of cats.

"Good to know you at last," the bald man said, holding out his hand. "I know of you, of course, but somehow we never met while you were still with the company." We shook hands; his was soft and clammy. "Let me take your coat," he said.

He helped me out of it and hung it on a coat-tree made of antlers. Beside it was a hollowed-out elephant's foot that held two umbrellas. Over it a needlepoint motto pronounced, *He who enters as a Mate Is never too Early but always too Late.*

"Meet my wife, Matilda. This is Commodore Harinxma, dear."

"Commodore, how do you do?" She was short and plump, dressed in a maternity smock, which seemed on the late side as she must be in her fifties. She had shrewd, bulging eyes, a bee-stung mouth and a beehive hairdo which looked somewhat the worse for wear, as if it were still inhabited.

"Come in, Commodore," she said. "How about some tea? Would you like to wash your hands first?"

"Thank you, that might not be a bad idea." I was grateful for her understanding of the problems of aging males.

"It's at the end of the passage, second door to your right."

The small toilet seemed smaller because of a profusion of needlepointed mottos on the walls. Over the cistern, facing the male visitor, was a large sampler of laughing faces with, in gothic lettering, *Show me a man who laughs all day, Who never gets in a rut, Show me a man who laughs all day, and I will show you a nut.* The mirror over the miniature washbasin was encased in another sampler, this one of playing kittens with *Meow, meow, meow, meow,* in diminishing letters. On the inside of the door as I left was another one, of a top hat, gloves and a walking stick, saying, *Stop! Did you take care of Jack the Zipper?* Maybe there were no children and Mrs. Bartels had spent the lonely hours needlepointing samplers while her husband was at sea.

When I opened the door, the bald man's voice called from a distance, "In here!"

The living room, in which he sat waiting for me in an over-stuffed armchair, was decorated with more samplers and African statuary of elephants and ostriches. In the corner a small Christmas tree nervously blinked its colored lights.

"Sit down, Harinxma," he said, indicating another overstuffed chair. "My wife sits on the couch."

"This is very kind of you, Bartels."

"That it is," he said bluntly. "If you'd been ten years younger, I would have told you to go fly a kite."

"Would a younger man have had less of a problem with this assignment?"

He contemplated me for a moment through his tinted glasses, then he said, "I would have left a younger man to face the consequences of his own choice. Ah! Here it comes."

With a tinkling of china cups the woman with the beehive hairdo came in, carrying an overloaded tray. I tried to struggle out of the suction cup of my chair; she said, "Don't bother, Commodore, stay where you are. Make some room on the coffee table, Daddy."

Her husband collected various magazines, which he stacked onto a book entitled *Cats on Cats*. When she put the tray down, I saw it was going to be a real Dutch tea, with gingerbread, angel cake and petit-fours. Two of the cushions on the sofa sprang to alarming life and came stalking the tray; she cried, "Oops!" as a third one burst from under her smock and leaped onto the coffee table.

"Matilda," Bartels said with strained forbearance, "take these animals away and lock them in the kitchen."

"But, Daddy—"

"Please, Matilda! I mean it."

She pouted, took two of the pillows under her arms and cooed, "Come, darlings, Daddy has important business to discuss with this nice old gentleman, so . . ." The third cat, on the coffee table, reached for the petit-fours.

"All right," Bartels said with grim determination. He collected the scavenger none too gently and carried it, struggling and hollering, into the passage.

"I'm sure you wouldn't have minded, would you, Commodore?" Her voice sounded pleading.

"No, no, not at all. What breed are they?"

"Persian," she said, pleased. "We always have Persians. They're so intelligent and so affectionate. But, of course, if you treat them like children, they'll *behave* like children, won't they?"

Bartels came back, rubbing his hands on his hips. "Now let's have some tea and talk turkey."

"Shall I pour, or would you like to do it yourself, Daddy?"

"You pour and I'll see to the rest."

"Very well."

While she poured the tea, he watched her as if he were judging a tea-pouring contest. "That's fine. Thank you, dear. Now . . ."

"Yes, yes," she said, "I'm going. Will you take your own sugar, Commodore? Do help yourself to everything."

"I will, Mrs. Bartels, thank you."

"If you gentlemen need anything else, just fire a shot at the ceiling."

"I will," her husband said with such matter-of-factness that I couldn't help glancing at the ceiling. The moment the door was closed behind her, he continued, "Now, what is it you want? Information, or my advice?"

"Information first, I suppose."

"Well, I'll give you my advice unsolicited: don't touch it. If you've signed a contract, tell them you've had an angina attack and make your family doctor draw up a statement that lets you off the hook. If you don't, you're a fool. As the saying goes, no fool like an old fool."

His bluntness began to lack charm. "All right, Bartels," I said, "let's have it. What's wrong with the ship?"

"Ah—that's a good question!" He leaned over, grabbed a petit-four and bit its head off. He continued, chewing, "That's what everybody's been trying to find out, from the architects down to yours truly. If we knew that, it would be a different ballgame. As it stands now, your guess is as good as mine. All I know for certain is that whoever sails her as master had better be on the ball twenty-four hours a day, for if he turns his back on the bitch, chances are she'll kill him."

His dramatics turned me off. I have a low tolerance for people milking situations for their theatrical effect; to make that statement while munching pastry furnished by a servile wife had an adverse effect on me. Off the top of my head I would have said that one of the problems of the *Isabel Kwel* had been her first master. "Explain it to me."

He wiped his mouth with a paper napkin off the tray. "You do realize that what I'm going to tell you has to remain between ourselves?"

"Depends what it is."

"There can be no exceptions," he said firmly.

"Let's start with the facts," I suggested. When he looked as if he were about to have second thoughts, I added, "You'll agree that in order to arrive at a rational decision I need a little more than the statement you just made."

He eyed another petit-four, then grabbed it as if it had been about to get away. This time he didn't bother to bite its head off, but stuffed the whole thing into his mouth. "Well," he began, "let me tell you my own story." At the 't' of 'story' he spat a crumb onto my lap. Good shooting; it was quite a distance.

"Take your time," I said.

He mistook my meaning. "Oh, I'm not going to cut any corners, don't worry." He wiped his mouth. "When I was given command of the new ship, of course I was pleased. I'd seen the drawings, I'd read the description, I'd visited the ship in the yard, I'd taken a special course in computerized navigation. I was as excited and well prepared as an astronaut before his flight. I was sure that this was the future, that the old ships had had their day, that I was going to open up the twenty-first century for the ocean towage business. Her maiden voyage was from the Clyde to Central West Africa, towing a hotel structure with crew quarters and heliport, four hundred and fifty thousand tons. It was to be a landmark trip: for the first time in history, Lloyd's of London allowed a single tug to tow a structure that big all by herself. At the outset we had the usual gremlins that every new ship has, but nothing serious. Our first oiling station was La Coruña. Up to then, everything had gone beautifully. The weather was fine, the wind moderate, the sea moderate, the ship handled like a dream. She would do anything, everything except fly, and was more than strong enough for the object. She towed the thing, unwieldy as it was, at a speed of four knots. Pretty impressive."

He waited for some audience reaction, so I said, "I should say so."

"We bunkered in the bay of La Coruña, picked up the tow again and headed out. I don't know if you're familiar with the Ría de La Coruña?"

"I've been there a few times."

"Well, then you'll remember that the channel runs virtually true north, and that at a given moment you have to make a ninety-degree turn heading for Point Herminio or you pile up on the shoals."

"I remember."

"Well—" The third petit-four bought it. Chewing, he continued, "I completed the maneuver. Everything was hunky-dory. I was right on course, slightly north of west. When I came out of the shelter of the shoals, a moderate northwest swell caught me on the starboard bow. And then it happened."

He gave me an expectant stare, so I asked, "What did?"

He snapped up the last of the petit-fours and popped it into his mouth. "She went crazy." Smack, smack, smack, smack—it was like watching a nature movie, *A Day in the Life of an Iguana*. "Suddenly the ship started to roll. She had rolled quite a bit before; I mean, she's definitely a tender ship, but all of a sudden, out of the blue, she started to roll out of control, dipping deeper and deeper, from one ear onto the other. Everybody on the bridge had to cling to the nearest handhold merely to remain upright. Downstairs was chaos. In the galley a ten-gallon pan of soup was flung off the range, scalding the cook's legs. In the engine room an oiler was thrown across from one side to the other. Members of the off watch were tossed out of their bunks. And all that in a matter of minutes, seconds. I had no time to reflect, my instantaneous gut reaction was to take the ship off automatic and kick her off course. That took care of it, but I had no idea what had happened, nobody had. It was stunning, totally unexpected: a three-thousand-ton vessel suddenly rolling like a barrel. I knew that if I'd waited a minute longer, she would have turned turtle." He paused, reached over the tea tray, found there were no petit-fours left, gave it a look of contempt and leaned back in his chair. "Well?" he asked, as if I had missed a cue. "What do you say about *that?*"

"Incredible."

I must in some manner have failed him, for he gave me the same look he had given the tea tray. "I'll sum it up for you in one word: unseaworthy. I realized at that moment, unbelievable as it seemed, that the newest, most expensive, most powerful tugboat in the world was unseaworthy."

"My God," I said, picking up the cue this time.

"I wouldn't believe it at first. It was total nonsense that a ship of such complexity, incorporating all those new ideas, should have something so basically wrong with it. Every boy who's ever built a sailboat out of a wooden shoe knows, for God's sake, that his first and main problem is how to keep the damn thing upright! Isn't that so?"

"Of course."

"Who could believe that the keenest brains in the profession, the cream of the engineering crop of the Technical University, designed a ship costing scores of millions that won't remain upright?"

I wanted to hear the rest of his story, so I asked, "Then what did you do?"

"Well, I'll tell you. I'm not saying I did the right thing, but, I mean, what else was there? I told myself that every ship has an angle of incoming seas at which it may start to over-roll. I told myself not to make a drama of it. I didn't even mention it in the log, for I didn't know how to put it without making myself look like a fool. More tea?"

"No, thanks."

"Well. To cut a long story short, it happened again. Off the coast of Africa, in one of those sandstorms that are worse than fog. That's why I was on the bridge, although it wasn't my watch. It blew! From zero to force nine in ten minutes, and the sea picked up just like *that*." He snapped his fingers. "So I said, 'Let's take her up a couple of points. Three points. Four.' We must have been about four points up from our course when, *whammo!* She started to cycle again, with a vengeance, much faster and more —more malevolent than the first time. As if she *wanted* to, as if she'd been waiting for the opportunity. Well, I don't want to sound melodramatic. She just did it again: rolling out of control up to capsizing point in two, three minutes flat. Less than that: one minute, thirty seconds, I don't know, I lost perspective. It was one of those occasions when time stretches out, when drowning people see their lives reel off in front of their eyes. But this time, at least, I knew what to do: I kicked her off course with the bow thruster. I don't think I'd have made it on the wheel alone, she was that fast, that—well—wicked: '*Got you, buster!*' But I brought her back under control, with my heart in my mouth and—well, I don't mind telling you. Minutes later, when everything was back under control, I realized I'd wet my pants. Now—what kind of reaction is *that?* Do I look like a man who's in the habit of wetting his pants?"

[28]

"Hardly. Go on."

"Well, to start with, I stayed on the bridge during my off watches from then on. I had a deck chair rigged up and slept there. The weather was good, she behaved beautifully again, but I couldn't trust her anymore. I knew that if the same set of circumstances occurred she'd do exactly the same, and this time I might have gone to the john and she'd turn turtle. It happened *that* fast, I want to impress that upon you. Something should be done about her, obviously, so I started to write a report in which I summed up the whole thing. But then I realized: dammit, if I report this in black and white and it gets into the wrong hands, what'll the result be? If the union, or the insurance, or a spy from the competition gets a peek at this, she'll lose her certificate of seaworthiness, and the moment that happens she'll be worthless, the company will never be able to sell her other than for scrap. So I tore up the report, burned it in the ashtray and wrote another one in which I said how satisfactory the ship was, blah blah blah, but that there were some morale problems among the crew which could of course be explained as unfamiliarity with their new surroundings, but there might be an underlying cause which, I thought, could best be discussed in a private meeting with the directors. Now, wouldn't you think that was a normal, rational request?"

"I would."

"Believe it or not, they never picked up on it. More than that: nobody from the head office would speak to me. Fransen, the head of operations, who's a Judas goat for the directors, shunned me as if I had the plague. I was relieved of my command, and they gave the ship to Rufus Bron. What do you say to *that?*"

"Incredible."

"Ah, but I'm not through! More tea?"

"No, thanks. What happened next?"

"I was so insulted at being ostracized that I thought, 'The hell with them! The hell with the lot of them!' So I resigned and accepted this job, for which—er—I'd had an offer earlier."

It was obviously a lie, but I went on looking at him with the eyes of a spinster gazing up at a preacher in his pulpit, to keep him going. He certainly had my attention now.

"After Beast Rufus, who had her only for a few months, Spooks Haversma took over the *Isabel*. As I liked him— Did you ever meet him?"

"No."

"Well, a great guy. A widower, a nice colleague, a humble man, one of nature's noblemen. So I thought I owed it to him to tell him about this. I went to see him on board, with his canary and his weird books and his Ouija board, the day before he sailed for the Gulf. 'Spooks,' I asked, 'have you noticed anything funny, handling the ship?' He said, 'No,' but then, he'd taken her on in Durban and sailed her straight home without a tow. 'Well,' I said, 'in that case there's something I have to tell you,' and I gave him the whole story. He listened—how shall I say—respectfully, he was that sort of person, but I had the feeling he thought I was a bit overexcited. I simply couldn't get through to him that this incredible vessel, on which he was installed in a suite with a hi-fi and palms and a glass statue, this tug-driver's heaven, was a killer. And the oddest part of it was this: the men who had been on board when it happened, the bosun, the chief, the engineers, had all been scared out of their wits by the rolling, but the moment I hinted that the ship might be a killer: Bingo! I was stonewalled. They simply refused to face it, it was as if I had committed treason by mentioning it. I've never been able to understand the psychology of that. Can you?"

I could, but I wanted to keep him going. "No."

"Well, there I was: the only man in the entire world who had this bee in his bonnet about the *Isabel Kwel*. She left for the Gulf with a string of barges, and for a couple of weeks there was no news; then I heard that Spooks had been shot by a mugger in Aden. At first, of course, I thought, 'Gee, I'm sorry, he was a nice guy.' Then the rumor began to circulate that he hadn't been mugged at all but committed suicide. I asked myself, 'If so, why?' I couldn't find out if an incident similar to mine had taken place on the way to Aden; all I know is that his mate took over and continued to the Gulf. Shortly after she came home, she was sold to the Third World."

"What was the mate's name?"

"Slobkous. Maybe now you understand why I said to you: 'Don't touch it.' If you take on this assignment, you need to have your head examined. Someone your age has no business on board a ship that has to be watched twenty-four hours a day or she'll sneak up on you and turn turtle. You're married, are you?"

"Yes."

"Be wise, go home and enjoy your wife, the way I'm doing.

It's like being in heaven, after all those years of banging around the globe—"

As if she had waited for the cue, the smiling Mrs. Bartels came in and beamed at her husband. "Anything else?" she asked coyly.

He didn't answer her question. "What do you think—should we tell him about the visit from the Chinese?"

She gave me a look, a swift, expert appraisal. "Why not?"

He looked doubtful. "All this is extremely dicey stuff, Harinxma. If you don't keep this to yourself, I may be in serious trouble."

His wife had rummaged in a sewing table and handed him a visiting card. He hesitated, then held it out to me. "This was the man."

It was a discreetly expensive business card with black-and-gold raised letters: *Kao Hsiung Steel and Shipping Cy, Charlie S. Chung, President,* and two addresses at the bottom, one in Kao Hsiung, the other in Brussels.

"He turned up a week ago in one of those limousines you see at the airport, twice as long as normal, with a chauffeur—"

"And a television set," his wife added. "I saw it when I walked the cats while they were in here talking."

"He was charming, very interested in the cats, studied my wife's samplers and asked her about them, and made notes of books on embroidery my wife mentioned, saying he'd have his secretary look for the English edition. A perfect gentleman."

"But what did he want?"

"He came to ask me if I'd be interested in the job they've now offered you: to sail on the *Isabel* as an advisor to the Taiwanese captain and his staff, as far as Rio."

"And what did you say?"

"Well, you'll understand now that the last thing I wanted was to get back on board that bitch, but I had to watch my step. I didn't want to mess up whatever deal KITCO was arranging with him. So I said I'd have loved to do it, but that I was a teacher now. He said, 'How about taking her as far as St. Vincent during your Christmas holiday?' "

"I was there at that moment," his wife said, "so I tried to give Daddy an out by saying I wanted him home with the family for Christmas—"

"Then the guy said, with one of those smiles—you know, all teeth: 'Family?' As if he meant: 'What family?' And that's when I

[31]

realized, sort of chilly-like, that he didn't want me for that job at all—"

"He just wanted to find out about the ship," his wife concluded.

"I don't quite get it," I confessed.

He looked at me as he must at one of his pupils who had dropped a clanger. "It's elementary, Harinxma: all the time he was watching my reactions—"

"Our body language," she explained.

"He tossed that bait at me to see if I'd spit it out. He waited for me to say: 'On *that* ship?' and then he'd press for details."

"Why did his asking about your family make you conclude all this?"

"He knew we *have* no family. He knew all about me!"

"He was very clever," his wife added, "but we had his number pretty quick."

"Then the telephone calls started," he continued.

"That's why we were so cagey when you called," his wife explained.

"The first was a rough, coarse voice, very brief. It said, 'You blab your mouth off to that Chink, Bartels, and you'll regret it for the rest of your life. Stay with your dumb kids, don't mess with big business or you'll get hurt.' I asked, 'Who is this? Who *are* you?' But he hung up. I'm almost sure it was Fransen."

"It was," his wife said positively. "I had picked up the other phone. I know him, he came to see me once to deliver some letters from Daddy."

"And then, a few days later, another bird called, another male voice, but this was a smoothie, like a salesman. 'Oh, Captain Bartels,' he said, 'this is Allied Marine Insurance Limited. I'd like you to answer a few questions on the tugboat *Isabel Kwel,* if you don't mind. To start with: does she have any problems you know of, and if so, what are they?' So I waved my wife to the other phone and stalled him until she could listen in; then I said, 'Why do you want to know?' And he said, 'We're conducting a survey of the new tugs for our company, and as you were master of the *Isabel Kwel*—' I said, 'Mister, I don't give out any information on ships without written instructions from the company.' And he said, 'But you're no longer *with* the company!' I said, 'No. Thank you,' and slammed the phone down."

"I said, 'Daddy, call the Better Business Bureau! Find out about Allied Marine Insurance Limited—' "

"I did, and what do you know? There *is* no such company!"

"Not in the *entire* world," she added.

"Well, well," I said. "Then what happened?"

But they had run their gamut. "You haven't had any cake!" she cried. "And no gingerbread!"

"No, thank you, Mrs. Bartels. So you think, Bartels, that the new owner of the ship knows she has a problem?"

"Of course he does. He must have a spy in the head office, they all have. But my guess is he doesn't know exactly what the problem is, and, frankly, neither do I. She's either top-heavy or has a fault in her underwater design that results in her going into that cycle under certain circumstances. And that not once every fifty years, or once every twenty-five years, which seems to be acceptable nowadays in naval architecture, but at least once every trip. It happened to Spooks Haversma who knows how many times, enough to scare him to death—"

"Are you suggesting he committed suicide because the ship has a fault?"

He looked peeved, as if I had taken something away from him. "Harinxma, I am not *suggesting* anything. I just put two and two together: a lethal fault that exhausts the captain the way it exhausted me after three weeks of working, eating and trying to sleep on the bridge; then the fact that you can't report it in writing or even in the log because you may cause her to lose her certificate—"

"Captain Haversma was a very unstable man," she interrupted. "After the death of his wife he went in for spirit contact, all by himself in his cabin. We know. His steward came to tea once. Very nice man, very concerned. He was sure Captain Haversma had killed himself. But not on board—somewhere on the waterfront, at the end of a jetty. He had her portrait with him."

"We don't know that, sweetheart."

"We do too! His steward said it was never found. He *must* have had it with him. It wasn't among his possessions. That's why the police wanted to know if it was in a silver frame or something that could have attracted a thief. But it was just one of those department-store frames, you know? Nothing special."

"Well, be that as it may," her husband said, slapping his thighs to indicate I had used up my welcome. "How about that dentist's appointment, sweetheart?"

She picked up the ball after a brief glazed look. "Ah! Yes. You won't try my gingerbread, Commodore?"

"I'd love to, Mrs. Bartels, but I'm afraid I must hurry and catch my train. I have a dinner appointment."

As I moved to the door, the cats came trooping in, hollering, "Meow!" and one leaped onto the coffee table. I went out to the hall and took my raincoat off the antlers.

Both Bartels and his wife came after me. Our farewell was warm and insincere. He offered to phone for a taxi, but I said I'd catch a bus, now that I knew where I was. He didn't insist; when I had my hat on, he opened the door with ill-disguised alacrity and bade me farewell. As I was going down the garden path, holding on to my hat in the strong wind, he shouted, "Mind what I said, Harinxma! All this was strictly confidential!" His wife hauled him back inside. The plastic sheet covering the garden furniture snapped at me like pistol shots.

6

When I arrived at the station, I found that I had to wait twenty minutes for the next train back to Rotterdam, so I went to the coffee shop on the platform and got myself another cup of tea and something to eat. There were no petit-fours; I had a doughnut. Sitting by myself at a little table, watching the crowd on the platform and trying to tune out a leather-lunged toddler yelling blue murder, I thought about Bartels' story. It sounded like emotional nonsense to me. Those two must have propelled one another into ever higher spirals of drama and sensationalism until their feet left the ground.

But once I was sitting in the train, watching the rain-swept vastness of the flat land reclaimed from the sea, which gave small Holland the aspect of a different planet, it occurred to me that the man's presentation and his personality might have put me off. It must be a familiar problem to police inspectors: some witnesses turn you off to the point where you disbelieve anything they say.

But was it possible that a modern vessel, certified seaworthy by Lloyd's of London, could be a time bomb in the way Bartels had described? Maybe he had been scared of the ship and dramatized her tenderness to vindicate himself; maybe the *Isabel Kwel* was what is known in the trade as a "ball-crusher," a ship that defeats captains until she hits one that licks her into shape. I had seen it happen, I had had one of those myself.

Bartels' anonymous telephone calls and Mr. Charlie S. Chung's visit by stretch limousine could all be explained. Mr. Chung had sincerely wanted a previous captain to serve as advisor to his staff, a logical choice. The fact that he had known the Bartelses had no family was not as sinister as the woman had made it sound; every owner worth his salt researches masters before entrusting them with capital ships. Fransen might indeed have been the 'rough, coarse voice' on the telephone; if a deal is in the making, captains shouldn't blab their mouths off on the subject of the ship under consideration. The 'Allied Marine Insurance Company' that turned out to be a hoax was probably a clumsy effort by a minor minnow among Mr. Chung's spies to collect information. It could all be toned down to decibels fit for the human ear.

Yet—there was a precedent: the first mammoth tankers. A number of them had mysteriously exploded while empty, after delivering their loads. It had been a baffling mystery, as there had been no fire, no spark, nothing that could have ignited the residual gases in the empty tanks. Nervous owners had started selling their new mammoths to the Third World; some of them even sold ships on the stocks. Then a boffin in some architect's office had come up with the answer: the built-in pumps that cleaned the empty tanks were the culprits; they swirled their fluid with such force and velocity that they created static electricity. No expert could have foreseen this and used it as grounds to deny the ships a certificate of seaworthiness; but once the fault was discovered, it was included in the standards for certification. Could it be that the *Isabel Kwel* also was suffering from a, so far, undiscovered lethal fault?

One element in Bartels' story made me believe she might be: the reaction of the members of his crew to his suggestion that the ship was 'a killer.' Their reluctance to admit it had mystified him; to me, it rang a bell: that was exactly how we had behaved on the Murmansk run during World War II. All convoys to Russia were

[35]

decimated by the German Navy and the *Luftwaffe;* of one convoy of forty-nine ships only two had arrived in Murmansk. Yet, to hear us talk in the pubs of Iceland and the Orkneys, it was all a huge lark. We behaved like the Spitfire pilots during the Battle of Britain: 'Death, where is thy stingalingaling?' Never, ever, would any of us admit that he was scared shitless; it would not only have been a gross breach of unspoken protocol but a totally self-destructive admission. For what could you do about it? Get off and walk? The crew of the *Isabel* had responded in the same way; if Bartels was right and they indeed had reason to be terrified, not only would none of them admit he was, but what could they do about it? Jobs were not that easy to find, and the captain, whoever he was, always found a way of dealing with it. What had really spooked them was his admission that he hadn't.

As I sat staring at the bleak landscape, at the slanting curtains of rain sweeping from the pitch-black sky to the glinting horizon, the challenging assignment unraveled in my mind. Whatever was the matter with the *Isabel Kwel,* she would need a topnotch tug-master of considerable cool and stamina, not a seventy-year-old with hypertension who woke up in the morning trembling with the beginning of God knew what degenerative disease. And why should I mess with her? I had a loving wife, a happy home life among congenial people, a fascinating hobby—

The train braked for the Central Station in Rotterdam. I took a taxi to the hotel.

7

When I went down to the lobby two hours later on my way to old Kwel's dinner party, I was determined to get out of the assignment. During the meal there would be an opportunity to do so gracefully and without making a production of it. My age was a good excuse; I didn't expect any problem.

When I emerged from the elevator, the hotel porter told me my limousine was waiting. The chauffeur must have been watching the revolving door, for the moment I came out he leaped out and opened the car door for me. There was one hell of a wind blowing; I had to hang on to my hat in earnest now.

As the car gathered speed, I leaned forward and slid open the partition. "Where are we going, may I ask?"

"Mr. Kwel's residence in Wassenaar, sir. It'll take us about twenty minutes."

"I see. Thank you." I leaned back in the cushions. I had never visited old Kwel at home before.

Eventually the car pulled up in front of a flight of steps leading to the pillared porch of a large, dark house surrounded by the tall cones of pines waving in the gale. At the top of the steps a butler in a claw-hammer coat and striped pants opened the front door for me.

"Good evening, Commodore. Mr. Kwel and his guests are waiting for you in the library. Allow me to take your coat. This way, please."

The hall was imposing: suits of armor crowned with plumes, the model of a paddle-wheel tugboat on an antique table carried by carved apostles. The butler moved across half an acre of Persian carpet toward a pair of heavy oak doors, which he opened; it was like the beginning of a British television series.

In a paneled, high-ceilinged room ablaze with chandeliers, three people were huddled in front of a fireplace. At my arrival, a woman in an evening gown crossed the room to greet me; she looked regally elegant, diamonds and all.

"Hello, Commodore."

"Hello, Miss Bastiaans. Nice to see you here."

"Let me introduce you to our guest. This is Mr. Chung, owner and president of the Kao Hsiung Steel and Shipping Company, Taiwan."

"Nationalist China, Miss Bastiaans," old Kwel snapped petulantly. He was sitting virtually on top of the log fire in a high-backed chair, a rug wrapped around his knees. A small, rotund Chinaman rose, wreathed in smiles, with the twinkling black eyes that make women want to adopt Chinese babies. "So happy to meet you, Commodore Harinxma!" If I hadn't heard Bartels' story, I would have been charmed; now I felt like a mouse being purred at by a cuddly cat.

The butler advanced on me with a tinkling glass of something on the rocks, on a silver salver. "Well, Harinxma," Kwel said, raising a glass of orange juice, "here's to our future cooperation."

Was this the moment to tell him? I decided not. "Cheers, sir—Mr. Chung."

[37]

"Bottoms up," Mr. Chung said, eyes twinkling as if this were the beginning of an evening with the Kama Sutra. Miss Bastiaans had disappeared; old Kwel, the Chinese and I were alone under the chandeliers.

"Harinxma, I told my friend Mr. Chung all about you, and he is pleased that you are the one to take the *Isabel* to Rio for him. He's left all the arrangements to us, but if you have any questions for Mr. Chung personally, this would be the time to put them."

Well, here it came. "I'm sorry, sir—Mr. Chung—but after studying the material on the ship and thinking over various aspects of the assignment, I have decided that it's not for me."

The old man shot me a furious glance. If I hadn't known he was blind, I would have been intimidated, as in the past; now, with again that unexpected sense of grief, I registered only his infirmity.

"What nonsense is this? What are you saying?"

"Mr. Kwel, I am seventy years old. I left the sea nine years ago. In those nine years, tugboats have changed beyond—"

Suddenly he let me have it, and despite his age he still packed a wallop. "Harinxma, I'm sick and tired of your posturing as an old man! God damn it, I'm twenty years older than you are, and look at me: I'm ninety, and I'm still in control of a company that employs over twelve thousand people!"

"But, sir—"

"You're knuckling under to the image of old age forced upon you and the rest of us by this idiot youth culture, this throw-away society we're living in! Do you realize what they've done to you? They tossed you out at the age of sixty, at the height of your powers in your profession, and now you find yourself in a ghetto called 'a retirement village' together with other discarded dodos. Everything you say, everything you do, your whole concept of yourself is imposed on you by the hucksters who make television commercials, in which we are pictured as loving granddads with rimless glasses hugging children who eat breakfast cereals, or staggering to the toilet with constipation, or powdering our dentures with glue. Are you being asked for the fruit of your experience? Consulted about the kind of problem you've spent a lifetime dealing with? No, sir! The young idiots claim the right to make their own mistakes, while you go in for half-witted pastimes like Bingo and shuffleboard and God knows what else fit for a ten-year-old. What you should do is what I'm asking you to do: get yourself on board that goddam tugboat my grandson rammed down my throat, pick it up by its ears and sail it to Rio!"

I couldn't help admiring a ninety-year-old blind man for unleashing this blast, but I stood my ground. "Mr. Kwel, in the time I've been away, tugboats have changed beyond recognition. I studied the literature on the ship; I cannot handle that computerized contraption. I wouldn't know where to begin."

"For God's sake, Harinxma! Who do you think you're talking to? I've been in this business for seventy years, I've seen ships develop from the age of sail! A ship is a ship, period. I don't give a damn what high-tech gadgets they load her bridge with, a ship needs a captain, and when it comes to that vessel you're the best captain I have. That's how I sold you to Mr. Chung. So, stop talking drivel, have another glass and start making sense. Mr. Chung, what do *you* say?"

Mr. Chung loved me; I could hear it in his voice when he purred, "Commodore, you'll be sailing under the flag of Nationalist China. In our culture, people your age are revered for their wisdom and their experience."

"And you won't be in actual command of the ship anyhow," the old man added. "The whole operation is meant as a training exercise for the Chinese captain and his staff. And you'll have plenty of assistance from four other advisors provided by us, all volunteers: first mate, chief engineer, radio officer and bosun. Your trainees will be experienced Chinese officers and sailors provided by Mr. Chung."

"A captain, two deck officers," Mr. Chung enumerated, "two radio officers, three engineers. The crew is made up of fishermen from a small island off the Chinese coast, their ancestors have been sailors for three thousand years. The supplementary crew is from a neighboring island and equally experienced."

"Supplementary crew?"

"The ship will be towing something minor. We need a supplementary crew to man the towed object."

Something minor that needed a supplementary crew. Like a battleship.

Mr. Chung cried, "Come, Commodore! Six weeks, purely in an advisory position! First-class flight home! And if you think your wife would enjoy it, a South American vacation. We'll be happy to fly her to Rio de Janeiro."

"In any case," the old man concluded, "you have a trial run

tomorrow. Take the ship out for a spin, find out how she handles. Then, if you still think she's too much for you, we'll talk again. Now let's relax and enjoy each other's company."

"Commodore?" It was Miss Bastiaans, smiling down on me; she had floated in unnoticed. "How about another one of these?"

Well, I might as well; my getting a little high wouldn't make any difference. "Very kind of you. Thank you."

"How interesting that you should be an *aficionado* of Scotch whiskey, Commodore," Mr. Chung said. "I thought Dutch sea captains preferred Geneva."

I explained to him that it depended on the circumstances.

Miss Bastiaans came toward me from the shadows in her long, pale gown, a tinkling glass in her hand. "Here you are, Commodore."

"Thank you, Miss Bastiaans." I raised my glass to Mr. Chung.

"Here's to the future," Mr. Chung said confidently.

It was the last time he referred to his offer that evening. During dinner in a candle-lit room, a flunkey behind each chair, he seemed interested only in me: my experiences during the war, my interest in ancient Rome. He drew me out on the subject of Theodosius the general and made a note of his name, saying he would order his secretary to get all the literature on the subject —the same treatment he had given Bartels. I told him there was only one contemporary historian who had done the man justice, but he was suspect because General Theodosius had been the father of the emperor.

Kwel allowed me to be the star turn of the dinner, with an occasional nod in the direction of Miss Bastiaans, who would instantly leap into the breach by saying, "How fascinating, Commodore! That's absolutely riveting!" before gesturing to my bodyguard to refill my glass with a white wine that made our local plonk seem like Kool-Aid.

The dessert was carried in on a bier: a flaming black confection in a white sauce. Kwel, to whom it was offered first, shook his head. Then Miss Bastiaans shook her head, then Mr. Chung shook his head; as I could hardly sit there stuffing by myself, I shook my head too with the thought that now, at last, I knew how the other half lived.

Kwel said, "Coffee and liqueurs in the library." Miss Bastiaans and the flunkey behind his chair helped him to his feet. When he was settled by the fireside again with the rug around his knees and Mr. Chung and I had sunk into our assigned chairs, the butler turned up with a huge silver tray with coffee, followed by a flunkey pushing a trolley with liqueur bottles. When we had all been served and I sat warming a balloon glass of Napoleon brandy between my hands, the old man cried, "Out! Everybody out! And no more disturbances! Close the door!" The butler and the flunkey made a hasty exit and closed the doors to the hall. "Well, Miss Bastiaans," the old man said briskly, "how about some Chopin?"

She rose, a picture of svelte elegance, floated toward a grand piano in her shimmering gown, sat down, cracked her knuckles and started one of the great Pole's melodious pieces.

You should always mistrust your reaction to performers when you have been drinking; even the most hackneyed piano player in a bar will sound like Vladimir Horowitz after three Scotches, a bottle of wine and a Napoleon brandy. But there could be no doubt that she played very well. She had no great technical brilliance, but then the piece didn't ask for that; it asked for sensitiveness, femininity and the capacity to identify with its shifting moods of hope and melancholy.

I sat gazing at the old man in his corner, as straight as a ramrod, head back, his imperious profile back-lit by the flames of the log fire, and suddenly I was overcome by a sense of loss, of farewell. To my surprise, I discovered that I was fond of him, despite the fact that he was an unmitigated bastard. My father had died when I was twelve; I had never had a substitute father except, I now realized, this old man who had dominated my life for over forty years. There he sat, daring death with his wasted body, his indomitable angry pride and a will like Moses' when he commanded the waves of the Red Sea to part. More than anyone else, more even than my beloved Sylvia, he had been the central figure in my life during my years at sea. Now, mellowed and maudlin with booze, I had the strange feeling that I was looking at him for the last time.

I glanced at Chung, who was gazing politely at the woman at the piano. His face was genial, almost impish; why was I so wary of him? Maybe it was the stretch limousine with the television. No shipping tycoon of repute would be caught dead in an ostentatious vehicle like that, for fear of looking like a pirate. Maybe he was one. In any case, he was not the innocent victim of the old lion in the corner; no one could sell that little man a lemon if he didn't want to buy a lemon. Why would he have wanted that flawed ship? Had the price been that low? Did he have a particular use for her in mind? Whatever the answer, I concluded I'd rather grapple with the old lion than with this smiling panda from the mysterious East.

Suddenly, as the woman at the piano started a new, rebellious variation of the melancholy theme, I was overcome by anger. Why, goddammit, couldn't these two bastards have given me the kind of straightforward assignment I had been led to expect? Why poison my last chance to go back to sea, to spend six weeks on an exciting modern tugboat, reveling in the memories of my past and trying to come to terms with my future? Why did they have to trick me into this hall of mirrors in which nothing was as it seemed, in which I was no more than a pawn in a game between two tycoons? Despite his dramatizing and his stuffing himself with petit-fours, I could see now why Bartels had resigned. For, indeed, what do you do as a master when you discover that your ship, the pride of the fleet, the most expensive salvage vessel ever built, is unseaworthy and the owners refuse to accede to your request for a private meeting in which to give them the news? Do you go on sailing the ship you no longer trust?

The old *Isabel,* my first command during World War II, had had a mysterious flaw too, which no one could explain and which had eluded all efforts to pinpoint it during a test run. That flaw had ultimately killed her, even though it later turned out to have been not the ship but human error. But the fear had been the same, the constant awareness of something wrong, something elusive, menacing, deadly. I had been young and inexperienced; I had shrugged it off and reveled in being Master After God of the most powerful tugboat in the world at the age of twenty-nine. But now?

Ah! How I would have loved to take on this assignment! Damn the two perfidious man-traders now gazing soulfully at the woman confiding her most private emotions to the piano. God, I was drunk.

When the last melodious cry of pain faded into silence, the two men applauded politely and I joined in rather passionately.

"Harinxma," the old man said suddenly in clipped tones, "whatever you do, don't allow them to play music for you on your deathbed. It'll drive you crazy."

Miss Bastiaans' voice asked charmingly, "Another brandy, Commodore?"

I looked up at her, shimmering in the light of the chandeliers, an allegorical angel without wings. I should have had the sense to refuse, but I was so smitten by her that I said, "Thank you. Thank you *very* much." I tried to make it sound full of meaning, and handed her my glass in defeat.

8

When the evening was over, I needed the butler's discreet assistance to make it to the front door. Outside, the gale nearly turned me into a missing person; both the butler and the chauffeur were needed to catch me before I took off and insert me into the limousine. Tears rolled down my face as I sat in the back seat alone, laughing.

I was piloted through the revolving door of the hotel by the chauffeur and into the elevator by the hall porter; from the look they gave each other, I concluded I must be pretty far gone.

But I didn't give a damn; I felt good, I felt terrific. It was a long time since I had felt like this. As I stood in the corridor upstairs and the door of the elevator closed behind me, I realized that I had forgotten to ask for my key. Then I found it in my hand; the porter must have put it there.

I managed to find my room; the sunny feeling that pervaded me made me want to call Sylvia, but maybe I wasn't in a fit condition for a marital conversation. I opened my suitcase and found inside a small package with two mince pies and a note: *Have a happy, happy trip, my darling man. I think you're wonderful to do it. Know that I'm aware of you all the time, day and night. I'll be thinking of you, praying for you, already I'm longing for the day you come home. Much love, more than I can put into crosses and circles. S.*

Tears welled in my eyes as I munched the mince pies; after this, I had to call her. The connection was made in a flash, the phone rang only twice before she answered, "*Madame Harinxma. Qui est à l'appareil?*"

"The mince-pie monster," I answered. "They were wonderful! Only an Englishwoman can make pastry like that!"

"Martinus?"

"Who else?"

"Are you drunk?"

Oh, it was going to be one of those conversations. "No, love," I said, "I just had an evening with the beautiful people. What was your day like?"

She told me, and didn't mention my condition again. I didn't mention the problem with the ship. But when it was over, my sunny feeling had dissipated.

I woke in the middle of the night, fully dressed, and discovered it was a bleak little room. Surely Kwel with all his money could have afforded something better for his one surviving commodore? But it was a good thing I woke, because now I could take the blood-pressure pills which I should have taken after dinner.

I undressed and settled down to sleep again. My last feeling before I passed out was one of pride: I had not signed anything. Despite the machinations of the evil empire, I was not going to tow a thing, not even a rowboat, across the Atlantic to Rio de Janeiro. I was going home, uncorrupted, to my dear wife and darling dog.

[Chapter Two]

1

The telephone roused me from a deep sleep. It was still dark and I had a splitting headache. I croaked, "Hello?"

A male voice asked, "Harinxma? Are you ready?"

"Who's this?"

"Fransen, head of operations. We're having a test run this morning, remember?"

"Jesus . . . What time is it?"

"It's early, but we have to leave now, Flushing is an hour away. I've got a taxi waiting outside with one of the architects. Come on, pull on your pants and come down. The sooner we get there, the better." He put the phone down.

I swung my legs out of bed and rested my head on my hands as the room swam around me. My God, it seemed I had hardly slept at all; my head felt as if there were a billiard ball loose inside. I had a tongue like a dead rat; my stomach acid would have corroded a doornail. I thought of calling Fransen back to the phone and telling him I was sick. But I couldn't do that; I was committed now and had to go through with the charade.

So I hoisted myself upright, had a quick shower to wake myself up, staggered around pulling on my shirt, my boxer shorts, my trousers, took my blood-pressure pills; when I bent over to put on my socks and my shoes, I was hit by an attack of hiccups. I must have really hit the bottle last night.

Walking down the empty corridor smelling of sleep, I tried to suppress the hiccups by holding my breath, but all I achieved was to make myself dizzy. In the elevator I tried once again, and succeeded momentarily because of the jolt when we hit the ground floor. The lobby was dimly lit; a scarecrow rose from one of the club chairs in the murk and loped toward me. "Well, there you are! Ready for a bit of fun?"

All I could do was look at him with bloodshot, baggy eyes. He took me by the arm and asked, "Are you okay?"

"Of course. Why shouldn't I—hic—be?" It sounded convincing but for the hiccup.

"I see," he said. "Dinner with the old man. Did he give you brandy?"

"He did."

"That's what does it," he said, guiding me to the revolving door. "Before he went blind, he must have got a kick out of seeing his guests swim out the door underwater, singing, with long hair."

The moment I stepped outside, the gale grabbed me; it had picked up considerably overnight and must be force ten by now. "Hang on, Harinxma," Fransen hollered against the wind, "in you go!"

He opened the door of the taxi, which was nearly ripped out of his hands by a gust, and shoved me inside. I landed sprawling on the lap of a dim passenger in the opposite corner, who helped me find my seat with what felt like tenderness. "Did you hurt yourself?" a girl's voice asked.

"No-oh," I said with a hiccup. "I'm fine. How do you do? My name's—hic—Harinxma."

"This is Baron Balthasar van Beusekom and Beverdingen," Fransen said from the front seat.

"To make it easier, most people call me B.B.," the voice said apologetically.

"I see. Well, how do you do."

The taxi took off; I sank into the corner of the back seat and closed my eyes, feeling miserable. My head throbbed, my stomach seared and I was still plagued by hiccups.

"Okay, Harinxma?" Fransen asked.

"Yes, thanks." I cursed myself not only for the stupidity of getting drunk, but also for the crazy notion that I would have taken on this assignment even under the best of conditions. I belonged home now, getting up gradually as the first daylight began to seep through the shutters, putting on my slippers, finding my glasses, turning off the illuminated alarm clock that projected the time on the wall, shuffling to the bathroom, gazing at Goya's Bridegroom in the mirror before putting in my teeth, combing my hair, then slowly making my way down the stairs to the kitchen to put on the kettle, let out the damn dog, put some Meow Mix in the cat's dish to make it shut up, prepare the tea tray, put on an overcoat over my pajamas and shuffle down the garden path to pick up the newspaper. *Jumbo Jet Flies into*

Mountain. President Mitterrand Admits Preferring English Muffins to Croissants; Bakers of France Outraged. Sunny, windy and warm.

It seemed a vision of heaven. Maybe I had needed this brief excursion into the world of youth to realize how fortunate I was, how beautifully my lifestyle suited my condition. Old Kwel couldn't have been more wrong when he said that my concept of myself was imposed on me by our youth culture; I couldn't sail a tugboat any more than I could perform a twenty-meter swan dive. I was not forced to behave like an old man, I *was* an old man, and bloody well liked it. Well, just one more hurdle to take and I would be on my way home. These hiccups were a bore; I went on holding my breath. The baron with the three-tier name beside me gave up the uphill struggle to engage me in conversation. Fransen took up the slack by shouting stories from the front seat while the taxi was shaken by the storm, drowning out his voice.

"You don't know Beast Rufus, do you?" Fransen bellowed, calling me back from a daydream of walking Héloïse in the perfumed hills of home.

I groaned, hoping to discourage him; but he went on, "You're in for a treat, Harinxma! He's a character, all right! He's probably the best salvage captain around, but we're having a hell of a time trying to keep him operating within the law! He's a card!"

About the last person I fancied meeting this bleak, unspeakable morning was 'a card.' Well, I would be the taciturn old grouch. One of the few advantages of growing old is that you're given a choice of roles with which to shut people up: cantankerous old bastard, stone-deaf old bore, senile jokester or frail stumbler permanently on the brink of tears. This morning I felt like all four; I prayed that the trial run would be short. All I needed to make my bliss complete was to be taken out into a gale by a card on board a rolling tugboat smelling of diesel fuel and be seasick.

After an hour's drive we arrived in the deserted streets of the harbor town of Flushing. It was a dismal place at any time; now, with its empty, wet streets lit by overhead lights swinging in the gale, it looked bleaker still. When the taxi drew up on the deserted quayside, I saw the silhouette of a tugboat outlined against a wild sky full of racing clouds turning blue in the dawn. Fransen had been right: at first sight she did indeed look like a pig. Her two stacks, side by side and close together, crowded the bridge and looked as if they were leaning outward, like ears. The squat snout, the ungainly body, the absence of the long, low sweep of an aft deck which to me had always been associated with tug-boats confirmed my overwhelming first impression: ugly. The photograph on the brochure had dolled her up with a bow wave and incongruous smoke pouring from her stacks so she had at least looked like something afloat; the contraption I contemplated from the taxi seemed a land-bound object, a space-age machine left behind on the surface of the moon. Her 'Paradise tree' with its dish antennas, radar reflectors, globes, coils and whiskers, a mysterious complex of electronic eyes, ears and tentacles, glinted faintly in the dawn.

Fransen helped me out of the taxi. The storm was fierce; I had to take my hat in my hand and started toward the *Isabel Kwel,* stumbling on the cobbles, my hair whipping in the wind. To approach her was a surprising experience. Neither from the photographs nor from my first glance at her silhouette had I realized the sheer size of the thing. She was colossal; as we entered the stillness of her lee, she towered above us like a pier with a lighthouse. There was a gangway; refusing Fransen's aid, I climbed the steep incline on my own, hiccuping. Those hiccups were a real pest; I hoped I hadn't done myself any serious damage. I couldn't remember their having lasted this long before.

When we arrived on deck, we found it empty. For a tugboat about to leave, this was unusual. There should be sailors at the bollards, a bosun checking the winch, engineers getting a last breath of fresh air before descending into their hellhole.

"This way, Harinxma," Fransen said, stepping across a high threshold into a dimly lit corridor. I followed him and caught a first whiff of the smell of diesel fuel.

There was more: the faint stench of overflowing toilets, the odor of breakfast hash being slung by a disgruntled cook somewhere below decks, smells that would have filled me with nostalgia if they hadn't confirmed my conviction that I was going to be seasick the moment the ship nosed outside.

Fransen opened a door and said, "Well, here it is: the bridal suite."

He let me step first into a cabin the size of a living room, with a wide view of the wild morning outside. A leather settee, leather club chairs, a coffee table and a room divider on which stood potted palms and the glass statue of a winged nude about to take off with a tugboat under her arm. Raunchy music panted from a loudspeaker among the palms; a cowboy wailed to the twang of electric guitars, "I gave you the ring, you gave me the finger."

"I'll see if he's awake," Fransen said and disappeared behind the palms.

I looked around the captain's dayroom. The walls were adorned with lithos of previous *Isabels;* I found my own 1940 one among them: an ungainly bull of a ship with everything livable bunched up forward. It seemed incredible from this distance in time that as a young man I had been in love with that ship. It was suddenly a moment full of meaning: an old man, holding his breath to suppress the hiccups of geriatric inebriation, face to face with the ship he had loved, the young man he had been. *Sing me a song of a lad that is gone; Say, could that lad be I? Merry of soul he sailed on a day—*

"Good morning."

I turned around and found a huge, red-bearded man with mean little eyes standing behind me, who sized me up with the sunny charm of a rampaging gorilla. "I'm Rufus Bron," he said, holding out a hand that somehow managed to look corrupt, as if he expected a banknote to be transferred in our handshake. "You want to take the old girl out for a spin?"

"That's the idea. How do you do, Bron."

His extraordinarily discomforting little eyes drank in the spectacle of the old wino before him, then he said, "What you need, Harinxma, is a hair of the dog."

"No, no! Thanks, but, for God's sake, no!"

My cry must have lacked conviction, for he went to an icebox, grabbed a crock of Dutch gin and a couple of frozen shot glasses, filled them with surprising dexterity considering he was holding two in one hand, held out his fist to me and said, "There you go: never again." He plucked one of the little glasses from his fist and tossed it back. I had no choice but to do the same.

The neat gin hit my stomach lining like liquid fire; I needed all my capacity for shame not to howl like a dog.

"Here," he said, proffering the crock. "Have another one."

"No, for God's sake . . . !"

"Believe me," he said with the authority of a specialist, "it takes two."

I knuckled under and committed suicide right in front of his eyes by knocking back another dose of the national beverage which Sylvia, even after forty years, refused to ingest, adamant in her conviction that it came straight from the lamp.

"Well, let's go upstairs and kick some ass," my host said sunnily. "The weather's just right, nice swell rolling out there. I'd better tell you, she separates the men from the boys. What this ship needs is a horse-trainer, not some egghead clutching a computer manual." I gathered this was a delicate dig at his predecessor Bartels. He turned to Fransen. "I hope the skeleton crew you dug up for me is up to this," he said as if he hoped they weren't. "Has any of them been on board this bucket before?"

"Oh, yes," Fransen said with ready assurance. "The chief has, the mate has. I'm not sure about the bosun or the second engineer."

"What about the ABs?"

"They'll be okay. All they have to do is cast off, haven't they?"

"Come and see," Beast Rufus said, putting an arm around his shoulders and taking him outside for what seemed like the execution. Startled by a wolf whistle behind my back, I looked around and saw it was a canary in a cage suspended from the ceiling in a corner of the bridal suite; I had missed that one. I followed the others down the corridor to a companionway which led to a lower bridge looking like the promenade deck for first-class passengers on an ocean liner. Then up another companionway, which emerged into the wheelhouse.

I recognized it from the photographs in the brochure, but they hadn't done it justice. The space was much larger than I had expected, glassed in on all sides and filled with an esoteric assortment of computerized equipment. Over the aft windows were five television screens. Two showed a winch seen from above; the third, the engine-room command post, with men in white coveralls surrounded by dials. The remaining two showed pieces of machinery I couldn't place. I was welcomed by the baron called B.B. and two middle-aged characters, one of them in white coveralls, who were introduced as Mate Valk and Chief van der Molen. They looked like participants in a wake.

The baron started to explain the electronic gadgetry to me: the radar scanner, the television screens, the weather-chart machine. Bron interrupted him. "Don't listen to him carrying on about his toys, we won't be needing any of them." He turned to the mate. "You Number One? Okay, let's get out of town. Somewhere quiet first, so Harinxma can find out what kind of sled he has strapped to his ass."

"The outer harbor okay?" Fransen asked.

"As long as there aren't any loose ships around; I'm planning to let him do a few sweeps. Better put out a bunch of lookouts before we swipe some herring farmer. You can cast off, Number One."

Mate Valk pulled the mike down from the ceiling and gave orders to take in the mooring lines; then he asked, "Will you take her?"

"No," Bron said, "you take her first. I just want Harinxma to see how she handles."

He and I stood in a corner while the *Isabel* headed out into the inner harbor ruffled by the wind. Low, shredded clouds raced overhead; the wind-frisked water was restless, with small, angry waves glinting like fish scales in the early light. The scene had an operatic quality, like the beginning of one of Wagner's Teutonic daydreams.

The moment the ship, buffeted by gusts, entered the open space of the outer harbor, Bron said, "Okay, let's do some baton-twirling," and took the wheel from Mate Valk. "Harinxma, come and stand beside me until I tell you to take over."

I obeyed.

"Chief?"

"Right here."

"Grab hold of those thrusters."

"Which one do you want?"

"Both. I'll tell you which, and when. Number One, give me half-speed on both engines."

"Half-speed." The mate worked the engine telegraph; the ship gathered speed.

"Okay, give me a starboard bow thrust, full speed."

"You're going too fast for that," a girlish voice said. It was the young architect.

"Shut up," Bron said. "Okay, Chief, do as I say."

The chief pulled the handle of one of the thrusters. The ship veered sharply to port, heeling slightly as she did.

"Okay, that's enough. Give me full speed on both mains."

"In here?" Fransen asked incredulously. The space was indeed limited.

"Who's sailing this ship, you or me?"

"Pardon me, I just thought that—"

"Look, friend, either I put this thing through her paces or you take over now. Make up your mind."

Fransen threw up his arms and walked away, joining the baron in the corner. Two down, three to go.

"Okay, full speed ahead."

The engine telegraph rang out; the ship shivered and gathered speed, heading straight for the quayside. Bron allowed her to virtually climb the basalt; then he ordered, "Stop engines," strolled over to the thrusters and did something that made her veer away at what seemed to be the last moment.

"Okay, Harinxma," he said. "You take the wheel and feel what she's like. I'll handle the thrusters. You do what I did and you'll be in for a surprise."

"What kind of a—hic—surprise?" I asked as I moved to take over the wheel.

"You'll find out," he said with a mischievous grin. "If you're half as good a sailor as they say you are, you'll know within the first few minutes."

'Well,' I thought, 'what the hell, I might as well put this monster through its paces and see what twenty-first-century tugboats are like.' I had no use for the knowledge, but I was curious all the same. So I got hold of the wheel, startled by its tiny size and its total lack of resistance. It spun as easily as a sewing machine, yet the three-thousand-ton colossus responded instantly.

"What speed do you want, Harinxma?" Bron asked at the controls.

"Let's start with half ahead."

"Both engines?"

"Yes."

The monster moved massively ahead; I worked the wheel and felt the huge body swing to starboard instantly. "All right," I said, "full ahead on both engines."

"Coming up," Bron replied.

With a surge that took my breath away, the giant ship blasted off for the opposite quay. I headed her away toward the open, with my heart in my mouth; she responded with such abandon that she heeled in the bend and stuff on the chart desk started to slide. I straightened her out and said, "Starboard half ahead, half astern port."

[52]

"Too brutal!" the architect's high voice keened from his corner.

"Shut up, boy," Bron said as if he were silencing a pet. "Try the thrusters, Harinxma, stern to starboard, bow to port."

"Okay, give me that."

Bron worked the handles of the thrusters, and the result was almost magical: the giant ship spun around like a London taxi. I was so taken aback by it that I let her make a full turn before I took her back in hand. "Jesus!" I said. "How about that?"

"I told you." Bron grinned with satisfaction. "And this is only the beginning. Sweat her some more, then we'll take her out for a spin. You're not going to believe this."

So, with mounting exhilaration and a feeling of awakening I cannot describe, I proceeded to put the *Isabel* through her paces. It was my introduction to the twenty-first century, all right. The ship's technology went way over my head. The workings of her innards were a mystery to me. Bartels' description of her had made me decide to shun her like the plague. Yet here I was: in tug-drivers' heaven. I felt her respond to a touch, a word, a daring command as if she had been waiting for just this: to swirl on a dime, whip around, charge, double back, trot, gallop, skitter and stop dead within a ship's length—and that over and over again. It was like joining a square dance with a diesel locomotive; never before had I handled a ship so enormously powerful and yet so responsive.

The gale swept the outer harbor. The spray of the fury outside streaked through her rigging, bursts of silver in the steel-blue morning light. Rain lashed the windows of the wheelhouse, squiggling down the panes, but through her clearview disk I had an unobstructed view of the world outside. There was not a moment in which I did not feel totally in control.

"Well?" I heard Bron ask by my side. "What do you say?"

"I've never known a ship like her. She's incredible."

"Welcome to the club," he said, "of two." He slapped my shoulder. "Now let's take her out into the real world. Chief, you'd better go down to your shop, we're about to start riding her in earnest. Be prepared for a few wild kicks, and warn the galley as you go down. As for you two," he said, addressing Fransen and B.B., "you'd better find a corner to jam yourselves into." Fransen obeyed; the baron shook his head. "All right, take her out, Harinxma."

[53]

I headed her toward the pierheads, where the foam was flying. The angry sea looked like the last place a man would want to be; white horses came storming toward us, manes flying.

"Hang on," Bron said, clutching the handles of the thrusters "this is where Bartels needed a change of underwear."

The ship nosed out; after a few wild rearings, her bow reaching for the clouds, she suddenly started a stomach-sinking lunge over starboard. It was totally unexpected. The violence and the suddenness of the lurch took my breath away. The baron came hurtling by like the daring young man on the flying trapeze and ended up in Bron's arms. I wanted to head her into the seas, but Bron shouted, "Let her do her worst, Harinxma! You'd better find out now!"

The ship, of her own accord, swung slowly to port and took the incoming swell on the starboard bow. She heeled over deeply, making everyone on the bridge reach for a handhold and hang on. But instead of swinging back, she went on heeling to an alarming degree. Things started to slide, fall, crash to the deck. Finally, at what felt like the last moment, she hovered on one ear, seemed to hesitate, then swept back with sickening speed, like a swing returning. She remained on even keel for only a second or two, then began to heel over starboard. I clung to the wheel as she lurched deeper; incredulous, I felt my grip slipping. I admit I was scared; no tugboat I had known had ever behaved this way.

Then Bron stopped the engines. That really made her do her worst; she wallowed in the troughs of the wild, confused swell like a sick cow, making us all hang on to our handholds for dear life. Fransen cried, "Bron!"

"Shut up!" Bron bellowed. "Harinxma! Let her shake her guts out!"

There was little else I could do. Down below, I could hear cries of anguish. Everything loose in the interior of the ship must have started a life of its own; the cook had probably fled the galley altogether. When the next row of white horses came storming toward us, everybody on the bridge braced himself for another sickening roll, but suddenly, magically, she righted herself and rode the waves like a gull.

It seemed a fluke. A second row came storming at us; again, instead of making a sickening lunge over starboard, the *Isabel* straightened up and rode the rolling hill of water like a seagull. Then I realized how Bron was doing it: with the thrusters. He was compensating the ship's wild gyrations with their tremendous counterthrust, and that not just once but continuously. "Take the thrusters, Harinxma!" he shouted over the roar outside. "Wait for me to call 'yes,' then give full power on both thrusters, countering her swing!"

We changed places, and Bron started to dare the sea. Full speed, half-speed, full speed astern, swerving, sweeping, playing with those killer waves a brontosaurian game of bumps-a-daisy. Each time she started her suicidal rolling cycle, he yelled, "Yes!" and I gave counterthrust from bow and stern, full power. The ship shuddered and shook; each time one of those waves slammed into her, I expected the Paradise tree above us to come crashing down; but she obeyed him like a broken-in horse. It was one of the most ingenious feats of seamanship I had ever witnessed. And so simple! Why hadn't Bartels thought of this?

"All right," Bron shouted, "your turn!"

I waited for the ship to hover on even keel before I made a dash for the wheel; Bron skidded to the thrusters.

"Ready?" I shouted.

"You bet!"

"Here goes!"

Now I started to dare the sea. The feel of the ship was different: there was a controlled frenzy to her power, a nervousness incongruous in so massive a monster; she felt like a racehorse straining to start down the track. I searched for the critical angle of attack of the incoming seas; when she started her stomach-sinking cycle, I shouted, "Yes!" and she instantly obeyed, without hesitancy or disorientation.

I started to put her through the twists and turns I had subjected her to in the inner harbor. I backed her, swung her, raced her astern, slammed her ahead, made her spin in circles, let her run away with the rudder midships and plow back without touching the wheel; finally I repeated the maneuver that coaxed her into starting her rolling cycle and had it squelched instantly by Bron at the thrusters. After about an hour of this, she had leaped through all the hoops I could devise for her. I headed back to port and looked over at Bron.

He nodded, satisfied. "Now put baby to bed." He lit a cigar.

"Take over the wheel for a moment," I said, "I'm going to take a leak, I'll be right back. Where's the john?"

"Right outside that door," Bron replied, pointing at the starboard wing of the bridge. "There's enough water flying around to wash away the piss of a herd of elephants."

As I came out onto the lee wing of the bridge, I spotted the baron throwing up over the rail, hatless, his hair a mad mop in the wind. I waited until he had gone back inside.

I took the ship back into port with Bron for a pilot. She moored like a dream; thrusters, I decided, were man's greatest invention since the wheel.

When the lines were ashore and snugged down, I felt forty years old, full of hormones, and realized I was hooked.

The alcoholic had fallen off the wagon.

2

After I had rung down 'Finished with Engines,' Bron took me along to his dayroom. He invited no one else; by then his authority was such that even Fransen didn't disturb the master's privacy. He groped among the palms, turned on the hi-fi, and a brow-furrowing number for choking baritone entitled 'Bouncing Balls' began to blast from the speakers. He poured two gut-zingers from the frozen crock, raised his shot glass at me and said, "Well, here's looking at her next skipper. Godspeed and happy sailing." He tossed back his drink, I tossed back mine; it nearly tossed me against the wall.

"Well, I don't know about that," I said, feeling as if I were speaking in tongues of flame. "She's supposed to have a Chinese captain."

He waved that notion aside. "You'll be the captain, Harinxma, don't kid yourself. No amateur can handle this bitch. It needs a man like yourself, with balls."

"Bouncing balls," I joked lamely.

"The tape? Oh, that's mine, I'm donating it to you. All Spooks had was fairy music. I took this one out of the car when my wife drove me to the ship yesterday. Hand me your glass." When I did so, he continued, "Just remember, don't let anybody handle the thrusters except you. The moment you feel she's getting the itch, streak up to the bridge, take the thrusters and put somebody you can trust at the wheel. Have a chair lashed right underneath the

[56]

handles so you're there when it happens. To you, she'll be a breeze, but that took—how many years?"

"As a captain? Thirty-five."

"Well, there you go." He handed me my glass.

I took it slowly this time, little sips which I rolled on my tongue before sending them down to the stokehold of my stomach. I was a crazy old man. Somebody would have to take me back to the hotel in a wheelbarrow. But I didn't give a damn. I felt terrific, I had not felt like this for nine years. I couldn't understand how I had survived; it now seemed I had led the existence of a two-dimensional ghost.

"Can you understand it?" Bron asked with an unfocused look. "Isn't this the most fabulous ship you've ever handled? And there the Kwels, those bow-legged, hairy moneylenders, go and sell this beauty to the gooks for peanuts! Because of a creep with tinted glasses and a spook-hunter with a Ouija board who should have been running ferries, not tugboats. Your glass."

"I haven't finished."

"Don't give me that." He topped it up from his frozen crock with such generosity that the ice-cold liquid splashed over my hand. I decided to feed it to one of his palms the moment his back was turned.

"Well," he continued, "I'll have this cabin straightened up for you. There's a dandy bedroom, a bathroom, television, the works. When are you coming on board?"

"I suppose tomorrow or the day after. But I'm not going to live here. It's the captain's."

"Well, you're a commodore, aren't you? Put on your gold rings and your cap with scrambled eggs and pull rank on the guy. Let him take the first officer's cabin, it's better than anything he's likely to have lived in up to now. Fransen seems to be leaving you the bird and Spooks Haversma's books. Have you seen them? Go and have a look while I hit the bathroom."

He disappeared behind the room divider with the palms; I strolled over to the bookshelf to look at some of the titles. Bowditch's *American Practical Navigator. Kinship with All Life. Recollections of Death. Human Personality and Its Survival of Bodily Death.* Haversma had been a serious man indeed.

I took *The Occult* by Colin Wilson off the shelf; as I opened it, a sheet of paper fell to the floor. I picked it up; on it was written in a schoolmastery hand: *Death is like the leaving of a ship. She unfurls her sails in the red of the sunset and heads for the horizon, leaving behind a group of mourners on the quay. As she disappears over the horizon, someone sighs, "There she goes . . ." But at the same moment, on a distant shore beyond the horizon, another group is waiting and someone cries delightedly, "Here she comes!"*

"You see," he said behind my back, "you're studying them already."

As I put the book back on the shelf, he came at me with his crock again. I had forgotten to feed my drink to a palm, but found to my surprise that my glass was empty. I put my hand over it. "No more, Bron," I said firmly. "I've got to get back to Rotterdam, and God knows what else I have to do this afternoon before I can hit the sack."

"Okay," he said with understanding. "At least I cured your hiccups. Have you ever had a bird before?"

The canary was contemplating me with a beady black eye, its head on one side. "Can't say I have."

"Well, we have one at home. The watchman has been feeding this one twice a day, he says; the seed is in the lefthand drawer of the desk. Keep its water topped up; if you've got people in here for drinks and it gets jealous and starts to drill like a dentist, throw a slipper at the cage. Like so." He took off his cap.

I felt it was time for me to leave.

The canary started to warble with a fierce, throbbing sound; Bron hurled the cap at the cage, hit a bull's-eye and the bird went into a frenzy, feathers flying. "If that doesn't work, cover the cage with a towel."

"Okay. I'd better get on my way. Thank you for this morning, it was very instructive. Where are you going from here?"

"First I'll take this bucket to Rotterdam, to the Park Harbor; later today I ship out on the *Fiona* for Cherbourg, where I pick up a tin dredge for Billiton. I'll do some pushing and pulling in Indonesia while I wait for a hotel structure that has to go to the Marquesas out of Singapore. So I'll be busy."

"Well, if I don't see you before you leave, Godspeed and happy sailing. And thanks again."

"You bet," he said. We shook hands.

In the corridor I ran into Fransen; I had the impression he had been lying in wait for me. "Are you ready?" he asked. "I won't be going with you, I need another couple of hours here. But I'll see you tonight, around dinnertime at your hotel."

[58]

"And the architect? Is he coming?"

"He's left, he had to get back in a hurry. You can call for a taxi from the harbormaster's office at the end of the dock. Lunch at your hotel; at fourteen hundred you're expected at the outfitters', half an hour later at the doctor's for your medical, then at the water bailiff's for the signing of the Articles. At eighteen hundred you interview your chief engineer, mate, bosun and radio officer at your hotel. I'll be there to tell you about them. See you then." He knocked on the door to the dayroom; I heard Bron bellow, "Come in!"

I set out for the harbormaster's office, leaning into the wind, my head ducked into my collar. I would have to call Sylvia from the hotel and tell her the trip was on; then I remembered I had never told her it was off. I entered the smoky intimacy of the harbormaster's office and asked the young man on duty if I could use his phone. I was given a mug of hair-curling overnight tea and listened to the story of his three-year-old singing 'Trees,' while waiting for the taxi to take me to the station.

3

In the station, on the empty platform, I found the baron waiting for the next train. I joined him on his bench and asked, "Well, how do you feel?"

I expected him to be pleased, relieved that his ship's flaw had turned out to be manageable; I was surprised when he gave me a teenage look of rebellion. "How do you *think* I feel?"

"Delighted, I'd say. You've designed a beautiful ship. She's without doubt the most responsive and nimble tugboat her size I've ever handled."

He shook his head. "Martinus, I'm not in the business of designing toys for megalomaniacs to show off with. She was designed to be a ship, not a death-defying contraption that can only be handled by a stunt man. I want sober, well-trained men to be able to handle my ships with ease and common sense. Those thrusters were never intended as stabilizers. There's a fault in her hull design, and we must find out what it is before we start building her sister ship."

[59]

"How far are you on that one?"

"She's in blueprints, ready to go on the stocks." He lit a cigarette. "Basically," he continued, waving out the match, "it's a matter of guts, of vision, and Arnold Kwel hasn't got it. This ship is a prototype, her hull embodies an entirely new concept. So she has a fault. It not only happens, it's routine."

"Any idea what the fault is?"

"Well, it's not just that she's tender. A ship can be tender." He looked around the empty platform; there was no one to be seen, but even so he lowered his voice. "Her problem is that under specific circumstances her MG suddenly diminishes, for no apparent reason."

"What are those circumstances?"

"That's just it! We could only find that out by field tests, or in the experimental model basin at Technical U., but old Kwel ruled out field tests and didn't want to pay for the basin."

"How long would that have taken?"

He shrugged his shoulders. "Anything from a month to a year. At five thousand dollars a day."

I began to see Kwel's problem.

"Not only did he turn down field tests and the model basin, he wouldn't even hear of any corrective measures."

"Such as?"

"Like giving her rolling fins. Kwel said the drag would increase fuel consumption and limit her maneuverability. Then, increase her MG by turning her fuel tanks into dual-purpose tanks, to be filled with sea water when empty. Under the law, this would involve scrubbing the ejected water with separators, as water mixed with oil pollutes the sea; Kwel said the separators were too expensive. We suggested pouring concrete into the bilges; Kwel said it would only increase her deadweight and thereby her fuel consumption. We suggested taking down the Paradise tree, but Kwel said removing her electronic gear would take away the ship's reason for being. I think he was just going through the motions. Basically, he's worried about her losing her certificate of seaworthiness. So he sold her before that happened. And here we are, my colleagues and me, suspended in mid-leap, so to speak. We begged him to give us the ship for just a month, a week, two days, days like today. But he wouldn't hear of it."

"What could you have done in two days?"

"Test her, test her, the way you did. Get you or Bron or

somebody in your class to put her through her paces in weather like this, and we would be there with our instruments making observations. Actually, of course, we should test her not in one but in a whole series of gales, gradually increasing her MG by taking down first the Paradise tree in sections, and if that doesn't solve it, working our way down."

"Let me get this straight," I said, not quite believing my ears. "Are you suggesting that you should crash-test the ship by demolishing her from the top down?"

He dropped his cigarette and ground it out with his foot. "Never mind," he said, "It's a pipe dream anyhow."

"I'm serious! How much did she cost to build?"

"Twenty, in U.S. dollars."

"Twenty *million*? You expected old Kwel to allow you to break up a ship of that value just to find out what's wrong with her design?"

"Martinus, forget it. Sorry I drew you into this. By the way, all this was strictly confidential. If any of this ever got to the wrong ears . . ." He lapsed into a gloomy silence, his head ducked into the upturned collar of his overcoat.

The train arrived. We found window seats opposite one another and sat gazing at the bleak, flat landscape swept by squalls. I wasn't keen to engage him in conversation, I had plenty to think about. The euphoria of the trial run gradually ebbed away; the time had come for some sober reflection, untainted by emotion.

I understood now why Bartels had resigned and maybe why Haversma committed suicide, although I found that hard to believe. They had been unable to handle the ship; she had filled them with the same dread I had gone through on that second run to Murmansk. But as far as I was concerned, all this didn't present a reason for me to turn down the assignment. With luck, we would have reasonable weather through the Bay of Biscay at this time of year; after the Cape Verdes it would be plain sailing. I was confident now that I could handle the ship. However, was it wise to let myself be drawn into this mare's nest of one tycoon selling another an unseaworthy ship?

I mulled over the whole business, gazing out of the window at the rising day; then another thought struck me. Somebody should warn the Chinese captain of the *Isabel*'s suicidal quirk, explain it in detail at the first opportunity, demonstrate to him how to cope with it once she started her dangerous cycle. The one to do that would be me.

As the train entered the reverberating vault of Rotterdam Central Station and came to a halt with a squealing of brakes, I decided not to tell Sylvia the whole truth. She would react very differently indeed to this pleasant little assignment if she knew that the *Isabel Kwel* was a killer.

4

The uniforms they gave me to try on at the outfitters' later that day were embarrassingly gaudy. The blue one had gold rings up to the elbows and the white one solid-gold shoulder tabs; the cap was the size of a helipad, its visor encrusted with scrambled eggs. As I stood gazing in the mirror wondering what I reminded myself of, the attendant came with a double bank of battle ribbons; after he had pinned them on, I knew what I looked like: a Soviet admiral about to review the May Day parade from the top of Lenin's tomb. I called Miss Bastiaans.

"Miss Bastiaans, sorry about this, but I'm at the outfitters' and I can't wear the uniforms they have prepared for me. They make me look like Admiral Rossopowski."

"I know, Commodore, but this is what Mr. Kwel ordered. He wants you to make an impression on the Chinese."

"Give them value for money, you mean?"

"Mr. Chung suggested it."

"And those battle ribbons! Where the devil did you dig those up?"

"Mr. Kwel did, Commodore. He looked up your movements in the old files. Let me see . . ."

"But they're music-hall stuff by now! You can't seriously—"

"Here, I found the list: convoy duty North Atlantic, salvage duty Western Approaches, convoy duty to Murmansk twice, so that's the one with the star, battle duty D-Day, battle duty Invasion South of France—"

"I've never done salvage duty on the Western Approaches. If I had, I'd be dead. They're all dead."

"Mr. Kwel said—"

"I don't give a damn what Mr. Kwel said! I'm not going to walk around looking like a—"

"You don't have to, Commodore, do you?" Her voice was full of sweetness and girlish mischief. "No one will be there to check whether you're wearing your Russian admiral's outfit once you're at sea, will they? So why not go along with it for just the next couple of days?"

I sighed. "Miss Bastiaans, you belong in the Paradise tree."

"Excuse me?"

"Never mind. Sorry I bothered you. I'll suffer through this fitting and get on with the serious business."

"Have you had your medical yet?"

"No, but I'm going there next."

"Well—good luck, Commodore, to us all."

Before I had been able to query that sentiment, she hung up. I acquiesced to the admiral's uniforms, but ordered a blue jacket without distinctives on my own account. The white one could be defanged by taking the tabs off.

The medical examination was conducted by a young doctor, incongruously tanned and aggressively thin. He called me "Pop," gave me the fastest checkup known to medical science, said, "You're okay, but too fat," listed my hypertension medication on the form and commented, "Keep up these pills or you'll be in serious trouble."

While I had him, I thought I might as well ask about my overnight tremors. "I suspect I may have the beginning of a degenerative problem, Doc. I wake up in the middle of the night sometimes with a sort of trembling inside my muscles, mainly my arms. And in the mornings it's very evident."

"Oh?" he said. "Hold out your hands." I did. "Are you a heavy coffee drinker? A teetotaler?" I said I was neither. "Well, it would need a full neurological workup, but I'm pretty sure I know what your degenerative disease is."

"Ah?"

"It's called booze. Like most other heroes of Holland's Glory, you're a lush, Pop."

I protested that I hardly drank at all, at home. He shrugged his shoulders. "I'm not going to argue with you, all I'm saying is: lay off the booze and you'll stop trembling. And while you're at it, lay off all coffee, sugar, fats, cholesterol and salt—I mean *all*. Exercise daily, and chances are you'll be able to cut down on your medication after a month and toss the lot overboard after three. But you'd rather take the pills, no?" When I didn't protest, he signed the form, slammed a stamp on it and bellowed "Next!" before I had been able to take care of Jack the Zipper.

In front of the water bailiff, whose office was next door, I did solemnly swear that I was over fourteen years old and would honor and uphold the conditions and restrictions of the agreement so help me God, then signed the Articles. As I did so, I discovered my rank was 'Salvage Inspector.' Well, it was better than pastry cook.

By the time I got back to my hotel, I was ready to collapse for an hour, but there was a message at the desk that a Captain Fransen was waiting for me in the bar. I found him installed in a booth with a bottle of whiskey and two glasses.

"Well," he said, "the pig's in the Waal Harbor, waiting for Daddy, so she's all yours. I gather you've signed on?"

"Yes."

He poured himself the glass of the lonely; it needed a lot of experience to drink it without going down on your knees first to slurp off the top. "If I were you," he said, "I'd move on board tonight. Bron had the bridal suite readied for you. Why don't you nip over there after the interviews and establish squatter's rights before the Chink shows up?"

"Interviews?"

"The skeleton staff, remember? In about ten minutes you get your first mate, here in the bar, man by the name of Slobkous. Then Bosun Schoonmaker, Radio Officer Harlingen and Chief Alberts, twenty minutes apart. If you don't like any one of them, let me know and I'll see if I can come up with an alternative."

"Is this man Slobkous the one who took over the ship when Haversma was killed?"

He looked up sharply. "How do you know that?"

I saw no reason to involve Bartels. "I have my sources."

"I see. We're being mysterious, are we?"

"Come on, Fransen! There's a great deal more to this assignment than you saw fit to tell me."

"Is there?" He gave me a tired look. "Well, in this business there usually is. But it certainly doesn't concern you, friend. Take my advice: stay out of it. Just do your job and everything will come up roses."

I was tempted to crowd him a little more, but wisdom prevailed. I was faced with the choice of either sailing a ship or turning into an amateur sleuth. One would cancel out the other; so I let it ride.

He lit another cigarette, pulled out his dog-eared notebook and flicked the pages. "Now, tomorrow. Janitors at six hundred hours, then caterers, linen, bedding, fuel, water, health inspector, rodent exterminator—the whole shebang. And to make your bliss complete: at fifteen forty-two—some hope!—your crew arrives from Taipei by KLM. Thirty-five bodies, all Chinks, comprising the following: one captain, two mates, one chief engineer, two ranking engineers, two radio officers, one cook, three cook's mates, two mess boys, one captain's steward—the only one of the lower ranks who speaks English—one bosun, one donkeyman, twelve ABs and six oilers. There'll be a bus to bring them to the ship, so be prepared."

"I'd like to meet them at the airport."

He gazed at me, his glass halfway to his mouth.

"I always made it a practice to welcome relief crews at the airport when they were flown in."

"But these are Chinese!"

"What difference does that make?"

He shook his head. "Harinxma, you're— Well, it's your baby. But tomorrow morning you're also going to have the compass adjusters, apart from all the other stuff. If you can find time to hand flowers to a bunch of Chinks at the airport with all that going on, you're a better man than I am."

"My mate will be on board."

He shrugged his shoulders, speared a gherkin and continued, "Okay, so I have to get you to the airport as well. I'll send—no, not a taxi: I'll send the bus to pick you up. Fourteen hundred all right?"

"Fine with me."

"Now, day of departure. One hour before cast-off: pilot on board and the captains of the *Polly* and *Jenny*, who are going to help you leave town. Out with the tide and off to Antwerp, where you pick up your tow: one thirty-thousand-ton dry dock for Talcahuano. Don't worry," he added, seeing my face, "the *Isabel* could pull three of them and never know the difference. Anyhow, you're getting off in Rio; up to there it's going to be a breeze."

"And thereafter?"

He shrugged his shoulders. "That's not your concern." He polished off his drink and put the bottle in the pocket of his raincoat. "Well," he said, rising, "I'm off to Bahrein. If I get back in time, I'll come out with the Belgian pilot to meet you. Here—the list of names of the characters you're about to interview. Have fun." He put his fedora on the back of his head and walked to the doors. I watched his somehow disreputable back disappear into the lobby.

A thirty-thousand-ton dry dock through the Roaring Forties? Those Chinese had better be good.

5

Ten minutes later a thickset, middle-aged man with a bulbous nose entered the bar, clearly a sailor. He looked around, sat down at one of the tables, shook his head at the barman and mumbled something. I observed him for a while as he sat there, looking around. He was neither drumming his fingers on the table nor glancing at his watch; he just sat there, as placid as a ruminating cow. I went to join him.

"Mate Slobkous?"

He rose, we shook hands. The barman came back for the order; when offered a drink, Slobkous shook his head and said, "No, thank you. I'll have a tomato juice."

"You don't drink?"

"I don't like what the stuff does to a man. I've seen too many examples of it."

"Well, you know the job: to act as advisor to the Chinese officers of the *Isabel* between Rotterdam and Rio. You'll have to be prepared to take control in situations when their unfamiliarity with the vessel may make it necessary. That should be no hardship to you; you know the ship."

"Yes," he said. His face expressed nothing.

"I gather she can be quite a handful."

He shrugged his shoulders. "They all can."

"This particular one has a few quirks I'd never come across. I ran a test with her this morning."

He nodded in a vacuous sort of way.

[66]

"Did you or Captain Haversma ever run into her rolling cycle?"

"Excuse me?"

"She shows a tendency to over-roll at a certain heading, under certain circumstances. You never came across that yourself?"

"Never."

He gave me a fish-eyed stare. It was not just that he was lying; there was something else that I couldn't put my finger on. My first impulse was to turn him down, but the fact that he knew the ship and even had commanded her, however briefly, was of paramount importance. At least someone would know what all the knobs, dials and switches stood for when we sailed.

"What other ships have you sailed on recently?"

He gave me an overview of his past few years; I observed him as he talked. He sounded all right, the list was respectable, I liked his temper and his manner, yet there was something. His lack of ambition struck me; in itself, that might be an advantage, but it might also be sheer laziness. Well, with two Chinese mates at his beck and call, he could spend his watches on the bridge in a hammock, as far as I was concerned, so I hired him. He seemed pleased in an offhand way; he said he would be there the following day, sometime in the late afternoon. He did not ask if there was anything he could do before then.

"Make it tomorrow morning, six o'clock. I have to meet the Chinese crew at the airport and we'll be having a carousel on board: fuel, water boat, janitors, linen service, chandlers, exterminators, adjusters, you name it. I want you to stand in for me while I'm gone."

"No problem," he said laconically. The perfect mate, if you didn't mind a hammock on the bridge.

The moment he left, a huge hulk loomed over me; I looked up and saw a Nordic face with high cheekbones. He must be the bosun. He held out a hand the size of a frying pan and said, in a voice loud enough to stampede cattle, "Hi there, Ome! How are ya?" He pumped mine; when he put the other one on top of it, I winced.

"Sit down, Bosun, sit down!"

He sat down; the barman turned up to take his order.

"Beer?" I asked. "Gin?"

"What are you having, Ome?"

"What's this 'Ome' business?"

He suddenly became self-conscious. "What? Oh—oh, I'm sorry, I meant Commodore."

"Come on, Bosun, I'm just curious. Is that my nickname now?"

"Hasn't it always been?" he asked, amazed. "I thought you were always called 'Ome Tinus.' You don't mind, do you?"

"Hell, no. I just thought—Well, never mind." The last I had heard, the name they had given me on board was 'Fancy That.' But that was a long time ago; at some moment in the intervening years, without my knowing it, 'Fancy That' had changed into 'Ome Tinus.' 'Ome' was the colloquial word for 'Uncle' and without malice, but it suggested an avuncular presence bringing candy for the baby. Well, maybe that was what I had become.

"When did you sail with me, Bosun?"

"Years back, Ome, as a kid. I was snotboy on the *Henrietta* when she went round the Cape to Priok and back. You wouldn't recognize me, I was a skinny kid then. But you gave me a book to read, *The Sea Wolf* by Jack London."

"Fancy that," I said. "Well, tell the man what you want to drink."

"What are you having, Ome?"

"Tea."

"I'll have tea too," he said loyally. The barman departed, disenchanted.

"Well, what do you know!" he said. "Off to Rio. It's going to be a pleasure, Ome."

"Thank you, Bosun. Now let's talk business. Have you been told what your job is going to be?"

"Well—sort of."

"You have the rank of bosun, but you'll act as an instructor to your Chinese opposite number."

"Chinese?" he asked, raising massive eyebrows.

While I explained it to him, the barman came with the tea. The bosun dumped sugar into the glass, stirred pensively and asked, "Are we going to have our own cook? I mean us whites?"

"Why?"

"We can't eat *their* crap, Ome. I've sailed with them before. What they eat isn't what you get in a Chinese restaurant, it's things like slime pie, noodles and cat's piss, with chopsticks. You can't eat that stuff, it would make you sick. How many whites are we?"

[68]

"Five."

"Oh," he said, "in that case *I'd* better do the cooking for us. I used to cook on the old *Josie* after the regular cook took off in Houston. Everybody seemed satisfied."

I foresaw a problem with the Chinese cook if he started to use the galley, but decided to cross that bridge when I got to it. "That's very kind of you, Bosun—beyond the call of duty."

"Nothing to it. Give me some money now and I'll do the shopping for tonight and tomorrow morning."

I gave him a hundred guilders and made him sign a chit.

"How long before I can shop again?"

"Day after tomorrow, in Antwerp."

"Okay. I'll stock up on some *nasi goreng* and *bami* now, the rest in Antwerp. You like it hot?"

I winced at the prospect. The difference between Chinese cuisine and his version of Indonesian cooking must be theoretical. But he was so keen to please that he sat there virtually wagging his tail, so I let it ride and got down to the technicalities that were his province: hawsers, mooring lines, parceling, grease, paint, rust-picking hammers, wire brushes, all part of the tender loving care of a ship. Suddenly he asked if I had a personal steward; when I replied that only the captain had, he said, "Let me take that on, Ome. I'll go on board now and see that you're comfortable."

"That's very kind of you, Bosun. You might start by cleaning out the canary's cage. We'll talk about the rest tomorrow."

The canary was good news to him. "What's her name, Ome?"

"I don't know. I don't believe it has any."

"*Is* it a she?"

"Bosun, I frankly—"

"I'll go and find out."

"How? With a magnifying glass?"

"You have to wait until the bird sings, then you know. Is she a good singer?"

"Loud and persistent, I gather. It used to be Captain Haversma's bird."

"What kind is she? A Yorkshire roller?"

"I honestly—"

A tall, blond young man appeared at our table. "Excuse me— are you Commodore Harinxma?"

"I am. Who are you?

"My name is Joop Harlingen, sir. I'll be your radio officer. That's to say . . ."

I greeted him more effusively than was warranted; the bosun rose to his feet. Towering over us after having pumped the young man's hand, he said, "Don't you worry, Ome. By the time you come home tonight, she'll be all cleaned up and happy and I'll know about her sex."

"Splendid," I said, glancing at the young man. "See you later, Bosun." After he had left, I explained, "He meant the ship's canary."

The young man grinned. "Tough luck, Commodore. Do you want to see my dope sheet?"

"Sure."

He pulled a sheet of paper from his pocket and handed it to me.

I was interested to see one trip with Captain Bron on the *Fiona* on his list. "Well," I said, folding the sheet and handing it back to him, "you know it's not going to be a normal run? We have a Chinese crew, unfamiliar with the ship . . ."

I explained the setup again, including the Taiwanese flag; he listened intently. The barman came; this time I ordered a glass of Amontillado; Harlingen followed my example, although it must have been a while since he last had a glass of sherry. When it came, he raised his glass. "Well, Commodore, here's looking at you."

"Cheers, Harlingen. The Chinese marcos probably have no experience with the equipment on board the *Isabel*. How about yourself?"

"Oh, I'm familiar with it. But I'll go and take a look at it now, if that's all right with you. I mean, if I'm hired?"

He was an amiable chap and I saw no reason to be persnickety about him, but there was something: nervousness, an uncertainty. It might be the ship. I asked casually, "You know about the *Isabel?*"

He gave me a sliding look. "Oh, yes," he said. "Everybody does. Doesn't take long for that kind of thing to get talked around in the fleet."

I hadn't intended to interrogate him, but he behaved as if I were doing that. He folded his hands and cracked his fingers. Then he said, "I mean—about her problem and so on."

[70]

"What problem?"

"Well—you know. Stability and so on. She isn't very popular. Whenever somebody was detailed for a stint on her, people commiserated."

"Then why did you volunteer?"

He looked surprised. "I'm sorry, Commodore, but I didn't volunteer. I was told to make this trip or else."

"Or else what?"

"Well—I might as well tell you. I had a problem in the past. A sort of a black mark. Nothing serious, but—well, you know the way it is."

"Would you mind telling me?"

"Not at all. I was serving under Beast—er—Captain Bron on board the *Fiona* in the Med. We picked up an SOS from a Swede who'd run aground in a fog just outside Skikda. You know how it is, other salvage tugs on station in the area picked it up too and they all came running: a Frenchman from Algiers, a German from Brindisi, the Englishman from Gib. The company got us the job, not just because we were the biggest but because we would be there first—or so they told the Swede. I damn well knew we couldn't be, we were too far away; even with a weight on the safety valve, it would take us twelve hours, and they said five. There was another boat of the company's within range, the *Hester*. She was towing. I knew her marco, we'd been chatting. Stupidly, as it turned out, I said to him something like, 'How about that bunch of liars in The Hague?' and mentioned the twelve hours. Well—it seems a lot of people were listening in, and there were—well—problems. Captain Bron threw me off the bridge, then I got hell from the company when we came in. They didn't fire me, but all the same it's a black mark, you know. So if you feel that you'd rather not have me . . ."

"I don't give a damn," I said. "This is a teaching job. The two Chinese marcos may not speak any English, by the way."

"Oh I don't mind that," he said. "As a matter of fact, I think I'd have liked the job, even if they hadn't forced it on me."

"Why?"

"Well, the *Isabel* isn't exactly a dream boat, but she has a lovely radio station. I'd like to get my hands on that. And as to the risk—well, you've been at it much longer than Beast—than Captain Bron has, and he licked her into shape all right."

So the *Isabel* was a penal colony, and this voyage a punishment for past misdeeds.

"I don't think you have anything to worry about," I said. "The run to Rio via the Cape Verdes is not called *La Route des Dames* for nothing."

"H'm," he said with another of those sliding glances. "Anything else I should know?"

"Well—there's a rumor that we may be asked to stay on as far as Talcahuano. And that I wouldn't like: through the Forties with the *Isabel*."

"I signed on as far as Rio. Didn't you?"

"Yes—but if in Rio they tell me, 'Stay on or else,' what can I do?"

It was getting more interesting by the minute. I wondered what was wrong with the other four. "Well, let's cross that bridge when we get to it," I said. "As far as I'm concerned, I'll be happy to have you on board."

"Thank you, sir."

"When can you move on board?"

"I've said my goodbyes and I have my gear with me, so I could move on right now."

"Very well, she's moored in the Waal Harbor. I'll join you there later tonight. See you then."

"See you, Commodore." He rose. "And thanks a lot," he repeated, as if I had done him a big favor.

I watched him walk away; then I wandered over to the bar. I needed a bit of exercise after all these disclosures. The bosun seemed straightforward enough, but I was pretty certain that something about Mate Slobkous was not quite kosher. I wondered what the chief engineer's criminal record would be, or, God knew, his trail of broken engines. But that was not the only thing that bothered me. There was Jim Kwel saying, as I entered the office, 'So you're the one who's going to take our *Isabel* to Talcahuano." At which his grandpa had snapped, 'Rio! And mind your manners,' or words to that effect. Well, curiouser and curiouser. I had better start watching my back, rather than indulge in nostalgia about the blind old man. Blind or not, he still had his sleeve full of aces. I might also have to revise my opinion of Mr. Chung's ability to look after himself; maybe he should be advised not to play cards with strangers.

"Commodore?"

I caught sight of him grinning at me in the mirror behind the bottles, and it gave me a shock—it was like seeing a ghost. But when I turned around to face him, the spell was broken; he just looked like someone I had known. "Hello there," I said. "You must be the chief engineer."

"Yessir!" He grabbed my hand and shook it warmly. "Glad to know you at last, Commodore! I've been waiting for this!"

"How so?" I asked, wondering what I was in for now. He was a keen, brown-haired, blue-eyed boy in his late twenties. Very young to be chief; but then, the policemen these days looked barely out of high school. "Sit down, have a drink."

He climbed onto a bar stool next to me and gazed at me with a spaniel look. "Gee," he said. "How about that! At last!"

"What'll you have?" Anything to get that soulful look off his face. I beckoned the barman; he strolled over, rubbing a glass.

"I'll have a Harvey Wallbanger," the young man said.

The barman asked, "I beg your pardon, sir? What was that?"

He described the Wallbanger; it sounded lethal. "It's what we sailed on when I was stationed in Elizabeth, New Jersey." He sounded like a bad actor in a movie about the British Navy.

The bartender took his time preparing the drink, writing down the ingredients as if he wanted to be covered for the insurance. He put the glass in front of the young man, who raised it and said, "Well, here's looking at you, sir."

"Cheers. By the way, what's your name?"

"Pieter Alberts, but my shipmates call me Porks."

I stared at him, thunderstruck; I *had* seen a ghost.

He added, "It was my dad's nickname too, as you know. Nobody knows what it means, but—well, everybody just picked it up. You do remember him, don't you? He talked about you a lot."

I had had time to recover. "Of course I do. Good engineer. Where is he now?"

"I'm afraid he passed away, a year ago."

"Sorry to hear that. What of?"

"Just old age, I guess. He was sixty."

"Oh. Sorry to hear that."

"Well, he had a good run for his money. You were together on the Murmansk run, weren't you?"

"Yes."

"I know all about that. My dad never stopped talking about how you tried to tow the last remaining freighter while all hell was breaking loose and how the old *Isabel* went down."

"I see." I wondered if Porks had ever owned up to his son that he himself had been the cause of the old *Isabel*'s sinking, by getting his engine signals mixed up under stress.

"That torpedo must have been just a lucky hit," the boy continued, looking in the mirror behind the bottles as if his father were gazing back at him.

I decided not to mess up old Porks' reputation. What he had told his son was his own business, and the whole thing was more than forty years ago anyhow. "Lucky for them," I said, emptying my glass and shoving it across the counter. "Another beer, please. How about you, Porks?" It was odd to call the boy by that name. It was as if I was caught in a time warp and gazing at his father in his bunk before we set out from Iceland, off Cape Langanes. *'You're sure we're going to be all right, Skipper?'* I didn't care for it.

"How did you know it was going to be me?" I asked. "Did the office tell you?"

"Oh, no. It's all over the grapevine, as far as the Firth of Forth."

"And what made you join this ship?"

He gave me a boyish grin. *"You* did, sir."

"I?"

"When I heard that you were going to be in on it, I decided I wanted to find out who my dad had been talking about all these years."

It was a touching remark, and I would have been sincerely moved if I myself hadn't heard about this whole affair just two days ago. Despite the speed of the grapevine, there was no way he could have heard about my involvement, volunteered to join the ship and come down from the Firth of Forth in forty-eight hours.

I wondered what the charming boy had done, for KITCO to send him to the penal colony called *Isabel Kwel.*

6

After young Porks had left, I should have gone to the restaurant and had dinner; but I decided to call Sylvia first, from the room. On the way I told the reception that I would be checking out tonight; they took it in their stride—they must be used to sailors and their unusual timetables.

By then I had been on my feet since four in the morning; after a brief loving talk with Sylvia while lying on my bed, I barely managed to reach up to put the phone back before I dozed off. When I woke up after what I thought had been a few minutes, it was ten o'clock. I packed in a hurry, went down to sign the bill and asked the porter to call a taxi.

On impulse, I told the driver to pass the gate to the dock where the *Isabel* was moored and drive down the next quay. When we were opposite the ship, which was lit up by floods like a seaside gambling joint, I got out and walked to the water's edge to have another look at her.

She was indeed stunningly ugly. Again I was struck by her top-heavy silhouette, her angular lines, her stacks like pointed ears. My old *Isabel* might have been ungainly, but her grandchild was a Frankenstein monster among tugboats. I had commanded ugly ships before and proceeded to fall in love with them; this time there seemed to be little danger of that—she was indeed a pig. I went back to the taxi; presently I was offloaded at the *Isabel*'s gangway. The ship looked wide awake with those floods, but I saw nobody on deck. The driver carried my bags to the bottom of the gangway and drove off; the car's headlights swept over a stack of lumber covered with tarpaulin and a bright blue telephone kiosk like a surrealist painting. I lugged my bags on board and headed for the companionway to the forecastle deck and the captain's quarters.

It took me a while to find them; finally I opened the right door and stepped across the high threshold into the dayroom with the palms and the winged glass nude with the tugboat under her arm. The room seemed shabbier somehow than it had earlier; the sofa and the chairs looked chafed; the palms on the room divider had obviously not been watered for quite a while, one of them was dead. In the cage in the corner the scruffy canary warbled its unpleasantly tuneless and grating song; there was a smell of dead cigars and unwashed bodies, like a motel room after a stag party.

I carried my bags around the room divider into what seemed to be an office, with a desk and a swivel chair, a computer on a stand and a couple of filing cabinets. From it a door led to the bedroom suite. It was spacious, with a wardrobe and a chest of drawers and a low bunk, wider than the ones I had been used to;

[75]

connecting was a bathroom with toilet, washbasin and shower. Above the bunk had been pasted a picture of two reclining nudes engaged in mutual gynecological exploration; my first act as advisor was to peel it off the wall, crumble it into a ball and toss it into the wastebasket. After that I went back to the dayroom, sat down on the couch and watched the canary hop around in its cage.

After Fransen's cynical statement in the bar and my meeting with the staff members, of whom only the bosun struck me as being of solid value, the thought of calling the whole thing off recurred to me. Rationally speaking, I was out of my mind to undertake this assignment. The ship had a serious problem, to put it mildly. The staff had obviously been put on board as punishment for past transgressions. Old Kwel and his grandson were involved in some underhand business in connection with the deal; I had been unable to detect exactly what, but it was certain to be something I should not be a party to, however innocently. And a thirty-thousand-ton dry dock was one hell of a mass to haul across the Atlantic with a bunch of inexperienced Chinese—they must be inexperienced or they wouldn't have needed me.

Yet here I was, Adam under the Paradise tree, seduced by a big, shiny apple—the ship. Looking at her across the water and thinking 'ugly' and 'a Frankenstein monster' had been pure camouflage; the pathetic part had been that the one I had tried to hoodwink was myself. Now, while staring at the canary hopping from perch to perch with a musical sound, I faced the truth. To go on this trip would be stupid, reckless and possibly dangerous. I was being manipulated by experts without conscience or compassion. Yet there it was: anyone who wanted to stop me taking this ship to Rio would have to shoot me.

I asked myself why. Was it because I yearned to be forty again and full of hormones? Because I longed to booze with the participants of Happy Hour again? Probably; but the main attraction was the ship, not despite her fatal flaw but because of it. I wanted to pit my wits, my experience and my tenacity against her deadly secret; I wanted to be the one to ultimately tame her, not Bron, who had, when all was said and done, tried to make the best of a bad job by inventiveness and exhibitionist ballyhoo. As the architect had said, those thrusters were never meant to keep her upright, merely to increase her maneuverability. There must be a way, or a combination of ways, to keep her from a suicide attempt each time nobody happened to be watching. What it would need was an act of identification on my part . . .

I brought myself up short. This was romantic nonsense. I should not try to rationalize or rhapsodize an act of willful folly, but, once I had decided to do it, get on with it. In Beast Rufus' immortal words, I should now go and find out what kind of sled I had strapped to my ass. I took from Miss Bastiaans' portfolio the brochure meant for potential customers, which had a detailed plan of each of the eight decks, and set out on a tour to familiarize myself with the ship's layout. I had to do it now, for tomorrow she would be swarming with people and I would be up to my eyes in other business.

Deciding to start from the top and work my way down, I followed the plan and took a series of companionways all the way up to the flying bridge. Good thing the floods were on; in the dark it would have been a risky expedition. As I emerged in the windy, wide-open space of the top deck, I suddenly found myself caught in another time warp.

It was the fire-fighting water cannon that did it. There were two of them, one on each side of the bridge, as there had been on the old *Isabel* during the war. Only those had been Bofors guns, for use against strafing aircraft and, in a pinch, surfacing U-boats, although we had been forbidden by stern instructors to depress them that far. With their familiar and somehow comforting silhouettes, there was the war again, all of it: the fear, the brotherhood, the sense of timelessness, of living through an episode with a clear beginning and certainly a clear ending, whichever way it turned out. A part of your life that would never form a whole with the rest of it, but remain an interlude of terror and heartrending sorrow and occasionally euphoric joy. Ah, well—old men and their wars.

There was more to take in on the flying bridge. On the inboard side of each stack was a set of rungs that led to the walkway on which was rooted the Paradise tree. From there a series of ladders gave access to three platforms, one above the other, with the multiple radar scanners, dish antennas and other esoteric equipment, as well as four searchlights and the air horn. The Paradise tree was very much larger and higher than it had seemed from the quayside, even from the navigation bridge deck one story below.

There seemed to be a permanent hum or rather a throb in the air; I looked for the source and discovered a screened air-intake in the aft part of each of the two stacks; they must be part of the ship's air-conditioning. Apart from the hum, this uppermost bridge must be pretty quiet during the voyage, a good place to put up a deck chair and take the sun after Cape St. Vincent.

The navigation bridge deck, one flight below, was in effect the wheelhouse I knew. But I used the opportunity to go round it once more at my ease, taking in all the equipment, the chart desk, the bank of dials and instruments almost as wide as the wheelhouse itself, the nerve center of the ship. Then, one flight below, the bridge deck proper: the covered part a storeroom containing the steering engine and some other machinery I couldn't place, the open part a wide deck with the tanks of compressed air, the cradle of the foremast boom and the navigation lights. One floor below that, the forecastle deck with my quarters and those of the first officer and the chief engineer, as well as the hospital, which was where I probably would end up if the Chinese captain insisted on the master's cabin: clean, aseptic, a sink with surgical taps, a pharmacy cupboard with a red cross, a bed high enough to change the patient's sheets without having to bend over, the floor-covering a vinyl imitation of marble. Not the most attractive place, but it would have to do. This night, in any case, I would spend in the captain's bridal suite.

As I explored the rest of the accommodations, opening doors and turning on lights, I came upon the radio room and spotted the first sign of life since I had come aboard: a smoking cigarette on an ashtray beside a typewriter keyboard that, I assumed, served the Telex, with a swivel chair in front of it. The room was much larger than the ones I remembered; every square inch of wall space was taken up by banks upon banks of radio equipment, all of it a mystery to me. "Sparks?" I called.

"Looking for me?"

He peered around the edge of a door behind me, which seemed to lead to another cabin. There was a look of bewilderment on his face and I remembered that radio officers were no longer called 'Sparks' in the fleet but 'Marco.' "How are you making out?" I asked.

"Oh, okay—only I don't have a mattress in my bunk. I suppose my predecessor had some orthopedic deal that he took with him when he left. Okay if I use the hospital for tonight? I suppose they'll give me a mattress tomorrow."

"Help yourself. I'm just looking around to get my bearings. That your cabin?"

"Yes, want to see it?"

I followed him inside. It was a pleasant little bed-sitter with a double bunk, a couch, a desk and an armchair. Over the desk another lurid color photograph of a gynecologist's view of the female genitalia was taped to the wall. He saw me look at it and said, "I've been trying to make it look a little more like home."

It made me wonder about his home life, but I kept my counsel. As he was the only one who had owned up to having had 'a minor problem,' I felt I could broach the intriguing subject of the penal colony with him. "Just as a matter of interest: I gathered you wouldn't have accepted this job on this ship if you'd been free to choose?"

"God, no," he said with feeling.

"I suppose the others feel that way too?"

"I don't know them, really; I never sailed with any of them. But they must have blotted their copybooks some time or other or they wouldn't be here."

"Any idea why?"

"Because it's a so-called volunteer job, this trip. Seems the union prohibits placing its members on foreign-flag vessels unless they volunteer. There simply weren't any volunteers, so they shanghaied the ones who had a black mark against them."

"Is her reputation that poor in the fleet?"

"Poor? Everybody knows she's a killer bitch. I was planning to resign altogether and get a job ashore until I was told they'd hauled a real old expert out of the mothballs—out of retirement to take her in hand, and I thought, 'Well, let's give it a whirl.' I love this radio room, lots of new stuff."

"Expert in what, exactly?"

"Ships like her. The handling of killer bitches. Are you? Sir?"

"I have survived to be seventy, that may be indicative of something."

"Seventy?" His face was a study. Then he said, "Well, President Reagan is seventy-two . . ."

"And Victor Hugo was eighty when he wrote *The Hunchback*

of Notre Dame. So you're going to be all right. Good night, Marco. See you in the morning."

"Good night, Skipper."

It was a long time since anyone had called me that.

I continued my tour of the ship. Finding my way through a maze of corridors to paint room, salvage store, fan room, winch-control room and officers' dayroom, I came upon a second sign of human life in this vast rabbit warren: the smell of coffee. It guided me to a galley like the well-equipped kitchen of a modern hotel; the homely bulk of the bosun loomed among the gleaming array of pots and pans, ranges and microwave ovens. He was pouring black coffee into three white ship's mugs from a comfortably old-fashioned enameled pot. "Hi, Ome!" he cried as he saw me standing in the doorway. "Just making some Java for the two officers. I didn't know you were on board yet. Would you like some?"

"Don't think so, Bosun; I'm planning to turn in soon. Thanks all the same."

"Pleasure, Ome. You go to bed and I'll bring you up a night-cap. It'll help you sleep."

"Very kind of you. Tell me, how come you ended up on board this ship?"

He looked up sharply, then went on pouring. He put the pot back on the stove, wiped his hands on his pants; finally he said, "I stood up for a drunk."

"How so?"

"Chap by the name of—well, never mind. He's gone now. But it wasn't his fault he drank too much; his wife was no good. He worried, you know? Good sailor, the best. I knew if I reported him he'd be out on his ear. He only drank when he wasn't on watch, so I let him get away with it. Then, suddenly, Captain Fransen came down on me like a ton of bricks. Somebody must have squealed. He said I'd endangered the ship, broken the rule that alcoholics have to be reported, run a sloppy crew, shielded shirkers—that sort of thing. I was taken off the *Henrietta* and put to work painting the basement of the head office in The Hague. Then I was ordered to volunteer for this job and told it was my last chance. The company isn't like it used to be, Ome. It's like the Navy now, or worse. It's—well, I talk too much. But you must know all this from my dope sheet. Don't you?"

"No, and it doesn't matter to me. Happy to have you aboard, Bosun. See you later."

Now all I needed to know was why Porks and Mate Slobkous had been sentenced to serve time on the *Isabel* and I would have the complete set. I came across Porks on the next deck down, the main one, after having worked my way through crew's quarters, laundry, shower room and 'recreation area': a state-of-the-art gymnasium with rowing machine and stationary bicycle adjoining a hobby room with workbench, shelves of paint pots and tools. Next door I found myself in a vast space dominated by three sets of winches with flanges higher than a man. The man was the charming young engineer, in a white boiler suit, brandishing an oilcan.

"Evening, Porks." It still felt odd calling him that; he looked very much like his father, who must have been the same age when he sank the old *Isabel*.

"Hello there, Commodore! What brings *you* here?"

"Just nosing around. This is the towing-winch room, I gather?"

"Yup. Those two babies hold about a mile of nine-inch hawser each, and that one a hundred and eighty feet of double nylon stretcher with a forty-two-inch waist. They're worked from the control room upstairs and observed by television cameras with screens on the bridge."

"Quite a plant." As a matter of fact, I had never seen anything like it; it was like the engine room of a science-fiction Mars rocket. I found myself in the role of advisor to Captain Kirk of the starship *Enterprise*.

"Come and have a look at the generator room," he said. "You haven't seen anything like that either, I bet."

He opened a door on the other side of the monster winches and took me down a passage with a series of humming pieces of machinery that I couldn't place. "Transformers," he said. Then we entered what I, with my outdated concepts, would have taken to be the engine room. In the center of a high-ceilinged space stood a veritable Minotaur of an engine, growling away with a throbbing rumble and a high-pitched whine that hurt the eardrums. "There she is!" he shouted. "The main generator!"

I contemplated the rumbling, shrieking machine with a feeling of disbelief. The engine of my first tug, the *Anna*, had been the same size and was considered to have the pull of three locomotives. Forty years later a piece of machinery the same size was merely an auxiliary engine, generating electricity. "This thing must produce enough current for a town!"

"It does!" Porks shouted with the proprietary pride of all chief engineers. "It's meant to provide electricity for the salvage equipment—cutters, welders, air pumps, water pumps—and the current for any disabled vessel we're assisting. If the *Q.E. II* lost power and called for our help, we could give her all the juice she wants."

"But why run it now? We're still connected to the shore."

"I want to try everything out before the Chinks arrive. Now come and see the engine room."

He led the way down the corridor and through a door at the far end. The engine room, or rather its control center, was an observatory separated from the engines by a double glass wall. It was lined with banks of dials and switches; on the plastic back wall was another female flasher offering her all, this time with calendar. The month was last November; the first thirteen days had been crossed off one by one, as in prison. The window overlooked a room painted gray that few would have recognized as an engine room; there were no engines, just elongated elevations which looked like hatch covers.

"When we're running full-power," Porks said beside me, "we'll need earmuffs to go in there, for it's a screaming hellhole, like vaults with demons in them, shrieking to be let out."

It was a romantic statement. Maybe he wasn't a liar but a poet, like Renoir, who had stated that the artist must correct nature.

"What exactly was the trouble you had, Porks?" I asked it casually, as if we had been discussing it.

He became quite still, like a deer listening. After a moment he said, "Who told you?"

"You did."

He turned to look at me; his face was his father's. "I?"

"When you said you signed on for this trip to find out who your father had been talking about all these years. I was only asked to take on this ship day before yesterday. There was no way you could have known. Now tell me the real reason."

He seemed unconcerned, but there was something there. At first it looked as if he wasn't going to answer; then he said, "I threw a wrench at him. It just grazed his scalp. But he yelled as if I'd knocked his teeth out."

"Who was this?"

"My chief. On the *Antonia*."

"Any particular reason?"

"He was a bully. He'd been bugging me ever since I came on board. We were on station in the Firth of Forth when it happened. He just had ridden me sore, after months of it. He said something about my being a bucket of warm shit. I happened to have that wrench in my hand and—well, you wouldn't believe the song and dance. Captain Fransen flew in, and I was sent home and put on standby. And now this. It just isn't fair."

"What's wrong with this?"

"Wrong? To be shipped out on her is like being sent to Alcatraz! She's been a killer from the moment she was launched; they knocked the pin out of the shackle before everyone was out from under. As she came down the stocks, she crushed a hunchback. She's had a curse on her ever since."

I didn't ask him where the hunchback came from; they are not usually employed by shipyards. His outburst sounded like classic sea-babble: a cursed ship, a shanghaied crew, the Flying Dutchman of the tugboat fleet. But there was more to follow. One of the designers had fallen off the bridge in the yard and broken his skull; he was a vegetable now. A bosun had had his brains splattered all over the forecastle by a swinging boom during her first trial. 'Lulu' Bartels had been so scared he had run off after her maiden voyage and left the sea. Beast Rufus had walked off in Durban. Spooks Haversma had shot himself rather than continue the tow. "And when they couldn't find anyone for the graveyard voyage, they manned her with us convicts. We were given the choice: ship out on the *Isabel* or you're out in the street. How would *you* feel?"

"Who told you all this, Porks?"

"A colleague of mine who sailed on her for one trip."

"Which particular trip?"

"The one under Spooks Haversma, to the Gulf."

"Did he tell you by any chance how he felt down here in this glass coffin, waiting for the ship to capsize and go down with all hands?"

He looked at me the way his father had done, off Cape Langanes. "Think we're going to make it, Skipper?"

His father had been sitting on the edge of his bunk in his long drawers when he said it, his dogtag glistening in the lamplight on his chest. 'Don't worry, Porks,' I had said, 'everything's going to be all right.' When I had turned to leave, he had grabbed my hand and pressed it with such fervor that I winced. He hadn't noticed I was scared stiff myself.

"Don't worry, Porks," I said. "Everything's going to be all right."

When I turned to leave, nothing happened. I left him staring after me, leaning motionless against the wall.

7

I made my way upstairs, back to the bridal suite, and barely had had a chance to undress when the bosun turned up with a bowl of Jell-O. Looking at the quivering blob with the tuft of imitation cream on top, I had a feeling of destiny.

"Try it," he said.

"H'm. What is it?"

"Cherry. My favorite. I brought ten boxes. Look." He showed me a box in gaudy colors. *Mrs. Horsting's Homemade Cherry Pudding,* all natural fruit, sixteen chemicals, artificial coloring, artificial taste. Apart from a cherry tree, Mrs. Horsting must have a lab the size of an atomic plant.

"Ome? Do you want your nightcap right away?"

"Nightcap?"

"Hold on, I'll be right back!"

It was very touching. I climbed into the bunk, drifted off to sleep, woke with a start and found the bosun standing by my bed with a mug. "Chocolate and rum. It'll make you sleep."

I slurped the hot, syrupy liquid with him hovering over me.

"Now, what did I hear you say? You want to move to the hospital tomorrow?"

"The Chinese captain may want these quarters. It's his ship."

"Over my dead body," he said fiercely. "Who does that slit-eye think he is? You're a commodore, he's just a lousy captain."

It was time we all came spiraling back to earth. "Bosun," I said, "those are the facts of life. This ship is sailing under the

Taiwanese flag with a Taiwanese captain. He has a right to this cabin. And don't call them slit-eyes, let's start on the right foot."

"Well, we'll see about that," he said darkly. "All I know is that nobody else is going to use this cabin, not while I'm around. You leave him to me; me speakee pidgin."

"Look, Bosun—"

"You go to sleep. You need it, you're an old man; if you won't look after yourself, someone has to do it for you. And don't worry: the others won't come in. I'll put this on your doorknob."

He showed me a plastic sign, DO NOT DISTURB, with a fancy silk cord.

"Where did you get that?"

"Oh, I picked it up," he said offhandedly. "I had to go to the men's room when I was out today, so I went into a hotel and found this hanging on the doorknob of a room. I'll hang it outside."

"But—"

"Hush, Ome. Now you settle down, go to sleep."

I should have voiced a moral protest, but exhaustion got to me. I was vaguely aware of the mug being taken from my hands, then the soft click of the door.

I was about to go under when I became aware of a tremor in my left hand. It was not that of my degenerative disease, but the vibration of an engine deep down in the ship, the giant generator. I lay there, my mind a blank, feeling that faint vibration, the living body of the ship. I tried to catch an elusive memory, in vain, before drifting off into sleep.

Chapter Three

1

When I awoke the next morning, I found the bosun standing beside my bunk as if he hadn't been away, proffering a tray with my breakfast. In all my forty years as a tug-driver I had never had breakfast in bed.

He put the tray on my lap. "I hope you like these," he said, pointing at a box of cereal called Looney Loops. He poured a generous helping into the bowl; they were multicolored animal shapes. "I tasted three different kinds, these were the best. Try 'em and tell me."

I chewed a mouthful. It tasted like pure sugar. "H'm," I said.

"Good, eh?"

Apart from the cereal, there were rolls, two kinds of jam, cheese, two boiled eggs and three slices of gingerbread. Enough to incapacitate a horse.

"Mmm!" I said.

"Coffee coming up."

By the time he came back, I had given up on the Looney Loops and was picking at the eggs. "This is splendid," I said, "but too much."

"Aw, come on, Ome! You've got a busy day ahead, you need your strength. Well, I'll leave you to it. Take your time." He went to the door. "I'll leave the sign on while you're having breakfast."

Young Porks proved immune to the bosun's veto; he came in after a peremptory knock, reeking of fuel oil, in his smudged white boiler suit with a wad of cotton waste in his back pocket. "Well," he said, "that cooling water pump of the generator is okay now, but I don't like the little tick it still has. Listen!" He lifted a grimy finger.

I dutifully listened. I could barely discern the humming of the generator itself, but I had dealt with engineers long enough to know the form. "I hear what you mean," I said.

"I'm going to leave it alone for the time being, but you'd better get hold of Fransen and tell him I want a spare."

"Spare what?"

"I'll give you the part number. Are you going to see him today?"

"I don't expect so, he's in Bahrein. But someone from the office will turn up."

"There are a few more things I'd like to add. Do you know that the fore and aft bearings of port number-three injector pump don't have any nipples?"

"Fancy that," I said.

"I won't bother you with the rest, not while you're having your breakfast. Just don't let 'em leave without that list. Sooner or later the generator's going to pack up, and without spares there won't be any electricity for the duration. We don't want that to happen."

"Of course not."

"I don't want to put down my predecessor, but there's been some very sloppy maintenance down there." He went to the door.

"Have you had your breakfast, Porks?"

"In contrast with our friend the radio freak, I have no time for breakfast," he said self-righteously. "Ha! Speak of the devil. Morning, Marco."

Harlingen must have entered the dayroom. I heard him ask, "Is the old man awake?"

"Holding court," Porks said.

Harlingen took his place in the doorway, holding a mug of coffee. "Morning, Skipper."

"Morning, Marco. Had your breakfast?"

"Yes, but my night wasn't too good. If you ask me, that hospital bed has fleas."

"The exterminators should be here any moment."

"It's strange, you know," he said musingly, leaning in the doorway, "but this ship feels different, peaceful. Maybe any ship does, without Beast Rufus."

"Marco," I said, putting my tray aside, "I'm going to move along. We'll talk again when we're under way."

"Sorry." He gulped down his coffee and put the empty mug on my tray. "See you later."

I wondered, while dressing, where Mate Slobkous was; he obviously hadn't arrived yet. I also wondered what the reason was for his being sent to the penal colony. I would no doubt find out in due course, but it might be too late. Well, I'd cross that bridge when I got to it.

2

I barely had my jacket on when they arrived all at once: the fuel barge, the water boat, the safety inspector, a man with a clipboard from the health department, a truck full of mattresses, pillows, blankets, sheets and messroom linen. Everyone wanted my attention, everyone had chits and forms for me to check and sign in triplicate; in the midst of it all, the launch of the Nautical Institute arrived with two adjusters who wanted me to cast off and mosey around the outer harbor so they could compensate my compasses. I told them to hang around and stay for lunch, or come back at fourteen hundred hours. Finally there came the sloths from the janitor service, who should have been there at the crack of dawn. In the meantime, no sign of Mate Slobkous; maybe he'd had an accident.

Despite the bedlam, the bosun managed to set up a sandwich lunch for fourteen in the messroom. If it represented a sample of the menus we could expect for the rest of the trip, it spelled massive constipation. Sharing the meal were the adjusters, the three-man crew of the fuel barge, the safety inspector, the skipper and engineer of the fire-patrol boat which had to be present by law while fuel was being loaded and an old salt whose function I failed to pinpoint. Porks, Harlingen, the bosun and I were there, but no Mate Slobkous. I was due to be picked up by the airport bus in less than an hour and couldn't leave the ship with this three-ring circus in full swing; I simply would have to call the office and find out where the hell the man was.

I was halfway down the gangway, headed for the telephone kiosk, when a taxi drew up and Mate Slobkous climbed out, as relaxed as a slow-motion movie. The driver unloaded his luggage from the trunk and the front seat without his passenger lifting a finger. He had a lot of gear with him, in suitcases and cardboard boxes. I strolled over, fit to be tied, but decided to play it cool.

"Slobkous," I said, "you'll have to put the ship through her paces for the adjusters. I have to leave for the airport to meet the crew."

He said calmly, "No problem," and paid the driver.

The bosun came down to help him bring everything on board; I went to dress up in my new uniform with the gold-leafed cap, which had been delivered that morning. I was putting the finishing touches to a black tie with a rash of little white K's, compliments of the company, when the bosun banged on the door, stuck his head in and said, "Slit-eyes' bus here, Ome!" I told him to stop this slit-eye business or he might find himself with his throat slit; then I went to board the bus.

It was a long ride to the airport and my mind buzzed with a swarm of minor problems, among which was how to remember Chinese names. Over the years I had developed a knack of remembering the names of crew members by tying them in with some aspect of the bearer, like rhyming 'De Beers' with 'jug ears.' How was I going to apply that to thirty-five variations of Chung, Chang and Hung? I'd have to work out something.

At the airport I found only the Taiwanese consul, a pompous little man, and his Girl Friday waiting to welcome the travelers. No one was there from the head office. The girl from the consulate had a crew list with her, full of Chinese characters.

The plane was on time; I readied myself like a parson taking up position at the door of his church to shake the congregation by the hand. They came through Customs lugging cardboard boxes tied with rope and string bags with clothing; all of them had new bright yellow oilskins over their arm and were, despite the winter cold, wearing T-shirts with the names of American universities. There seemed to be an awful lot of them; they lined up in a double file in the arrival hall, blocking traffic. I was looking for their captain when I spotted a woman, a grinning old crone with stringy white hair and tiny eyes in a wrinkled face. I turned to the consul. "Are these all crew members?"

"Yes, yes," the consul said, preoccupied, checking the list.

"Would you kindly introduce me to the captain?"

"Ah, yes, of course." He whispered to the girl, who consulted the list and pointed to a name; the consul called, "Captain Cho, please! Captain Cho!"

A very young man in a new-looking business suit disengaged himself from the ranks and came toward us. He seemed far too young to be the master. "Captain Cho, this is Commodore Harinxma, your advisor."

The young man gazed at my white hair, the massive gold rings on my sleeves, the fruit salad of battle ribbons on my chest, the cap with scrambled eggs, and muttered something that sounded like "Jesus!"

I held out my hand. "Captain, it's a pleasure to be of service to you."

He looked at the hand, the battle ribbons again, the cap's visor garlanded with gold leaf like Caesar's; for a moment I thought he was going to run back to the plane. But he took my hand, gingerly, like a child told to say hello to Santa Claus, and said, "Honored Commodore, it—it is an honor." He bowed.

I thought it might help if I chatted him up a bit. "Tell me, Captain, who is the lady?" I nodded at the old woman surrounded by solicitous Chinese.

"Ah, the cook, Honored Commodore, Ma."

"Ma?"

"Ma Chang, relative of all lower ranks, except those gentlemen over there."

He indicated a group of ten men standing ostentatiously apart from the rest. Instead of university T-shirts, they wore dark jumpsuits and looked menacing, like karate instructors.

"They are from a different island," the captain said in a whisper. "They are not like the others, the others do not like them. Good luck they are hop-hops."

"Excuse me?"

"They go on towed object. Hop-hops."

"Ah, runners. Now, would you be so kind as to introduce me to your staff?"

"Yes! Yes, Honored—"

The consul cut him short by shouting something in Taiwanese. He must have ordered everyone into the bus, for they all picked up their belongings, slung them over their shoulders or lugged them along as they followed an airline stewardess like a herd of clockwork gnomes a Barbie doll. My handshaking ritual had gone by the board; the whole situation was without precedent. How was this crowd of primitives under a den mother going to sail a ship as sophisticated as the *Isabel?* How was the earnest young man in the new business suit going to assume command of

[90]

the ship, with her computerized control panels, her television screens, her Paradise tree, her deadly secret?

I followed them outside, waited until they had piled into the bus, and then sat down on the front bench, the multitude behind me tweeting and chirruping. There were indeed an awful lot of them, for some had to stand. Then I saw the ten grim men in black seated at the back of the bus in splendid isolation; they were surrounded by empty seats.

The ride back to the harbor seemed long. The Chinese captain, sitting beside me, did not appear to be interested in conversation. I wondered what had possessed Mr. Chung to select this obviously inexperienced crew for a difficult tow of many months, part of it through the worst storm zone of the globe. I wondered if old Kwel or efficient Miss Bastiaans had any inkling of this.

Halfway through town, I asked the young man beside me, who was gazing out the window in fascination, "Tell me, have you sailed with these people before?"

He looked up and gave me a toothy smile. "No, Honored Commodore. They are fishermen, Mr. Chung got them from the government. They have no work, all the fish are dead. Mercury. The sea around their island is full of bellies. The government helped them find work."

"They have never sailed on board a tugboat?"

"No, Honored—"

"Just 'Commodore' will do."

"Ah, yes. Commodore." He looked away, back at the traffic, especially the bicycles. "Good," he said. "Good sight. Good place."

"And the others, the runners? They're from another island, I gather?"

"Yes—Commodore. Other island, close by. But bad. Bad people. They rape, steal brides. In past. Now no more. Now the government helps them."

"They were fishermen too?"

He thought that over, then he said, "As they say in the English: of sorts. They did sea work of sorts. Not good, but good. I mean, good sailors, but good luck they are hop-hops and not with the rest." He looked at me gravely. "We, I hear, have cabins?"

"Yes. You can have the suite."

"Sweet?"

"The captain's dayroom, bedroom and bathroom. Very nice, you'll see."

For some reason that seemed to worry him.

By the time we arrived on the quayside I had decided to call the office at the first opportunity, for to start towing a thirty-thousand-ton dry dock with these people seemed foolhardy. But first I had to get them out of the bus and installed on board.

They all formed a line again the moment their feet touched the ground; in the center stood the old woman. The ten black jumpsuits lined up a short distance away, scowling. Captain Cho gathered around him a group of other young men in new business suits; together they advanced on me.

"Honored Commodore, these are the officers," the captain said with obvious pride. "Number One!"

One of the young men stepped forward and bowed. "Greetings, Honored Commodore." After we had shaken hands, he stepped aside to make room for the next one, Number Two.

"Greetings, Honored Commodore."

"Welcome. Pleased to have you aboard."

So it went: Chief Engineer, Chief Two, Chief Three, Radio Officer One, Radio Officer Two and the bosun, one of the T-shirt brigade, a huge brute with BRYN MAWR stretched across his breasts. After this I went to welcome the jumpsuits, who glared at me with varying degrees of detestation when they saw me coming. I went up to the most hostile of them, held out my hand and said, "My name is Harinxma. I am the senior advisor. Happy to have you with us."

The man looked at me as if I had spat at his feet. He did not utter a word, just stood there and glowered, his eyes black with hatred. I went over to the crowd of happy fishermen, jostling each other between the railroad tracks, giggling, and went from one to the other, starting at the far right. I shook hands with them all: Amherst, Vanderbilt, Cornell, Yale, Harvard, Oberlin, Wellesley, Carleton—the T-shirts would make it easy for me to keep track of them, as long as they didn't get mixed up in the laundry. When I reached the lady cook, I saluted and said, "My name is Harinxma, I am the senior advisor."

She looked up at me with an odd, unfocused gaze and lifted both hands as if she were about to touch my face. Then she smiled, showing she lacked four front teeth, and bowed.

"You speak to me, Captain, I speak the English," a cheerful

voice said. "She no speak the English, I speak the English very good."

It was a grinning little man in jeans with a nameless T-shirt. He looked so unsavory that if he had accosted me in the street, I would have put my hand on my wallet. "My name is . . ." He pronounced some sounds I could not memorize. "I your butler. Speak and I will tell her what you say. Speak. Now."

Captain Cho joined us. "He is number-one steward, Commodore. He will look after you."

"Steward," I said, "welcome. Glad to have you on board. Please tell the lady likewise."

The steward quacked and lisped at her. While he did so, I called at the ship, "Slobkous! Porks! Harlingen! Bosun! Join me, please!"

They were all watching from the bridge deck, fascinated; the first to turn up was Porks. He came down the gangway in a hurry, the planks rumbling. Mate Slobkous followed, taking his time, then Harlingen and the bosun. When they joined us, I said, "Captain Cho, Madam: Mate Slobkous. Chief Engineer Alberts. Harlingen, radio officer. Schoonmaker, chief petty officer." The bosun looked pleased at that. "Would you be kind enough to introduce them to the gentlemen of your staff, Captain?" Turning to my men, I said, "You sort out who belongs in your department, then show them their quarters. Bosun, here's your opposite number —er—Bryn Mawr." They sized each other up.

I headed back for the hate-filled leader of the runners. "Would you and your men please follow me on board? We'll show you your quarters. Tomorrow you'll move on to the dry dock."

He did not respond, but stared at my jugular. I turned and looked for the steward. I couldn't recognize him among the crowd, but I remembered the blank T-shirt. "Steward!" I called when I spotted it. "Come here a moment, will you?"

To my amazement, he shook his head and made a gesture as if he were throwing something away. Behind me, I heard a grunt. The glowering headman aimed the guns of his black eyes at the crowd of happy fishermen. It was as if he hit them physically; they all fell silent and stared at him, their faces blank, their chirruping cheeriness silenced. Then he slowly lifted his hand, pressed a nostril shut with a finger and blew a blob of snot onto the cobbles. It was a gesture of such contempt that I could not mistake its meaning.

One thing seemed obvious: I could not put the two groups together in the confined space of the crew's quarters or there would be problems. The head office would have to find lodgings for this lot for the night. In the meantime I had better put them back on the bus until I had sorted things out with The Hague. I said, "I'll try to arrange hotel accommodation for you. Would you kindly go back on board the bus until I have done so?"

The headman fixed his baleful glare on me. It looked as if he were going to blow snot at me too, but the consul intervened.

"Commodore," he said sharply, "these men cannot be herded back on board that bus. They are not slaves to be shunted around. Mr. Chung is responsible for providing them with cabins on board your vessel."

"Consul, as you have witnessed, it's obviously unwise to put the two groups together. These ten men will go on board the towed object tomorrow; until then they'll be given other accommodation. While I arrange that, I suggest they go back on the bus. I'll order some coffee for them and telephone my office in The Hague for instructions."

He gave me a stony look. "In that case, sir, my place is with these men until the matter has been settled to their satisfaction. They are not slaves. Whatever arrangements—"

I saluted and left him to act out his role as protector of the downtrodden without me in the audience. I headed for the telephone booth. The tension on the quayside was tangible; all the officials and workmen on board the tugboat were lined up at the rail, watching the spectacle, spellbound. I walked past the now motionless rows of fishermen, entered the bright blue booth, closed the door behind me and dialed the number.

I was put through to Miss Bastiaans, who said Mr. Arnold wasn't at his desk. She didn't know if he would be back in the office today. No, she had no idea where he was. Had I tried Captain Fransen's office? She gave me the number. I tried it; he wasn't at his desk either, he was in Bahrein and no one in Operations knew about the crew arrangements on board the *Isabel*, it wasn't the company's responsibility. I called Miss Bastiaans again and said, "I think you'd better trace Mr. Kwel for me. I have over thirty-five Chinese here, which means they're spilling out of the portholes, and ten furious runners spoiling for a fight. I'm willing to improvise, but this one has me stymied. Besides, I have a few other things to do. Find Mr. Kwel and tell him it's urgent."

"Could you give me those details again, Commodore?"

I ran them through for her again; she was obviously making notes. "Very well, Commodore, I'll see what I can do. You do realize that the *Isabel* is no longer the company's responsibility?"

"Miss Bastiaans," I said, nicely because I liked her, "do as I told you."

I crossed the now empty quayside to the gangway and glanced at the bus. The runners were sitting inside in taut repose, staring ahead. The consul and his secretary stood at the door, radiating pique. He asked, "Could you tell me, please, what the arrangements are?"

"I'm in touch with my company, Consul. They're trying to contact the chairman of the board; he'll call back shortly. In the meantime, would you, and you too, ma'am, do me the honor of joining me in my dayroom?"

He gave me another stony look. "Our place is with the men on the bus, Commodore."

"As you wish," I said, and went to my shipful of problems.

At the top of the gangway I was welcomed by Slobkous, as cool as a cucumber. "Everything is under control," he said. "They're down in the cabins, nesting two to a bunk. I showed 'em how to pull them out to turn them into doubles. Everybody's taken care of except the captain and the steward, they're waiting for you in the dayroom."

"Have the compasses been adjusted?"

"Done."

"And the rest?"

"Everything's on board except the Chinese food from the caterers."

"Have you called them?"

"Yes; it'll be here before dark."

"Good work, Slobkous. Happy Hour at six for the staff, Chinese included. Spread the word."

"Will do."

I went to my cabin. Slobkous was turning out to be a capable fellow, and, thank God, no emotional life. Not so young Harlingen; he stopped me in the corridor. "Commodore! I checked the new crystals, they're wrong! South Africa instead of—"

"Call Radio Holland and tell 'em to replace them."

"But that's not all! The—"

"Call them, it's your department. Let me know how it works out. Happy Hour at six in my quarters."

In the dayroom I found Captain Cho and the rogue steward waiting for me. I asked the captain, "Is everyone settled below?"

He said, "Yes, Commodore." I had the impression he wanted to speak to me privately, so I said to the steward, "Go and find the bosun, he'll instruct you how to serve drinks and so on."

"I know how to serve drinks. I was barman in Mah-Iot Hotel, Kao Hsiung! Very fine, big tips!"

"Well, splendid. Now get out."

He stared at me as if he couldn't believe his ears.

"Go find the bosun," I said. "This is not the Mah-Jongg Hotel."

"Mah-*Iot*, not Mah *Jongg*."

"Look, friend, if you and I are to get along, do as I say. Go find the bosun now. Leave us alone."

He said, "Wah!" which must be pretty strong language, for Captain Cho looked embarrassed. But he left.

"Captain," I said, "I gather we have more than thirty-five men on board. That's too many, we don't have room for them."

"We come to learn, Commodore. We all want to learn."

"Maybe so, but I can't have men sleeping two to a bunk."

"Why not?" He seemed genuinely amazed.

"For one thing, this ship is not—" I realized I was getting onto thin ice—"not meant for that many people."

He smiled. "Commodore, do not worry. We are happy to share beds. We have everything worked out. Do not worry. You will see: work out fine."

"All right," I said, "you're the captain. Tell me about yourself."

"Excuse?"

"What's your background?"

"I was captain of one of Mr. Chung's tugboats. Number One was my mate. The engineers are off other tugboat. Big tugboat."

"Harbor tug, I take it?"

"No, we sail out to sea to pick up big bodies. Hulk, battleship, whatever comes. Sometimes bad weather, very bad. But not big as this. This is beautiful ship, Commodore. Very honored. Very honored." He bowed sitting down.

"Thank you. You are used to standing watches at sea?"

"We here to learn. We all learn."

[96]

"Well, Mate Slobkous will give you the details. He and I alternate, four hours on, four hours off, for the first week we're at sea. I suggest you and your Number One join my watch and your Number Two mate Slobkous's. Would that be agreeable to you?"

"Oh, yes, Commodore! Oh, yes. Now, I do not know about new deep-sea navigation. My mates do not know also. You have satellite?"

"We have, and I suggest you and I go up to the bridge in a moment to look at the layout. But, first, this suite is yours by rights. You are the captain, these are the captain's quarters."

He appeared horrified at the suggestion. "No, no, Commodore! This is *your* cabin! I wish not to be here! I am not real captain, only tit-you-lar. You are captain until I have learned."

That was not what had been arranged, but I didn't want to enter into an argument with him. I'd take it up with old Kwel when he called. I rose. "Very well, then, let's go upstairs."

He followed me to the bridge. There was a lot of activity in the corridors, the usual pre-departure racket of people yelling at each other down stairwells. The engines were being tested; the ship writhed and bucked in her moorings. Someone was testing the foghorn; its massive blast hit us when we entered the wheel-house.

Captain Cho stared at the display of controls, dials, scanners, viewers, television screens and flashing electronic figures. The first time I had set eyes on this wheelhouse, it had looked to me like the control room of a nuclear plant; no wonder the young Chinese was awed by the thought that he would have to start manipulating this space vessel tomorrow at the crack of dawn.

I was not prepared for the intensity of his reaction. He looked at me, aghast, and cried, "No! I cannot!"

"Excuse me?"

"I cannot command this ship! I am not qualified! I have license up to one thousand tons, I cannot take command of this—this Gol Yath!"

"Excuse me?"

"Gol Yath! Giant! This is not my—my competence! I did not know, not expect!"

"Captain, I understand your reaction. I myself—"

"No!" he cried, no longer terrified but indignant. "No way! Mr. Chung tell me big, very big, but he did not tell me—this!" He made a sweeping gesture.

"Captain," I said soothingly, "don't be intimidated by this space lab. I was as alarmed as you are when I first came up here. What these gadgets are meant to do is make life easier for you. Look—look at this . . ." I chose one of the switches, marked POSITION. "All you have to do to find out the ship's position is flick this and: presto!" Alas, nothing happened; the little display window remained dark. "The generator must still be off," I said lamely. "Sorry about that."

He walked away, crying, "No! I will *not* accept command of this! I have been mislaid!"

"Excuse me?"

"Mr. Chung mislaid me! He said: 'Tugboat is tugboat, Dutch one is like the one you now command, only bigger.' He not said —*this!*" He made another sweeping gesture.

"But I assure you—"

"No! I will not!" He walked to the companionway; there he turned to face me. "You are a commodore. You are a learned man. You sail this. I cannot. I am not qualified. I am licensed only up to one thousand tons. All these buttons, switches, clocks, I not understand. I refuse. Hear me, Commodore? I refuse. Point. Blank." He started on his way down.

"Hold it, Captain! We must talk this through before the director of my company calls. He may do so any moment."

"But I will not—"

"Now you listen to me!" I had to put some power behind it or he would have walked out on me. The effect on him was unfortunate. He looked up at me with a face reminiscent of that of the headman of the runners, frozen in an expression of contempt.

I could not let this farce continue. "Captain," I said, "if you do indeed have a tonnage restriction on your license, then we have a problem."

"I told you! One thousand tons. No more. I go now."

"No! This is serious."

He froze altogether. His eyes took on a faraway expression.

"Captain, you may not be qualified, but neither am I. My master's license became invalid at the age of sixty. I'm supposed to be your advisor, I cannot accept any responsibility beyond that. So let's look at the situation soberly. You have to settle the matter of your qualification with Mr. Chung. Call him on the telephone—"

"No," he said tonelessly. "I have dispensation."

"You mean you're licensed up to one thousand tons, but received dispensation from that restriction?"

"No matter, I *feel* not qualified. I come here, I look and see, and I say: not qualified. I will not accept. No."

"Okay," I said, tired of him, "when my director calls, I'll report all this to him. You do as you see fit."

Back in my dayroom, I took a deep breath and crossed to the window to have a look at the quayside. The bus was still there with its hostile runners. The whole thing was ludicrous. Two crises already before we were even under way! I should collect my gear and walk off before old Kwel talked me into staying on for more. There was a knock on the door.

"Come in!"

It was the bosun. "The bus driver wants to see you, Ome. He's pretty steamed up."

I had forgotten about the coffee I had planned to send down. "Where is he?"

"Right here in the corridor."

"Show him in."

The bus driver was furious. "For God's sake, Captain, what am I supposed to do with that bunch of characters? I can't sit on the quayside all night! I asked the Chinese gentleman, but he won't even answer me. The bus is supposed to be back at the depot before dark!"

"I'll telephone the office again. How about some coffee in the meantime? I'll have it delivered to the bus right now."

He muttered, "I can't keep this up forever," but seemed pacified for the moment.

It was a good opportunity to give the Chinese steward something to do. I opened the door, called him, and heard a noise behind me. He came out of my bedroom with a false smile, as if he had just burgled the place.

"What were you doing in there?"

"Unpack clothes. Very neat. Everything very neat. I was valet—"

"Go to the galley, order a pot of coffee with a dozen plastic cups and take them to the bus."

His smile vanished, he suddenly looked like the cutthroat I suspected him to be. "Nah! No coffee for *them!* Dogs! Pregnant dogs! Wah!" Before I realized what he was up to, he pressed a

[99]

nostril and blew a blob of snot onto my carpet. I looked at him, speechless, then I yelled, "Get out!"

He ran off.

I fetched a wad of tissues from the bathroom to clean up the mess before it was trodden into the carpet. When I found myself on my knees, cleaning up my steward's snot, I sat back on my heels and asked myself what in hell I was doing. Then something caught my attention, some change. The ship had fallen silent.

I was about to get to my feet to find out what was going on when there was a knock on the door. Miss Bastiaans entered.

"Commodore?"

"Yes, Miss Bastiaans, I'm here." I rose, stuffing the tissues into my pocket.

"Mr. Arnold is here."

"Where?"

"In the limousine on the quayside. He is not good at climbing gangways."

"I'll come." I made a move to the door.

"Just one second, Commodore." She stopped me and closed it behind her. "Mr. Arnold has had a very busy week, like any executive, but he is in his nineties and can only do so much."

"But I must talk to him! This situation—"

"You will talk to him in a minute." She was handling me in the same way I had been handling the panicking young captain. "He's very much on top of things, but he has to be protected from emotional ups and downs. If you are disturbed and need to debrief with someone, it would be better if you did so with me. I gather your problem is serious. Would you mind running through it with me?"

Her calm self-assurance had a beneficial effect; I could see her point. "How about a drink?"

She gave me a quick look. "Not for me, thank you. But do help yourself."

"Is there time? I don't want to keep Mr. Kwel waiting."

"Please."

I went to the icebox to get myself a small shot; I needed it. Luckily, Bron's crock was still in the freezer.

"Your problem has to do with the crew, you said. I saw a bus with some men on the dock. Are they part of it?"

"Those are the runners. They now turn out to be the least of my problems. Cheers."

[100]

"What's the worst?"

"The Chinese captain is licensed only up to a thousand tons. He has a dispensation, but when I showed him the bridge, he panicked and said he'd been given to understand I would be the actual master. He called himself 'titular' master only. That, clearly, is a situation I cannot let myself in for."

She thought it over. "Well, you should certainly put *that* to Mr. Kwel. What about the crew?"

"They seem to be primitive fishermen without any experience of tugboat work. Combined with a captain who refuses to function, that makes for a pretty package when it comes to sailing tomorrow."

She thought it over while I sipped my drink.

"I don't think you need bring them up," she said. "It'll probably work out better than you expect. They are experienced sailors, they'll adapt soon."

I smiled at her; I began to feel like an uncle. "Sorry, Miss Bastiaans, but I'll have to mention them to Mr. Kwel. It takes even experienced merchant-marine sailors a year to adapt to the specific demands of this job. We don't want to lose any legs on the aft deck when the hawser starts to scissor on the bars, do we now?"

"All right, Commodore," she said, "but do remember what I told you. Make it a matter-of-fact report, don't get emotional. Mr. Kwel will have the answer, as long as it's handled objectively."

I polished off my drink. "Let's go."

"Are you sure you—"

"Don't worry, I'll go easy on him."

I opened the door for her; we went down the corridor together. Again I was struck by the silence on board; a few minutes earlier the ship had sounded like a bazaar, now you could hear a pin drop. The old man must have decked out the limousine with flags of the royal house.

When we came out into the open and started down the gangway, I saw the limousine. It was without flags, but the way it was parked did seem regal: smack in the middle of the railroad tracks. Any train clanging down the quay would have to stop and ask permission to proceed.

When he saw us, the chauffeur got out and opened the door. The old man was sitting in a corner of the back seat, a rug over his knees.

"Commodore Harinxma is here, sir," Miss Bastiaans said.

"What is all this?" the old man asked testily, gazing at me with his oddly youthful eyes which saw nothing at all. "Why have I been called here?"

No wonder the ship had fallen silent; it was like an audience with the Pope. "Sorry, sir, we have a problem."

"In the past you were always able to solve problems on your own, Harinxma. It's no longer my ship, we're just providing services."

"It's a case of an unqualified captain, sir. I don't think I can sail under the circumstances."

"Don't talk rubbish," he said. "Come in. Sit down. You too, Miss Bastiaans. Close the door."

We obeyed.

"Well?"

I said, "The Chinese captain insists he is only the titular master and will not assume command, so instead of serving as advisor, as agreed, I would in effect be acting master. That is not our agreement."

"It's not an agreement between you and myself, Harinxma, it's between you and Mr. Chung."

"But you represent Mr. Chung."

"I do not. Mr. Chung is represented by the consul. Address yourself to him."

I knew him well enough to realize he was playing for time; behind his porcupine act he was in the process of working this out.

"It means that I would be given all the responsibilities of a master and none of the rights," I said.

"No, Harinxma. You'd be given all of the rights and none of the responsibilities. The Taiwanese captain is responsible by law, as he is listed on the manifest as the master. You have been assigned to assist him with counsel and advice and a practical demonstration whenever verbal advice proves inadequate. What you do is this: you take on factual command until further notice, but before each decision or order you ask him if he wishes you to demonstrate the procedure. At the end of the watch you enter in the log that Commodore Harinxma in his capacity of advisor took charge of the operation at the request of, and in the presence of, the master. It will cover you, and you can go on acting as master for as long as necessary. Just make sure the man is physically there, and defer to him whenever feasible."

It sounded reasonable, but I didn't want to end up in an ambiguous situation. "I'm afraid I can't go in for that, sir."

He gazed at me; even though I knew he was blind, I couldn't help feeling the weight of his regard, as in the past. Then he said, "Miss Bastiaans, leave us for a moment. Go for a walk, take the chauffeur with you."

"Yes, sir."

She opened the door and slipped out.

"Harinxma," he continued after hearing the car door close, "what I am about to say is to go no further. You *must* sail this ship for me as far as Rio de Janeiro."

"But, sir—"

"The deal has not yet been finalized. Mr. Chung will pay in full only after arrival of the tow in Rio de Janeiro."

"But—"

"Stop butting in! Therefore, it is of the utmost importance that the ship get to Rio without any complications. Your task is to see to that. It's not going to be difficult. You may have some rough weather at this time of year as far as St. Vincent; there you enter the trades. With a minimum of vigilance on your part, her flaw is not likely to show up. Start by assuming command; if you handle it the way I suggest, you won't have any problem. The Chinese captain should be ready to take over in Rio; it sounds like a mere case of stage fright."

My first reaction was anger. Mindful of Miss Bastiaans' warning, I tried to sound bland when I said, "Sorry, sir, I cannot be a party to that."

"Huh?" He gazed in my direction.

"I'll have to warn the Chinese captain about her flaw. I cannot undertake to keep it from him."

He took so long before answering that I wondered what he was up to. "Harinxma," he said finally, "you have sailed for me for over forty years. I expected you to have acquired some loyalty toward the company during that length of time."

"Sir, if the company sustains a loss, it will survive. The men who sail the *Isabel* without warning may not."

"What makes you feel responsible for them, may I ask?"

"The fact that I know the truth."

"If knowing the truth made people responsible, Harinxma, history would look very different."

"Sorry, sir."

He went in for another silence. Miss Bastiaans and the chauffeur strolled past; she glanced at the car with obvious concern. The more I thought about it, the more determined I became not to be a part of this. Either I would coach the Chinese captain, step by step, in how to cope with the ship when she started to cycle, or I would back off here and now. The ship would sail with another captain, one less concerned about the niceties than I was.

Suddenly the old man said, "Right. Let's see if we can reach a meeting of minds on this. What exactly were you planning to tell the Chinese captain?"

"That, for reasons unknown, the ship has a tendency to roll out of control under a certain combination of circumstances. There is a way of counteracting this, but it needs practice and constant vigilance. Anybody who isn't made aware of this is sure to come to grief in the Forties when he's hit by a gale. I'll put the man through the drill as often as is feasible, until he has mastered it. Always supposing he pulls himself together and starts to function as a master within a reasonable period of time—say, before the Cape Verdes. If in St. Vincent he still refuses to accept responsibility, that's where I get off."

He thought it over. "That sounds reasonable. Just don't dramatize. Tell the man she is tender and has a tendency to over-roll under certain conditions. Show him how simple it is to correct that. Cast off the tow somewhere between here and St. Vincent and demonstrate it to him. There is no reason to go in for dire warnings. Stay with the facts."

"The fact is that she will capsize unless the cycle is broken."

"Who says so? You?"

"Bartels tried to discuss it with you. Bron—"

"Bartels is trying to explain away the reason why he retired early, which was that he was afraid of the ship and couldn't handle her. Bron wanted to perform the same circus acts with her as he did with the *Fiona* and all the other ships he's had. When he was told he couldn't, he walked off like a petulant child. Now, what else did you want to see me about?"

"The runners, sir. There is so much tension between them and the crew that, even if I could find room for them, I can't have both groups on the ship without danger of trouble. What do I do with them? They're waiting in a bus, over there. The consul is with them, he refuses to budge until they are, as he says, properly looked after."

"Send them ahead to Antwerp and detail your first officer to accompany them. Miss Bastiaans will take care of lodging and transportation. Talk to her."

"But I'll need Slobkous tomorrow morning when we leave, what with this inexperienced crew and an inactive captain."

"You'll be taken out by two tugboats and have a pilot to see you out to sea. Once you're in the open, the ship virtually sails herself, that's what she was built to do. Tell your mate that after he has settled the runners on the dry dock and handed them over to the runner captain, who is already there, he comes out to meet you with the Belgian pilot. That way he'll be back on board for the arrival in Antwerp. Anything else?"

"No, sir."

"All right." He sank back into the cushions and closed his eyes. "Call Miss Bastiaans."

I opened the door. Miss Bastiaans was standing within earshot; she came at once. She asked softly, "How is he?"

"He's asking for you."

She was about to step in; then she said, "I arranged with the consul that we'll take over the runners and send them ahead to Antwerp. If you could delegate someone to accompany them—"

"Mr. Kwel suggested I send Mate Slobkous."

"Ah, good. Godspeed, Commodore, happy sailing."

She slipped inside and closed the door. The car moved away, leaving me standing center stage, master of the *Isabel Kwel.*

3

After telling the consul to wait for Mate Slobkous, I went back on board, yearning for a few moments of peace and solitude in which to reflect, undisturbed. But when I closed the door of my dayroom behind me, it was opened again by my rogue steward, carrying an armful of bedclothes.

"Who was that in automobile?" he asked, beady-eyed. "Boss man?"

"Where are you going with those blankets? My bed has been made."

"These are for *me*," he said smugly. "I sleep here." He pointed at the couch.

"Like hell you do. You sleep below with the others, in your own cabin."

"No sleep here?" He sounded offended. "I am butler! I follow you like shadow! Otherwise, lose face."

"No! And here—" I handed him the wad of tissues from my pocket. "Clean up your mess on the carpet. No more snot-blowing on board this ship. Understood?"

The bosun came in the moment the Chinese had left. "Ome, can I have a word with you?"

"What is it?"

He gestured at the door. "I was supposed to take care of you. Weren't you happy with what I did?"

"Bosun," I said, "please!" But I should take him seriously. "Okay, this much I can tell you: he's not going to take your place where it matters."

"I've been asking myself what's left for me to do anyhow, with that slit-eye bosun running around making himself busy. Why do you have to have a Chinese in here too?"

"You're supposed to instruct their bosun, not stand pouting in a corner. Show him the ropes."

"Skipper?" This time it was Porks, looking as if he had crawled through a sewer.

"Yes?"

"I'll be late for the Happy Hour, I had a back washer blow out on me."

"Don't worry, we're not going anywhere."

And there came Slobkous. "Can we have a look at the charts now?"

I told him about his assignment: to take ten surly Chinese to Antwerp, put them in a hotel or on board the dock and meet me with the pilot in the Western Scheldt the following morning.

It did not faze him. "No problem," he said. "Do I sign the chits for the hotel?"

"Yes. If there's a problem, call Miss Bastiaans at the head office."

"Sure you'll be all right without me tomorrow morning?"

"I'll find out. Have a good trip."

"Likewise." He left as if he were leaving for a weekend of tennis. When I looked at the quayside from the dayroom a few minutes later, the bus was gone.

At last I had the opportunity to think things over in privacy.

The canary trilled and warbled in its cage. I filled its little tray with seed from the bag the bosun had bought. While doing so, I began to realize that I was in an unenviable situation, to use an understatement. Thanks to the old man's manipulation, I was now virtually in collusion with KITCO, the architects and whoever else in this murky business had an interest in getting the ship out of their hair with no questions asked. What bothered me was Mr. Chung's role in all this. During the evening at Kwel's house he had struck me as a tough and astute operator; now it began to look as if he had had a flawed ship foisted on him—deadly flawed. Or was that just Bartels' hyped-up version? Bron's expertise was equally unreliable; to him, tugboats were just sleds strapped to his ass, which was fine as long as you didn't mind living for months on end with a sled strapped to your ass and sleeping on the bridge with your wrist tied to a thruster handle. In any case, Mr. Chung was either a provincial dude who had bought a status symbol, or he had outsmarted old Kwel, having his drydock towed to Rio by a boat on which he had only an option, where he would cancel the deal on the basis of the ship being unseaworthy, with his tow halfway to Talcahuano—for free.

I wished I could have talked it over with the late Spooks Haversma; it sounded as if he had been a sane and sober man despite his Ouija board, not a dramatist like Bartels or a prima donna like Beast Rufus. Maybe Sylvia could see clearly in this thicket of intrigue and supposition; I would call her later today, once the ship had quieted down; it was likely to be a long conversation. For the time being, the carousel was in full swing: after a peremptory knock Harlingen came barging in with a gripe about walkie-talkies that should have a range of at least two miles if we were going to tow a thirty-thousand-ton cookie tin; the set Radio Holland had sent down was kid stuff.

And so it went, until darkness fell and we all gathered in my dayroom for Happy Hour. Porks turned up in his blues, and Harlingen brought in the radio officers, two smiling Chinese youths. The bosun trained the steward in the use of doilies and how to serve drinks. "Not so much gin, Rin-tin-tin! They've got a ship to sail!" The steward dropped two glasses, then a bowl of peanuts; each time he said, "Hopla!"

The Chinese mates and engineers did not show up, but they joined us for dinner in the officers' lounge. After the first awkward minutes a conversation started among the engineers, leading to the drawing of engine parts on paper napkins. The bosun served spaghetti and Mamma Mia Meatballs with Chunky Tomato Sauce. He was assisted by the Chinese rogue steward; in the process something seemed to be resolved.

After the meal we dispersed for the night and the ship quieted down; I saw my chance to call Sylvia from the phone booth on the dock. It was dark by then; there were giggles and alien chatter among the crates and the tarpaulin-covered stacks of lumber; cigarettes glowed briefly in the night like fireflies. It was not exactly privacy, but then, they did not speak Dutch. I hoped none of the Dutch staff was ashore taking a breath of air before turning in; I would have to keep my voice down.

Sylvia picked up the phone at once, as if she had been waiting for my call. When the operator had cleared the line, I told her, behind my cupped hand, what had happened that day: the arrival of the Chinese, the T-shirts, the woman cook with the gap teeth, the steward blowing snot and crying 'Pregnant dogs,' the captain who refused to take command. Told in sequence, it sounded unreal; Kwel's instructions, however, presented a very real dilemma. "Should I get involved in this or back off? If I want to do that, I should probably do it now." I didn't mention the ship's fatal flaw.

She listened without interrupting, then remained silent for so long that I thought I had lost the connection.

"Sylvia? Are you there?"

"Yes, love. I'm thinking."

I let her think for a while, the phone's meter ticking away. "Well?"

"I don't know. I don't like it. I don't like any part of it. But I want to think it through. Let's give it twenty-four hours, we'll both see much clearer by then. Now, are you all right? Not too tired, under too much stress?"

"I'll take a sleeping pill when I turn in, that'll take care of it."

"You've taken your blood-pressure medication?"

"I'll do that when I get back on board. Night, love."

"Night, dear one. We'll talk when you're in Antwerp. Take care."

"You too. Night."

I went to my quarters, undressed, took a sleeping pill and

climbed into bed. The harbor tugs were due at four in the morning; I could do with a good night's sleep.

But my mind was churning, it was hard to settle down. Also, there was an unholy racket on board. Porks and his Chinese colleagues were trying the engines again, jerking the ship back and forth, setting the mooring lines screaming. There were Chinese noises everywhere: laughter, giggles, tuneless background music. All the floodlights were on, turning night into day behind my window. I went to see what the devil they were up to and saw, in the harsh light of the floods, Asian figures scurrying in and out of shadows at a crouching run, as if they were making a movie on the Boxer uprising. Then some joker set the foghorn blaring. I rang the bridge.

Somebody picked up the phone and said, "Meow? Sing kwan, meow."

"Whoever you are, stop that noise! And cut those damn floods! Go to sleep, man, we sail before sunrise!"

"Meow, kwang."

It became quiet.

Then dark.

The engines stopped.

It was a miraculous transformation. I had said 'quiet' and it became quiet, 'dark' and it became dark.

I was, once again, Master After God.

Chapter Four

1

Early the next morning, before daybreak, two large young men with blond mustaches turned up in my cabin, filling it with a smell of self-rolled shag. They were the captains of the *Polly* and the *Jenny*, about to take us out onto the river. They seemed very young despite their mustaches.

The Chinese steward served coffee under the eagle eye of the bosun. This being a workaday operation, there was not much to discuss, but tradition had not changed: captains of harbor tugs about to take an ocean-going sister out of bed turned up for coffee if the departure was before eleven; after that, for gin. They looked around the dayroom while sipping their coffee. This must be the future they dreamed of: a sitting room with club chairs and a couch, a canary in the corner, a bookshelf with weighty volumes, a steward who served coffee with gingerbread. They asked where she was bound; when I said, "Taiwan," I could see it in their eyes, though one of them said, "Too far for me," and the other, "Same here."

The bosun opened the door. "The pilot's here, Ome."

"Send him in. And ask the steward for some more coffee, please." I wondered where Captain Cho was.

The pilot, a hearty fellow full of early-morning cheer, smoked a cigar smelling like a smoldering haystack. The steward served more coffee and gingerbread; I sent him to find Captain Cho and ask if he would please join us in the dayroom. When after ten minutes there still was no sign of the young man, I said, "Well, gentlemen, it's time we got out of town. Excuse me a second while I check on Captain Cho. He should have been here by now."

"Captain Who?" the pilot asked.

"The Taiwanese master. I'm the senior advisor, he's in command."

"Well, well," the pilot said.

The harbor captains finished their coffee and went back to their tugs; the pilot relit his cigar to leave a memory. I followed his smoke trail down the corridor to the first officer's cabin, where Captain Cho had taken up residence. I knocked on the door.

[110]

After the third knock I heard a sound inside that I interpreted as an invitation to come in. When I opened the door, the first thing to hit me was the sickly-sweet smell of alien tobacco smoke. Captain Cho, in loud pajamas, was sitting upright in his bunk, reading a little red book. When he saw me, he scowled and sucked his pipe.

"Captain, your presence is needed on the bridge," I said.

He stared at me, smoking, before he deigned to speak. Then he said, "No."

There comes a moment in this type of situation when something has got to give, so I said without regard for his losing face, "Captain, this crap will not get us anywhere. If you refuse to sail this ship, even with my support and guidance, I'll have to send the harbor tugs home, dismiss the pilot and call Mr. Chung in Brussels. Make up your mind."

The mention of Mr. Chung seemed to make a difference. He gazed at me through the smoke. "He is in Brussels?"

"I understand he is," I lied.

"Oh," he said.

I picked up a pair of trousers off the chair. "Get some clothes on and come to the bridge. I'll sail the ship, but you must be there, and I must ask your permission before I can give any commands or make decisions. That is the law." He went on staring at me. Maybe the trousers weren't his. Well, I had done my best.

On the bridge, in the dim green light of the chart lamp, I found the pilot and the Chinese first officer. The bosun was at the wheel; the Chinese steward, with the keen interest of a pickpocket, lurked in a corner with a full view of the proceedings. I began by sending him packing; then I went to the for'ard windows to have a look at the forecastle deck bright with floodlights. A bevy of Chinese sailors, in T-shirts despite the bitter cold, were standing by at the bollards under the supervision of Bryn Mawr, the muscle man.

"Number One," I said to the first officer, a slight young Chinese with intelligent eyes, "Captain Cho is due any minute. Your place during this maneuver is on the fo'c'sle to keep an eye on the mooring lines. Number Two should be on the aft deck."

He said, "Yes, Commodore," and was about to sprint off; I had to stop him if I wanted to play this by the book. "Hold it!" I called. "Wait until Captain Cho is here, he'll give you the order. In the meantime I'll check with the engine room."

I went to the phone and punched the number. Porks' voice answered, "Engine room!" He sounded flustered.

"How about it, Chief? Ready to roll?"

"Well, I'd have liked another ten minutes to run through the procedure once more with these characters, but I suppose they've got it now. So, as far as I'm concerned, ready for take-off."

"All right. Stand by."

I put the phone down; still no Captain Cho.

"Where is the—er—master of this vessel?" the pilot asked with heavy irony. "We're going to lose the tide if he keeps this up."

"He'll be here presently," I said. A little more was needed; the silence weighed heavily on the bridge. "He's shaving," I added.

As impromptu excuses went, this one struck the wrong note. "Shaving, eh?" the pilot asked. "Makes you wonder what."

"They all shave 'em," the bosun contributed.

I was about to put a stop to this when Captain Cho appeared, looking as he had the previous day, his face turned to stone. "Captain Cho," I said, "meet the pilot."

"Morning," the pilot said past his cigar. "Hope you didn't cut yourself."

The bosun sniggered.

"Enough of that," I snapped.

Captain Cho turned his stony gaze on me; obviously, he considered me to be part of a conspiracy intended to make him lose face.

"Captain," I asked, "do you wish to take over, or would you prefer me to go through a demonstration of this vessel leaving port?" It was a ridiculous question; in no way could I make it sound realistic.

"Proceed," he said stonily.

"Thank you, Captain." Well, that was that; from now on I could forget about him. "Number One, to the fo'c'sle," I said; the young man darted off. I went to the aft window and checked the situation on the poop; Number Two was there in the white cone of the floods, so were Brandeis, Radcliffe, Loyola and Carleton.

The pilot yawned with his fists beside his shoulders and said, "Sorry. Had a late night last night, bringing in a pregnant mammoth. All right if we get under way now?"

"She's all yours, Pilot."

"Thank you." He pulled the mike down from the ceiling and said, "Let go fore and aft."

From the loudspeaker overhead came a variety of noises: quackings, chortlings, giggles. It was as if by some turbulence in the ether he had tuned in to the dormitory of a girls' school. Number One was not on the fo'c'sle yet.

"Excuse me." Captain Cho, *redivivus*, had come up behind the pilot. "I will tell them."

"You mean they don't know what 'let go' means?" the pilot asked, amazed.

"They speak no English at all. You wish the mooring lines taken in?"

"That's roughly what I had in mind," the pilot said. The bosun listened with fascination.

From the loudspeaker came a sharp hiss, then a jolly voice. "*Isabel*, this is *Polly*. We're all set." Another hiss. "*Jenny* all set."

"Roger, *Polly*. Roger, *Jenny*," the pilot said. "We're casting off. Stand by."

He gestured at the mike. "Go ahead, Captain. Fore and aft decks are on one circuit."

Captain Cho took up position underneath the mike, which turned out to be too high for him; I pulled it down as far as it would go. He gave the mike a blast of high-pitched chatter; the Chinese on both fore and aft decks sprang to life. The moorings were whisked on board and coiled on deck with the speed of an Indian rope trick; the pilot, who had been watching, had to tear himself away from the spectacle when he realized the ship was now drifting free of the shore. He pushed up the mike and said, "Okay, *Polly*, *Jenny*, ease her out."

"Roger, *Isabel*—Roger." The *Polly* swung ahead of us, churning; the *Jenny* dropped astern.

"Easy now, *Polly*, easy."

"Roger, *Isabel*."

"Steady as she goes."

"Steady."

We started down the harbor to the river, which was hidden from sight behind a distant shed. The ship moved slowly past sleeping freighters, with here and there a lighted crane.

"I think I'll give an early warning," the pilot said, "we have a liner coming downriver. Excuse me, Captain."

Captain Cho moved aside; the pilot pressed a button, the wail of the foghorn roared in the early-morning stillness, echoing off the facades of the warehouses.

The ship nosed out into the open, handled by the two tugs. The river opened before us, pewter and black. The liner the pilot had announced was passing as we came out, a gigantic cluster of stars. There was a lot of traffic of small fry: lighters, motor barges, private little ferryboats pushing bow waves almost as big as themselves, jammed with people on their way to the yards and wharves downriver.

"Well," the pilot said, "we can let the tugs go now, if that's all right with you."

"I'll tell the engine room," I replied. I took the phone; Porks answered. "Okay, Chief, we're on our way."

"All set."

I nodded to the pilot.

"Who has the wheel?" he asked.

"I have," the bosun said.

"Stand by." The pilot went to the mike. "*Polly, Jenny,* this is the *Isabel.* We're ready, you can let go. Thank you."

"Roger, *Isabel*—Roger."

My attention was caught by an altercation on the foredeck. A crowd of Chinese sailors was leaning over the rail, looking down at the *Polly,* screaming cat language. Someone on the deck of the *Polly* shouted, "Let go, you bastards! Let go! They're *ours!*"

"Oh, boy," the pilot sighed, shaking his head. "I don't believe this."

"Captain Cho!" I called.

He materialized. "Yes?"

"There seems to be a problem about releasing the lines." I pulled the mike down for him. "Could you tell your men that the ropes belong to the tugs?"

He took the mike and exploded in a torrent of guttural sounds. They let go of the *Polly*'s lines.

"Well, as the saying goes," the pilot muttered beside me, "it takes all kinds."

The *Polly* had cast off, so had the *Jenny;* they both gave a farewell blast on their foghorns. I let the *Isabel* wail in response.

"All right, Helmsman," the pilot said, "two forty-eight, and watch the small critters."

"Aye, aye."

[114]

The pilot, who seemed familiar with the space-age equipment, rang for half-speed; we headed downriver with our backs to the dawn. The steward brought coffee; he had forgotten the condensed milk.

The bosun growled, "Stupid orang! Where's the fucking milk?"

"Have nossing to make fucking holes," the Chinese hissed.

"Men," I said, "that'll do. Would you like milk, Pilot?"

"As a matter of fact, I would," the pilot said.

"All right, steward, get the milk and we'll make the holes."

"Don't do that, Ome! I *told* the bugger where to find the piercer!"

"Well, tell him again. But take it easy."

"Orang!" the bosun bellowed, and I cringed.

The steward came back and asked gently, "You called, big mouth?"

I said, "Stop that!"

The rest of their discussion was carried on in gestures.

"Lovely day," the pilot said in a tone that was full of meaning.

"It is," I agreed.

So it went, all the way downriver. Coffee was served, sandwiches were served, half of which the steward dropped on the floor, saying, "Hopla!" He wiped them on his pants before putting them back on the plate. There was a lot of traffic; some of the small fry dared us on the principle that right of way is right of way, whatever your opponent's size; but they were the pilot's problem. All I had to do was stand there and exude benign authority. Captain Cho pouted in his corner.

It was daylight when we reached the open sea. As we passed the outer buoy, the swell hit us and the *Isabel* came to life. A black launch slung with tires came pitching and wallowing toward us, dipping the big white letter 'P' on its bow in the water.

"Well, Commodore," the pilot said, "I think this wraps it up. It was a pleasure taking you out. Now if you'll sign this chit for me, I'll mosey off." I rang down the speed to Dead Slow for him and said, "That should be signed by the master."

"Oh, I see." He took his book of chits to Captain Cho, who frowned at it.

"Sign here, Captain," he said, indicating the spot. "If you can't sign your name, make a cross. The commodore will certify it's yours."

[115]

"What is this for, please?"

"Now, don't make any problems, Captain, just sign. My trolley is waiting."

While Cho signed, the pilot looked at me morosely. "She's a Taiwanese ship now?"

"That's right."

He took his book back. "Captain, Commodore, Godspeed and happy sailing. And *lots* of luck," he added.

"Thank you, Pilot."

I went out onto the port wing to watch him leave. He went down the Jacob's ladder; the launch departed. I gave them a thank-you wail on the horn, went back into the wheelhouse and rang up the speed to Full Ahead, with demonstrative self-confidence. No point in advertising the fact that I had had no more than a two-hour crash course by Beast Rufus on the spaceship's bridge and knew, in fact, as much about her esoteric gadgetry as did Captain Cho by now—if he had been watching the pilot, which I doubted. He looked totally turned inward standing there, frozen in his corner, thinking alien thoughts.

"All right, Bosun. Another mile or so and I'll give you the course. For the moment, steady as you go."

"Aye."

"Captain Cho, let's have a look at the chart."

I went to the desk and plotted the course for the Scheldt River entrance, staying within the coastal traffic zone. He watched me without a word, then retired into his corner again. I gave the bosun the new course and strolled out onto the port wing. The weather was clear but cold; the white beaches of the Dutch coast shimmered in the early sun. Seagulls circled over our wake, screeching and diving. The Chinese sailors on the aft deck were scuppering buckets of sea water on board and started to wash the deck. I was about to call Number Two to tell him to stop them; steel decks should not be washed with sea water because of rust. But there had been enough confrontation for one day; this once would not hurt.

In the distance I heard the ship's bell strike four twins. A voice beside me said, "All right, Commodore, I'll take over the watch, if you're ready." It was mate Number One. Captain Cho had disappeared.

This was a surprise. Young Number One looked completely at ease, as if for him to take over the watch was the most normal thing in the world. Well, I couldn't sail the ship all by myself; in any event, initiative should be encouraged. So I said, "Very well, thank you. The course is two ten. We're running full-speed. Call when you sight the Scheldt pilot."

"Yes, Commodore." He went back into the wheelhouse.

The bosun came out, furious. "Ome! There's a slit-eye who wants to take my place at the wheel!"

"Bosun," I said, "that's the idea. And stop calling these people slit-eyes, dammit!"

"But the man doesn't know what to do! He stands looking at the wheel as if it's something he's never eaten before!"

I went into the wheelhouse and saw Number One arguing with a tiny Chinese sailor labeled Whittier.

"He's too short, Commodore," Number One said.

"Bosun, get a crate or something."

Mumbling, he lumbered off.

I asked, "Maybe you'd be kind enough to man the wheel until he turns up, Number One?"

"Yes, Commodore."

The bosun came back with an empty crate saying MOUTH-WATERING NAVELS FROM ISRAEL. "Try that, boy-o," he said.

The little helmsman climbed onto the crate and clapped his hands in childish delight. It infuriated the bosun, who came toward me with a face of thunder. "All we need now on this bridge is a skipping rope!"

"They have to work it out among themselves, Bosun. Don't try to run their lives for them. We have troubles of our own."

"Ain't that the truth!" He looked around to see if anyone was listening. "Can I have a word with you in private? There's something I think I should tell you."

"Number One, if anything unusual comes up, call me. I'll be in my dayroom."

'Yes, Commodore."

"Good watch, gentlemen."

I took the bosun along to my quarters. The canary was trilling its heart out in the corner.

"Well, Bosun?"

"I don't know if it's my place to tell you, but somebody should."

"What is it?"

"When Mate Slobkous arrived on the quayside yesterday in

[117]

that taxi and unloaded his gear, I helped him carry it on board. I don't know if you noticed a bunch of cardboard boxes."

"Well?"

"Did you read what was printed on them? 'Bols Dutch Geneva.' When I carried them on board, they clinked."

"So?"

"I know it's none of my business, but five boxes of a dozen each? That's enough to put a regiment under."

"I'm sure there's an explanation. I'll ask the mate about it when I see him. Thanks."

"Yes, Ome."

He left me listening to the canary with a troubled mind. So that was what had seemed wrong with the man when we first met in the café: they had saddled me with an alcoholic. Hallelujah.

2

I was prepared to confront Slobkous the moment he was back on board, but it didn't work out that way. After he arrived with the pilot in the Western Scheldt and the ship was on her way again, he took me aside. "I have news for you. The dry dock we're taking on is pregnant."

"I beg your pardon?"

"A thirty-thousand-ton derelict, and a yacht welded inside, derelict too. That tow is going to fall apart at the first blow."

"But that's ridiculous!"

"You're telling *me!*"

If I hadn't had the option of leaving in Antwerp, I would have reacted with shocked indignation. "By the way," I said, "I gather you carried five boxes of gin on board."

It didn't faze him at all. "Oh, that's a bit of private merchandise. A man has to make some money on the side, with our wages."

"Where were you planning to make that money?"

"Rio. I sell it to an agent, he pays three times the cost price. You don't mind, do you?"

"Why should I? Suit yourself." Well, one worry less; at least I hoped so. I would know if he started drinking; Dutch gin on a man's breath is impossible to disguise.

The Western Scheldt pilot joined us and asked how things were in Rotterdam. I told him. The bosun, back at the wheel, yawned and asked if I'd had a look below, it was like Ketèlbey's 'In a Persian Market.' It turned out that he was a music buff; his wife had won first prize on the program *Name That Tune*. We talked about music and wives until the Antwerp harbor pilot came on board with Fransen, who entered the wheelhouse in a chain-smoking frenzy, shook me by the hand, waved at the Chinese mates and said hello to Slobkous. Captain Cho was not on the bridge.

"Sorry, Harinxma," Fransen said, "I intended to come on board earlier, but I just flew in from the Gulf. I'll set you on your way, then I'm off to Glasglow, where the *Hilda* is picking up a tin-ore dredge for Billiton."

"I gather the dry dock has a yacht inside."

He lit a new cigarette with the stub of the previous one and muttered, between puffs, "Chung will tell you all about that in Brussels. You have a car waiting at the quayside to take you there."

We were approaching the city of Antwerp, a Brueghel painting of red-tiled roofs and medieval churches. The river was choppy with the wakes of tugs, fishing smacks and bumboats. The pilot moored the ship at a quay in the heart of town, where a stretch limousine with uniformed chauffeur was waiting, seagulls circling overhead. After we had made fast, I changed into my uniform with the commodore's rings and put on the cap with the gold scrambled eggs. When I came out, the Chinese crew gathered on deck gawked at me; someone gave what sounded like a wolf whistle. Glancing over, I guessed it to be the female cook, who grinned at me with the gap in her teeth. The chauffeur of the limousine saluted; I returned his salute, sank into the cushions of the back seat and found myself, in a space like the cabin of a cruiser, facing a small table laid for one, complete with linen, plate, cutlery and basket of fruit. A miniature television set showed a Belgian matron boning a chicken and addressing her listeners as *"Dames."* By the time I had taken all this in, the limousine was on its way.

We left town; just for the hell of it, I peeled a banana. As I brought it to my mouth, I seemed to catch the eye of the Belgian matron, who stopped boning her chicken and stared at the camera in apparent disbelief; I put the banana down with the unnerving feeling of having passed through the looking glass.

I was deposited in the resplendently illuminated Grand' Place of Brussels, outside a seventeenth-century restaurant with a swan over the door. Mr. Chung, waiting at a candle-lit table, rose when he saw me. A chair was pulled out for me by a waiter in gaiters.

"Delighted you could come, Commodore. My secretary managed to find some literature on your Roman general. I can see now why you are so fascinated by the man. An extraordinary story, very meaningful for these times." He smiled; Little Red Riding Hood's grandmother, with teeth.

"I gather your dry dock has a yacht welded inside it, Mr. Chung."

"The yacht goes to Punta Arenas, the dry dock to Talcahuano."

"In that case, you may expect problems in the Forties."

His smile remained sunny. "There is no need for concern on your part, Commodore. You are not going any farther than Rio de Janeiro."

"I'm not thinking of myself, but of the crew and the captain."

"Ah?" His smile did not change, but his eyes did. "Any particular reason for your concern?"

"Well, sir, the ship may be manageable for a man who knows what to do and has the self-confidence to do it, but your Captain Cho is not in that class."

"Interesting that you should say so. Captain Cho happens to be the most experienced master of my fleet."

"Within the restrictions of a one-thousand-ton license, I gather."

"He received a dispensation of that restriction for this voyage, as he probably told you."

"He did."

"Then why your reservations, Commodore?"

"Captain Cho has refused to take on any responsibility for handling the ship. As a matter of fact, it takes a good deal of persuasion to get him even to leave his cabin."

"And why is that?"

"His understanding was that I would sail the ship. I told him that was impossible, as I no longer hold a valid license and am supposed to act only as his advisor."

[120]

"I see. First, would you like an aperitif?"

"Scotch on the rocks, please."

The waiter from the seventeenth century took the order; when the man had left, Mr. Chung beamed at me benevolently. "Hasty judgments are rarely accurate, Commodore, as many philosophers have told us."

"One philosopher disagreed when he said, 'Beware of first impressions, for they are the right ones.' I think it was La Rochefoucauld."

He positively radiated. "I must write that down! Excuse me one moment . . ." He took a small notebook and a gold pencil from an inside pocket and made a note. "La Rochefoucauld, you say? I'll ask my secretary to check it out." He pocketed the notebook and the pencil. "Now, where were we?"

"On board a space-age tugboat with a crew of Stone Age fishermen and a captain who refuses to leave his bunk."

"Ah, yes." The drinks arrived, he waved away the *maître d'* with the menu. "Your good health, Commodore."

"Thank you, sir. And yours." The Scotch was as smooth as children's lemonade, but its after-kick that of a Port Said hoofer.

"Now, Commodore, your problems. Let us take them one by one and see if we can shed some light."

"That would be welcome, sir."

"Captain Cho. Like most of us, a complicated man. A superlative sailor with a fear of being put upon that borders on paranoia."

It sounded like a healthy attitude, in present company.

"Also, an inferiority complex. It may be necessary to take that into account at times. How did you get the ship to Antwerp, by the way, if he refused to function?"

I told him.

"That arrangement will not be necessary for long, Commodore. Captain Cho is a born sailor, and once you are under way, he will be unable to resist the—how shall we say?—the persuasive power of a ship like this. And that is where *you* come in." He sipped his drink, which was pink and looked about as innocent as a hand grenade. "It would be a good idea if you were to make him fully aware of the ship's problems before he leaves for the Forties."

Well, what do you know? "Sir," I said, with the sudden feeling that the entire restaurant was listening, "the *Isabel* is one of the

[121]

most advanced tugboats of our age. She is a beautiful ship, nimble, responsive, enormously powerful, economical, incredibly versatile—"

"And tender," he added, smiling. I thought he would add, 'Isn't she, Commodore?' but he just let it hang there as he looked at me with that genial smile.

Now that he had me cornered, I saw no reason to be cute about it. If Kwel had hoodwinked him, that was no business of mine, but I owed the frightened little captain glowering in his bunk and the den mother with the gap in her teeth some fraternal consideration.

"If I were you," I said, "I would not send her through the Forties. Certainly not with that crew and that captain."

"Ah?"

"If you were looking for a combination certain to fall prey to whatever problems the ship may have, you couldn't have made a better choice."

I thought that was telling him a great deal more than Kwel would have wanted; to my surprise, he reacted the way Captain Cho had. His face froze into a mask.

"I resent that, Mr. Harinxma," he said. "That was uncalled for." His voice had lost its warmth.

I had no idea where the man was coming from. Here I was, out on a limb, telling him the truth about the *Isabel,* or beginning to, and got put down for my pains. "Let me put it this way, sir. If your Captain Cho is as good as you think he is, he'll have ample opportunity between Rio and Punta Arenas to show his mettle."

He gave me a look I could not interpret. "Shall we order?" He beckoned the *maître d'*.

While he went through the menu for me and made chic recommendations, I wondered what made the man tick. Old Kwel had tried to swear me to silence; now, by merely hinting at the possibility that there might be a problem, I had managed to step on his toes. Obviously, this was where I should leave it.

But no more was said by my host on the subject of the *Isabel.* It was a splendid meal, with lots of wine, of which I partook liberally as well as regaling him on the subject of General Theodosius. He made notes in his little book for his secretary to research. By the time I was served coffee, liqueurs and a cigar, I was sure I could sail the *Isabel* to Rio single-handed with just Porks, Slobkous, Harlingen and the bosun.

And that, I realized in the limousine on the way back, was exactly what I would be doing. Well, it was only for six weeks. The pay was very good indeed, and not many seventy-year-old inhabitants of retirement villages found themselves being driven through the night in a stretch limousine with television, smoking a cigar.

I flicked on the little set, which, to my surprise, was now showing a nude chorus line. I gazed at the pink wrigglings on the miniature screen, fascinated, while the limousine whispered down the freeway.

3

Halfway to Antwerp, I hit upon the daft idea of calling Sylvia now. There was a telephone in the car, but when I picked it up, it didn't seem to be connected. As we approached a floodlit gas station, I tapped on the partition and told the driver to pull in.

I found a telephone booth, one of those that leave your bottom exposed, and placed a collect call to the South of France. Sylvia answered and I told her, at the top of my voice because of a diesel truck that had just pulled in, about the yacht inside the dry dock, the reluctant captain, Chung's bizarre reaction and how I thought I had handled both men rather well. She listened without interruption, then said, "Love, you've let yourself be . . . rhubarb rhubarb . . . again!"

"Let myself be *what?*"

"Ma-nip-u-la-ted!"

The diesel roared.

"By whom? You must speak up!"

"By both of them! They . . . rhubarb rhubarb . . . out of you!"

"But how?!" I shouted as the diesel was revving up.

"What did you say?"

"How? How? How could—" The diesel tried its air horn. This was patently ridiculous. "All right, Syl!" I yelled. "I'll call you later! There's a truck right next to me!"

"You *must* call! Apart from everything else, you . . . rhubarb rhubarb . . . the children! . . . rhubarb . . . Christmas!"

"What's that? About Christmas?"

"It's Christmas Eve!"

My God—so it was. "Love," I said, "I'm awfully—" The diesel demonstrated what it thought was wrong with its air horn; it certainly was not the volume. "Happy Christmas!" I yelled. "I'll call later! Bye, love!"

Christmas Eve. I would have to call the family from somewhere near the ship.

When I climbed back into the luxurious little living room of the limousine, the chorus line had been replaced by a religious service in a cathedral. It seemed full of wriggling pink figures too, but it may have been the wine.

The limousine reached the outskirts of Antwerp. Instead of heading toward the center of the city, it began to skirt it. We dipped into a tunnel; I couldn't remember passing through any tunnels on our way to Brussels; then I realized we were passing under the River Scheldt. The tug must have been moved across the river to the yard where the dry dock was moored while I was knocking back Margaux and gorging myself on Zabaglione Manneke Pis.

A few minutes later we emerged and drove through the gates of a huge shipyard, floodlit from one end to the other. In the artificial dusk I saw the *Isabel*'s familiar Paradise tree at the far end of an alley between the sheds. I suddenly felt tired; but then, what with one thing and another, it had been quite a day.

I found the bosun waiting for me at the top of the gangway, like a worried parent. "Hi there, Ome! I thought I'd wait up for you, considering I had nothing better to do."

"Is Captain Fransen on board?"

"He's waiting for you in the dayroom."

"For God's sake, I want to go to bed! Well, all right, bring us some coffee."

"Yes, Ome."

I opened the door to my quarters and there was Fransen, sprawled on the couch, a bottle of beer in his hand. The rings around his eyes were so dark they looked like targets for gun practice.

He asked, "Well? How did it go?"

I told him about Chung's bizarre reaction to my readiness to tell him about the *Isabel*'s fatal flaw; it shook him badly.

"For Chrissake, Harinxma!" he cried. "Stop yelling 'fatal flaw' all over the waterfront! If you must talk about it, call it 'FF' or 'effing FF,' but shut up about it, now the Chinks are on board. And anywhere else, for that matter, anywhere at all! In this business the walls have ears. And what are you talking about anyhow?"

"Friend, I'm stuck with the job of teaching that incompetent tug-driver from Taiwan how to handle this ship when she starts her cycle. You were there when Bron demonstrated that she can be a death trap to anyone who's not an expert."

He took a swig of his beer. "It's none of your business. It's not your place to tell the Chinese they bought a pig. Let the owners fight it out." He tossed the empty bottle into the trash basket and stood up. "Right now, let's start taking this box of goodies out of town."

"Fransen," I said, "have a heart! I've been at it since four o'clock this morning and I've just come in from a heavy meal, full of expensive wine. I must have some sleep or I'll keel over. The tow has to wait for the incoming tide anyhow, or I'll be side-swiping the locals with that dry dock barreling downriver."

"Don't worry," he said, "slack is at two hundred hours. I've ordered the tugs for three hundred. The Belgians start holding up traffic in the narrows at four hundred. So you've got three hours after we've had a look at the dock. That won't take us a minute."

I sighed. "All right. I'll hold you to that."

In the corridor we met the bosun with his coffee; I told him to put it on the table, we would get it later. He said he would do no such thing, he would keep it warm. Behind him hovered the Chinese steward, in a huff. And there came Porks: "Is it true? Are we going around the Horn?"

"No. We get off in Rio."

"You, maybe! I signed an open-ended contract! I'm not about to go around the Horn in this bitch with a curse on her!"

"Come on, Harinxma," Fransen called helpfully from the end of the corridor. When I joined him, he said, "You have to watch young Alberts. He argues."

"Well, this time he has something to argue about."

"He'd better shut up or he'll get himself fired. By the way, for a runner captain you have a man called Harry Keerie, known as Harakiri. He's good, but as ornery as a mule."

"How big is the dock?"

"Big."

"Slobkous says thirty thousand."

"Bigger than that. Thirty-five."

[125]

"And what about the yacht it has inside?"

"Come and see for yourself."

We walked down the alley between the sheds to the main basin of the yard, where a huge dry dock was moored. Lit up by the yard's floodlights, it looked to be in a terrible state of neglect. Its ribs showed, its plates were buckled and streaked with rust. High up on its flank I spotted the remnants of what must have been a company name: A.G., the rest obliterated by rust, and, a yard or so lower: NES. This brute was at least forty thousand tons.

"Don't break your neck," Fransen said as he led me across an acre of scrap iron to a gangplank slanting upward to the floor of the dry dock. The interior was lit up jerkily by the blue sheet lightning of welding. I caught my first glimpse of the yacht: a beached whale trapped inside a steel canyon. It looked ancient, much larger than the silly little thing I had imagined. This was a substantial vessel with a clipper bow, a bowsprit complete with figurehead, and a name: QUEEN OF PERSIA. I estimated it at a thousand tons, yet it looked small in the canyon between the dock's walls.

The dock floor was crowded with welders and longshoremen, dragging chains. A figure detached itself from a group around a welder and advanced on us, throwing a long shadow. "Hi there, Slobbo!" the creature cried. "How are you?"

Someone behind me said, "I'm okay. How are *you?*"

I turned around and saw Slobkous standing behind me. "Harakiri, meet the commodore," he said. "You know Captain Fransen, don't you?"

"Do I know Fransen! Who's this, you say?"

"Commodore Harinxma," Fransen said. "Advisor for this convoy."

"Glad to meet you, Keerie," I said. "I gather you're the runner captain for this trip."

We shook hands, he looked me over. I could see him more clearly now: a wiry, probably straw-blond character in his forties; in the welding light he looked like a demon with a blue face and green hair.

"You know we're due to leave at three hundred hours?" Fransen asked.

"If the Belgians are through welding on my extra eyes by then," said the blue demon.

"How are they doing?"

"Slow. Tell me, Commodore, Captain—what do you want me to call you?"

I had dealt with runner captains all my life; they were a proud and independent lot. "Harinxma to you."

"Okay. Want to check the struts, Harinxma?"

"I did that," Fransen said.

"I'd like to have a look at them myself, if you don't mind." Despite my tiredness, I had to establish a relationship with the runner captain in charge of the dock before we sailed, for I wouldn't meet him face to face again before Mindello, our next bunkering station, in the Cape Verdes. Until then our only contact would be by walkie-talkie.

"Harinxma," he said as we walked down the length of the ship, "have a good look at these struts, now. The structure seems solid enough, but the struts themselves are on the light side, if you see what I mean."

The distance between the flanks of the yacht and the walls of the canyon was about sixty feet. Horizontal struts, supported by vertical stanchions every twenty feet, had been welded on at the height of the yacht's deckline.

"Leaves a lot of play, if you see what I mean, Harinxma. Where's this box going anyway?"

"Punta Arenas is the destination of the yacht, the dock continues to Talcahuano," Fransen said.

"Good night! So I'll be hitting the Forties twice with this coffin?"

"The second time there'll be no yacht inside."

"Well, what do you think, Harinxma? Is this structure going to be secure in bad weather? If we get one of those gales with this pig's bladder, there's going to be blue water in here."

"Not enough to give flotation."

"Even so, I'd be happier if we could weld both anchor chains to the dock floor, instead of just the eyes I ordered."

"We don't have time for that," Fransen said. "If you want that done, it'll have to wait until Rio. In Mindello it would take a week. Will that satisfy you?"

"I suppose so. Now, Harinxma, would you like to have a look at the yacht? I've bedded the gooks down in the staterooms."

"We don't have time for that," Fransen said. "The man has to sleep. Show it to him later."

But my relationship with Keerie had only this half-hour in

which to establish itself, so I said, "I think I'd like a quick look. Are you coming, Fransen?"

"No, I've seen it. Don't be long, or you'll hit the deck when we sail and I'll be in trouble with the Belgians."

"You go ahead, Skipper," Slobkous said, "I have to get back to the ship."

"All right, Keerie, lead the way."

A narrow articulated gangway led from the dock floor to the deck of the yacht. The runner captain climbed it at a good clip; I followed him at my ease. I had a limited amount of vital energy to spend; this must be why the old captains I had sailed under had all moved at the maddening pace of turtles. When I reached the deck, Keerie was waiting for me.

"How are you getting on with the Chinese?" I asked.

"Okay. They know their job. For the rest, they can smoke opium as far as I'm concerned and bugger each other. They've got plenty of room to do it in."

He took me down a dim corridor lit only by an oil lamp at the far end. "There you go," he said, pointing at closed doors. "Card room. Library. Dining room. Lounge. And these: private state-rooms, one for each gook. I'd show them to you if we had the time." The corridor smelled of toadstools, like the bilges of the old *Anna*. There was an imposing door at the end, which he opened with a flourish.

"Welcome to Titsville."

It was a large stateroom. Its ceiling, covered with ornate gold scrolls, reflected the light of two oil lamps. One wall showed a mural of nude female figures, some of them disfigured with mustaches and beards below the belt. The centerpiece of the room was an oval bed with a narrow, unmade mattress like a dog's nest; this must be where Keerie slept. There was a built-in dressing table and mirrored wardrobes; the floor was covered with a carpet pockmarked with burn holes and dark spots of dampness. The place smelled like Roquefort cheese. "What this needs is a couple of broads," Keerie said. "Mind if I import some talent?"

If he'd really been planning to bring women on board, he would have kept it to himself. I replied, "Do whatever you like, Keerie, as long as you have a second-in-command to take up the slack."

"As a matter of fact, I think I may have. He looks like a mean bastard, but he knows his way around."

"Who's that?"

"Their mandur, or whatever you call him. I don't have to tell him a thing. He had the lamps filled and lit, his people housed, watches organized before I could say a word. He may slit my throat while we're under way; apart from that, I think I drew lucky. At least he won't be boring me about his love life." He gave me a look. "Aren't you too old for this?"

"They may have to bury me at sea."

He slapped my shoulder. "Just queen it, Harinxma. Don't lift a finger. Let Slobbo do the work for you and you'll be okay."

"I have to get back to the ship," I said. "Thanks for the tour. How do I get back to the gangway?"

"But you haven't seen my bathroom!"

He pushed open a door among the mirrors. It had been a palatial bathroom at one time; now it looked like a bombed-out building. The mirrors were cracked, the ceiling had holes in it, the toilet was broken and where once there had been a bath was now a cavity in the floor. The washbasins were still there, but had no taps.

"They must have been gold," he said. "Everything was gold. There must have been a gold pisspot in the bedside table. Who did this thing belong to?"

"No idea."

"Pity to let this beauty rot away. Well, glad you could manage a visit." He slapped my shoulder again. "This way."

He took me back into the corridor with its closed doors. One of the doors opened and I found myself face to face with the steel-eyed Chinese who had confronted me on the quayside. He had not gained in charm in the meantime.

"Good evening," I said. "Good to have you aboard."

He gave me one of those looks that are supposed to kill.

"I hope you found everything all right for you and your crew?"

He didn't reply, just stared at me.

Keerie helped out. "If he didn't, he'd be the first to tell us, by the look of him. Wouldn't you, baby?"

Baby did not react, other than by shifting his killing gaze to the man with whom he would have to spend two months on board this hulk. When I wished Harakiri Godspeed and happy sailing before going down the companionway, it was more than an empty phrase.

Downstairs, I found Fransen waiting for me. "For God's sake, go to bed, Harinxma," he said, rubbing out a cigarette with his foot. "I suggest you let the harbor tugs winkle this thing out of here and you take over in the channel."

"All right. Let them prepare the bridle with throw line attached, and I'll take over as soon as I have room."

"You'll have plenty of room," Fransen said as we walked back to the edge of the dock. "I told you, they're holding up traffic. They can't hold it for more than an hour, though, so you'd better not hang around."

"Tell them not to hold it up until the dock moves out of this yard. I want to see the bridle in place and inspect it myself."

"Look, Harinxma, everything's been arranged—"

"Fransen, I'm not going to be hassled into hightailing it out of here with my shirt hanging out. I want to see the bridle in place, I want to check the shackles. Once I give my okay, we move; not before. All right?"

He stared at me, the blue lightning of the welding twitching behind him. "Okay, Harinxma, I'm not going to get a perforated ulcer over you. Let's go back to the ship."

We edged down the gangplank, stumbled across the acre of scrap iron in the dark and walked back to the *Isabel*. As we approached, I saw a white delivery van parked at the foot of the gangway with on its side panel, in arty letters, LODE BEUKELMANS, PÈRE ET FILLES, PRIMEURS ET FRUITS EXOTIQUES. Two little girls looking like twins peered at us from the window of the driver's seat, one sucking a lollipop. I said, "Girls, what are you doing out this late? Is your dad on board the ship?"

They stared at me; the one with the lollipop pulled it out of her mouth and stuck out her tongue at me.

A man came down the gangway. "You Commandant Harinxma? I put the basket in your salon."

As we entered my dayroom, I found on the coffee table a handsome basket of fruit with a business card attached to its handle: *Happy Christmas and bon voyage, Charlie Chung.*

"Well," Fransen said, "you have to hand it to him. The Kwels wouldn't do this in a thousand years."

"That reminds me: I have to call my family to wish them Happy Christmas. Where do I find a phone?"

"Too late, man. Call them once you're under way, by ship-to-shore. Go to bed, dammit!"

Slobkous stuck his head around the door. "Is it going to be three hundred hours, the tugs?"

"Probably later," I said, "but where's Captain Cho? He should be in on this."

"In his bunk," Slobkous replied without interest. "He's feeling poorly, I was told."

"All right, I'll see him before we leave. In the meantime, start getting things ready while I take a couple of hours off. I want to check the bridle before we make fast; has it been made up yet?"

"Yes. Sixty-foot reach, double shackle both ends, to be attached to the bollards on the dock floor they're reinforcing now."

"Let me know when it's all set to go, and I'll come and check it out."

"Jesus, Harinxma, that's going to take forever!" Fransen moaned. "The Belgians—"

"Stop worrying about the Belgians. *They* don't have to get that dock to Rio. Now I'm going to sleep."

I ushered him out and locked the door of the dayroom; if I didn't, there would be people in and out every few minutes. I undressed, as I knew from experience that this was the only way to coax my body into relaxing for sleep. A few minutes later I was bedded down and went out like a light.

4

I was wakened by banging on the dayroom door, told the banger I was coming, pulled on my pants and opened up. It was Slobkous with the Flemish tugboat captains. They turned out to be thirsty; I put the Chinese steward to work fueling them while I paid a visit to Captain Cho.

I found him sitting up in bed in his striped pajamas, smoking his pipe, reading his little red book. He welcomed me with his stonewall look; he seemed younger than ever, a recalcitrant teenager. I wondered what the little red book was. *Quotations from Chairman Mao?* Hardly, on board a ship flying the flag of Nationalist China. But it would fit the picture of adolescent rebellion.

"Well, Captain, how about coming with me to inspect the bridle before we sail?"

He puffed at his pipe.

I had always had a problem with teenagers, but suffered them as gracefully as I could in the happy knowledge that they were not part of my world; I could leave them behind for my wife to wrestle to the mat. Now I had one on board.

"Look, Cho," I said flatly, "if you don't want to accept command, that's your problem. I'll sail the damn thing. But, goddammit, I need your body on the bridge to satisfy the law, or I can't get this tow moving. So make sure you're there, or I'll have you dragged out of that bed. We sail in twenty minutes."

I had made more diplomatic speeches than that in my time, but it would have to do. I left to pay a hurried visit to the dock to inspect the bridle. After checking the reinforced bollards and the freshly welded eyes with Harakiri, I went back on board and found my staff gathered in the dayroom for a pre-departure Happy Hour around the fruit basket.

Slobkous was having an apple, Porks and Harlingen were into gin. Porks seemed to be worrying about his engines; his Chinese engineers were used to MAN diesels on which everything was the other way round, so he had to watch them like a hawk. Harlingen reported that his radio officers had started by freezing in their booties, then started to pull out all the stops; Harlingen had let them play to their heart's content after turning the power off. The Chinese steward dropped two bowls of peanuts and one gin and tonic, yodeling "Hopla!" each time; Porks started to call him Hopla. It was not exactly an atmosphere of international brotherhood, but I did not feel like preaching at them.

Finally the Flemish captains left with so much gin in them that it seemed impossible they could navigate the high threshold, let alone their vessels. I sent Slobkous to present my compliments to Captain Cho and request his presence on the bridge. If he was still in bed, I was to be advised.

When I reached the bridge, he was standing in his corner, like a statue. The pilot was there; I introduced them to each other. Then I spoke the magic formula: "Captain Cho, do you wish to take charge of this operation, or do you wish me to demonstrate the departure procedure for you?"

He made a gesture which I interpreted as acceptance. I said to the pilot, "Well, let's get this show on the road," and forgot about the silent figure in the corner.

"Let go fore and aft," the pilot said into the mike. This time Bryn Mawr, Brandeis, Whittier and Loyola knew what the command meant; all Number One had to do was watch.

I revised my opinion of the Stone Age fishermen, they were very good; for once La Rochefoucauld had been wrong. Out in midstream, we made fast to the dry dock: an angular mass ten times the size of the ship blacking out the glitter of the waterfront. The Chinese worked the lines deftly; there was no scurrying to get out of the way of the formidable forty-inch nylon when the stretcher was paid out in the harsh light of the floods. Slobkous came back to the bridge and said, "Well, at least the Chinks know a rope from a noodle." I alerted him with a nod to the silent presence in the corner.

The four Belgian tugs churned away to keep the dock in the center of the channel while the *Isabel* gave it forward momentum. On the bridge the mood was relaxed. The pilot let me do the maneuvering, as this was out of his league; he simply gave the headings. The bosun had the wheel; Number Two was on the aft deck; Number One hovered near me throughout the operation, following my every move.

Once again I was startled by the tremendous power of the ship. To tow a dry dock this size with just one tug was in itself an innovation to me; in my time it would have taken at least three. But I couldn't remember having come up to speed this fast even with three ships; when I put on Full Speed Ahead to get the massive load behind me moving, the *Isabel* seemed to growl and hunch her shoulders, then proceeded to whisk the dock and the four tugboats along with a forward surge that took my breath away. The channel was by no means straight, we would have to negotiate a few tortuous bends and narrow passages; a runaway dry dock of over thirty thousand tons at this skittish clip would be a bull in a china shop. I rang the speed down to half.

The pilot said, "We can put on more speed, if you wish."

"What about the narrows at Parel Shoal?" I asked.

"Plenty of room. We halted all traffic."

"Even so, I prefer to take it easy until we're past Fort Liefkenshoek. I've got a lot of mass behind me, I don't want to swipe one of your buoys."

"We've a lot of vessels held up beyond the narrows, Commodore. They've been told to proceed at five hundred hours."

"Would you like to take over this maneuver?"

"No, no, you go ahead. I'll inform the police." He went to a corner of the wheelhouse and started to mumble into his walkie-talkie.

I felt as if I had never been away. The process of identification that always occurs when you start to tow a large object was taking place again. I knew by a sort of osmosis what the cumbersome mass behind me would do, and I knew that if we were to barrel through the narrows at Parel Shoal at full speed, the dock would have too much forward momentum for me to keep it center channel. Sideswiping a buoy would do no harm, but I didn't want any sloppiness with Captain Cho watching. Besides, I was taking no chances with this monster.

"Captain, tea." It was the Chinese steward.

"Thank you." Nice feeling, to hold a heavy ship's mug again. I went to the aft window of the wheelhouse and looked at the black citadel behind us. Red and green flashers were winking among the stars. In a matter of days I'd be thinking about the rusty mass as 'good old dry dock,' later still by a name we would bestow on it. Tugboat crews usually attribute a personality to the object they are dragging along, a need rooted in our distant past.

5

I stayed on the bridge well past the end of my watch. The stars were paling in the blue of the dawn and the River Scheldt had widened into the vast pewter plain of the estuary when the tugs cast off. I gave them the farewell-and-thank-you blasts of our horn; when they responded, their braying sounded puny in the immensity of water and sky. I put the engine on Full Ahead; the short hawser was whisked out of the water. By then Slobkous, who had turned in for a shut-eye an hour earlier, was back on the bridge.

"You're going to be all right, Slobkous?"

"Don't worry, Skipper. I know the ship. You turn in."

"If anything comes up, don't hesitate to call me. I'll just be having a nap on the couch in my dayroom."

"Will do."

"Good watch, gentlemen."

Captain Cho had disappeared; I hadn't seen him leave. The bosun reluctantly handed the wheel to little Whittier on his orange crate and accompanied me down the companionway.

"I'll bring you a nice mug of hot cocoa, Ome."

"Good idea, Bosun. But no rum this time."

"Are you sure? You should sleep for a couple of hours. The rum helps."

"Quite sure, thank you."

As I entered, the canary was peet-peeting at the dawn. I could see Haversma's point in having the bird on board; it was somebody to come home to. I filled the feeding cup and said, "Well, here we go, another trip. How about some breakfast?" The bird came fluttering down with the sound of a small pigeon and started to peck furiously, throwing most of the seed on the floor.

I wondered if I should pay a visit to Cho, but decided to let it be. I was on call, so I just took off my shoes and jacket and lay down on the couch in the dayroom. Surprisingly, I did not feel a bit tired. On the contrary, I had not felt so stimulated and alert in years. But I should try to sleep, or exhaustion would sneak up on me. Then I remembered it was Christmas Day. I should call the family. I picked up the phone and punched the number of the radio room.

"Radio. Harlingen."

"Harlingen, Harinxma here. Could you get a number in the South of France for me, or are we still under shore restrictions?"

"No, that's okay. One second . . . Okay, let me have the number."

I gave it to him.

"Right-o. It'll take just a couple of minutes. I'll call you back."

The bosun came in with a mug. "Here you go, Ome. Nice and hot. Have you taken your pills?"

"Who told you about my pills?"

"Well, I watched that slit-eye unpacking—"

"For God's sake, Bosun! Stop calling these people slit-eyes! And tell anyone you hear doing it to call them by their names."

"Have you *heard* their names?"

[135]

"Call them what it says on their T-shirts. Thank you, by the way. This is delicious."

"Pills," he said, like a wife.

"They're in coin envelopes in two boxes on the top shelf of my wardrobe. Bring me a white envelope from one box and put the other in the fridge."

As I shook the pills into my hand, he asked, "What's in the brown envelopes?"

"They're for suppertime. The whites are breakfast."

"Do you have enough for the trip?"

"Each of the boxes holds four weeks."

He frowned thoughtfully. "H'm. That should take us as far as Rio. Now, how about your teeth?"

"Bosun, I appreciate your concern, but leave my teeth to me. How did you know about them anyway?"

He looked down on me with a smug expression. "I'm not blind," he said. "I unpacked their little bath and those tablets. That's to say, the slit—the Chinese did."

"Well, I'll take care of them myself."

He turned at the door. "Happy dreams, Ome. I'll cover the bird. By the way: he's a male. I'm calling him Pete."

It was maddening, and yet comforting. In a sense, I was his canary. *The sea is so big and my ship is so small.* We all need the comfort of tender loving care, the giving of it as well as the receiving.

The telephone rang. "I've got France for you, Skipper. You can talk normally, no need to say 'over'; just like a telephone ashore."

"Dad?" It was my daughter Helen's voice.

"Hello, honey! Nice to hear you. Happy Christmas!"

"Happy Christmas, Dad! We miss you! Are you all right?"

"Sure. This ship is a lazy captain's dream. I'm lolling on a couch in a bridal suite right now."

"You're what?"

"Never mind. Are you okay? How are the kids?"

"They're fine. They all want to talk to you . . . Jackie, come here. *Come here!* It's Granddad on the phone . . ."

"Hi."

"Happy Christmas, boy!"

"Yeah. Here's Suzy."

"Suzy, love! Happy Christmas! How are you?"

[136]

"Fine, Grandpa."

"What presents did you get this morning?"

"I got more cows for my farm and a floppy doll and—oh-oh! The dog's eating the pies! Mam! *Mam!*"

So it went, one installment of grandparental bliss after another, including the dog, which they somehow got to bark, for God's sake. Man was not worthy of his own inventions: a whole Paradise tree full of electronic wizardry to hear a dog bark on the Riviera. My heart flowed over with gratitude for Mr. Kwel. The only one I would really have liked to talk to was my daughter.

I went to get a glass of water and took my pills, but I should eat something with them or they would lie on my stomach like pellets. I went to have a look at the fruit basket. Apart from fruit, it contained portions of different kinds of cheese in individual wrappings and a small bottle of Kirschwasser. The cheese was tempting; I chose a portion of Brie, but found that the underside had been nibbled by mice. I put the piece back and picked up an apple; it too had a piece nibbled out of it. I checked the others; all had been chewed at by mice and displayed with the good side up. I turned the basket over on the couch; half the space inside was taken up by a false bottom with a hole in it. On closer scrutiny, it looked as if that too had been gnawed out by little teeth. I pulled the cardboard out and—"Holy God!"

There, leering at me, sat a small rat.

The door opened, the bosun came in. "Ome! What the hell—"

"Look!"

We both stared at the rat incredulously. It was sitting among the chewed-up remains of the fruit basket, as cool as Slobkous. It yawned, scratched itself, stretched, totally unfazed by our proximity. Rabies! That's how wild rodents behaved when they had rabies!

"Hold it!" The bosun ran into my bedroom, came back with a boot and raised it to clobber the beast. The rat looked up at him, unimpressed, then it looked at me, yawned and hopped onto the back of the couch.

"You filthy—"

"No! Don't!"

I stopped the bosun, not out of tender feelings but because of the mess it would make. The rat strolled along the back of the couch, laying a row of little mines.

A voice said behind me, "Him house rat." It was the Chinese steward.

The bosun advanced on the rat and reached out to grab it, but recoiled.

"Stroke him," the steward said to me. "Him know people."

When I hesitated, he fetched one of my pencils from the desk and scratched the rat's back with the eraser. The rat seemed to like that; it rolled onto its back.

"I'll get a bucket," the bosun said. "Then I'll whack it one and toss it over the edge." He made for the door.

"No, Bosun! It's obviously tame. It must have belonged to the fruit merchant's little girls."

The creature jumped onto the bookshelf and perched on top of Bowditch's *American Practical Navigator.*

"Well?" the bosun asked. "What do you want me to do with the filthy varmint?"

I looked at the rat on the Bowditch. It looked back at me. "Let's leave it there, for the time being."

He snorted. "Well, you're the skipper. And now go to bed, man! Here, Rin-tin-tin, take that to the galley." He handed the tray with the empty mug to the Chinese, who made off with it.

I said, "The man's name is Hopla."

"It isn't," the bosun retorted defiantly.

"It is now. So knock it off; you have to live together as far as Rio."

"You're telling me," the bosun said gloomily. We were both trying to behave as if we were unaware of the rat watching our every move from its perch on the Bowditch.

After he had left, I lay down to sleep. The rat observed me like a sphinx, with what looked like contentment. The canary squealed in its cage and rattled its beak along the bars in what seemed to be a frenzy of jealousy. I heaved myself back to my feet, went to fetch a towel from the bathroom and covered the cage with it.

To help me fall asleep, I took a book from the shelf at random. It turned out to be *Human Personality and Its Survival of Bodily Death.*

I did not even open it; sleep came at once and totally, the moment I lay down, as if someone had covered my cage with a towel.

[138]

6

The telephone rang; it took a few moments of orientation before I answered it. "Harinxma."

"Skipper, sorry to wake you." It was Slobkous. "We're entering the Channel and there's a lot of traffic. I thought you might like to be around. I'm turning in."

"I'll be right up." I looked at the clock; I had slept three hours. The rat was asleep on the Bowditch.

In the wheelhouse Mate Number One welcomed me, smiling and bowing. "Good morning, Commodore." No sign of Captain Cho.

"Good morning. What's the course?"

"Two sixty," the bosun at the wheel said, claiming the privilege.

"Let's have a look at the scene, Number One."

It was cold on the outer bridge, a chilly day. Massive cumuli, pregnant with rain, came sailing across the slate-colored sea from the cliffs of North Foreland on the horizon. It was the edge of a cold front; before long we would have a bit of wind. I looked at the dry dock. We were still on the short hawser; the citadel, tigered with rust, loomed right behind us, with inside its ramparts the ancient yacht. In the dark I had not realized quite how ancient: two tall masts, a thin ocher stack crowned with a doily of frilly ironwork. She looked like a dragonfly caught in a web, with all those struts and stanchions welded onto her from the walls of the dock and, higher up, the trelliswork of the dock gates. Through the binoculars I saw runners at work on the starboard wall, at the foot of a flagpole with three black balls, the international sign for a tow. Their trousers billowed in the wind; Harakiri, in jeans and duffel coat, was directing them with gestures. They must be belaying an additional bridle on the bollards on top of the dock. It seemed excessive, but gave me the reassurance that my runner captain was a stickler for security.

Suddenly it got home to me that we were at sea. "Well, gentlemen," I said, "Godspeed and happy sailing."

"Godspeed, Ome," the bosun replied, heartfelt.

Number One seemed puzzled for a moment, then he said, "God's speed, Commodore."

I looked at the dry dock through the binoculars and saw that Harakiri and his crew had left the starboard wall. They must be back on board the yacht by now; I decided to try to raise him and switched on the walkie-talkie.

"Dry dock, this is *Isabel*. Do you read?"

I had to try three times before his voice replied, "*Isabel*, this is *Agnes*. I read you loud and clear, over."

"Who is *Agnes*?"

"This box I'm on, Harinxma. That's what it says on her flank, doesn't it?"

I remembered the odd letters on its flank, partially obliterated by rust: A.G. . . . NES. So the ritual process was taking place: the inanimate object had received a name. "Righto, *Agnes*. All well on board?"

"Affirmative, *Isabel*. As you may have seen, I put a backstop on the bridle, over."

"Affirmative, *Agnes*. Make sure you give it plenty of play, though, before we start paying out the full hawser, for that will increase its dip, over."

"*Isabel*, when will that be?"

"Off Gris-Nez. I'm expecting a bit of wind and plan to keep you on a short leash in these confined waters. We don't want to end up athwart the shipping lane, over."

"As far as I'm concerned, we're all set. Let it blow. Godspeed and happy sailing, *Isabel*, over."

"Godspeed and happy sailing, *Agnes*. Over and out." I turned to Number One. "From now on, write '*Agnes*' in the ship's log when referring to the dock. Tell the next watch."

He looked nonplussed; then he said, "Very well, Commodore."

To him, it must all be part of the Mysterious West.

[*Chapter Five*]

1

During the days that followed, I discovered that to sail with a Chinese crew was a novel experience indeed.

They filled the corridors with the smells of their cooking and played on the intercom, interminably, Bron's tape of *Bawdy Ballads for Lusty Lovers*, which I had given them, at three times the normal speed. Meanwhile they led a separate existence from which foreigners were excluded. They were polite and smiled a lot, but it was as if all companionways down to their deck had a NO TRESPASSING sign on them.

The Chinese officers were courteous and correct, but declined to take part in Happy Hour and announced, the second day out, that they preferred to take their meals with the crew in the messroom. We got the impression that we were not welcome there; the tables were already overcrowded anyhow, so we decided to have our meals, cooked by the bosun, in the officers' lounge.

Captain Cho regained self-confidence to the point where he took a regular watch in rotation with his two mates, but each time he turned up on the bridge there was a notable change in the atmosphere. From the moment he appeared, he strutted and snarled and made what were obviously snide remarks to crew members, who reacted with good-natured bewilderment and proceeded to ignore him. He did not seem to notice; he continued to swagger and posture with set jaw, his hands clasped behind his back, admiral on the bridge of a pocket battleship. Now and then an unfamiliar development would stop him in his tracks; on those occasions he did not hesitate to call me, regardless of the hour, and demand rather imperiously that I enlighten him. I did so without comment; it served to restore sanity to our relationship, for, after all, he was the master. But we stood different watches, and for the rest of the time I forgot about him.

I shared my watch with Number One, the keen young Chinese first mate. He never lost sight of me, followed me wherever I went, but we rarely exchanged more than a casual word. The only Chinese member of the crew with whom I had any personal contact was Hopla, the steward. He was much in evidence, eager to serve sandwiches, polish shoes, press clothes and gossip. What little I knew of the private lives of my Chinese staff I picked up from him. Chief Liu had seventeen children; Captain Cho was Mr. Chung's very, *very* good friend; Mate Number One's father had a farm with a thousand hens that laid multicolored eggs; the second radio officer had had an operation that had left him safe with other men's wives. All this, I discovered, had to be edited: Chief Liu had seven children, Captain Cho got on well with Mr. Chung and Mate Number One's father, who was retired, had a few chickens that laid eggs which he colored after they were laid. As to the second radio officer's operation, Harlingen spent some time trying to persuade the young man to teach him the Taiwanese national anthem in order to find out if he was a soprano, but without success.

Inevitably, the Dutch staff closed ranks and became a tightly knit group more quickly than would normally have been the case. All crews new to a ship develop a private language; in our case, 'pencil' soon became 'rat-scratcher' and the dayroom—where the rat, now called 'Louis,' ruled the roost—became 'Louisville.' Louis turned out to be an amazing creature, as bright as a well-trained dog and as friendly. He was well-mannered; when drinks were served, he would hop onto the coffee table and eye the snacks but always wait to be offered one. He and I became friends, probably because we shared my quarters. His daytime roost was on top of the Bowditch, where he lay in wait for me from the moment I left. On my return he would make a flying leap and land on my shoulder—a startling experience the first few times, but I soon got used to it. Thenceforth, while in my quarters I walked around with a rat on my shoulder. During the night he had a tendency to turn up unnoticed, sneak onto the pillow and start to sniff my scalp. I locked him out, but had to make damn sure he was not inside when I went to bed or his inquisitive wet snoot would start probing my ear, which resulted in the high C Harlingen had tried in vain to get out of the second radio officer.

Considering the time of year, we were lucky with the weather; after Gris-Nez the convoy proceeded slowly southward through lovely frosty days of silver light and sky-blue sea. The dry dock was far behind us now on the long hawser; the sun's reflection colored its rusty flanks with changing stripes of light and shadow, shifting from orange at sunrise to gray during the day, red at sunset and deep blue at dusk, gradually fading into black, festooned with red, green and white lights flashing in the night. I didn't see much of Harakiri and his crew through my binoculars, only an occasional scurrying of tiny figures on one of the dock walls, but Harakiri himself was much in evidence in our private world. Every day during Happy Hour I would make contact with him via the walkie-talkie, and the crackly voice from the instrument on the coffee table became a regular feature of our gatherings. He would want to know what the news was on board the tug and in the outside world, as he had no contact with shore stations. We told him every detail, such as the rat now accompanying me to the bridge, which drove Pete the canary berserk with jealousy and set him shrieking like a drill until I put a drop of Kirschwasser in his drinking water, which made him sound like a nightingale. In return, Harakiri gave us a daily report on the archeological discoveries he was making as he slowly dug his way through the innards of the old yacht, which, he had discovered, once belonged to some Eastern potentate. He found secret compartments behind walls, little trapdoors in ceilings; one day he reported the discovery of someone's private diary under the floor of his wardrobe. His quotes from the diary sounded like stories from the *Arabian Nights:* exotic adventures in outlandish places like Zanzi in Japan, Olifantspoot in South Africa, Oola-Poola in the Gilbert Islands, all interspersed with descriptions of perverted activities in the oval bed. Harlingen looked up the place names in the Pilot, but drew a blank; when challenged, the crackly voice answered, "Oh, those names were changed after the war, of course. You know how it was: the natives took over and renamed everything. But let me tell you the latest . . ." It was his way of coping with what must have been an exceedingly tedious existence.

Meanwhile, during the peaceable days and nights between the English Channel and the Cape Verdes, I made the bridal suite my home and came upon some archeological discoveries myself. In one of the drawers underneath my bunk I found, folded down, Spooks Haversma's Ouija board, with planchette. In the desk I made a more welcome find: a whole bunch of classical tapes, which must have belonged to Haversma too, which gave considerable class to my dayroom, compared to 'Bouncing Balls.' I also discovered, after being initiated by Slobkous into her electronic innovations, that the *Isabel* was indeed a lazy captain's dream. Satellites took care of all navigational calculations. The automatic pilot steered the ship. On the desk in the dayroom was a computer which, after a few simple manipulations, produced in a flash the day, date, hour, position, barometer reading, temperature, sea, wind, speed, course, miles made and miles remaining. There was a subsidiary little screen over my bunk; no need for the master to even leave his bed.

I also telephoned Sylvia every few days merely by calling the radio room and saying, "France, please." In minutes I had her on the line, thanks to the wizardry of the Paradise tree. She and I spent more time chatting, during that first week, than if I had been home. The rest of my free time I spent watching TV from the comfort of the couch: *Dallas, Wheels, Shape Up with Shana,* picked off some satellite by the inventive Harlingen with the ship's dish antennas. While we were off Portugal, I, or rather Louis, became hooked on a serial called *Peeling en Paradiso,* a nature documentary on the Amazon in which a bespectacled Dr. Peeling lectured among the lianas on insects and furry creatures. It was full of squeaks, squawks and crunching noises as the furry creatures consumed the insects or each other. Every afternoon between three and four we sat watching it, eating peanuts, Louis perched on my shoulder, until the ship moved out of range of the station.

Throughout those dreamy days and star-haunted nights the *Isabel Kwel* behaved impeccably. Not a roll, not a quirk, nothing but *Meeresstille und glückliche Fahrt.* But I was too old to be seduced by the voice from the Paradise tree. Maybe Adam had thought he could have his apple and eat it; I knew that the day of reckoning must come sooner or later. My self-imposed reason for being on board this ship was to prepare the Chinese captain for that eventuality, but the chance did not present itself. The weather was beautiful, the sea like a millpond; who said that the *Isabel Kwel,* biggest and most sophisticated tugboat in the world, was a killer? I had difficulty believing it myself, let alone the cocky young man strutting on her bridge.

I remembered a similar light-hearted, careless atmosphere on board the old *Isabel,* forty-three years ago, on her way to Langanes. Two months later she was dead.

2

Three days before the Cape Verdes, when I arrived on the bridge for the afternoon watch, Slobkous said, "I've some interesting news for you, Skipper."

"Oh?"

"Our little friend the captain. Seems he flunked his driving test."

I glanced at Number Two, who was writing in the ship's log at the chart desk.

"Don't worry about him, he doesn't understand Dutch. Even if he did, he's the one who told me. Seems the bungler lost a tow a year ago, a destroyer from Japan. He was caught in one of those blows you get in the Sea of Japan that come out of nowhere, just as he was rounding the Nanatsu Islands. It caught him with his pants down; he wanted to head into the wind, didn't give the tow enough time to swing, bust his stoppers and nearly tripped the ship. He was towing from a hook with an explosive device, so he pulled the trigger and detonated the charge. He lost his hawser. And the destroyer."

"How did he get away with it? Anywhere else he would have lost his license!"

"Apparently the whole thing was swept under the mat."

This was bad news. To end up with your hawser at right angles is a classic disaster situation while towing; if the hawser isn't released at once, the tow will pull the tugboat over until it capsizes. No tugmaster worth his salt would be caught in such a situation; it was strictly for amateurs or, indeed, bunglers.

But how could such dangerous incompetence have been hushed up? And what in the world could have possessed Mr. Chung to appoint someone with that dismal record as master of the *Isabel Kwel?* Maybe Fransen would know the answer; I would take it up with him in Mindello.

We arrived off St. Vincent Island just before nightfall. As I didn't want to enter the channel between the islands in the dark with the dock, I stood off Antão until daybreak; when we rounded Dos Pássaros early the next morning, the pilot came on board.

Fransen was with him. He brought the mail: three letters from

Sylvia, one from my daughter and a handful of Christmas cards from the grandchildren.

A local tugboat came out of Mindello to stand by *Agnes* after she had been moored to the buoys in the Porto Grande; we went to the fuel dock behind the breakwater for oiling. After we had passed through Customs, Fransen took me to a quaint little restaurant in the quaint little town of Mindello.

After we had ordered drinks, I said, "Well, the Chinese captain is a dud."

He shrugged his shoulders. "So what? It's you who's running the ship, and you're legally covered. What does he do?"

"He stays in his cabin most of the time. When he does take a watch, he carries on like Lord Nelson at Trafalgar. But his actual value as a master is zero, and now it appears he may be dangerous as well."

"How so?"

I told him about the lost destroyer. "Now what?"

"Now nothing, Harinxma. You take the ship to Rio and let the Chinese take it from there."

"But you can't let that bungler sail into the Forties with this ship, this dock!"

"Who can't? It's got nothing to do with us, he's Mr. Chung's baby."

"But, Jesus, Fransen! You represent the owner, you run shore service on the ship! Surely that includes reporting—"

He threw up his hands; the black-mustachioed waiter mistook it for a gesture of impatience with the service and belligerently brought the menu.

Fransen, sidetracked, started to leaf through it and ordered something with tentacles; I settled for a steak and contributed a bottle of local wine.

He said, "You realize it's probably goat steak here?"

"All right, make it an omelet." After the waiter had left for the kichen, I picked up where I had left off. "I insist that you report the captain's incompetence. We all have a serious responsibility here, I particularly."

"Look, it's none of our business. The ship is registered in Taiwan, the crew is Taiwanese, so, legally—"

"If you don't report it, I will."

He sighed. "Harinxma, I hate to be blunt about this. You may have been brought in for this special assignment, but you're still an employee of the company, like everyone else."

"I'm an employee of Mr. Chung."

"Same thing, as far as procedure is concerned. You report to me, I report to KITCO, they report to Chung. *Your* job is to see to it that ship and tow get to Rio. Is the man stopping you from doing that?"

"No, but—"

"Are the other deck officers okay?"

"Yes, but, like the crew—"

"Then you've nothing to worry about, and neither have I."

"But these Chinese are totally inexperienced!" I cried. "Think of what they could do with the dock!"

"What? Hit something? Everybody spotting that tow on his radar is going to give it a berth of miles. Tows are protected by the laws of the sea."

"Don't joke about it! What about the ship's flaw? He'll never make it through the Forties!"

He sighed and threw up his hands again. This time the waiter came spoiling for a fight. "Senhor! We try to please, but good cooking takes *time!* This is not McDonald's!"

Fransen muttered, "Oh, fuck off." Then he asked, "What's his problem?"

"Fransen, I can't leave it at this. If you won't report—"

"Now you listen, old buddy!" Suddenly he was laid back no longer. "Your instructions are to advise the captain. It's nothing to do with you if the man can't take advice, or won't, or is incompetent, or a baboon. You advise, and report to me. You've done that. If Chung wants to know more, he'll ask. Until he asks, you shut up. You're messing in a delicate situation, and I won't let you do it." He raised his glass. "Cheers."

I was getting mad. "You ought to be ashamed of yourself! Delicate situation? It's like sending a carful of kids out into a rainstorm with a drunken driver. Tell the man-traders to go to hell!"

"Thanks. And then what?"

"Then you retire, as you've told me you want to."

He looked at me with compassion fatigue and took a swig from his drink. "How's Slobkous shaping up, by the way?"

"Okay. Good mate. But—"

"Let me tell you something about him that maybe you should know. He could have had a ship of his own years ago, he had one offered to him on several occasions. But he won't accept. Do you know why? During the war—this he told me confidentially over a drink—"

"I thought he didn't drink."

"During the war he was as keen as butter to have his own ship. He and the captain of the tug he was on couldn't stand one another. Then, during an air attack on the convoy, the captain was either hit or blasted overboard, and Slobkous has felt guilty ever since. He blames himself for not fishing the man out in time. I think he did what anyone else would have done, but he doesn't think so, and that's what counts. He's always refused to accept a ship of his own. He says he doesn't want the responsibility."

It was nimbly done. He had pulled this trick before, back in Rotterdam, when I had pressed him too hard about the sale of the *Isabel*. He had taken off at a tangent, telling me about the two hulks he had nearly lost while taking them around the Horn. I realized that to press him harder would serve no purpose this time either; I would have to take care of it myself.

The waiter turned up with the food. I was served my omelet; Fransen was left to serve himself, but the slight did not register.

"How's the pig been behaving?" he asked, chewing a tentacle.

After three weeks in a lazy captain's dream I no longer looked upon the *Isabel* as a pig. "She's behaved well, but the weather has been good."

"No swell?"

"No swell."

"Well, good. Now let's talk business. You're oiling right now. That should be through by around midnight. I've arranged for the caterers to deliver tomorrow at six hundred hours; by then you should be back with the dock and ready to sail . . ."

We talked shop during the rest of the meal; Captain Cho was not mentioned again. After dinner Fransen walked me back to the ship. The *Isabel*, at the fuel dock, was lit up like a spaceship before take-off. When I arrived on board, first Porks intercepted me and then the bosun, each with a minor problem that could have waited until morning. I entered my dayroom; Louis leaped onto my shoulder from the Bowditch. The canary trilled blue murder; it had to be fed and watered before the towel went on. I plucked Louis off my shoulder, which took some doing as he clung like a burr, put him on the floor and opened my daughter's letter first, while he clambered up my trouser leg and settled on my lap.

Dear Dad!

Well, Christmas is behind us, thank God. We had a jolly time, but, heavens, it was cramped! Mother says you are planning to build an extra room onto the house, which I think is a super idea, and I understand you took on this job to be able to pay for it. I was sorry you weren't here, though. It was like in the past when I was little and we had Christmas with just Mother and your empty chair and your place laid at table, and all of us saying: 'Happy Christmas, Daddy!' raising our glass of Bishop Wine or whatever it was. Jolly, but bleak at the center, if you see what I mean. I really missed you. I miss you, period. Are you all right? Mother worries about your high blood pressure and taking on too much responsibility, but I have never known her not to worry about you. Will you write to me? Just to me, not one of those mass letters for the family which always end up being addressed to the littlest ones? Tell me how you really are, how you feel, what it's like to be back at sea, if you think of us occasionally, if you love me. I love you, Dad. I really do. But you know that. Don't you? So fast, childhood passes. So fast you find yourself suddenly old . . .

It was a moving letter, unlike any she had written me before. On impulse, I sat down at my desk to respond in the same vein, with the same honesty: about my loving every minute of this voyage despite my age, maybe because of it; about old Kwel and his idea of society imposing on us its concept of being old; about my suddenly recognizing that he had been a father figure to me all my adult life; about how happy I was that at last she and I were able to express our affection for each other instead of being self-conscious about it, stuck in our traditional roles of father and daughter.

I stopped halfway, read my letter again and suddenly thought of her trying to read it while the children were quarreling or the telephone rang with the plumber on the line, or just reading it and wondering what had got into me all of a sudden. So I tore it up and started afresh.

I discovered the real reason only after I had done so: a sudden sense of loss, almost of mourning. During all those years of home-comings and leavings I had spent much more time with the two boys, talking about life, listening to their problems and admonishing them to obey their mother while I was gone; meanwhile the little girl must have been waiting for me to give her the same quality of attention, to treat her as an equal, a fellow human being rather than, first, as a sweet, cuddly doll and later as a beautiful young woman. Then she had married and I had given her away in the approved manner, and then there had been children, and then she had divorced the ass and become too busy and too preoccupied for us ever to see each other alone again. How could I possibly make up for the lost opportunities of a lifetime by correspondence? They were the years the locust hath eaten.

So I wrote her a chatty letter which, when all was said and done, consisted of *Dear Helen,* followed by an extract from the ship's log and the weather report, signed *Your ever loving Dad.*

3

After the Cape Verdes we hit the trades. Wind and sea didn't amount to much, as both were moderate; but to do what I had to do, this was the best I could offer between here and Rio de Janeiro.

I began by calling Captain Cho to my dayroom for a preparatory talk. In doing so, I managed to step on his toes again, either by the way I called him in or by what I said, which was to the point, considering he knew nothing about the ship and so far had not betrayed the slightest interest in her. I explained the problem of her suicidal rolling and the thruster operation in detail, with drawings; his attention was almost caught despite himself, but Louis chose that moment for a flying leap onto his shoulder from the Bowditch. That tore it; Captain Cho jumped to his feet with a shriek and shook the rat off as if it had been a boa constrictor. After that my efforts were ineffectual. He sat there scowling, jaws working, eyes smoldering, while I carried on about self-feeding rolling cycles. I had worried about the fine line between calling the *Isabel* a death trap and sounding too casual about her problem; I needn't have worried, subtleties were lost on him. The only hope of getting through to him was by showing him in practice, with his hands on the thruster handles, the kind of mischief the ship could be up to. I invited him to accompany me to the bridge for a demonstration. He did so with ill grace.

An hour earlier I had given Slobkous the order to bring the tow into the wind, a slow, laborious process; when we arrived on the bridge, everything was set. The demonstration went smoothly, but not dramatically enough to bring home to Cho how dangerous the self-feeding cycle of the *Isabel*'s rolling could be under more severe conditions. Had I known those conditions precisely, I might have hit the exact angle of incoming seas or the exact speed and wave train; but whatever I tried, I failed to get her to roll the way she had during the test run off Flushing. All I could do that morning was to make her lurch heavily and to compensate the lurches with the thrusters, the way Bron had done. I had remembered the anguished cries from the galley on that occasion and sent Hopla to tell Ma Chang to secure whatever she had on the range; I had also warned Porks in advance. As a consequence, there were no sounds of protest from either the galley or the engine room. Maybe it was this lack of drama which made the whole thing appear rather tame and abstract. I let Cho have a turn at manipulating the thrusters; he behaved as if he did so to humor me.

After my portentous preparations the actual exercise took no more than half an hour and was a distinct anticlimax, from which Captain Cho walked away as if he had resisted the overtures of a soothsayer. He really was a pompous little ass; I stared after him with a mixture of anger and incredulity. In my wildest dreams I had not foreseen that I would end up facing the stone wall of an owner who did not want to hear and a captain who would not see. I could understand his being intimidated by the ship; what I had a problem with was his sneering disdain for her without even trying to take her in hand himself. Obviously, nothing short of her going to the point of capsizing would convince him that she was a potential death trap. The likelihood of that happening before Rio de Janeiro was minimal.

In contrast, Number One, bright, ambitious little chap that he was, took it all in, beady-eyed. But although he had the makings of a good master, he was far too inexperienced to take *Agnes* through the Forties, let alone with this ship. I decided to stop pussy-footing around and simply write Mr. Chung a sober but blunt letter telling him, as diplomatically as that allowed, why his pet captain was a public danger. The decision gave me a measure

[151]

of inner peace, and I set about writing it. But I had barely started when, nine days out of St. Vincent, something happened that blew me right out of the water.

Breakfast in bed had been served as usual by the bosun. Louis was ogling the tray, ready to jump onto it for his treat of Looney Loops as soon as the coast was clear. The bosun had gone to get my pills from the wardrobe. I was holding Louis back, whispering, "Not yet!" when the bosun came back and said, "Sorry, Ome. No more pills in that box, only empty envelopes."

"Okay, get the next one from the icebox."

I went on eating while he went to the dayroom and came back with another box, which he held out to me.

"Look at this," he said.

"What?"

"Nothing but empties in this one either."

"That can't be! I packed two, we finished one! It must be full!"

"It is, but all these envelopes are empty."

My heart skipped a beat.

"What are you taking them for, Ome?"

"High blood pressure."

"What happens when you don't take them?"

"Jesus! I don't know . . ." Then I realized I should make light of this or it would spread through the ship like wildfire: 'The old man may have a stroke any moment!' "Oh, it's nothing, really. The pills are a backstop, a safeguard. I don't really need them at sea, while I'm on a regular schedule. I just have to make sure I take a nap every day . . ."

I saw he didn't believe me.

"I'm going to be okay, Bosun, on condition you don't start any rumors. Don't tell anyone, it'll only upset them and create a stress I can do without right now. Promise it will remain between the two of us."

"Sure." He gave me a worried look. "Are you okay now? Can I give you a hand to get to the bridge?"

"For God's sake, man, I'm not an invalid! Remind me to take my nap every afternoon, that's all! Now let me have my breakfast in peace."

He left, reluctantly. I heard him open the door to the corridor and say, "You better stay out this morning, Rin-tin-tin. He isn't feeling too good." So he was off and running with his message of doom, promise or no promise.

I stared at the two boxes of empty envelopes. There had been a four-week supply in each. Like every elderly man who has to take two lots of pills each day, I had worked out a system; but an excess of zeal for economy had made me put the envelopes back into the box after swallowing their contents so I could use them over and over again until they were worn out, instead of throwing them away and getting a new lot each time. I had met my doom by saving the expense of a box of coin envelopes. In the hurry of my packing, either Sylvia or I must have picked up a box of empties, thinking it was full.

What now? I remembered the young doctor with the suntan in the water bailiff's office: 'Keep up these pills or you'll be in serious trouble.' What kind of trouble? I had never gone without pills since a specialist had diagnosed mild hypertension fifteen years ago. It had not remained mild; new pills had been added and their dosage gradually increased over the years until I arrived at my present hefty load, which must be enough to poison a healthy person. What would abruptly cutting them out do to me? All I could do was wait and see; in the meantime I had better work out the fastest way of getting a new supply.

First, I thought of turning the tow around, heading back to St. Vincent and asking Sylvia via satellite to send me a full box by express airmail. But I discarded the idea; we were just about halfway to Rio, I might as well have her send it there. Our ETA was ten days from now; by then whatever I had coming in the way of dramatic developments would be over and done with. Maybe I had been right when I said to the bosun off the top of my head that I didn't really need pills at sea, certainly not on this luxury cruise. I would soon know. How about my transferring to an oncoming ship, one that would take me back to St. Vincent in a matter of days? Or to an overtaker that would take me to Rio? Harlingen could broadcast an emergency call, surely someone near would respond, and most ships made at least fifteen knots as opposed to our speed of five. But there was little traffic on this course; few freighters or tankers made South America via the Cape Verdes. Otherwise—what? Have the parcel dropped from an airplane? Who would pay the fortune that would cost?

The whole thing was getting hysterical. 'Wait and see,' I told myself. 'Maybe nothing will happen. Maybe you can do without pills.' It was not true; the young doctor had warned me. Well, I had no choice but to behave as if nothing were the matter. And just to put my mind at ease, why not take my blood pressure now? It was sure to be normal; all that had happened so far was that I was ten minutes late with my breakfast pills. So I took it, as a base line to measure from in case it went up.

To my surprise, my blood pressure was high. Why should it be? I had done nothing, just lazed around; last time I took it, a day or so ago, it had been low, for me. Nerves, obviously. I should take my mind off it, go to the bridge and do some gawking and strolling, as I would normally do at this time.

I did, but going to the bridge didn't take my mind off it. I busied myself with the chart, checked the compass, asked Number One what kind of training he had had. I realized from the way he looked at me that he had told me this before, but he politely reeled off his *curriculum vitae* again.

I was only half-listening. I must have been wrong. It had to be a mistake. I should go and take it again. But I couldn't walk out on Number One before he had finished his life's story. He took his time; finally I saw my chance and said, "Very interesting. Well—I think I'd better go down now and finish that—er—report." I hurried back to my dayroom and took my blood pressure again.

It had not been a mistake. It was higher than it had been half an hour earlier. I should lie down, put my feet up, read a book. I took one at random from Haversma's collection; when I lay down on the couch with my feet up, I saw it was *Experiences of Death* by Dr. Sabom. Interesting book, full of case histories of people who had clinically died of heart attacks and floated above their bodies while being carted off to the emergency room. They looked down from the ceiling on doctors trying electric shocks, opening their chests to massage their hearts. *The Occult* sounded better; but when I opened it, the folded paper dropped onto my chest: *Death is like the leaving of a ship. She unfurls her sails in the red of the sunset . . .*

I took my blood pressure again; both systolic and diastolic were higher than the last time. It was little more than an hour since I had discovered I had run out of pills, and already my blood pressure was soaring. In the few minutes I had been lying here it had risen two points. A Valium was the answer: take a Valium— this must be psychological, it couldn't be anything else. I couldn't have elevated blood pressure within an hour because of lack of medication.

I took two Valiums and lay down on the couch again. It was uncomfortable, so I went to lie on my bunk. That was uncomfortable too with my clothes on, so I undressed, put on my pajamas and went to bed, taking the blood-pressure gauge with me. As I lay there, gazing at the ceiling, clutching the gauge, I calmed down. The Valiums were taking effect; I was beginning to feel drowsy. Just before I slid into sleep, Louis stuck his wet nose into my ear, so that took care of that. I tossed him out, locked the bedroom door, took my blood pressure again and sat bolt upright: it was even higher! This time it really must be a mistake. I took it again. And again. The reading remained the same. Whatever I did—rest, read a book, take Valium—the pressure was creeping up. I had the proof right in my hand. I had been depressing my blood pressure artificially for fifteen years; now my basic pressure had manifested itself, and it was life-threatening. My God! What could I do? Nothing. Lie down. Go to sleep. Sleep. Sleep . . .

I awoke feeling I had slept for hours, looked at my alarm clock and saw it had been seven minutes. I took my blood pressure again. It had risen another point. My God! Where would it stop? I tried to remember cases of people with catastrophically high blood pressure. I remembered they had headaches, giddiness, were invalids who had to stay in bed. I was getting into a panic. I was ready to hurl the damn blood-pressure machine against the wall. This had to stop! I must *do* something, get a hold on myself.

I got up, put the blood-pressure machine in the desk drawer, slammed it shut, dressed and went back to the bridge. Nothing had changed, only the sun had risen a little higher above the horizon. In its low light *Agnes* threw a long shadow on the glassy sea. We had passed through the trades; there was not a ruffle, no flying fish, in waves this low they could not take off. Porks appeared on the boat deck below in his shorts, taking a breather before the change of watch. He spotted me and waved; I waved back, hoping it wouldn't be interpreted as a need for sea-babble. But he was late as it was; little Whittier left the wheel to trip to the pinger and strike four twins. Porks had better hurry, but he probably wanted the Chinese engineer to go through the shuffle of the changing of the watch before he came sweeping in. They were all prima donnas at that age. I had been one myself.

Before I knew it, I was steeped in memories of youth, the melancholy of farewell. Suppose I died at sea? No corpse in the freezer; Slobkous would bury me. *'Inasmuch as we are gathered together to say farewell to our beloved brother Martinus Harinxma . . .'*

"Another nice day."

It was Slobkous; I hadn't noticed his arrival. "Yes. Yes, marvelous day. Splendid."

He gave me an odd look. "You feeling all right?"

"Of course. Why shouldn't I? I'm feeling fine."

"Okay. I'd like a word with you about the Chinese ABs. Something is going on. I don't know if they're buggering one another in those double bunks or what—"

"Look, Slobkous, let's talk about that some other time. Unless it's urgent. Is it?"

"No."

"In that case, I think I'll go below."

He gave me that look again. "Are you sure you're feeling—"

"Dammit, Slobkous, I feel fine! There's nothing the matter with me! I'm—I'm in the middle of a long, complicated letter, rather tricky. Sorry I snapped, I was preoccupied. See you at Happy Hour."

This was ridiculous; first I exacted the promise from the bosun that he would keep it to himself, now I went hamming it up in front of Slobkous, of all people.

Back in my dayroom, I took my blood pressure again. Higher still! Jesus Christ, how high could it go without popping a vein in my brain? I had no idea. It might go on rising until the top of my skull came off. Worrying and taking my blood pressure every few minutes sure as hell wouldn't help. I should forget about it, for God's sake. Or call Sylvia, ask her what the hell I could do. No, not that under any circumstances. Nothing she could say or do would make any difference; I would just start to worry about her worrying. She didn't expect my next telephone call until day after tomorrow. Forgetting about it was indeed the only answer.

I discovered it was as easy to forget as walking naked in a crowd. I could think of nothing else. It was an addiction: every ten minutes or so I took my blood pressure. And it got worse. How I lived through Happy Hour I had no idea; I brought it off somehow. The moment they were gone, I took it again.

I kept taking it all day, all evening. After supper, when my watch came up, I had a headache. I didn't feel like going to the bridge to walk around and lean on the rail and gaze at *Agnes* and the starry sky; I went to my dayroom instead.

The bosun was there, observing me unobtrusively. He was like an elephant trying to hide behind a palm tree. I said, "For God's sake, Bosun, what *do* you want?"

[156]

He looked hurt. "Nothing, Ome. You don't look well to me, that's all. I just want to help."

"All right, get Mate Slobkous. And Mate Number One. Tell them to come and see me."

He left. I was standing in my bedroom in my robe and pajamas, holding on to my bunk, when Slobkous and Number One came in. I told them I wasn't feeling well. That I wouldn't be coming to the bridge for a while. I was going to bed. I asked Number One if he could handle things; the Chinese took it in his stride, but Slobkous looked worried. There wasn't much else he could do.

I climbed into bed, lay staring at the ceiling for a while, then took my blood pressure again and looked at the little dial in disbelief. I had never registered a pressure like this before, ever. It wasn't just high, it was astronomical.

What in the name of God could I do? So far I had been alarmed, but hadn't quite believed it; I had felt I was getting carried away. Suddenly I was brought up short: it hadn't been just a bit of drama when I had thought of Slobkous burying me at sea; he was going to. My God: Sylvia! She had warned me that I was taking my life in my hands, that an old man with hypertension had no business venturing out of his own environment. Or had she? I couldn't remember. Anyhow, I *had* taken my life in my hands, and now, suddenly, incredibly, it was drawing to a close.

"Co'dore?"

I didn't want to see him. I didn't respond, but lay there, eyes closed.

"Co'dore, sir . . . ?"

I opened my eyes. Hopla was standing beside my bunk, a small, wizened man of an alien race.

"Co'dore sick?"

"Not sick," I said. "I'm going to sleep. Good night." I turned my back on him and lay there with my eyes open, staring at the wall. I was going to die. No man could have blood pressure that high and live. I would never make Rio. I would be buried at sea by Slobkous. He would be spooked by the responsibility of having to take over the tow, he knew how dangerous the ship was when she started her cycle. I felt tears welling up, a flood of tears over everything: Sylvia, my beloved daughter, the grandchildren I would never see again, this poor ship. I put my hand on the wainscoting and felt the throb of her engines like a heartbeat, as I

[157]

had on board the old *Isabel* in the summer of 1942, at the beginning of my life as a captain. Now, here was the end. It seemed pointless, mindless. And yet, why not? Statistically, I should have died with the others who had perished in the wastes of the Arctic Ocean. What had I done with my forty-odd years of borrowed time? Sailed a few ships, towed a few objects across the ocean. The one time in my life when I had had a sense of meaning was when I shielded that young German boy we had fished out of the oil slick of a sunken U-boat, when he screamed in terror at the sight of the Stuka diving out of the sun to strafe us with machine-gun fire. When I had pressed his face into my shoulder to protect him from the sight of death, I had briefly touched upon the meaning of it all, the essence of my existence. But the plane had passed overhead, death had drawn away, and both Heini Rabenschnabel and I had gone on living.

That should have been the moment for me to go; I would have died with a feeling of acceptance. Now, shivering with terror, I was dying like an old dog in a corner. I felt a terrible sense of sorrow, of waste. I had wasted the forty years that had been granted me.

Abruptly, I sat up. I would not just lie there and stare death in the face like a paralyzed rabbit. I had to do something, get up, go out, die in the open.

But I couldn't face the starry sky, the phosphorescent sea. I took three sleeping pills, gulped them down and zonked out, falling like a stone into oblivion.

4

In the middle of the night, groggy with pills, I had a vision. A horrible old crone with a toothless grin was bending over me, touching me. I cried out and tried to struggle free of the hallucination, but it persisted. Then I heard a voice. "Co'dore! Let her look at you! She doctor! She help you!"

I stared at the vision in disbelief. It was the old Chinese cook with the gap in her teeth, saying, "Wang kwai. Wang kwai." Beside her stood Hopla. There was no sign of the bosun.

"What—what does she want?"

"She doctor. You tell her where pain is."

The old woman held up a small white carving of a male figure and pointed at its stomach. "Kwai?"

I couldn't believe this. It seemed a final, cruel irony. I wanted to get rid of her and was about to do so, but part of me, a mindless, primitive part, reached out to her as a ray of hope.

"She want to know: pain there?"

I found myself shaking my head. "Hypertension," I said. "High blood pressure."

They frowned in puzzlement.

Wearily, I pointed at my heart, made a gesture of squeezing an artery with my fist. "Woosh, woosh!"

Both of them looked baffled.

"My heart pumps—woosh, woosh!—but my arteries—" I pointed at one in my neck—"too tight." I made a small hole with finger and thumb and blew through it. "Woosh! Too tight. So: pressure . . ." I pointed at the ceiling.

They conferred in earnest whispers. Then he said, "We not know, Co'dore. We not understand. Head hurts?"

How could I tell them? I had to tell her something. I pointed at my ears. "My ears whistle because my blood pressure is too high. Tinnitus!" Despite my headache, my terror of death, I suddenly saw myself: a dying old man yelling 'Tinnitus!' at an old Chinese woman with a doll in her hand.

She rose on her toes and blew in my ear. Her breath smelled of alien spices. "Kwai?"

Wearily, I nodded.

She seemed delighted and talked to Hopla, a string of birdlike sounds. Proudly, he translated it for me. "She say: old age. She say: will pass if you live long enough. She wish you long, happy life."

I closed my eyes and said, "Go away."

There was more whispering. She moved toward the foot of my bunk.

"She want to see feet, Co'dore."

"My feet? What the hell does she want to see my feet for?"

She looked at me, the gap between her front teeth bared in a smile. She pointed at my feet.

The door sprang open and there was the bosun, larger than life. "Are they bothering you, Ome? Want me to throw 'em out?"

"No, Bosun, it's all right."

"Can't you see the commodore is sick?" the bosun shouted. "What are you two doing in here? Fuck off, Rin-tin-tin! You too, old bag-lady!"

"Bosun," I said, "please! She's a doctor."

"A doctor?"

Hopla lifted the bedcover and bared my feet.

"Please, Co'dore. She read feet to find why you ill."

"Just give the word, Ome," the bosun said.

"It's all right, Bosun."

The old woman took hold of my left foot and started to press the sole. "Kwai?" She pressed another spot. "Kwai?"

"What's the matter with your feet, Ome?"

"Bosun! Let her—ouch!" A fierce pain shot up my leg.

"Kwash, kwash!" she said, and pressed the sole of my foot again. I howled with pain. The bosun loomed behind her, ape hands at the ready; but she grinned and babbled Chinese.

"What does she say now?" I asked Hopla.

"She say she find trouble. Now ask permission to do one more thing."

"Ome, don't fall for their hocus-pocus! I've been sailing with slit-eyes—"

"Bosun, do me a favor: go away. Just go and wait outside. I can't cope with the three of you at the same time. Wait outside."

He turned away and strode out, offended. I gazed at the gap-toothed old woman. She seemed to go into a sort of trance; then she produced a wooden bead dangling from a string, put her left hand on my abdomen and, eyes closed, let the bead swing back and forth. She slowly moved her hand up my abdomen; suddenly the bead swung clockwise. She opened her eyes, then moved her hand higher up my body, the bead swinging. Her eyes had a faraway expression. When her hand was over my heart, she closed her eyes once more.

She stood like that for a while, eyes closed, bead swinging, then she opened her eyes, gave me a toothless smile and babbled something.

"She say: she know trouble now. She say: can cure."

Babble-babble.

"Food. Special food she will cook for you."

More babble.

"You not eat, not drink anything else. She cook small meals."

She held up six fingers.

"Six times a day."

She went on babbling in short bursts, and he translated. "She say: you cured in two moons . . . She say: you better tomorrow or next day . . . She say: you healthy, strong man . . . She say: you wrong food, many years. Wrong drink . . . Smoke too, very bad . . . She say: bad food, bad drink, bad smoke insult spirit of heart . . . She say: spirit of heart ready to say bye-bye . . . She say: like woman, heart need attention, compliments, praise . . . She say: if you insult spirit of heart more times with bad food, bad drink, spirit will be angry and say poof! Then you dead."

"But tell her I *am* dying! It's incurable! It can only be controlled by pills, and I'm out of them! I'm *dying!*" I cried it in anguish.

She looked at me with kindness while he tried to translate my cry of despair. He obviously did not know the words and ended up trying to express what I had said by turning up his eyes and letting his head drop in a gross pantomime of death.

She nodded and smiled at me. Hopla said, "She say: no, Co'dore no die. No, no."

"But she nodded!"

"She nod: no."

"What?"

"She nod: mean no. Co'dore no die. No. No." He nodded vigorously, then shook his head. "This mean: yes."

Suddenly the whole thing had turned into a farce. What could an ignorant old woman from a remote Chinese island who nodded 'yes' for 'no' possibly know about modern medicine, about hypertension?

"She say: you must make peace with spirit of heart . . . She say: think of it as healthy, young, strong, beautiful . . . She say: you must tell heart, 'Sorry I offended you, heart. Forgive me, heart. Heart, beautiful, healthy, young heart, return me to health, youth.' "

"Ha! Ho!" she cried, pointing at her biceps.

"You say: 'Ha! Ho! Heart, you strong!' You must flatter spirit, make heart forgive."

[161]

"Thank you," I said to her, feeling sick. "You're very kind."

She gave me her toothless smile, packed up her paraphernalia and turned to leave. Hopla respectfully opened the door for her, bowing; she did not respond. He followed her out, closing the door behind him.

I gazed at the ceiling. My head throbbed. My ears whistled. I could feel my faltering heart labor in my chest. I grabbed my blood-pressure gauge and put on the cuff. Higher still! It was as if death was standing in the doorway, like a man.

Before I knew what I was doing, I found myself on my knees beside my bunk, praying, "Heart, old heart, please forgive me! Please be young, please be strong, stay with me, stay alive . . ."

When it penetrated to me what I was doing, I wearily climbed back into my bunk and lay with my face in the pillow.

I had lain like that for a while when I heard a voice: "Ome? Want your cocoa?"

The bosun was standing by my bedside, looking down at me with worried eyes.

"No, thank you," I whispered. "Later . . ."

"She's a witch, Ome. You shouldn't let her. She'll put the evil eye on you."

"She'll cook me a special diet."

"You're going to eat her stuff?" he asked, aghast. "The junk they eat? It's hocus-pocus, Ome! You can't do that! It'll make you sick!"

"Bosun, I'm sick already. Now let me get some sleep. Thank you."

"Ome," he said, "you're a stubborn old man." I heard him open the door. Then he said, "Now, don't you go and kick the bucket on us. This ship would be a real mess without you."

"I won't. Good night."

I dozed off; suddenly I realized Slobkous was standing beside my bed, looking at me, aghast.

"How are you feeling, Skipper?"

"I'll be all right."

"Of course," he said, but I saw he had a realistic notion of my condition. "Anything I can do for you?"

"No, thank you. I'm being looked after."

"Take it easy, now."

He disappeared. I drifted off again, not into sleep but into a strange, glasslike peace.

[162]

5

I had no idea what time it was when the first witch's meal was brought in by Hopla: three small bowls, each filled with a different-colored sludge. There was a strong smell of cats. Hopla looked triumphant.

I tasted a spoonful of the concoction; it tasted of nothing, but the smell of cats was overpowering. "Get the salt shaker, Hopla. It's with the glasses, in the dayroom."

"No! Ma Chang say no salt! No sugar! No nothing! Only what she put on tray."

"A dash of salt is not going to make any difference. Get it."

But he stood his ground. "No! If you eat salt, spirit of heart will be offended."

Weakly, I ate it, saltless, in his presence. Each of the three dishes contained a revolting sludge that slithered slimily down my gullet.

When I had finished, he said, "Good. Ma Chang happy. Very good. Back in two hours with next meal. Lie down, Co'dore." He left with the empty bowls; the cabin stank as if a cat had defecated in a corner.

After a while I took my blood pressure. At least it was no higher. Still above the danger point, but the night's rest seemed to have brought the continuous rise of the day before to a halt. A reprieve . . . ?

I lay listening to the soft tinkling of the lamp with the throbbing of the engines, the creaking of the wardrobe as the ship heeled in a slow roll, the footsteps overhead on the bridge. I dozed off.

After a while I woke up and took my blood pressure. It had gone down a little. My God . . . My God!

I ended up on my knees again, touched by an inexpressible grace.

6

I stayed in bed for what seemed like days, nights, eating cat-smelling sludge with a sense of devotion, dozing off at intervals. I wondered why no one came to see me. I would have liked to see Slobkous or the bosun. Someone must be keeping them away.

Someone did come in later. I was half asleep in semi-darkness and couldn't see who it was; the apparition disappeared as silently as it had come. It might have been Number One. There had been no sign of Captain Cho.

I dozed off again and woke with a start as someone touched my hair. It was Louis. He curled up beside my head on the pillow. I fell asleep again.

I woke up at dawn. Next day? Two days? I didn't know. Louis woke too, yawned, stretched, rolled onto his back, lashing his tail, waiting to have his stomach scratched. As I did so, I became conscious of high, piercing squeals in my dayroom accompanied by rattling. Pete the canary had probably not been fed. I swung my legs cautiously out of my bunk and stood up, expecting to keel over. But there was no sense of giddiness. I walked slowly into the dayroom. There was Pete, screeching, hopping around in his cage, throwing out sawdust. As I stood filling his cup, Louis landed on my shoulder, wanting his share of the birdseed. I put a little heap of it on the coffee table. Suddenly I realized it was the morning watch; it should have been myself and Number One. Maybe I should put in an appearance, it would reassure him to see me on my feet again.

On my way back to the bedroom I passed the desk with the computer. I switched it on. The small black screen came to life and rolled out its luminous green lines. I stared at it, transfixed. It couldn't be . . . But there it was: the day, the date, the hour. I had been sick and half unconscious for no more than eight hours.

I wandered back into the dayroom and sat down on the couch to think it through. Could the computer be mistaken? No. *I* must be. But what had happened to me? Had the whole thing been a dream? A hallucination? Ma Chang, the foul sludge, the blood-pressure crisis? No, there were the empty dishes on the coffee table. There was the stench of cats. Then I remembered: the sleeping pills. I had taken two of them. Plus two Valiums. It had not been an illness. It was impossible that within a few hours after taking my last medication I should have had catastrophically high blood pressure. I had got into a blind panic and knocked myself out with two Valiums and then two sleeping pills. No wonder I had lost all sense of time, I was lucky to have woken up at all. I had better get myself to the bridge and see what was going on. Let the staff and the crew see me, which was more important. I dressed, then I was overcome by a strange reluctance. It took me a moment to realize it was shame. I was the commodore, commander of the convoy, and I had panicked like a hysterical hypochondriac, throwing the fear of God into the entire ship. I must go to the bridge, the engine room, the radio room at once to reassure everybody that I was not dead, had not been ill even, just—what?

Drunk. It was not something to be proud of, but something everyone would understand. The skipper had had a couple of glasses too many and needed eight hours to sleep it off. Or had it been twenty? I opened the curtains. Dawn was breaking. Eight hours, thank God.

When I opened the door, I found Hopla squatting in front of it, asleep. He leaped to his feet and asked with remarkable presence of mind, "Co'dore feel good now? Feel good?"

"Where is everybody? I haven't seen anyone for hours!"

He pointed proudly at his chest. "Me! Me say: No! Stop! Otherwise everyone go in: chief, Mr. Mate, Fat Bullock—"

"Fat who?"

"What you call? Bosun. Very angry, want to feed you hot chocolate. What do I do? Say not allowed, Ma Chang feeding him, Co'dore not eating anything else. Fat Bullock look like to bonk me and walk in over my corpse, so I say: you make Co'dore drink that, Co'dore . . ." He gave his alarming demonstration of death again: eyes upturned, mouth slack, head slumped.

I went down the corridor and up the companionway to the bridge. It was a glorious early morning, a young blue dawn with a new moon just above the horizon. The still hidden sun lit up feathery ridges of mackerel cloud, red and gold. It was like returning from a year in a dungeon. As if I hadn't seen the sea for years; it seemed to have acquired a new dimension.

The wheelhouse was still dark. I said, "Good morning, gentlemen."

Two singsong voices replied, "Good morning, Commodore," from the shadows. They were Number One and Number Two, at the chart desk.

"How are we doing?"

The light over the desk was switched on; its greenish glow lit up their faces. A delicate hand pointed at a cross on the pencil line of our course. "Our position ten minutes ago, Commodore. Course two eighteen."

"Good progress since the Cape Verdes, Number One."

"Yes, Commodore."

"Isn't this your watch off, Number Two?"

"Yes, Commodore . . ." He gave me a sliding look, then glanced toward the back of the wheelhouse.

Captain Cho was standing where he always stood when I was on the bridge, in the starboard aft corner by the radar console. The green light thrown up by the screen was faint, yet there was no mistaking the expression on his face. It was a look of triumph and contempt.

"Good morning, Captain," I said.

"You better have look at your Mr. Slobkous."

"Why?"

He didn't reply, just gazed at me with that look of contempt.

"He's in his cabin, Ome," a voice said from the shadows. I hadn't realized the bosun was there.

Something in his voice made me say, "Okay, let's go."

I accompanied him down the companionway, into the corridor to the mate's cabin. When we were out of earshot of the bridge, I asked, "What's going on?"

"He's—he's sick, Ome. He's lying on his bunk, unconscious. When I came in to tell him it was quarter-hour, he wouldn't get up. He couldn't. Well—come and see for yourself. Are you okay?"

"Yes, I'm okay."

It was dark when I opened the door; it took me a moment to adjust my eyes, then I saw Slobkous lying on his back on his unmade bed, one leg dangling over the edge. He indeed looked unconscious. I hurried to his side; his eyes were half open, the whites showing, his face looked flushed. Heart attack? Stroke? The ship heeled slowly; I heard a rolling sound behind me. I looked and saw it was an empty bottle rolling on the deck. The bosun picked it up and handed it to me without a word. *Odschi Dschornia Imported Russian Vodka, 100% proof.*

"And have a look at this," the bosun said. He lifted the dangling leg onto the bed and pulled out a drawer under the bunk. It was stuffed with empty bottles. There was enough there to floor a regiment. He was a drunk after all.

"Those boxes, Ome," the bosun said grimly. "Those boxes of Dutch gin in Rotterdam. I don't know what he told you, but that's what was inside. It wasn't Dutch gin, it was vodka."

He must be an alcoholic of long standing; as the Russians know from generations of experience, vodka is the one booze you can't smell on a drunk's breath.

"Did you know about this, Bosun?"

"Well . . ." He looked unhappy.

"He's a notorious drunk, isn't he? That's why he never made it to captain?"

"Well—I guess so, Ome . . ."

"Why the hell didn't you tell me while there was still time to ditch him? And don't give me any crap now! I want to hear the truth!"

"Well, I—I thought he'd kicked the habit, maybe. I couldn't believe they'd send you on this trip with a drunk. I got worried when I saw those boxes carted on board, that's why I told you. But I didn't know how much to tell you. I didn't know you that well, and it wasn't my place. I waited for Captain Fransen to tell you, but he never came before we sailed. Old Mr. Kwel came instead and *he* sure didn't tell you. Ome, I'm sorry about this, but I think he's out for the duration."

"Well, let's begin by ditching those damn bottles."

"Oh, that's not all of them, Ome. That's just one box."

"Well, go find the other ones!"

"I'll try, but he's smart. All drunks are smart. If he's hidden them, he's done it so no one can find them, not all of them. And if I find one and you face him with it, he'll turn nasty. Frankly, Ome, any way you look at it, after this he'll be no good to you. He'll either be out for the count or a roaring lunatic throwing things at anyone who comes into his cabin."

In the past I could have coped with that, but not now. I was too old, I couldn't be bothered. I had to face it: I would have to sail the ship alone. But why had he resumed drinking so suddenly?

Then I remembered his face as he had stood looking down on me sometime during the night. I remembered his expression of unmitigated horror. I had done it to him, he had thought I was about to die. It was his way of refusing to accept command of the ship.

"All right," I said. "I'll go and see the others."

7

Porks was delighted to see me. The rumor of my imminent demise must have made the rounds of the ship, for he was boyishly exuberant in his relief. I told him about Slobkous; he commiserated, but didn't seem surprised. Harlingen shook me by the hand as if I had been away for weeks when I entered the radio room; he too took the news about Slobkous in his stride; he seemed more interested to know if we were going to have Happy Hour that evening.

The only one really shaken by Slobkous' fall was the bosun. He caught me on my way back to the bridge and said, worried, "Maybe you'd better check on Slobbo again, Ome. I went in there just now and I don't like the look of him."

So I went back to the sad little cabin that smelled of urine and vomit and defeat. He was lying on his stomach now, his face on its side on the pillow, mouth open, snoring. I looked at him for a while, but there was nothing I could do to ease his misery; even if there had been, it was too late, he would probably not surface again before Rio. The only way I could help him was by not reporting this to Fransen; we would have to make a concerted effort to get him sober and spruce him up before we arrived. Until then I would sail the ship alone.

I returned to my dayroom; when I entered, it felt as if I had been away for days. Louis jumped onto my shoulder from the Bowditch; Pete hopped and warbled, ruffled his feathers and dragged his beak across the bars of his cage; when I reached inside, he hopped onto my finger. The feel of his tiny, fragile claws on my skin made me realize for the first time how lonely he had been, how desperately he wanted to be let out of his prison cell, how he yearned to soar and swoop in the boundless space of the rain forest and add his trill and warble to the myriad-voiced cacophony of the jungle. I talked to him, cooed, whistled; unwittingly, I must have hit upon something he recognized. He threw his head back, sounded a tiny discordant trumpet, strutted up and down on my finger, hopped off, fluttered away and came back, to the fascination of Louis perched on my shoulder.

"What do you think, Louis? Shall we let him out?"

He rubbed his head with its firm little ears against my neck.

"Maybe better not."

He nuzzled my earlobe with his small, wet snoot and tickled me with his whiskers.

I wondered what my blood pressure was. I went to fetch the gauge from my bedside table and was about to put the cuff on my arm when the thought struck me, 'What's the use? High or low, I have to see this through. I can't deliver this ship and all who sail on her into the hands of Captain Cho. So, better not to know.'

[168]

I opened the door, went down the corridor, out onto the deck, and with a mixture of recklessness and pathos threw the gauge overboard.

I didn't stay around for the splash.

Chapter Six

1

I hadn't been down to the main deck since Rotterdam. As I made my way down the companionways and the maze of corridors the next morning, I discovered that the *Isabel* had indeed changed into a Chinese ship. Pajamaed sailors squatted on the floor outside their cabins; they grinned and made room to let me through. The place smelled like the old town in Singapore.

The galley had changed beyond recognition. Instead of the kitchen of a modern hotel where order and efficiency reigned, it now was an Oriental mess. Ma Chang stood at the crowded range, her hair tied in a knot, dressed in a shapeless smock and perspiring heavily, which was not surprising as the place was as hot as an engine room in the Red Sea. A dozen pots and pans stood bubbling, clappering and hissing on the stove; on washing lines strung from wall to wall, bundles of dried herbs were swinging with the swell. On the table where the bosun had poured coffee, there now were Chinese bowls with chopsticks, a basket of what looked like severed ears, a teapot and a vase of flowers. On one of the shelves I spotted, among the white ship's mugs, a statuette with a smoking stick of incense in front of it.

The moment she saw me, she stopped stirring, bared the gap in her teeth and dried her hands on her smock. I was struck by how tiny she was. I took off my cap.

"I've come to thank you, ma'am. You probably saved my life."

She looked up at me with a smile, but didn't understand what I was saying; I should have brought Hopla along. All I could do to express my gratitude was take her hand and kiss it. It smelled of the sludge I was ingesting six times a day. When I looked up, I found her staring at me with an expression I couldn't interpret. Then she reached up and touched my cheek. "Woo poos," she said, as to a favorite cat. At least, that's what it sounded like. Hers was a cat world.

She took me by the arm, pointed at the table, guided me to one of the stools, poured a bowl of tea for me, patted me on the shoulder, pointed at the bowl, then returned to the stove and gave a startlingly raucous shout. The men I had seen waiting outside in the corridor appeared one by one in the doorway; each received one of the pots from the stove and took it away. After the last one had left, she wiped her face with her smock, dried her hands on it, went to a corner shelf, brought a second bowl to the table, pulled up a stool and sat down facing me. She poured herself a bowl of tea and raised it for a toast. I responded; we drank together; then she put her cup down and looked at me. Her face seemed to acquire the same trancelike stillness that had struck me during her visit at my bedside. She produced the bead on its string from the pocket of her smock, stood up and gestured to me to do the same.

She put her hand two inches from my chest and moved it slowly from left to right, from right to left, looking at the swinging bead. It oscillated back and forth, without changing into a clockwise motion. She went down my body as far as my knees, then moved around to my back, where I presumed she did the same. She reappeared and pointed at the stool; I sat down again. She made the same passes around my head; finally she seemed to be through with the checkup, pocketed the bead, patted my shoulder and grinned.

"Okay?" I asked.

She vigorously shook her head. After a startled moment I remembered that it meant 'yes' and breathed a sigh of relief.

"I owe it all to you, madam."

"Woo poos," she replied, grinning.

On an impulse, I said, "Meow."

That broke her up. "Hoo hoo! Hoo hoo!" she hooted, pointed at me and said, "Meow!" She seemed to consider it the joke of the century; tears rolled down her lined face, which she dried with the back of her hand. Then she raised a finger as if to say, 'Wait!' Shuffling back to the stove, she picked up one of the pans, took it to the table, filled a bowl with green noodles, put it in front of me and asked, "Meow?" She hooted with laughter as she returned the pan to the stove.

I stared at the steaming noodles, not knowing how to cope with them, as there was no cutlery. She gave me chopsticks; my messy first bite ended in my slurping an endless length of noodle. It tasted good, after the slimy sludge.

"Good," I said. "Very good."

"Woo poos." She pointed at the bowl. "Chunggi."

"Delicious." As I sat there, messily gorging myself while she gazed at me contentedly, I became aware of a number of faces in the doorway observing the scene with fascination. It was not, as I thought first, because of my august presence in their galley; from the way they looked, I realized that it must be a signal honor to have a meal served by their den mother. She seemed to have taken a liking to me; it was mutual.

She watched me wrestle with noodles swinging with the swell until the bowl was empty, then she raised her finger again: more treats coming. She fetched another bowl from a shelf, shuffled to the pantry and came back with it filled with white globules. She put them in front of me and said, "Mm-mm."

I managed to catch one between my chopsticks and actually bring it to my mouth. It tasted sweet and succulent; I ate it slowly, savoring it. "Good. 'Mm' indeed."

"Lie che," she said.

"Ah, yes. Lichee."

She shook her head vigorously.

"Woo," I said. "Very woo."

For some reason, that broke her up again. "Hoo hoo!" She hooted with laughter again until tears rolled down her face. The men in the doorway seemed to agree it was very funny.

She watched me like a young wife feeding her husband a new dish from the cookbook. I was flooded with a sense of well-being and gratitude. When I finished the dish, I wiped my mouth with my handkerchief and said, "Madam, you are a wizard."

She looked at me with her small, bright eyes and her face took on an expression that in my part of the world would have been interpreted as fondness. Then she reached across the table and once more touched my cheek.

Even though she could not understand the words, I tried to get across to her some idea of my appreciation. "You worked a miracle. For fifteen years I've been stuffing myself with pills, my stomach must have turned into a chemical factory. You gave me a series of mysterious dishes, and now look at me: better than I've felt in years." I picked up my tea bowl, raised it and said, "Madam, thank you. Godspeed and happy sailing."

She stared at me as if she had understood every word, took her own bowl, raised it and made a little speech of her own. I had no idea what the words meant, but the faces in the doorway which had followed her speech with rapt attention chorused what I took to be the equivalent of "Hear, hear!" So I raised my

[172]

bowl in their direction. "Godspeed and happy sailing to you too, gentlemen. May this be a safe and prosperous voyage."

I was getting carried away; it was time to get out of there. I put my cup down, smiled at her and was about to take my leave when someone appeared at my side. It was Bryn Mawr, the Chinese bosun. "Wa djin joh," he said.

I looked at her, eyebrows raised, then remembered she was unable to explain it to me. But she grinned and pointed at the door. He must want to show me something. I took her gnarled hand again, bowed and said, "Thank you, madam."

She sat quite still at the table, looking at me intently, then she said, "Shoo."

I obeyed, and followed my guide.

He took me out into the corridor, where the others joined us; we proceeded down to the far end, then rounded the corner to the messroom.

I had not been in the messroom since the Chinese crew arrived; now, here they were, a crowd of them, seated at the long tables, having their meal. There was a hubbub of laughter and conversation, but they fell silent when they saw me in the doorway. Everyone turned round and gazed at me with acute interest. I entered; Bryn Mawr took me to the nearest man, whose T-shirt said Swarthmore, told him something, pointed at me, then pointed toward the galley. I understood he was reporting what he had seen. The man rose, bowed and said, "Won Chang."

I shook him by the hand and, trusting my luck, said, "Glad to know you, Won Chang."

He smiled. "Han chi, Omi."

"H'm. Yes," I said, taken unawares.

The next man rose, bowed and said, "Ong Chang."

"Glad to meet you, Ong Chang. Godspeed and happy sailing."

"Han chi, Omi." Heaven knew when they had picked that up.

I went down the line, each man rising, bowing and introducing himself and saying, "Han chi, Omi."

Suddenly I came upon Mate Number One. He rose, smiled and said, "Happy to see you here, Commodore. This is a surprise."

"Why should it be? These men are all my nephews now. Or so it would seem."

He frowned, not understanding.

"*Ome* means uncle."

"Ah . . ." He turned to the assembled men and obviously relayed the information, as I heard the word "Omi" several times. They all laughed and applauded.

"Woo!" I cried, in an excess of zeal.

For a second they looked at one another, stunned, then they shrieked, raised their bowls once more and shouted in unison, "Woo! Woo, Omi!"

After the applause had died down, I asked Number One under my breath, "What does 'woo' mean?"

He hesitated, then replied, "In their language it means 'to perform the act of procreation,' Commodore."

"Fancy that," I said.

2

My visit to the galley and the messroom signaled a change in my relationship with the Chinese crew. When I appeared on the bridge, Captain Cho scurried, but Whittier, the little helmsman, in answer to my "Good morning, gentlemen," climbed off his orange crate, bowed and said, "Omi." When I happened to meet one of them in the corridor on my way to my quarters, his face lit up, he lifted a finger and said, "Omi." The 'Woo' joke was flogged to death by one of them, a low-browed AB called Wellesley, who could not meet me without bellowing "Woo, Omi!" and killing himself laughing.

To my surprise and somewhat to my dismay, Captain Cho had not used the opportunity of my temporary absence to assert himself as master of the *Isabel Kwel*. I thought that his disappearing when I first arrived on the bridge after my brief illness had been accidental; maybe he had wanted to go to the bathroom. But no, it had been quite intentional and became common practice: the moment I showed up on the bridge during his watch, he ran for cover in his cabin. God only knew what I had done to him this time; the only conclusion I could come to was that, apart from being incompetent, he was a neurotic youth in whom I inspired a sort of paranoia, forcing him to flee at first sight. It caused an additional paragraph to the letter addressed to Mr. Chung; the boy did not need an advisor, he needed a therapist, or a mother. I made a point of not appearing on the bridge during his watches, rather than making an issue of it. He was Mr. Chung's problem, not mine.

I suggested to the Chinese staff that they take part in our Happy Hour; after some coaxing, they did so—all except Captain Cho. They sat politely through the demonstration of Louis jumping from my shoulder onto the coffee table the moment the bar snacks were brought in and waiting until one was offered to him; after that initiation they became quite lively.

The Chinese chief engineer turned out to be witty, articulate despite his fractured English and almost embarrassingly erudite. Porks was more surprised at this than I was; they must hardly have exchanged a word during their watches, other than on technical matters. Young Marco Number One was no slouch either; at my urging he told us that he had started out by studying business administration, then switched to the Technical Institute in Taipei and shipped out as junior radio officer on a tanker before joining Mr. Chung's small tugboat fleet; his father taught economics at Taiwan University. What struck me most, I think, during this first social hour was their rather sophisticated wit, reminiscent of the British. Suddenly, Chief Liu said, "Seems you made great impression on crew, Commodore."

"How so?"

"They are very—er—clannish tribe out on those outer islands. They lived in isolation for thousand years. They are as—er —foreign to us as to you. You managed make them admit you into family. They now call you 'uncle.' "

"That, in their world," Marco One said, "is almost as good as father. They live, of course, in matriarchal society."

"So I gathered."

"The woman is—was—head of village. They all have her name."

"I seem to get on with her very well."

"That's what meant," Chief Liu said. "None of us hope to be accepted way you are. To us, she is—er—ice queen."

"Why don't they get on with the runners on the dry dock?"

Marco One replied, "They are from neighboring island and enemies for centuries, something to do with abducted daughters. In China, how say?—rural—to abduct daughter is considered service to parents, but in their island the women rule, it is capital crime. There have not maybe been abductions for many years, but they are still great enemies. I wonder why Mr. Chung put them together. He must have had reason."

After a silence Chief Liu asked, "How is Mate Slobkous? He be back soon?"

"Well, I don't know, Chief. I'm afraid he may be gone for quite a while."

"Give him our regards, Commodore," Chief Liu said. The others muttered their approval.

After Happy Hour, as I made my way to the mate's cabin, it struck me as surprising that the Chinese had not cottoned to the fact that Slobkous was a drunk; I had had the impression they knew everything that went on on board the ship. Maybe it was just politeness; calling the mate's ailment by its proper name might make him lose face.

The cabin was a mess, and it reeked like a men's urinal. I found Slobkous sitting on the edge of his bunk. He seemed momentarily sober, but looked like death.

"Well, how are you feeling?"

He gave me a bleary look and shook his head. "Sorry about this," he said hoarsely.

"I'm sorry for *you*, Slobkous."

He stared at me for a long moment, then he said, "Yeah."

"I'd advise you to lay off the booze, if you can, before we fly home from Rio. It would be better not to let the company doctor spot your problem."

He shrugged his shoulders. "He knows. Everybody knows. I thought you knew."

"I wish I had."

"Well, I suppose they wanted to give me one more chance and, hallelujah, I blew it. So back to the rest home, for all the good it does. I really thought this time I'd make it." His voice broke. "I really, really thought this time . . . but, hell, I'd better face it. I can't shake it, or them." He suddenly looked wild-eyed.

"Who, Slobkous? Tell me."

"Don't patronize me, Harinxma! They're real! As real as you are, and they won't leave me! They won't leave me in peace! The moment I hit the bottle, they pop up, day or night, and they won't let up! Why do you think I drink? Because I like it?"

"You mean—you see—er—things?"

"People! Look at him! Look at him right now, standing beside you! You brought him in yourself."

"But who are they, Slobkous?"

He started to weep. "Men who died in the war . . . Shipmates
. . . Girls I knew who were killed in the bombing . . . A brother,
killed in the battle of the Java Sea . . ." He noisily blew his nose,
then fixed me with a baleful stare. "I wonder who that is beside
you. You lost a ship through enemy action, didn't you?"

Poor Slobkous; it was delirium tremens. Others saw rats or
snakes coming out of the wallpaper. To humor him, I said, "Describe him for me."

"A sailor. Officer of some kind. Nice kind of guy, laughing
now. Thirties, jersey, duffel, fleece-lined boots. Looks like the
Arctic to me."

The Arctic convoys had been full of nice guys in their thirties,
laughing their heads off. At least in the beginning. "If you had to
describe him to a police officer as a suspect, what would you
say?"

He looked intently at his hallucination by my side. "Long nose,
eyes close together, cap on the back of his head. Brown hair. With
a curl. Skinny. Ring a bell?"

For a moment he took me aback; it sounded like my old
Sparks, who had been killed on board the *Isabel* the day before
she was lost. But how many skinny, long-nosed guys had there
been, knocking about on tugs? How many had never returned?

I said lightly, "Well, from what I heard, you and Spooks Haversma must have had a high old time together," and made for
the door.

His reaction was violent and totally irrational. "Get out!" he
screamed. "I don't need your goddam patronizing! Get the hell
out! Leave me alone!"

"Look, Slobkous, all I meant—"

"I don't want to talk to you! I don't want to talk about anything! Get the fucking hell out of my cabin and *stay* out!" He
looked as if, had he had the strength, he would have thrown me
out.

As I opened the door, he said, "You don't believe me, do you?
You don't believe the guy is there, do you? Well, he still is, and
he's ready to go with you."

"I'll have the bosun bring you some coffee. Take care now."

I closed the door behind me and went back to my dayroom.
Louis jumped onto my shoulder as I entered. Even though I didn't
believe a word of Slobbo's alcoholic hallucinations, the thought of

a ghost accompanying me was enough of an excuse to head for the icebox. Against the young doctor's advice and with the sneaking feeling that I was double-crossing the Chinese den mother in the galley, I poured myself a medium wallop.

The young doctor's advice . . . 'Lay off all booze, coffee, sugar, fats, salt, cholesterol, and I mean all, and you'll be able to cut down on your medication after a month and toss the lot overboard after three.'

That was, in effect, a pretty good description of Ma Chang's diet. Maybe things weren't as spooky around here as they seemed to be. Maybe there was an explanation too for old Sparks' ghost.

3

Apart from that one transgression, I stuck religiously to Ma Chang's and the young doctor's diet. The only part of his advice I was not following was daily exercise; so I set out into the lower regions of the ship in search of the gymnasium.

It was the first time I had been down this far after my lonely tour of the ship in Rotterdam; what I found was an overpopulated Chinese tenement. The long corridors of the crew's quarters, which comprised thirty cabins for the lower ranks, were crowded with people squatting on the floor playing Mah-Jongg, darning socks, ciphering on an abacus, playing with a cat and three kittens the existence of which I had never suspected—they must have picked up the pregnant mother in Mindello. In the doorways to the cabins, bead curtains swung with the swell in unison, hitting the jambs with a massive rhythmic clatter each time the ship pitched. There was a smell of sweet tobacco, spices, incense; over the hubbub of voices caterwauled the speeded-up Chinese version of Bron's *Bawdy Ballads for Lusty Lovers*.

When they saw me, there were grins and shouts of "Omi"; as I passed, some of them touched my ankles in a gesture of familiarity and, God knows, affection. I found the door to the recreation complex of the gymnasium and hobby shop at the far end of the corridor; when I opened it, it was obvious that nobody had been using it. There was a stale smell of bilges; one of the banks of fluorescent lights was blinking; in the gloom the rowing machine and the stationary bike looked like instruments of torture in a dungeon. I walked over to the bike, took off my shirt, climbed into the saddle and started to pedal away. It was a boring business; the bicycle faced a blank wall on which I tried to conjure up images of bicycle rides through woods and fields of my youth. Then I became aware of faces in the doorway.

They were looking at me with utter astonishment; they couldn't have had a clue as to the purpose of the health equipment. As I stolidly continued pedaling, their astonishment changed into hilarity. They giggled, they laughed, finally applauded; self-consciously, I changed over to the rowing machine. Suddenly Bryn Mawr, the muscle man, pushed the others aside, climbed onto the bicycle and started to pedal furiously. A few moments later, little Whittier worked his way in, hopped onto the back of the bike, and Bryn Mawr started to pedal faster, as if they were actually going somewhere. Everybody seemed to think that was a splendid idea; they started to shout encouragements at the cyclist, who was going faster and faster; in the meantime I went on stolidly rowing, feeling paternal.

After about ten minutes of this, when everyone had had his turn, I'd had enough. The moment I rose, Hopla came with a towel.

I thought it was meant for wiping my perspiring torso, but he beckoned and I followed him, together with most of the others. He opened a door and I found myself in the shower room. It was not built for prudes; there were no partitions between the showers nor between the commodes opposite; Bryn Mawr stripped and turned on the shower; soon we were joined by others, as it literally was a communal one: the water came down in a long curtain of rain from a horizontal pipe in the ceiling. Following suit, I took off my shorts, my moccasins and my socks and joined them in the rain, soaping my armpits and other details with casual ease as if I were jostled by naked Chinese every day. Chances were I would be, from now on.

The situation generated sentimental thoughts about the Brotherhood of Man, but when two of them took seats in the row of commodes and started to relieve themselves, singing the Chinese version of 'Bouncing Balls' at a startlingly high pitch, I suffered culture shock, dried my chalk-white body with Hopla's towel, put my shorts back on and left, shoes and socks in hand.

Out in the passage, Bryn Mawr, looking ten feet tall and three

[179]

feet wide and without a stitch on, handed me a bowl of tea and slapped me on the shoulder. The spectators of the game of Mah-Jongg, squatting in the corridor, made room and one of them patted the deck, inviting me to sit down. I did so; it wasn't easy with a bowl, shoes and socks; also, it had been quite a few years since I last squatted on the floor cross-legged. I slurped hot, sweet tea, tried to make sense of the game and felt my left ankle being patted. Suddenly I found myself thinking of my retirement village, The Cheerleaders, the golf club, General Theodosius. Of that whole complex only General Theodosius could have turned up at the end of the corridor; someone would have helped him take off his breastplate and his helmet and sent him into the shower room for a rinse and a crap to the tune of 'I gave you the ring, you gave me the finger.'

Suddenly this mixture of goodwill and clashing cultures, swinging bead curtains and friendly joshing without words became timeless. How dead old Sparks would have loved this! How I missed them all! How lonely I had been until, like Jonah, I was swallowed whole by this monster of the sea!

Chapter Seven

1

After twenty-two days at sea, we arrived off Rio de Janeiro. In the meantime I had finished my report on the unfortunate Captain Cho for Mr. Chung, whom I planned to telephone from the harbormaster's office for an immediate replacement; the report would be sent by special courier. My guess was that he would want to fly down to Rio himself to look into the situation.

It was early in the morning, the night was shedding its veils. The white high-rises of Copacabana and Ipanema were emerging from the morning mist; above them towered the mountains. I recognized the Sugar Loaf, the Pico do Coronado, vaguely discernible in the young light, with its statue of Christ. To the west, the Pedra da Gávea, shaped like an old square-sail. Standing at the rail outside the wheelhouse, I gazed nostalgically at the most beautiful city in the world. I had fallen in love with it when I first set eyes on it in 1948; that year I had come back three times, towing sections of a floating factory. The last time I had seen the city, in 1964 during a brief stopover on my way to Valparaíso, I hadn't had a chance to go ashore. To return now as an elderly man in uncertain health was a curious experience; reasonably speaking, this would be the last time. Remembering the young man who had drunk it all in with such solemn enjoyment—the beauty, the strangeness, the excitement—I felt a pang of envy. In a few hours I would be calling Mr. Chung, he would send a new captain; after hanging around for a few days waiting for the man and another day of familiarizing him with the ship, I would fly home. Héloïse, the Glee Club, 'What's in the mail today?' 'Goody, goody: the mail-order catalogue from the outsize-shoe factory!' Back to the evening classes at the Lycée: *Simii scandentis partes posteriores nudae videntur.* 'And, Monsieur Harinxma? 'Ave you come up with the translation?' 'Yes, Mademoiselle: "Monkeys climbing above their station show their bare buttocks to the nation." ' 'Very good, *mon commodore!* Captures nicely Valentinian's contempt for the sycophants in the Senate.'

The pilot launch, a black dot in the golden haze, came foaming toward us and swung alongside with Fransen and the pilot standing ready to grab our Jacob's ladder. Fransen waved, I waved. As they climbed on board, the launch swung free and headed back to the city; I gave it a polite blare of thanks with the foghorn.

"Good morning! You're headed for the general anchorage north of Enxadas Island," Fransen said as he appeared on the bridge.

"Ah, good morning. Good morning, Pilot. Enxadas Island? In the old days we used to anchor off Viana, where the docks are."

"Can't be done anymore, not for a tow this size," Fransen said. "There's a causeway now between Niterói and Rio. After your time, I'm sure. Built in '74."

"I haven't been back here since the middle sixties."

"You'll see a lot of changes. Especially when you get down to the beaches. You've never seen anything like the skyscrapers and hotels. Man, these people really know how to live. You must come back with your wife one day. Get cheap tickets from most anywhere. You'll have the time."

"Captain?" the pilot called.

"I'd better stand by," I said. Captain Cho stood, frozen and forgotten, in his corner.

We became involved in the intricacies of the operation. It was not all that complicated, but it was new to the Chinese crew and I was worried. As it turned out, they were as expert and as nimble as any I had known. We shortened the hawser and entered the bay, surrounded by busy police launches that treated us as if we were towing a floating atom bomb, and by a *bateau mouche* full of waving tourists which circled us several times as we slowly moved toward our anchorage. It was odd to see the long, pillared causeway straight ahead which now cut that magnificent bay in half, making it seem smaller and less striking than I remembered it. All modern-day bays with romantic pasts were beginning to look the same.

The day became hotter as we moved slowly up the channel. Four harbor tugs came barreling at us, the pilot's walkie-talkie began to speak and snarl in Portuguese. I offered him our VHF, but he waved it away; he obviously intended that his orders to the tugboats should be kept private.

The anchorage was roomy and cool in the breeze, but a long way from the nearest mooring dock for bumboats on the Ilha das Cobras; there would be no casual back-and-forth between dock and shore. But then, the runners would probably want to stay on board; they had done so in Mindello.

Once *Agnes* was put to bed by the tugs, secured to four-point buoys, the *Isabel* cast off and headed for the fuel docks. When the hoses were in and the fuel oil was gurgling down the pipes, Fransen said, "Well, I have some shore business to attend to, but you and I should talk, Harinxma. How about lunch at my hotel? Say, noon in the bar of the Lancaster, in Copa?"

"Okay, see you."

As I watched him hurrying down the dockside in his scruffy raincoat, fedora on the back of his head, it suddenly came to me what he had reminded me of all along: a corrupt union boss on the New York waterfront.

2

Because of the time difference, it was unlikely that Mr. Chung would be in his office in Kao Hsiung; but he might be in Brussels. I went ashore in my blues, which hung around me in folds as a result of Ma Chang's diet, and began by placing a collect call to the Brussels number on the business card Chung had given me during our exotic dinner in the seventeenth-century restaurant. I used the telephone in the fuel company's office on the dock—not the most private of settings, as the small room was filled with characters drinking coffee, desperate for entertainment; maybe I could arrange with Mr. Chung to call him at a later hour. The connection seemed to be a long time in the making; meanwhile I watched fully grown men with whiskers throw paper airplanes at each other. Then the operator said, "Your number does not reply, sir. Please try again later."

I placed another call, this time to Kao Hsiung, Taiwan. That stopped all activity dead in its tracks; the airplane throwers gaped at me as if I had dialed a phone-sex number on the public blower. This time the connection took no time at all; suddenly a mechanical voice, high-pitched and somehow old-fashioned in its hackneyed Chinese singsong, chirruped, "Velly solly, office closed at this hour. Please wait for peep, then give name and number so you can be call back. Thank you." After that it started to give

[183]

the message again in Chinese. I didn't wait for the peep; later would do.

Well, maybe better this way. It was a bit sneaky, doing this behind Fransen's back. As it was getting on for twelve o'clock anyhow, I called a taxi, changed some money with the cashier and set out for the Lancaster Hotel in Copacabana.

I found him at a window table in a bar overlooking the beach and the ocean. He had a glass and an ashtray full of stubs in front of him; when I reached the table, he looked up with a weary grin and asked what I would have to drink. As we waited for my glass of orange juice and another double Scotch for him, he made small talk about his coming retirement, while I gazed at the view of the ocean. Two girls in bikinis were walking down the black-and-white checkerboard pavement skirting the crowded beach; they had a black poodle with them that ran back and forth with a stick.

After the drinks had been served, I said, "Fransen, as I told you before, Mr. Chung cannot send that flawed ship through the Forties with her present captain. If he does, I'm going to raise bloody hell. I thought I'd better tell you."

"Ah?"

"I've come to know the Chinese pretty well during the past weeks. The crew are willing and capable, but haven't been tested. The staff is okay, the two mates will stand up in an emergency, but the captain, as you know, is a pompous little jerk who's scared of the ship, throws his weight around and appears to be totally incompetent. Once he hits the storm belt, God knows what may happen. If you ask me, there's a real chance that he'll not only lose the tow but turn the damn ship over. Now, are you going to tell Mr. Chung that, or am I?"

He didn't answer, but lit a cigarette, taking his time doing it. He inhaled deeply and said finally, with puffs of smoke, "I have to tell you something, Harinxma, which has to stay between ourselves. Mr. Chung, we found out, has insured the ship for her full replacement value."

"So?"

He frowned. "Come, now! A man buys a ship with a serious problem, at a bargain-basement price. He puts on her an untested crew from some remote Chinese island, which means no union and no next of kin who might raise a stink, a staff that still has to learn the ropes and a captain who's a dud. Then he insures her at full replacement value, strings a tow with maximum windage behind her and sends her into the Forties. Now, how does that smell to you?"

"Don't be ridiculous, Fransen. If that ship turns over in the Forties, nobody will come off alive. You're talking about forty-five people!"

"I'm talking about twenty million dollars. That's an awfully big jackpot."

As the concept sank in, I rejected it out of hand. "Look, Fransen, I may not be the best judge of human nature in the world, but I've worked with men all my life and under all sorts of circumstances, including war. In the case of Chung, I'm pretty sure that what we have is a provincial millionaire with dreams of grandeur who has over-reached himself. He tried to enter the big league by buying the largest, most powerful and most sophisticated tugboat in the world—"

"And manned her with a music-hall crew of Stone Age fishermen? A fart of a captain who's notoriously incompetent? And then insures her at full replacement value? Even you—"

"Fransen, setting up a ship for scuttling by choosing the worst crew and the most incompetent master is the stuff sea-babble is made of: villains and heroes, black hats and white hats. The fact that he's a Chinese adds to his image as a monster. No, I won't buy it. The way I see it, the whole history of the ship is one of bungling and last-minute improvisations. It's obvious that young Kwel rammed her through before her concept was tested, and when she turned out to be a lemon, his grandfather sold her to the Third World. Bunglers, the lot of them: both Kwels, the architects and now Chung, who bought her as a trophy. And insufferable, incompetent little Cho about to take her to her doom. Well, that's not going to happen. I'm going to tell Chung that the guy has to be replaced by an experienced, functioning captain. Even if Chung is the amateur with megalomania I think he is, he'll realize the danger. I'm phoning him this afternoon."

He pressed out the cigarette he had just lit, took an envelope out of his inside pocket and handed it to me. "You'd better read this first."

"What is it?"

"Read it." He ordered himself another glass while I tore open the envelope.

[185]

Commodore M. Harinxma, by hand,
private and confidential

To my surprise, the letter, although on stationery with company heading, was written by hand and signed *Arnold Kwel*. If I hadn't known he was blind, I would have been impressed; now it was obvious Miss Bastiaans had been told to write his dictation in longhand. Why? To make it look personal? Because he wanted to make sure there were no copies?

Dear Harinxma,

Only once before in the past half-century have I made a similar request to you; when I asked you to take command of the old 'Isabel' during the Second World War for the sake of the survival of the Dutch tugboat business. During that half-century our relationship has grown into one different from that between owner and master. Together, we have seen so much and lived through so many ups and downs in our profession that I think by now we have become friends as well as fellow workers in the same vineyard.

I liked that; it was like Baron de Rothschild telling one of the peasants pressing his grapes with their feet that they were united by a common purpose and in the process of becoming friends.

It is on this basis of our personal relationship that I want you to continue in your present position on board the 'Isabel' as far as Talcahuano. My reason for this request is as follows.

After the war, Holland never recovered her monopoly in the deep-sea towing business. We are still among the first, but we have to fight to defend that position. Given our limited resources as a nation, the only way we can remain competitive is by being at the head of the pack when it comes to modern, trend-setting tugboats, which means building bigger, more powerful, faster and more sophisticated ships. We have managed to do just that for the better part of a decade; now, with the 'Isabel Kwel,' we have run into what is potentially a deadly snag. The ship, despite or possibly because of her mold-breaking originality, has a design fault which renders her unsuitable for the kind of work in which we specialize, therefore we have been forced to sell her. However, we must find out exactly what that fault is and correct it in the design of the sister ship which is now on the drawing boards. Already the new ship is far behind

[186]

schedule; unless we locate and identify the fault within the next few months, we'll fall behind in the race, probably irretrievably. It would mean the end of Holland's Glory as we know it, to which you and I, each after our own fashion, have devoted our lives. Given the fact that you are now virtually in command of the 'Isabel Kwel,' I am asking you to continue as her acting master through both the Atlantic and Pacific storm belts, so as to give the architect who will join you in Rio ample opportunity to determine what exactly is wrong with the ship.

I can hear you say, 'I'm too old, too frail physically and emotionally to see a tow that size and a ship with her problems through the Forties!' Harinxma, you know my answer to that without my spelling it out. I know you, and, besides, growing old is a relative business. To me, the seventies are the best years of a man's life, on condition he can overcome the peer pressure to call himself 'old.' I hold no brief for the eighties, let alone the nineties, but the seventies are the crowning years of your life. Use them, Harinxma! Use them not just for your own good, but for the future of the profession to which you have devoted the years of your manhood.

At this moment, Harinxma, the future of Holland's Glory rests, once again, in your hands.

Confident of the outcome, I remain:

> *your friend,*
> *Arnold Kwel*

At first sight it looked like a sincere personal plea from one old man to another in a relationship that, while inherently antagonistic, had been mellowed by the years. But somewhere a bell rang. A word, a phrase, a thought. Then it came back to me: The Hague, the head office, Jim Kwel saying, "I gather you're the one who's taking our *Isabel* to Talcahuano.' They had planned it way back then. Once again the old buzzard had pulled a fast one on me.

As a rule, apart from surface ruffles like yelling at the dog and swearing at the Christmas tree, I was slow to anger; this time I was outraged. I folded the letter, put it back in its envelope, handed it to Fransen and said, "Well, you'd better come clean, before I do a Samson and bring the roof down."

He had the misfortune to smile. "On whom?"

[187]

"On you, you bastard! On you and those two conniving, chiseling crooks in The Hague!"

At least it wiped the grin off his face. "I don't understand—"

"Just answer my question! Why did old Kwel pick *me*, and not someone else?"

"Look, Harinxma. I'm not a party—"

"Fransen, I've been suckered by you and those two jokers long enough. If you don't come clean now, I promise you I'll do exactly what I said: I'll bring the goddam roof down and bust the whole shady deal wide open. So: why *me?*"

He stubbed out his cigarette again. "Because the old man felt you were the most capable."

"Crap! I'm a seventy-year-old retiree who's been out of practice for nine years. Bron is a hundred times more capable than I am. Why me? Come on, out with it."

"It had to be a captain not associated with the company," he said stiffly.

"But I *am* associated with the company! I get a pension."

"The lawyers must have decided that it had to be someone not on active service, so he picked you. And you can do it with one hand tied behind your back, you know that."

"I know no such thing. I had a blood-pressure crisis in mid-ocean. If I sail into a force-nine gale with that rig, chances are I'll kick the bucket."

He shrugged his shoulders. "Obviously, the Kwels don't think so. That's all I can say."

"Does Chung know that KITCO is planning to crash-test his ship in the Forties?"

"I don't think so."

"You don't think so. And the architect—when is he supposed to arrive?"

"He's here."

"Where, here?"

"Probably on board ship by now, with his equipment."

"Equipment?"

"He brought quite a load of stuff. Don't ask me what it's for. I don't know."

"And the tow is supposed to sail tonight?"

"Correct."

"With me as captain?"

[188]

"With you as advisor to the captain. Exactly the way you came."

"And the other members of the skeleton staff?"

"They'll stay on board until Talcahuano too."

"What makes you think *I* will?"

He gave me a pensive look. "Harinxma, the old man has been dealing with captains for fifty years. There are certain kneejerk reactions none of us can suppress. Give a seasoned master a crew of chimpanzees and he'll end up feeling paternal about them, on condition you keep them together long enough. He also knew that if he gave you a ship, any ship, even this pig, you'd be hooked by now and take her through the Forties. With pleasure."

I looked away and gazed at the beach. The girls and their poodle had started to walk away from the crowd, along the edge of the ocean. "Fransen," I said, "I don't want any part of this. I'm going to phone Chung."

He gave me a tired look. "You bull-headed old bastard, can't you get it through your thick skull that KITCO represents Chung, that I represent KITCO and that if I say: 'The ship will sail,' she sails, captain or no captain? By the time you hunt down Chung, which may take days, the ship will have left with your precious Chinese crew. If you want to protect them, you'd better be on board. That, my friend, is the bottom line."

So it was. The old man had known that if he had proposed in The Hague that I take the ship through the Forties, I would have turned it down. He had reeled me in slowly, in small increments, counted on my identifying with the crew until I had turned into a mother hen. Father figure indeed! The hell with him.

The girls and their poodle had entered the solitude beyond the crowd. They were all alone now on the lonely silver beach, which stretched into the haze on the horizon.

"How about some food?" Fransen asked.

"No, thank you." I rose. "I need to think this over, Fransen. I have to talk to my wife."

"Don't be stupid, Harinxma. Don't tell your wife anything. Just say, 'Guess what, honey! I've been asked to go on to Talcahuano. Nice trip. Just a few more weeks, and the money is very good.' It is, by the way. KITCO pays you the same salary Chung has paid up to now, plus a ten-percent bonus on arrival. You'll be able to build two guestrooms by the time you get back."

So they even knew about that.

3

There was only one place I knew of where I could get away from it all for a few hours. I took a taxi to the terminal of the funicular railroad that went up the mountainside to the giant statue of Christ; when I arrived at the station, a train was about to leave.

The long, slow ride through the dense jungle with its occasionally breathtaking views of the city was wasted on me. While the tilted carriage full of ooh-ing and ah-ing tourists slowly ground and squealed its way to the top, I thought of Chung, and Fransen's interpretation of his motives. I would have shrugged it off as pure sea-babble if I hadn't remembered my meeting with the man in the restaurant in Brussels. I remembered saying to him that if he had been looking for a combination certain to fall prey to whatever problems the ship might have, he couldn't have made a better choice than Captain Cho and his crew. His face had frozen into a mask and he had said, 'I resent that, Mr. Harinxma. That was uncalled for.' He had taken me by surprise, for I had wanted to tell him the truth about the *Isabel Kwel;* I had expected him to be grateful. I had concluded that I must have offended him by putting his judgment in doubt. Now the expression on his face came back to me. Could it be that, rather than being offended, he had been shocked at the discovery that his scheme was obvious even to a seventy-year-old tug-driver?

When the funicular arrived at its destination, I got out, climbed the steps and sat down at the foot of the colossal statue to look at the view. It was stunning; far below lay the city, a shimmering expanse of white stuccoed walls and red rooftops, studded with the spires of baroque churches and the slender towers of skyscrapers, looking small and elegant from this height. To the right, the immensity of the blue ocean; across the green-and-cobalt bay the mountains, shrouded by haze. In the center of the bay, close to the thin silver line of the causeway, the black matchbox of the dock; closer to the city, at the inverted 'L' of the fuel dock, the toylike *Isabel,* the trinkets on her Paradise tree glinting in the sun. Maybe it was the serenity of the bird's-eye view, but as I sat there, gazing at the matchbox and the little toy tugboat far below, the idea that Chung was a mass murderer became ludicrous. My first concept of him had been correct: a monkey who had reached into a jam jar to grab the banana and now found himself caught because he refused to let go. Old Kwel had run rings around Chung and used him for his own purposes; he had done the same to me until I found myself where I was now: gazing down at the matchbox and the toy, knowing that the real monkey with his hand clutching the banana in the jam jar was I. Of course I wanted to protect Ma Chang, Hopla, little Whittier and the rest from death by drowning; very commendable. I would have to fool Sylvia along those lines. But there was no point in trying to fool myself: I was going to take the ship through the Forties to Talcahuano because I wanted to, because I had fallen off the wagon.

I wondered if alcoholics went through the same process, knowing that they might be killing themselves and not giving a damn, helpless in the throes of their addiction. I knew that I might be risking everything I had in life: my marriage, my well-ordered retiree's existence, my daughter, my harmonious evolution toward old age and death—everything that constituted Martinus Harinxma ashore. And why? For what?

I wondered if any alcoholic ever came up with the answer to that question. To know that you were in the process of killing yourself must scare the hell out of you in sober moments, as it obviously did Slobkous. Now I would be forced to report his relapse to Fransen, for I couldn't possibly take him along through the storm belts, alternately roaring and puking in that cabin of his which stank like the men's room in a sleazy saloon. I had better tell the bosun to spruce him up for the flight ahead.

But still there was that question: why was I doing it? The sea? Possibly, but I had done without the sea for nine years. The crew? I could hold up our departure and lean on Mr. Chung to replace Captain Cho with a master who was better qualified. The ship?

Ah, now. I gazed at the sparkling little toy tugboat far below. I had no illusions about her. I knew that to keep her from sneaking up on me in the Forties would need constant vigilance on my part. I would have to be aware of her slightest move, even as I slept. Forty years ago I had very nearly been killed by the grandmother of the little toy glistening in the distance. But I had been young and inexperienced, trusting and overconfident; I had not known at the time that there was such a thing as a killer ship. I was looking at one right now. And yet, hard to believe as it must be to someone who had never had a ship of his own, I could know all that, *all* that, and at the same time realize that I had fallen in love with the pig. She might be a killer, she might be treacherous and ready to play me false, but I was utterly infatuated. I knew every twist, every quirk, every deadly threat that lurked in that unlovely body of hers, yet I couldn't leave her. It was almost as if the *Isabel* and I were engaged in a lovers' combat, daring each other in order to establish supremacy.

It was hardly a rational decision. It would certainly be hard to explain to any man who had never owned a sailboat which he took out for solitary jaunts, cooking meals for one at anchor in lonely coves, smoking a pipe in the cockpit afterward, watching the mast move against the stars, and then falling asleep on a narrow bunk listening to the strumming of halyards and the slapping of small waves against the hull, to dream of seagulls circling over a deserted beach somewhere beyond the horizon in another dimension to which she took him on a lovers' journey beyond time.

As I rode back down the mountain in the shuddering, gnashing little train and watched the toy tugboat disappear from sight, I found myself reflecting that every man should, at some point in his life, have a ship of his own, however small, if only to discover that it is better to have loved and lost than never to have loved at all.

4

The call home was a tough one. To begin with, I made it from the fuel company's office on the dockside; the line was poor and those airplane-throwing characters were still hanging around, drinking in every word. The line was bad, but even so Sylvia's distress and dismay came over loud and clear. She brushed aside my argument of having to protect the crew from the incompetence of the Chinese captain; all she heard was that I wasn't coming home but staying on to tow a dry dock through the storm belt. She didn't know about the *Isabel*'s problem; to her, experienced tugmaster's wife, the fact that the dock was a giant object with maximum windage was enough. I assured her that I had plenty of people to do the legwork for me, that all I was supposed to do was be present on the bridge to direct operations, but she didn't buy it. She wanted me to have myself checked by a doctor; she wanted me to hold up the tow until another captain had been found. When, finally, I had worn her down to weary acceptance, I had the uneasy feeling that I had strong-armed her and thereby betrayed the tenderness that had become the most important element in our life together these later years.

"Well, Marty, then all that's left for me to say is Godspeed and happy sailing . . ."

"Now don't worry, love, I'll be fine. Take care of yourself, and give my love to Helen and the others. We'll be in touch. Okay? Bye, Syl. Love you."

The audience grinned; one of them echoed 'Luv you!' He was lucky I didn't push his cigar into his mouth. And now I had better go and break the news to Captain Cho before someone else did.

The moment I came back on board, Porks jumped me as I stepped on deck; he must have been lying in wait. "Who told that boffin he could store his junk in my workshop?" he cried. "I need that place to work in! Now I can hardly move in there!"

"Steady on, man. I don't know what you're talking about."

"So he did it while you were ashore? I might have known! Let me tell you—"

"Let's go to my dayroom. And stop yelling."

As we made our way there, the bosun came down the corridor.

"*He* did it!" Porks cried, pointing an accusing finger. "*He* had them put it there!"

"Where else did you want me to put it?" the bosun yelled back. "'Ome wasn't here, it had to go *some*where!"

"Gentlemen, please! Not out here. Come in." I opened the door to the dayroom and ushered them inside. "Now, Porks— what's all this about?"

Porks took a deep breath to keep up the hog-calling contest. "While you were ashore, that hotshot architect who came on board had a truckload delivered and the bosun here had them pile it all into my workshop!"

"What kind of a load?"

"Junk! Garbage! A huge pile of it! All I know is that now I haven't got enough room to—"

"All right. Go back to your engine room and leave it to me. Bosun, go find the architect if he's on board. Tell him I want to see him. Say it's urgent."

They left, muttering at one another. A few moments later there was a knock on the door and B.B. came in, in a fancy dressing gown and embroidered slippers. "Oh, hello there, Martinus," he said jovially. "Nice to see you again! Well, what's the fuss about?"

"B.B., good to see you. Look, it seems you brought some equipment with you which the bosun put into the chief's workshop, so now he's hopping mad. What kind of equipment is it?"

"Oh, just a few odds and ends."

"Such as?"

"I don't remember, exactly. I can let you have the list, if you wish."

"Let me have it now, please. By the way, where did they put you up?"

"In the hospital. The bed's a bit high, otherwise it's spiffing."

He left; the moment he was gone, the bosun came in. "Ome, let me explain what happened—"

"I know what happened. You should have asked the chief's permission first." Before he could prolong the argument, I said, "I gather Captain Fransen has been to tell you that you're going on to Talcahuano."

He grunted. "Yes, but as I was saying—"

"Has he seen Mate Slobkous yet?"

His face fell. "Sorry, Ome. I couldn't stop him. I didn't know he was coming."

"What shape is the mate in right now?"

"So-so. Not unconscious, but he isn't all there either."

"See if you can spruce him up a bit. Get him some coffee. I'm afraid he'll have to leave with Captain Fransen before we sail. Better give him a haircut too. At least get him under the shower."

"I'll see what I can do, but he's not operational, Ome. Captain Fransen will need help to get him into a taxi."

"It'll probably be a bumboat first. As soon as we're through oiling, we're heading back for the dry dock."

B.B. came in with a sheaf of papers. "This is it, Martinus. I can't see what everybody is getting worked up about."

[194]

"Captain Fransen will be leaving later today, Bosun. See what you can do about the mate."

"Will do." He moved heavily out of the room.

B.B. said, "Here, have a look. It's not much, really."

The list ran to three pages. It contained a bizarre collection of items: one radio transmission and receiving set with Morse key and aerial; welders, welding hoods and acetylene cutters; rolls of number-zero tarpaulin; eight-foot lengths of heavy-gauge six-inch pipe; ten-foot lengths of twenty-two-inch pipe; rolls of thin stainless cable . . . No wonder Porks had hit the ceiling. It was indeed a truckload.

"What in the world is all this for?"

"Oh, just in case."

I remembered our conversation in Flushing station after the test run. "You're not planning to start dismantling the super-structure by any chance?"

"Of course not. It's just that the ship is heading into bad weather, we don't know what to expect, so—"

"So what?"

"It seemed prudent to bring along some stores for emergency repairs. We'll be thousands of miles from the nearest port."

"Never more than a hundred, and you're cluttering up the ship with all this stuff."

"I know we're not likely to need any of it, but I checked with the head office and they gave their okay."

It all sounded pretty shifty to me and I was about to take him on when the door opened and Fransen came in. "Ask *him!*" B.B. cried. "He'll tell you Arnold Kwel knows about it!"

"Okay, I'll discuss it with him, but chances are we may have to leave half your junk behind."

"Junk!" he said bitterly. "How's that for gratitude? Sailors!" He slammed himself out.

"What's that about?" Fransen asked.

"The truckload of stuff he brought on board. It's driving my chief around the bend; it all ended up in his workshop."

Fransen shrugged. "Find room for it someplace else."

"But what does he *need* it for? What's he planning to do with radio transmitters, rolls of tarpaulin—"

"Harinxma, it's none of your business. Let the man do his job, dammit."

"It *is* my job! I want to know what—"

"No! It's *not* your job to stick your nose in every goddam thing! You're charged with wet-nursing Captain Cho and that's *it*. Now, I've spoken to your staff—"

"So I gather."

"But I'm leaving Captain Cho to you. You tell him; I've never exchanged more than two words with the man."

"Gee, thanks. What do I say to him? 'Sorry, but I'm hijacking your ship'? I have to talk to Mr. Chung about this—"

"Dammit, Harinxma, stop fussing about Chung! He's *my* department. Now, about tonight—"

"Why should I be the one to talk to Captain Cho? You represent the owner, I'm just an employee."

He gave me an exasperated look. "Some employee! Look: just tell him that you're staying on in your present function to help him through the Forties."

"And that we're planning to crash-test his ship on the way?"

"He'll find that out in due course. No need to bring it up now."

"Fransen, I think all this should come from Mr. Chung."

He shook his head and sighed. "You didn't take in one word of what I told you at the hotel, did you?"

"About his wanting to scuttle the ship? That's nonsense."

"Harinxma, old boy, you may steamroller your staff, young Cho, anyone you like, but you're not going to steamroller *me*. I represent the owner, and I tell you to go and tell Captain Cho. That's all there is to it."

"You're pulling rank on me?"

"I sure as hell am! Jesus, it's like having a bull on a leash! Now, about your departure—"

"You'll have to take Slobkous with you."

"I know. Now will you *listen* to me?"

"Later," I said, tired of him. "I'll go and see Cho now."

I left him heading for the icebox, shaking his head.

5

When I opened the door after he had called "Come in!" I found Cho sitting up in bed, smoking his pipe, reading his little red book. The air was heavy with the sweet scent of alien tobacco; suddenly a memory stirred in the back of my mind and the thought occurred to me that this sickly-sweet smoke might not be perfumed tobacco, but opium. It would explain a lot of things.

"Captain," I started, "has Captain Fransen been to see you yet?"

His eyes narrowed. "No."

"In that case, I'd better tell you. The Dutch company that runs the shore service has decided that the skeleton crew will stay on board to see you and your staff through both the Atlantic and the Pacific Forties, as far as Talcahuano. Mate Slobkous is about to leave, so it'll be you and I who have to run the show. I hope that's agreeable to you?"

I could be imagining it, but, despite its protective immobility, his face seemed to take on an expression of melancholy. Suddenly I felt sorry for him. There he was, a young, ambitious captain, Chung's protégé, full of promise, and somehow it had all crumbled to nothing: golden future, self-confidence, faith. For a few moments he sat there with his little red book and his pipe, an image of defeat; then he rallied, stared at me with his small, dark eyes in stonewalling defiance and said, "I have no instructions from Mr. Chung to that effect."

"Captain Fransen is Mr. Chung's representative. I see no reason why we should go over his head. So, you and I should get together and decide what measures to take as we enter the Forties."

"You take all measures you want, Commodore," he said. "I want specific instructions from Mr. Chung that you people must stay on board and run the ship."

There was only one way to handle this. "Captain, I'm not planning to advertise it, but you know as well as I do that you're not capable of taking this ship and this tow through the storm belt. You still have a lot to learn, and learn, I promise you, you will in the coming weeks. Once we start hitting the gales, it's going to be a circus with that windjammer behind us. Now, why don't we talk it through and discuss what needs to be done before it starts to blow?"

He didn't buy it. He stared at me stone-faced and said, "No. You captured this ship. I will compose telegram to Mr. Chung that I am prisoner on board."

This was ridiculous. "For God's sake, Captain," I said, "don't be childish! Nobody is keeping you prisoner. I *need* you on the bridge, and you need me. You can't sail this dry dock and this tender ship under gale conditions any more than you could that destroyer you lost in the Sea of Japan. So, stop striking attitudes. Let's go to the bridge, take a look at the charts and prepare for the circus to come. Let's do it now."

I probably shouldn't have mentioned the destroyer, for he sat there staring at me with a look of puzzlement, presumably trying to work out where I could have picked up that information. Then he rallied. "Commodore, I will not leave cabin until I have instruction from Mr. Chung himself. If you sail before I have received instruction, I consider myself prisoner."

However grudgingly, I had to admire him for his stand. If I had been in his shoes, I probably would have done the same. He was an odd little bastard, but somewhere there was a core of steel. "Tell you what," I said, "you send a telegram to Mr. Chung, and so will I. I'm the advisor, and my advice will be that you are not competent to take this ship and this tow through the Forties. Let's wait and see what he says."

I got up to do it. Then, alas, he caved in. As I went to open the door, he said behind me, "Commodore . . ."

I turned around to face him, and there was that melancholy look again on his small, lineless face, the sadness of defeat in his dark eyes. "If those is Mr. Chung's instructions to Captain Fransen, I will accept. But Captain Fransen must tell me face in face."

"I'll tell him that."

I left him to confront his moment of truth in private, and made my way back to my quarters. I hadn't told him that we were going to crash-test Mr. Chung's ship in the storm belt, nor that Mr. Chung would be mad as hell when he discovered that a ninety-year-old blind man had been running rings around him. But Cho's defiance, brief though it was, had brought about my own moment of truth. I would not join in Kwel's and Fransen's shabby subterfuge. I had a contract with Mr. Chung, I owed him the truth. If he hit the ceiling, so be it.

I expected to find Fransen in my dayroom, but he had left. I went to my desk and composed a cable, which would have to be sent via a shore station as regulations prohibited our transmitting telegrams with our own equipment while in port. I made two copies, one to be sent to Kao Hsiung and one to Brussels, hoping that one of them would reach him before we were due to sail.

IN VIEW OF INEXPERIENCE OF STAFF AND CAPTAIN AS DEMONSTRATED

DURING ATLANTIC CROSSING, I JUDGE IT ESSENTIAL TO WELLBEING OF
VESSEL AND CREW THAT SELF AND DUTCH STAFF REMAIN ON BOARD
THROUGH BOTH STORM BELTS TO TALCAHUANO STOP FULL REPORT IN
MAIL STOP WILL HOLD DEPARTURE UNTIL REPLY RECEIVED SIGNED
MARTINUS HARINXMA COMMODORE END.

6

I sweated through five increasingly tense hours that afternoon,
procrastinating to the point of sabotaging our departure; finally
the answer was delivered by a youth in a bumboat. It was addressed to MASTER TUGBOAT ISABEL KWEL and therefore taken to
Captain Cho before I could intercept it.

I found him on his bunk, as always, telegram in hand. He
looked stunned; I knew the answer before he handed it to me.

DEAR COMMODORE HARINXMA, APPRECIATE YOUR FRANKNESS AND AM
IN TOTAL AGREEMENT PLEASE ACCEPT FULL FACTUAL COMMAND
THROUGH TALCAHUANO BON VOYAGE GRATEFULLY, CHARLIE S. CHUNG.

"Well," I said, "that clears the air. Now let's go to the bridge."

He set his jaw. "No. If I am not fit to command, I wish no part
of it."

"Cho," I said in what was intended to be a warm, fatherly
tone, "don't be an ass. We've all had to learn. Why cut off your
nose to spite your face?"

I saw from the look he gave me that he didn't know the
expression and that it spooked him. He clamped his pipe between
his teeth and picked up his little red book, as clear a signal as if he
had bared his buttocks at me. Well, so be it. I had other things
to do.

Fransen, whose return I had not been looking forward to,
seemed morose when he entered my dayroom an hour before
departure. "Mind if I help myself?"

"Be my guest."

He poured himself a stiff one from the icebox. "Those
mother-fuckers at the Health Department refuse to clear the
Chinks without individual checkups and tests, at fifty bucks a
piece. That means I'll have to go through the whole mating dance
again with the golliwogs in Punta. Want a shot?"

"No thanks. By the way, I think you should know that I had an exchange of telegrams with Mr. Chung."

He stopped pouring and stared at me. "You crazy, crazy bastard," he said calmly.

"Here, read this." I handed him a copy of my telegram and Chung's reply.

He read them carefully, folded them and put them inside his black notebook. Then, to my surprise, he grinned. "Good work, Harinxma. The old man will be pleased."

"He will?"

"So should you be. If ever you wanted proof that the murderous little Chink was counting on Cho to scuttle the ship, here it is."

I gazed at him in disbelief. "Run that past me again, will you?"

"Did you expect him to say, 'No, dammit, get off my ship, you old busybody'? In that case, if anything happened to the ship, there would be one expert witness ashore ready to testify that Mr. Chung had been warned, by cable and written report, and that the warning was ignored. It would amount to proof of criminal intent. Excellent! You're a chip off the old man's block, apart from providing work for unemployed assassins."

"Now, what's *that* about?"

"How do you think grateful Charlie will feel toward you now you've loused up his game, at least as far as Talca? I'd watch my back from now on while you're ashore. You wouldn't be the first to be rubbed out by the Chinese Mafia."

I was about to voice a protest, but there is no arguing with fanatics. To him, Chung's evil intent had obviously become an article of faith. *Credo quia absurdum:* I believe *because* it is absurd. There was no reasoning with that.

I said, "So now everybody's happy. *Gesundheit,*" and started to talk about more mundane matters, like the members of the Health Department with the Oedipus complex who had refused to clear our Chinese.

7

In the thick of our pre-departure flurry, with harbor tugs churning alongside, a pilot cutter banging against our flank in the wash of their propellers and the aft deck full of Chinese in the harsh light of the floods, a bumboat wormed its way to a free parking space alongside and Fransen, who had ordered it, got ready to leave. When he was about to go and collect Slobkous, I asked him to have a look at B.B.'s list, just to give him something to do while I went to say goodbye to poor old Slobbo.

When I got to the cabin, I saw that the bosun had shaved him and combed his hair with the parting in the middle. He also must have filled him up with black coffee and aspirin, for Slobkous was up and about and looked quite presentable, despite the phony suntan which was in effect hepatitis yellow. It couldn't be long now before his liver packed up, the alcoholic's suicide.

"Well, old fellow," I said with forced good cheer, "I'm sorry to see you go. I could have used you in the Forties."

He had been looking at me bleakly, with the absent-mindedness of his condition, but this brought him around in a hurry. "*What* did you say? You're staying on?"

"As far as Talcahuano. Young Captain Cho can't hack it alone."

He became quite agitated. "Don't do it, Harinxma," he whispered, grabbing my lapels, his face close to mine, "don't do it, for God's sake! It'll cost you your life!" Vodka might be scentless, but not in the quantities he had ingested; his breath smelled like last night's stag party.

I tried to disengage myself. "Kind of you to worry, Slobkous, but I'll be all right. Number One is on the ball now, and so is Number Two. And it isn't the storm season yet; we may sneak through without a blow."

He sighed; I couldn't help turning my face away. Then he whispered, "Don't tell anyone I told you. Swear it!"

"Told me what?"

"Swear it! Swear that you won't ever let on you know! The only one who could have told you is me."

"What *are* you talking about?"

He glanced at the door. "Spooks was killed." His whisper was almost inaudible.

"I know."

"No, no! Not by a mugger. Killed on purpose." He brought his face so close to mine that I could see the burst veins in the yellow of his eyes. "He was *murdered!*"

Poor sod, he might look presentable and *compos mentis,* but he still had the willies. "Look, Slobkous, I know there are rumors. Someone else told me under oath of secrecy that Spooks had committed suicide. I think it's best if we just let him rest in peace."

[201]

He was so close now that he looked from one of my eyes to the other. His breath stank like death; it was hard not to back away. "He was murdered because of the report," he whispered.

"What report?"

"On the ship! Giving it all away: the rolling, the—"

"Where is it?"

"Huh?"

"That report, where is it?"

"They took it!"

"Who's 'they'?"

"The ones who murdered him!"

"But how? When?"

"He was on his way to mail it. He'd hidden it inside his wife's portrait. The board had warned him they would be lying in wait for him, that he ran a grave danger—"

"Board?"

He took a breath to reply, then footsteps sounded outside. "Ouija board . . ." he whispered, stepping back.

He patted his hair into place and looked at the door like a man expecting his executioner. As the door opened, he whispered quickly, "Ask it yourself . . ."

It was Fransen, breezy with mateyness about as convincing as a loan shark's commercial during the *Late Late Show*. "Well, are we ready for the trip home? You look good, Slobbo. You'll pass."

"Pass what?" the beaten man asked wearily. "The hangman's weigh-in?"

"Don't be gloomy," Fransen sparkled, slapping his shoulder with such enthusiasm that it nearly felled him. "You'll see: once we're on our way, you'll enjoy it. Splendid airline, Varig. Lots of free booze."

"That'll be a real help," I said.

Fransen turned on me with startling anger. "You stay out of this, Harinxma! Goddammit, you've made enough waves as it is!"

A tart repartee came to mind; but I had no death wish that compelled me to grapple with him. He was bad news. "All right, Slobkous, old chap"—my cheerfulness didn't sound convincing either—"take care, now. Godspeed and happy flying."

He gave me a bleary look that, I knew, was intended to be full of meaning. Luckily for him, his eyes were so hangdog and shot with burst veins that the look was that of a spaniel turned down for a walk. I hated to think what third degree his genial traveling companion would have subjected him to if he had smelled a rat. As it was, he said, "All aboard, Slobbo! Off you go," and ushered his captive into the corridor.

I went to the port wing of the bridge to watch Slobkous being lowered into the bumboat and, to coin a phrase, spirited away. Fransen waved at me; I waved back, and there went poor Slobbo, off in a bumboat pitching and rolling among the harbor tugs and the police launches, with his ghosts and his alcoholic delusions. Haversma murdered? I was ready to take the modern world of competition seriously, but not to the point where I accepted that shipowners, of whichever nationality, hired assassins to kill tugboat captains who wrote unfavorable reports on one of their ships.

The *Isabel*, with *Agnes* in tow, sailed at midnight.

8

Yet, after the tow had been settled on its course and I had started the paying out of the long hawser for the two thousand miles to the Strait of Magellan, the specter of hired assassins with James Bond grapple irons disturbed my peace during the dark early-morning hour after I came off watch. It was nonsense, of course, but so are most nightmares.

Old Slobbo's alcoholic fairytale about Spooks Haversma's portrait of his wife with the secret report inside clearly came straight out of the wallpaper; but as I took clean pajamas out of the chest in my bedroom, I spotted the planchette and took it out to have a look at it.

It was no more than a small piece of plywood, a pointer on a caster. The board itself, which had lain folded up at the bottom of the drawer ever since I had come on board in Rotterdam, looked garish and phony when I pulled it out and opened it up. Two half-circles of letters, one from A to M and the other N to Z, a row of figures from one to zero, with underneath the word GOODBYE. In the top lefthand corner a smiling full moon and the word YES, in the other a pouting new moon and the word NO. A Victorian parlor game—that was how we had treated it in May 1944, mates and skippers of five ocean-going tugs tied up alongside each other in Shadwell Basin, London, waiting for D-Day. Every night we had gathered in my messroom, which was the largest, to while away the hours playing chess and checkers and Monopoly, cross-eyed with boredom, our stomachs sour with pre-invasion jitters, until one of us, I couldn't remember who, produced a Ouija board like this one. We started to fool around with it; for a few minutes the board spelled out moronic answers to our flippant questions. Then, suddenly, the hand that guided the planchette became guided itself and the pointer, moving at high speed, spelled out: HELP ME HELP ME HELP ME WHERE AM I BOYS WHERE AM I. In the sudden silence, Harmsen off the *Amalia* asked, 'Who are you?' The pointer, flashing from letter to letter at a frantic speed, spelled out: BULLFROG BULLFROG THIS IS BULLY WHERE AM I BOYS PLEASE GODDAMMIT HELP ME WHERE AM I THIS IS BUL—

'Enough already,' Harmsen said, pulling the board away and closing it. 'Let's go back to Monopoly.'

Nobody protested, for Bullfrog, or Bully, had been Harmsen's Number One, killed off Orford Ness by a strafing Messerschmitt just a week before.

Did I want to start fooling with all this now? God only knew what macabre nonsense the board would start to spout this time.

I closed the board as Harmsen had done, stuffed it together with the planchette back in the drawer with the pajamas and the socks, and went to bed. I no longer worried about hired assassins; I dozed off with Louis curled up between my ankles, relishing the life given back to the ship by the gentle swell of the South Atlantic in the summer night.

When I returned to the bridge a few hours later, dawn was breaking like a rose over the immensity of the ocean. We were well out in the open and had finished spinning out our long hawser like a black spider of the sea. Godspeed and happy sailing, gentlemen! We had a brief Happy Hour to celebrate the smooth departure, then the rhythm of shipboard life took hold as Whittier, bless his jolly soul, struck four twins on the ship's bell, starting another chapter in the brief, troubled life of the *Isabel Kwel.*

Chapter Eight

1

During the first week or so after Rio the weather remained beautiful and warm, the sky clear, the wind light and pleasantly cooling. But the moment we crossed the fortieth parallel and lost the Brazil current, which had been pushing us along at an added eighteen miles per day, we began to battle the Falkland current, which put us back twenty-four miles per day, and the trouble started.

It began with a beam swell that came heaving in from the southeast, rapidly growing in size until, for the first time on this voyage, I was forced to break the cycle of the *Isabel*'s rolling with the thrusters.

After feeling the change in vibration, B.B. came up from the hospital in a flash, cried, "Beautiful!" and hurried back to collect his measuring devices, which he proceeded to take up to the flying bridge. After a few minutes I saw Porks join him there.

During the past week those two had become fast friends, despite their initial run-in about the stores in the workshop. They were like boys in their enthusiastic hunt for the *Isabel*'s deadly secret; on a few occasions, on my way to the messroom, I had noticed them huddled together in the officers' dayroom, poring over blueprints, printouts and a hefty volume of Xeroxed pages which turned out to contain the ship's specifications. Porks had become young B.B.'s right hand, setting up his equipment on the bridge, finding outlets into which to plug various pieces of esoteric machinery; after hours upon hours of whispered conferences and endless drawings of electrical circuits, all of which were discarded, B.B. ended up installed for action: on a stool, lashed to the console of the starboard aft engine telegraph, surrounded by toys anchored to the bridge deck with adhesive tape. To see him sit there, bare-legged, slippered, his hair a boyish tangle, holding what looked like a toggle switch connected by a cable to an improvised outlet in the wheelhouse wall, made me shake my head; he and Porks were, in those moments, about twelve years old. Their main area of interest was the flying bridge, especially the foot of the Paradise tree, where I spotted them a few times during the first days. Each session in the wheelhouse was preceded by a visit to the flying bridge; heaven knew what crucial part of the treasure hunt they had found there.

This time they came down after twenty minutes and set up B.B.'s clock shop, complete with ticking counters taped to the deck and the toggle switch, clutched for dear life by a tense B.B., in the corner of the wheelhouse. Porks hovered over him, watching dials and whispering readings into his ear. After a quarter of an hour B.B. muttered, disgruntled, "Too damn tame!" But even so he started to cipher, topee on his nose, his beet-red sunburned legs propped up on another stool.

A few days later, after we passed Punta Pozos, the barometer began to fall. According to the weather charts produced by the machine in Harlingen's radio shop, a disturbance was coming from the southeastern quarter. This was unusual; I had been hugging the coast not only to avoid the thirty-seven-mile-a-day adverse current farther out to sea, but also to seek shelter from prevailing westerly gales. If we were hit by high winds and seas from the southeasterly quadrant, there was no way I could keep the dock from being blown into the Bay de los Nodales, an unhealthy place to be in and impossible to get out of.

So I went to put Captain Cho into the picture and to discuss with him the only way to safeguard both the ship and old *Agnes:* to take the runners off the dry dock and sink it.

When I told him that, he looked at me goggle-eyed, momentarily dropping his carefully studied mask of hostile superiority. "*Sink* the dock?"

"It's a standard operation, Captain," I explained. "Submerging it is not going to endanger it. Docks are meant to be submerged. That's the only way to keep it stationary; if we leave it to float, it will end up on the rocks with that windage."

"But—but shouldn't we ask Mr. Chung first?"

"Captain, we have no choice. We're too close to the coast, and we had better start now. Gales in this region have a tendency to jump you before you see them coming. After the gale we'll have to pump the water out of the dock again and that's a pain in the neck, but we have no choice. Also, I intend to cast off. I want this ship to ride out the gale on her own, not with her ass tied down."

"But what about the yacht?"

[206]

"We'll cut her loose and let her float free, attached to the dock with a hawser which will keep her headed into the seas."

"But what if she breaks loose?"

"We'll give her a sheet anchor." I said that only to pacify him; realistically, if there were to be a gale and the yacht broke loose from the dock, she would almost certainly end up as jetsam among the rocks and the gulls on the beach of the Bay de los Nodales. But that was the name of the game, and no doubt she was well insured.

His jaw set, his face back in its imperial scowl, he stated, "I cannot permit that. I forbid you to put the yacht at risk. I command you to ride out the gale with the dry dock afloat."

So far I had been careful not to throw my weight around more than was strictly necessary; this time I said, as pleasantly as I knew how, "Captain, all I can say is: enter your protest in the ship's log. Now, if you don't mind, I'd like to get cracking."

I left and went to the bridge, where I raised Harakiri on the walkie-talkie.

The crackly voice responded, "This is *Agnes*, this is *Agnes*, do you read?"

"Good evening, *Agnes*, this is *Isabel*, this is *Isabel*. I'm going to submerge you and cut you loose. We have a full gale threatening from the southeast. I want you down and ready to ride it out before it gets dark. Over."

There was a silence full of static, then the voice crackled, "I read you, *Isabel*. What about the yacht?"

"I suggest you start cutting the supports and stream her, two lines and a bridle, to ride out the gale. You might also prepare a sheet anchor with a piece of number-zero sailcloth, if you have such a thing, otherwise a weighted hatch made up of two-by-fours—you know what to do. Do you read?"

"Affirmative, *Isabel*. Glad you're ordering this in good time. I'd hate to be marooned on this pig's bladder close to the coast. Over."

"Go ahead, *Agnes*. Let me know when you and your runners are ready to be picked up. I'll have a boat standing by, over."

"Roger, *Isabel*. Give me a couple of hours. Over and out."

"Over and out."

I took the wheel from Whittier, hove to into the freshening

wind, put the engine on Dead Slow to maintain steerage and paged the bosun on the tannoy.

A few minutes later he came running; I told him to prepare a boat and then go to the aft deck, as I was about to start to winch in the hawser. Through my binoculars I spotted runners scurrying on the walls of the dry dock, opening valves and air vents. On the dock floor a few of them were dragging acetylene tanks about; welding cutters started to flicker in the gathering dusk.

I was watching the stretcher being winched in on one of the television screens when the bosun turned up in a huff. "Dammit, Ome, I can't get those Chinks to prepare the boat! They refuse!"

"What's that?"

"The men refuse to prepare a boat! It's mutiny!"

I went to the aft window to have a look; the men on watch were standing about on the boat deck, looking surly and defiant.

"Number One," I asked, "what's going on? What's the matter with those men?"

Before he could answer, Hopla piped up; I hadn't noticed him coming to the bridge with coffee. "They do not want dogs here," he cried dramatically. "No room for pregnant dogs! Wah!" Before I realized what he was up to, he blew snot onto the deck.

"Damn you!" I cried. "Get that cleaned up! I forbade you to do that!"

Number One started to talk to him in Chinese; then the telephone on the chart desk shrilled. It was Harlingen. "Skipper? We've got the dock on the blower. Would you take it?"

"Thanks, Harlingen." I picked up the walkie-talkie. "Yes, Harakiri?"

"We have a problem, Harinxma," the crackling voice said. "My Chinks refuse to leave the yacht. Over."

"Did they give a reason?"

"They don't want to join your crew. Over."

"That yacht is a derelict! If we get the kind of seas I expect, she's not going to stay in one piece. I won't allow them to risk their lives, so tell them to get ready. I'm sending a boat. Over."

"They're an ornery bunch, Harinxma. If they don't come, it won't be because I haven't tried. Over."

"How are you getting along?"

"Another hour or so and we'll have fifteen feet left. I'll be the last one off and close the valves and the vents. Over."

"What's the yacht doing?"

[208]

"Standing free now; the moment it has flotation, it'll be off and running. Over."

"Sheet anchor ready?"

"Affirmative. Triangular sheet of number-one tarpaulin, weighted, rigged up and ready to go. Over."

"Bridle in place?"

"Affirmative."

"All right. Expect a boat. Tell your men to stand by on the lee side. Over and out."

Five minutes later he was back on the blower. "*Agnes* calling *Isabel*, *Agnes* calling *Isabel*. Do you read?"

"Yes, Harakiri. What's up?"

"I've had an argument with the mandur, now he's turning ugly. They're staying aboard the yacht, period. Over."

"But her deck may stove in if she's broached!"

"I told them that, but they won't listen. They refuse to join the Chinks on the tug. What do I do now?" There was a silence while he waited for my answer, then the scratchy voice repeated, "*Isabel*, do you read?"

"Yes, I read. Hold everything. I'm coming over myself. Over and out."

I switched off the walkie-talkie, turned to put it down and found Number One and the bosun staring at me. "You can't *do* that, Ome!" the bosun cried. "You can't go out there! Look at those seas!"

"I have no choice, Bosun. I must convince those idiots that they're about to commit suicide."

"But, man, you . . . you . . . Send someone else! Send *him!*" He pointed at Cho.

I turned to Cho. "Think you could convince them, Captain?"

The Chinese quickly shook his head.

"Well, I'm going to give it a try."

As I turned, I saw Hopla scurry off the bridge and wondered why; then it came to me. I picked up the walkie-talkie. "*Isabel* to *Agnes*. *Isabel* to *Agnes*."

"*Agnes* here, I read you, over."

"Harakiri, does the mandur speak English or do I have to bring an interpreter?"

"You'd better. He and I communicate in sign language. Over."

"Thanks. Keep an eye open for the boat. I'll board on the lee side. Over and out." I turned to Cho. "I'd ask you to come, but I can't leave the ship without a captain. I'll take my steward. Bosun, you go to the boat while I corner Hopla."

I found him in my bathroom, backed into the corner. When he saw me, he cried, "No, Co'dore! No, no, not me! I cannot!"

"Why not? You translate for Ma Chang."

"Different language! I not understand!"

"Don't talk rubbish, Hopla."

"Dogs! Pregnant dogs!"

"Come along." I reached for him, but he climbed into the shower. I realized it was no use, and had no more time to spend on him. In half an hour the sea would be too rough; leaping onto a heaving dock from a plunging boat would end up with Ome in a cast. I picked up the phone and called the engine room; Porks answered. "Porks, can I see you for a moment on deck? I'm in a hurry."

"Coming."

I met him as he came up from the engine room, wiping his face with cotton waste. "Jesus, it's hot down there. How are we doing?"

"Everything's fine, only the runners won't leave the yacht. I can't allow that; when she starts riding out the gale, her old timbers won't stand up to the jerking of the towline. So, I'm going over there myself, but I need an interpreter. Do you think one of your officers—"

"You're going *where?!*" He looked at the sea, the half-submerged dock. "You're not going across in this weather? Let them drown! Let the bastards drown if they refuse to leave!"

"You can't be serious."

"Of course I am! If they refuse to leave the yacht, let them drown! You're not going to risk your neck and this ship to plead with those bastards not to commit suicide!"

I turned my back on him. On the boat deck the bosun was waiting for me. He said somberly, "No deal, Ome. None of the sods will come along. This is mutiny."

"Oh, for God's sake, Bosun!" The light was beginning to fade, the sea seemed angrier; I didn't want to be out there in the dark. "Come on, you and I'll go. We can handle this boat between us."

At first he looked doubtful, then the spirit of the occasion got to him. "Sure," he said. "Step right in, Ome. We'll show 'em." He leaned against the flank of the boat, his hands knitted in front of him for me to step up in. I heaved myself over the edge, grunting and huffing; he climbed inside with the ease of a gorilla.

"Can you lower us, Bosun?"

"No problem."

A voice beside the boat called, "May I come, Martinus?"

I looked over the edge and found B.B. standing there, holding fluttering oilskins, the back of his short-sleeved shirt bulging in the wind.

"Have you handled boats before?"

"Ever since I was a boy!"

"All right, hop in. Let's go, Bosun."

The bosun reached down and hauled him on board, then switched on the electric motor that worked the davits. Both Chinese mates came running belatedly.

"Okay, Bosun, start the engine."

"Not until we're in the water, Ome. These water-cooled deals heat up fast. It'll run, don't worry."

When the boat was down and the pulleys had been cast off, the seas seemed larger and angrier than they had looked from above. The wind was picking up; if I spent too much time on the dock, we would have a problem getting back; even now I needed all my strength to hang on to the gunnels. Maybe it *was* a bit crazy for me to attempt this. I was no longer the man I had been.

Agnes, as we approached, looked way down; but the yacht was not yet afloat even though the dock floor was awash. The boat swerved into the lee of the starboard wall like a roller-coaster; the swell was running high and fast—there *must* be a big blow on its way to generate this surge. The bosun maneuvered the boat in for a mooring; I told him and B.B. to stay where they were. Harakiri stood waiting for me in whipping oilskins, occasionally up to his calves in the water that came slopping down the length of the dock floor. He threw a line, which B.B. caught; then he pulled the boat in. I grabbed his outstretched hand the moment a surge brought me level with the dock floor. I should have put on boots; I had stepped out of my cozy little world of tame rat and canary straight into the wild blue yonder. Before I had found my balance on the dock floor, I was soaked up to my knees. "Let's go," I said manfully.

"Good of you to come!" Harakiri shouted into the wind. "Let's hurry! Going to be dark soon! Careful on this ladder! It's loose!"

[211]

When we reached the yacht, I saw that the companionway had been taken down. My heart in my mouth, I climbed the slippery Jacob's ladder against the flank of the yacht. The wind, funneled by the dock walls, tore at me; I felt I wasn't going to make it to the deck, I didn't have the strength. But I managed to get to the top somehow, was hauled over the rail and welcomed by staring Chinese faces. After living all these weeks in shipboard intimacy with my crew, I now saw the difference in their features. These men were members not only of a different community but of a different clan. I had thought I knew how the Chinese mind worked by now, but looking at the faces of these men made me realize I would have to start from scratch.

Harakiri joined me; I asked, "Where is the mandur?"

"In the lounge with his cronies."

The inside of the old yacht seemed to reek more pungently of toadstools than it had in Antwerp. Harakiri slid open a glass door; I stepped inside and found myself in a large solarium. A row of windows overlooked the foredeck of the yacht; the opposite wall was covered with a mural of defaced nudes, similar to the ones I had seen in Harakiri's stateroom. Lolling in broken-down lounge chairs with the innards hanging out and chaises-longues with gutted pillows were some black-pajamaed men; one of them got up and came over to us. I recognized the iron-faced mandur who had confronted me on the quayside in Rotterdam. He ignored my outstretched hand.

"You must leave this ship, Mandur. Your lives will be in danger unless you do. Do you understand what I'm saying?"

He gazed at me with the same pebble eyes as on the quayside in Rotterdam.

"Don't waste your breath," Harakiri muttered beside me. "He doesn't understand."

The temptation to leave them to their fate was strong. "Why do you refuse to come? Do you understand what I'm asking? Why?"

He stared at me. I was wasting my time. Then he went to the vandalized mural on the wall, pointed at an obscene twosome engaged in the act of sodomy, put his finger on the one bent over and said, "Ma Chang," with such contempt that, for the first time, I sensed the depth of the hatred these bizarre people must harbor for one another.

"Listen," I said. "Wind! Wind is coming: hoo, hoo! Waves:

whoosh, whoosh! This ship: glug-glug! If you stay on board, you're going to be dead, all of you." I pointed at him, then made a throat-slitting gesture. "So, come with me. Come." I went to the door, beckoning.

The mandur made a gesture as if he were ripping off a mask and nodded vigorously.

"What does he mean?" I asked.

"He means that if he went on board the tugboat, he would lose face. Well, it's his face or ours. Let's beat it, Harinxma."

I was overcome by anger. I had, somehow, managed to make myself understood by his compatriots on board the *Isabel* at least some of the time, so he had to understand the gist of what I was saying. "Friend," I said, "I understand that you and the people of the other island have a feud of long standing. I understand that you'd rather risk your life than lose face to them. But *I* am commander of this convoy. All souls under my command are my responsibility. If you don't come with me, you'll die. And if you die, *I* will lose face. Do you understand that?"

Behind my back, Harakiri said, "Come on!"

The cast-iron face remained implacable. He stared me down with those black pebbles, without recognition, without response.

"Very well," I said. "As you wish." I turned away, sick at heart. "Let's get out of here."

Outside, I shouted against the wind, "Can you finish lowering the dock and make it to the boat?"

"No problem! Hang on for another ten minutes, I'll close the vents! After that she'll go on filling until the air pressure puts a stop to it! Have we got ten minutes?"

I nodded, but didn't like it. Time for us to get back on board the *Isabel* with some visibility left was running out. Harakiri's presence in the boat would be a help; when they saw us return without any pregnant dogs, the crew might assist us by hoisting the boat back on board.

In the boat I found B.B. and the bosun, B.B. as green as a frog.

"Are you okay, Ome?" the bosun shouted over the sound of sea and wind.

"Yes, thank you!"

"Are they coming?"

"No!"

"Good riddance!" he yelled with conviction.

We waited in the restless boat while Harakiri clambered up

and down the walls of the dock with impressive agility. It was going down fast; despite the whistling and hooting of the wind, I heard the roar of air escaping through the vents overhead. Then the yacht started to move.

The bosun saw it first; I was watching Harakiri turning the horizontal wheel of a giant gauge. "Watch out!" the bosun yelled. "Here she comes!"

So she did. There were splashes of iron beams crashing into the water as the yacht, with groans of shifting iron, started to drift astern, her bowsprit scraping along the dock's starboard wall with a screeching sound, striking sparks. We cast off to get out of her way; from a distance we watched the old vessel float out of the dock, listing over starboard, dragging the hawser attached to her anchor chains. For a few moments it looked as if she would broach to; she rolled heavily, loose objects slid off her decks, doors slammed, windows reflected the sunset in brief orange flashes. Then the hawser sprang taut; the bridle was whisked out of the water and the old ship straightened out with her bow in the seas. She began to rise and pitch like a giant bird; she looked like a good sea ship, as long as she held together. I saw men on her foredeck working lines; then I heard a whistle over the roar of the wind; Harakiri beckoned to us from the top of the starboard wall. "Let's pick him up, Bosun!" I shouted.

We did, with difficulty; when Harakiri was in the boat, we set out toward the *Isabel* rearing and plunging in the distance, black diesel smoke whisked from her stacks. "Let's go and hit the booze!" Harakiri yelled. B.B. threw up over the edge.

Alongside the *Isabel*, Harakiri and the bosun managed to hook in the pulleys simultaneously and a few seconds later the boat was swinging above the water. The Chinese at the winches were on the ball; we were hauled home before the next roller came snorting by, as big as a bungalow.

"All right," I said when we were secure in the blocks, "let's get into some dry clothes and meet in my dayroom. This calls for a moment of relaxation before the gale hits."

Harakiri looked back at the yacht, now sheering behind the dock, streaked by bursts of spray. "Good luck to them, the crazies," he said.

As I passed the door to the main deck, I saw a small, huddled figure staring at me. I had never seen Ma Chang out on deck before, not since Antwerp. I stopped, concerned, to find out if she

[214]

was all right, why she was there now; but something in the way she stared at me made me change my mind.

We had a brief Happy Hour in the dayroom, then I took Hara-kiri down with us for supper. I discovered he never ate with his Chinese, but usually had something out of a can by himself. He seemed to enjoy the communal meal, but for some reason the crew was unusually silent. I took it to be Harakiri's presence until, when dessert came around, Ma Chang placed a new dish in front of me. It was half a canned pear with a little bit of white fluff on top; in it was stuck a thin black stick. Only when she lit it did I recognize it as incense. Pear with incense? I sat looking at it in dismay when, suddenly, there was a sound of hand-clapping. I looked up to find everyone applauding, grinning at me. Wellesley bellowed, "Woo, Omi!" Ma Chang stood in the doorway to her galley, clapping her hands, showing the gap in her teeth.

"What's going on, Harinxma?" Harakiri asked. "Is it your birthday?"

"No, it isn't," I replied. "I think they're just pleased to see me."

Pear with incense had its drawbacks, but it was the thought that counted.

2

A few hours later the full gale hit with the impact of a freight train. We had cast off from the dock and I was lying on my bunk for a catnap when the windows were lashed by the first bursts of spray. I had hoped that the old yacht wouldn't be subjected to a force-nine blow, but we seemed to be in for one.

I dressed, hopping about on one leg, grabbing hold of ward-robe and bunk to keep my footing. When I entered the wheel-house, the windows were opaque with spray. Night had fallen; when I peered through the revolving clearview disk, I saw, in the light of our for'ard floods, mottled black mountains combing to-ward us, crowned with phosphorescent foam. The low sky seemed to spew water; spray was whisked across the foredeck in horizontal sheets. The ship cleaved the combers with crunching blows, but her gyrations communicated joy rather than agony; she took the seas with ease. To the bosun, who was holding the wheel, I said, "Let me get the feel of her, Bosun." He stepped aside.

When I held her, I had the impression that she was in her element; she responded to the wheel without lurching or hesitation. It was as exhilarating an experience as the trial run with Bron had been.

"She takes it well, doesn't she?" I discovered B.B. was standing beside me. He still looked pale, but seemed to share the exuberance of the ship.

"Here," I said, "take her. You designed her, find out what she feels like in this weather."

He took the wheel. "What's the course?"

"Never mind. Just keep her headed into the seas."

It turned out he needed Whittier's orange crate.

"I gather you're beginning to like my ship," he said.

"I think she's a terrific sea ship. Just don't start her cycling."

"Let me get my instruments!" He handed back the wheel and hurried to the door.

Presently I passed the wheel to the bosun and went out onto the starboard wing to see how the dock and the yacht were doing. Oilskins snapping, lashed by spray and rain, I found it impossible to see what was going on in the dark beyond, so I went back inside and took Number One's place at the radar scanner. The dock was two oblong parallel echoes; the yacht, discernible only intermittently among the fluorescent ridges of the waves, seemed to have remained in place.

B.B. returned with his folding stool and attaché case and installed himself in the starboard aft corner. He opened his case; when it began to slide around on the deck, Harakiri put his foot inside the lid to hold it down while he applied the surgical tape. B.B. took out one instrument after another. Then Porks turned up. He appeared to be measuring list, pitch and speed of recovery; B.B., with some difficulty, made notes on a pad on his lap.

I asked Harakiri, "Did you give the mandur your walkie-talkie?"

"I did."

"Try to raise him."

He took the walkie-talkie from its wall case, flicked the switch and said, "*Queen of Persia*, this is the *Isabel*. *Queen of Persia*, this is the *Isabel*. Can you read?"

There was a crackling silence.

"He doesn't speak the lingo," Harakiri said. "Even if he'd switched the damn thing on, which I doubt, what good would it do?"

I called Number One over from the radar scanner. "Here, you try."

Number One started to talk Chinese into the walkie-talkie; there was no answer.

"Let's put the thing on 'Listen,' " I said. "Maybe he'll try to raise us."

At that moment we ran into a wave that seemed to stop the ship dead in her tracks with a shuddering crunch; a moment later the for'ard windows were hit by a whiplash of spray that sounded like buckshot. B.B. came scootering toward us on his stool; Porks and I caught him, Harakiri picked up his toggle switch.

Once back on his feet, B.B. was ecstatic. "This is invaluable, Martinus," he said. "Let's see if we can pinpoint the danger zone by making a few sweeps."

"Wait until this gale's over. I don't want to push our luck."

"But this is perfect!"

"Too rough, B.B."

"But we may never—"

"B.B., no!" I went to the phone and dialed the radio room, while he and Porks collected their toys, muttering.

"Radio, Harlingen."

"Harlingen, are you keeping up our bearings of the shore beacons to double-check the satellite input? I want to be sure we're not working our way into the Bay of Nodales."

"I'm doing that."

I put the phone down. "How's the yacht doing, Number One?"

He took a moment to detach himself from the radar scanner. "Come and look, please, Commodore. It seems— See for yourself."

I took his place and looked at the screen. Behind the two rectangular islands of the submerged dock the intermittent echo of the yacht, frequently obscured by the ridges of the waves, appeared to be sheering wildly.

"Harakiri! Take a look at this."

The runner captain peered down at the scanner for a long

time; then he said, "Looks to me as if one leg of the bridle's come loose."

"So she's hanging on by only one shackle?"

"It's belayed on an anchor chain. The shackle should stand up; the one that broke must have had a crack in it. One should be able to hold."

"Even when she's sheering like this?"

"I'd have liked to put in a stretcher, but I didn't have one."

"Those men on board must be pretty uncomfortable."

"You told them what the score was, Harinxma. It's their bed, they made it, they'll have to lie in it. Is it okay if I go below for a while? I'm not much good up here anyhow."

"Take the couch in my dayroom. I'd like to have you around, just in case."

"Let's face it, the only thing that can happen is that the other shackle breaks. In that case, there's nothing I can do. They'll be on their way to the angels."

"What about the sheet anchor? Won't that keep them headed into the seas if they break loose?"

"It may prolong the agony, but it won't hold in this wind. What's to leeward?"

"A reef, shoaled patches and a rocky beach. Wherever they end up, it's curtains, with this sea."

"Well, it won't be for want of trying on your part. Good watch, all." He did not sound as if worry about the fate of his runners would keep him awake.

Porks had gone down below; B.B. was making calculations in his corner; Number One was glued to the radar scanner; the bosun concentrated on the wheel. The wind and the seas seemed to be increasing in fury. There were now frequent crunches when the ship ran into the blank walls of huge waves; the whip-lashes of spray were continuous and drowned out all conversation. I charted the dock's position and ours every ten minutes; so far it seemed to remain stationary, maybe with a drift of less than one knot. I hoped the *Coastal Pilot* was right when it said: *Southeasterly winds bring strong but short-lived gales.*

Suddenly, Number One called out, "Commodore! Come here, please!"

I hurried to the radar scanner and peered down at the screen. The ridges of the waves now kept obscuring even the twin echoes of the walls of the dock. But behind them no speck arose, however briefly. The yacht's echo was gone.

Number One asked, "What do you think?"

"Maybe the seas are too high now for the echo to register, or maybe she's out of range. Put the scanner on forty miles."

The screen changed. The phosphorescent ridges of the waves ran closer together and became faint. The coast of the Bay of Nodales registered now: the rock towers on Punta Lobos, the mass of Punta Medanosa. The low islets Hiebres and Shag were occasionally obscured by what must be surf. Nowhere within the crescent of the coastline was there any sign of a ship. It might be that the distance was too far for it to register under present conditions, but the absence of the yacht's echo on either ring of the radar was ominous.

I looked up. "I'm afraid we've lost her."

Nobody appeared to be shocked, or even affected. The bosun said, gazing up at the compass, "They had it coming."

I made my way to the corner where B.B. sat ciphering, his stool lashed to the pedestal of the aft telegraph. "Seems we lost the yacht. Once she broke free of her hawser, that was it. This coast is full of rocks. They haven't got a chance."

"Well, you did all you could."

He continued his calculations.

3

I stayed on the bridge all night, occasionally dozing in a deck chair Hopla had lashed to the console with the thruster controls. From time to time I asked Number One—after the watch had changed, Number Two— if there was any sign of life on the radar. There was none. I slept fitfully, plagued by guilt. Should I have pleaded with Ma Chang to have herself ferried to the yacht and prostrate herself before the mandur of the runners, humiliate herself to prevail upon him to bring his men to safety? She might have done that, if there had been time for me to convince her before the seas had become too rough for the boat. But in my heart of hearts I knew that she would have refused, despite the friendship and mutual understanding that had grown between us.

By now there could no longer be any doubt: ten men were lost. The ancient yacht with its Tiffany lamps and obscene murals had foundered and was being pounded to flotsam by now on the rocks of the Bay de los Nodales. Once the surf was through with them, the ten bodies would be dismembered, their limbs strewn about the deserted beach for the gulls and the hermit crabs to feast on, leaving their bones to bleach in the sun.

But why? The question haunted me. Why had they deliberately sacrificed their lives to save face? Why had my crew, the men with whom I laughed and joshed and showered every day, to whom I was now tied by a bond of warmth, even rough tenderness, refused to lift a finger when it came to saving the lives of their compatriots on the yacht? It seemed barbaric, inhuman, to sacrifice ten men for the sake of some ancient feud. It had to be the essential difference between our cultures: their total disregard for individual human life. Maybe Mr. Chung shared the same lack of concern. Maybe Fransen's explanation of the mystery of the incompetent captain and the unemancipated crew was right after all.

All night long I fretted and grieved, like any captain who has lost members of his crew. It was like a parent losing a child. Captains may not grieve that long and that intensely, but we grieve, and blame ourselves, and search our memory with masochistic persistence for the exact point where we went wrong, where we might have forestalled whatever it was, where we should have seen it coming. I remembered from my wartime days the futile question as to the meaning of it all, the point of life, the reason for our being, the enigma of the rise and fall of our individual lives. A normally cynical MTB commander whom I had known when I was stationed in Dover once said to me, after a midnight raid during which he had lost two men, 'Each time I lose one, the Hound of Heaven is on my traces.' That night, in the Bay de los Nodales, the Hound was on my traces too. *I fled Him, down the nights and down the days; I fled Him, down the arches of the years; I fled Him, down the labyrinthine ways of my own mind; and in the midst of tears.*

Meanwhile the *Isabel* soared and plunged with sickening surges as the tremendous swell of the angry ocean lifted her to the sky and dropped her into the troughs. The wind lashed the

[220]

windows of the wheelhouse with whips of spray; spindrift smoked in spiraling clouds, white in the beams of the floods, green and red in those of the navigation lights. When a bleak sun finally rose through clouds like roiling smoke over an ocean in blind fury, I was exhausted with soul-searching and sour with age. I rose arthritically from my deck chair and looked out through the clearview disk at the scene of cosmic violence. It seemed, in the gray, smoking daybreak, that I had never seen such a wild and confused sea before. I went to the radar scanner, seeking refuge from the mindless violence outside in the green-shimmering order of man's technical triumph. The two islands of the dry dock were still there, though washed under continuously by racing mountain ridges of oceanic swell; there was no other echo, no ship, nothing but the ridges of the waves for miles around.

Around eleven the wind suddenly dropped. It was as if the elements were obeying a divine command. The hills of the swell went on heaving massively, one sliding range after the other, but spray no longer lashed the windows, no spirals of spindrift whirled about the laboring vessel. The wind ceased to whistle and shriek in the rigging; in that sudden stillness, like the miracle of creation, there sounded thin and fragile, but of an inexpressible beauty, the screeching of a bird.

I went out onto the port wing and there it was, planing over-head, white and beautiful, a seagull looking down at us. It seemed a messenger of grace, Noah's dove.

"Commodore!" It was Number Two.

"What is it?"

"An echo at ten miles, due west."

I went inside to check. At ten miles to the south-sou'west an echo flashed with each sweep. "Looks like a fair-sized vessel," I said. "Probably a Coast Guard cutter."

"I'll take a look," said Harakiri, who was now back on the bridge. "Where are the binoculars?"

"In the box."

He took them out onto the wing. Hopla came with coffee for the watch and a mug of Ma Chang's tea for me, followed by the bosun carrying a tray of sandwiches. After everybody had helped themselves, the bosun said, "Your cat's dinner's coming up, Ome."

Suddenly the door to the wheelhouse was rolled open and Harakiri hollered, "Harinxma! Come and have a look!"

I joined him outside; he handed me the binoculars. "There, on the horizon! Tell me what you make of it."

I had to readjust the binoculars before the image emerged of the inhospitable coastline of Argentina's most desolate region. Profiled against it—vaguely, blurred by haze—was a triangular sail like that of an Egyptian dhow. "What the devil is that?"

"I'll tell you what it is," Harakiri said, taking back the binoculars. "It's the fucking yacht."

"It's what?!"

"The yacht, I tell you! They must have *hoisted* the sheet anchor! She's under sail, heading our way."

If that was true, the ten dour men in their black pajamas would have done something worthy of Sinbad the Sailor.

The minutes ticked by. The triangular sail became clearer. Then the superstructure of the antique yacht rose from the horizon: a frilly extravaganza, a ship designed by Fabergé. There she came, rising and falling with the swell, her ungainly sail adding a note of panache. I was struck with admiration; then a sneering voice said behind me, "Dogs! Pregnant dogs!" and I heard a familiar sound. I whipped around and shouted, "Hopla, you're not a sailor, you're a *slob!* Clean up that mess!"

After he had scurried off, I set the *Isabel*'s foghorn roaring. It was an irresistible impulse—they must still be too far away to hear us. But a minute later a flare soared skyward from the yacht and burst into a shower of red sparks against the black backdrop of the Punta Medanosa.

"Well, well," Harakiri said beside me. "Now they're even setting off fireworks."

"Fancy that," I said.

4

My first impulse was to have myself ferried across to the yacht to congratulate the ten men who had pulled off this impressive feat, but the seas were too rough still and, what was more, B.B. was crowding me with his instruments and his eager, freckled face.

"We must test her now, Martinus! We must! We may never get another chance!" I was yearning for my bed, but I could see his point. So I called the engine room to warn Porks that we were about to do some extreme rolling, and that if he was planning to come up, he had better instruct Chief Liu. I sent Hopla down to the galley to tell Ma Chang to take her pots and pans off the stove and find herself a secure place until the rolling was over. When everything was set, I took the wheel myself, put the bosun at the thrusters and, for the first time since the gale started, let the ship's head fall away.

I thought I remembered how the *Isabel* could roll, but I was mistaken. I went through the same shock of disbelief I had gone through as she nosed her way out of Flushing. I had not approached anything like it in the trades; this time everyone on the bridge, including the bosun, was scared stiff when she finally moved into her suicidal cycle.

There is a particular feeling about a ship rolling out of control that is indescribable. The mind may not yet know she is in the process of turning over, but the gut does. Suddenly someone shrieked, "What's going on? What's happening? What are you doing? Stop that! Stop!" It was Captain Cho, clinging to the doorpost, eyes popping.

There was no mistaking the danger. At what felt like the last moment, I told the bosun to pull the handle of the bow thruster and kick her head off course.

B.B. shouted, "Again, Martinus! Let's have that again!"

"No, enough is enough."

"But I was just—"

The telephone shrilled.

"Bridge."

"Chief Liu here! It's madhouse! All tools came off wall!"

"The engines okay?"

"Engines fine, it's engineer! My Number Two got hit on head by flying wrench and has almost passed out. Could you ask Porks to come down?"

"Do you need help?"

"I could do with coffee, and my Number Two with glass of brandy."

"I'll send the steward."

"Thank you. Do not worry about us, we are doing okay. As long as this is end of it."

"It is. Keep me posted."

I put the phone down. "Porks, you'd better go to your shop. Number Two has been hit by a spanner."

Captain Cho came staggering toward me; the ship still rolled a fair bit. "I forbid you do this!" he shouted. "This is Mr. Chung's ship! I forbid!"

I suppose I should have handled it diplomatically, but after the night we had had, his outburst was the last straw. "Now you listen to me," I said, for once not worrying about his losing face. "You've been skulking in your cabin for most of this voyage, you've shown no interest in handling the ship or taking on any responsibility, I won't have you now suddenly throwing your weight around. I suggest you go back to your cabin and stay out of my hair."

He nearly had a fit. It was a Cho fit, so he turned into Lot's wife.

"I shall not forget this," he hissed.

"I hope you won't, for this is how she behaves when she rolls out of control."

He gave me a look of pure hatred, then zigzagged off.

"Ah, well," B.B. said, unsticking his toys from the bridge deck, "pretty inconclusive, but there'll be other opportunities before Talcahuano, I hope."

I said dourly, "I wouldn't be surprised."

He disappeared, taking his instruments with him. I was dead on my feet, but I had to make the rounds to find out how everyone had fared, and sent Hopla ahead with some brandy for the second engineer.

There was a lot of excitement in the crew's corridors; men stood together in clusters, gesticulating, imitating the tossing they had been subjected to. Ma Chang was unruffled, but then she had been warned what to expect; all she had lost was a jar of pickles. She laughed and poked me in the stomach—it looked as if she had enjoyed the excitement. The second engineer, when I got to him, was in less dramatic shape than Chief Liu had led me to believe. He had a sizable bump on his head where the wrench had got him, but the brandy probably did worse things to him than the wrench had.

When I finally reached my quarters, I found that the one who really needed soothing was Pete the canary. The cage must have whirled around like a spin drier. Kirschwasser in the drinking cup and some baby talk were a help. Then Louis leaped onto my shoulder. I could not produce any more tender loving care, I needed some myself, so I took him with me to the bedroom and fell asleep with him softly exploring my scalp.

5

The yacht slowly drew nearer to the *Isabel* during the afternoon; when I returned to the wheelhouse, it lay to at about three ships' lengths to starboard. Although there was still a fair swell running, I ordered the boat out and, despite the protestations of the bosun, had myself ferried across to the yacht together with Harakiri. We were swung aboard in a sling.

Dangling between sky and heaving sea with my heart in my mouth, I tended to agree with the bosun; but once I stood on the yacht's deck, I did something I had rarely done before: I embraced a man. And not just one; while I was at it, I hit all ten; one of them had to put down a hammer and get up from his knees for it. After a startled first reaction, they all responded in kind, even the cast-iron mandur, who took Harakiri and me on a guided tour of the deck and showed us the jury-rigged sail. It was a marvel of creative invention; not only had they lashed it professionally to the mainmast, they had even managed to create a boom by using the central spar of the awning on the aft deck. I wondered when and how they had been able to rig it up in such a professional manner; when the yacht broke loose from her starboard bridle, she had rolled like a barrel, broaching to at every third wave, before disappearing in the spume at the height of the gale. To bring in the sheet anchor—which they must have done, as I had seen it go overboard myself—meant risking broaching her altogether. Yet, under those catastrophic circumstances they had done a job that would have taken the senior class of a naval academy half a day to accomplish on firm ground. There could only be one conclusion: they were superlative sailors.

Afterward the mandur took us to the adult solarium, where we all sat down on the deck in a circle and went through an elaborate, oddly formal ceremony of passing cans of beer from one to the other. Each man took a polite sip, toasting me in the process; I toasted them back. All of this without a word, in front of the mural of staggering obscenity. The ship was lively, as the swell was still running fast and long, so we all sat swaying in unison, like monks at prayer. For some reason the whole thing brought tears to my eyes; it is a bewildering aspect of aging: suddenly you cry.

One of them brought in some sinister snacks on sticks that looked like worm-kebabs; I declined with a mute expression of regret. In order to prevent their losing face, I pointed at my stomach and violently nodded my head; they seemed to get the message, or maybe they forgave me in the general ambience of brotherhood. The beer turned out to have a kick like a mule. When I finally rose to leave, I was unsteady on my feet, as well as inclined to resume embracing; as I skated to the exit, I collided with the doorpost. I was helped by many hands into the sling that lowered me back into the bobbing boat below; I landed in an untidy heap at the bosun's feet. Harakiri yelled from above like a concerned parent, "Is he hurt?"

The bosun yelled back, "No! There's a God for drunks!" He heaved me into a sitting position and said, "Now you sit still, Ome, don't start leaping around! Man, you're lucky you didn't bash your skull in. You're one crazy old coot, do you know that?"

I forgave him and waved at the Chinese faces lined up at the rail; they waved back and shouted incomprehensible words between cupped hands.

I don't remember the crossing. At a given moment I found myself back in my bunk, being cradled with a sense of exquisite security, with Louis observing me from the shelf above me. I sang 'Be embraced, ye millions' from the final chorus of Beethoven's Ninth; it set Pete in the dayroom warbling the descant. Then I heard the bosun's voice saying, "Now you calm down, Ome. You're getting everybody upset. Go to sleep."

I obeyed, for he too was part of life, part of the yin of gloom, the yang of joy.

When I wakened, shaking like a leaf, it was dark. On my bedside table stood a tray with the three little bowls of Ma Chang's prison fare. Louis was curled up on my pillow; Pete was silent. The ship was silent too, apart from some secretive creaking and clanking as she slowly rolled in the tail end of the swell.

I looked at my alarm; it was ten o'clock. I drifted back into sleep with the happy thought that I knew where my children were, every single one of them: back under the wings of the hen.

6

We began raising the dock again the next morning. Still weary from my visit, I moved the *Isabel* alongside the submerged port wall; Porks and his Number Two were ferried across to the pumping shed to start the motor. But after the dousing the old engine had received, it was out of action, so we had to empty *Agnes* with our own equipment.

We towed across by boat our six-inch hose with bright orange floats, and Porks connected its coupling to the port bilge pipe. Then he and his Number Two were ferried back and he started our large-capacity pump, which proceeded to empty the dock at the rate of five hundred tons an hour. It would take us forty hours to bring it back to its original flotation.

The problem was what to do with the yacht. I discussed it with Harakiri on the walkie-talkie; he reported that his mandur was planning to sail it back between the walls of the dock while *Agnes* was still submerged. I decided against it; the swell, although it looked benign seen from the bridge, still had enough surge to slam the antique craft down onto the dock floor with her full weight, which might stove in her bottom and make offloading her in Punta Arenas a problem. I now trusted the seamanship of the Chinese runners sufficiently to have the yacht towed by the dock, this time with stretcher, double bridle and the heaviest shackles from our stores. If we were hit by another gale, it was likely to be from the west, which would take us out to sea instead of onto the rocks.

The weather had turned; as I looked at the sea now, the whole episode seemed like a bad dream. The sky was clear and pristine, as always after a big blow, the sea a glassy infinity of slowly heaving swell, as if breathing in its sleep. The *Isabel*, spewing a milky jet of water and foam, rolled lazily alongside the twin islands of the dry dock, which gradually rose as the water was pumped out. The yacht wallowed and walked to and fro behind

Agnes on a short leash; occasionally the runners adjusted her triangular sail to keep her from butting into the dock. On board the tug it was siesta time; I collapsed on the couch in my carpet slippers, vaguely aware of Louis climbing all over me and Pete cheeping at the beams of sunlight through the windows sweeping the wall with the dipping and rising of the ship. Happy Hour that day was well named; everyone was there except Cho and B.B., who, according to Porks, was ciphering in his hospital. I toasted our success with Alka-Seltzer. The next morning the ship's pumps finished bailing out the dock and I went to the bridge to move her into position to pick up the bridle. As there was still a fair amount of swell, it took some nifty footwork to avoid crashing into *Agnes.*

That evening we sailed into the night, still on the short hawser to give the dock momentum before paying out the full length. The yacht was streamed behind *Agnes;* now back to its normal height, the citadel looked forbidding with its rust-streaked ramparts, vermilion and orange in the glow of the setting sun. The yacht, lit up with lamps and lanterns, became part of the stars as darkness fell.

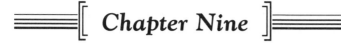

Chapter Nine

1

I had worried about the Strait of Magellan; I remembered it from the sixties as a tricky passage with fierce currents of up to eight knots with the tide, and sudden squalls of cyclone-like winds in the western section that could come whirling down the canyons at seventy-five miles an hour and up. The first two narrows on the Atlantic side I remembered as being veritable hell's gates.

As it turned out, Fransen showed his mettle as a professional this time. He turned up with a fleet of harbor tugs, five for the dock and one for the yacht, and took control of the operation. Four of the tugs sucked onto the flanks of the dry dock like leeches, two on each side, the fifth acted as tailholder, and so, with the *Isabel* roaring at full speed providing the momentum, the convoy churned through both narrows with the tugs providing steerage. It looked deceptively easy, as expert professional work can on occasion; we made Punta Arenas, the stark little harbor town at the tip of the continent, within forty-eight hours. There the yacht was moored and delivered to her owner, a man so rich, Fransen told me, that he collected antique yachts the way simple millionaires collected antique cars. The *Isabel* was boarded by a bevy of government officials from a launch.

They tried to persuade me to keep four of the tugboats as well as anchor the dock, for they were expecting the Panteonero, a local wind from the west-northwest which could reach force twelve on the Beaufort scale. I protested, on behalf of the mute Captain Cho moping in his corner, that there were adequate mooring buoys available to hold the dry dock even in a hurricane if I could make it a four-point mooring. Finally, thanks to Fransen's persuasive skills, we arrived at a compromise: I was allowed to make a four-point mooring on condition I lowered the dock ten feet to reduce its windage and kept the four tugs on standby in port. The maneuver was executed, the *Isabel* was permitted to tie up at the Muelle Fiscal; the yacht, moored at the old passenger wharf, was by then swarming with Customs officers.

Fransen took me, to meet the owner the moment we were cleared. We found him in the solarium of the yacht, surrounded by officials studying the murals with museumlike earnestness. He was blond, blue-eyed, in his thirties, wearing an open-necked shirt that revealed a gold chain and cross among the hair on his chest. "Hey," he said to Fransen when he saw us come in, "your Chinese won't let me stand them a drink! What do I do about this? I want to thank them for taking care of my ship!" Fransen suggested he give the runners money; the owner seemed disappointed. "I wanted to take them out on the town," he said, with the truculence of a spoiled child.

"Why don't you take *us*?" Fransen suggested shamelessly. "This, by the way, is Commodore Martinus Harinxma, senior advisor of the convoy. If anyone saved your ship, it was he. Harinxma, meet Mr. Salan."

"Oh," the owner said, with a marked lack of enthusiasm. "How do you do?"

I told him I was very well, thank you, but that when it came to going out on the town he should count me out, as I was on a very strict diet.

That perked him up. "Which one? Golden Door? Pritikin? F-Plan?"

"Ma Chang's," I replied.

"A Chinese diet? Oh, I want to know about that one! Please dine with me! There is an excellent restaurant in my hotel where they'll prepare any diet you wish! Please . . ." He moved toward the door. "Let's have a drink first, then dinner. I assure you, whatever your diet, they'll prepare it specially for you. I own the place."

I would have preferred to relax in my dayroom, read my mail and go to bed; I had been on my feet for the better part of the past forty-eight hours. But after a nudge from Fransen I gave in gracefully and the owner took us to his hotel, a yellow building I had spotted from the bay. There he tried to force some local hooch on me while waiting for the menu.

"I'm afraid that's out," I said. "I'll take a pot of weak Chinese tea."

"*Madre de Dios!* What *is* this diet?"

I explained, with as much reticence as courtesy allowed; it sent the man into raptures. He turned to call the waiter; as he did so, Fransen looked at me meaningfully, then nodded in the direction of a set of glass doors behind our host. It took me a moment to realize that he was directing my attention to the next room. At a small table sat Captain Cho; he was listening earnestly to a black-haired gentleman who sat with his back to us.

"Let's order," our host said.

While explaining to him why I was restricting myself to a salad and an apple, my mind was on the scene next door. Had Cho been to Punta Arenas before? How else could he know anyone here well enough to have a meal with him? Then the waiter brought them a second round of drinks and the other man turned. It was Chung.

The meal seemed endless. While Mr. Salan explained in stupefying detail what he was planning to do with the yacht, I asked myself why Fransen hadn't told me that Chung was here. And how had Cho heard? Harlingen would have alerted me if the information had come through the radio room. There must have been a letter to Cho from Chung that was delivered on arrival. Probably there was nothing to it; Cho was the captain, Chung the owner . . .

"Of course you can," I heard Fransen say. "They did the same with Rembrandt's *Night Watch:* lift it off the old canvas and transfer it to a new one. That mural would be an asset to any billiard room." It was time for me to retire.

I excused myself, promising Mr. Salan I would make sure to let him know next time I was in St. Moritz or Acapulco; I left him and Fransen ordering coffee and Tia Marias.

The moment I was outside I nearly took off like Peter Pan. I managed to remain grounded, but my cap started a life of its own, disappearing down a side street. There was a full gale blowing, howling down the street, which was empty even of cars. As I struggled downhill toward the harbor, the only living being I met was a cat trying to cross the street; screeching, it was whisked across diagonally when the Panteonero hit it. I had to admire the foresight of the officials who had insisted on my lowering the dock; had I not done so, it might now have been on its way to the eastern shore of the Paso Ancho, dragging four mooring buoys like Pekinese on leashes. Finally, I reached the ship, which lay straining at her moorings; propelled up the gangway, I stumbled down the corridor and into my dayroom. The canary was rioting in his cage, in a furious whistling competition with the wind in the rigging; Hopla, in one of the club chairs, was reading my mail. He leaped to his feet with the agility of a rhesus monkey and made a ritual gesture of dusting the envelopes, saying, "Co'dore, wind! Co'dore all right in wind? Where Co'dore cap?"

"Don't baby-talk me, Hopla," I said. "Next time at least have the courtesy to wait until I've read them first."

"Oh, that envelope open! I was just dusting—"

"Hopla," I said, "you're a good steward, but let's arrive at an understanding: your duties do not include dusting my mail. Now *beat it!*"

He did, at the same speed with which I had been propelled up the gangway.

I changed into my dressing gown, thinking about Chung. In this weather he was unlikely to turn up on board; probably he would call me to his hotel tomorrow for one of his little chats, as he had in Belgium. I was not looking forward to it; he was sure to carry on about the crash-testing.

There were three letters from Sylvia among the mail Fransen had brought on board. Before I had opened the first, there was a peremptory knock on my door and Fransen came in, hair tousled, tie wrapped around his neck. "Woof!" he said. "Some wind out there! Sorry to barge in, but you and I should have a talk. Am I interrupting?"

"Sit down, get yourself a drink. You know where it is."

"No, thanks. I won't stay long." He sprawled in a chair. "I've come to say Godspeed and happy sailing, for I'm off early tomorrow. You can handle the rest." He lit a cigarette and swallowed the smoke. "How about Chung turning up unannounced?"

"You didn't know he was coming?"

"No, sir. You'd think he might have told me, wouldn't you? After all, I'm his representative, or supposed to be. We're still running shore service for him. How did that little fart react to your crash-testing the ship?"

"The captain? He took it the way he takes everything from me: like a deaf mute, with murder in his eyes."

"Are you ready to receive Chung tomorrow? We have to agree on what you're going to say to him."

"I'll tell him the truth."

He threw up his hands. "Harinxma, for Chrissakes—"

"What do you think his captain has been telling him in the hotel?"

"Even so, don't rub it in. Don't tell him KITCO put you up to it. Say that your heart broke because the captain was patently incapable of handling the ship in bad weather and needed a demonstration. Explain you did it as an act of Christian charity."

"Do I give him a hymn book, with inscription?"

"Dammit, Harinxma, this is a delicate situation!"

"About as delicate as a hijacking, I'd say. Old Kwel had it all his own way, didn't he? Instead of crash-testing her at his own expense, he sold her to Chung and did it behind the man's back. Pretty neat screwing. Chung must be fit to be tied. Talk about losing face!"

"Okay, okay, point made. Now let's do some constructive thinking. How are we going to make sure that B.B. can get in one more test in the Pacific Forties? He says he needs more information, especially on large-wave action."

"Why make an issue of it? We'll just do it."

"That would create a bit of a problem if Cho told Chung about it."

I stood up. "Fransen, don't carry the sorrows of the world on your shoulders. Let the old man come up with an answer, and tell me tomorrow. I'm going to bed."

"Well, that's great," he said with heavy irony, crushing out his cigarette. "You'll have to whistle in the dark for that one, old cock. I'm leaving at six hundred hours tomorrow morning for Rotterdam." He struggled out of his chair. "I'm at the Hotel Cabo de Hornos if you need me. Otherwise, see you in Talca. Good night."

On his way to the door, Louis jumped him from the Bowditch; it gave rise to some strong language. "You should warn people about your damn rat! Let him try that on Chung when he turns up for a chat!"

"Louis, come here!" But Louis' feelings were hurt by the rough handling he had received; he jumped back onto the Bowditch and proceeded to stare at me, eyes wide with theatrical shock. He and I had come to know each other well; it was like living with a roommate in Naval College.

I started my mail by reading my daughter's letter.

Dear Dad

I hope this one reaches you before you fly home from Talcahuano. I am looking forward to your return, but are you? I have been lying awake recently, as Marijke had a bad cough, and found myself wondering what it must be like: going back to sea after so many years and then having to leave it all again. How are you going to handle that, Dad? Mummy never talks about that aspect of it, but I know it worries her. She must be asking herself whether you are going to be able to settle down among the retirees for a second time. Hard for both of you, I'd think.

My news is pretty downbeat. When Harry and I separated, I told myself that it was probably a passing phase, that sometime in the future we'd get back together. Now Anna Engelhart tells me he has a girlfriend with two kids of her own, and that they are talking marriage. When you first retired, did you too think that maybe it was just a passing phase? There are so many things you and I should talk about! We never talked, really; we were kind to each other and loving, but we never sat down to talk about real things, things only a father can talk about to his daughter, and vice versa. Like beginnings and endings, the growing awareness that each new beginning is the beginning of an end. Sorry to sound gloomy, but this is new to me: to have a father at sea at this ripe age. It is different. I used to dream about writing you this kind of letter when I was little, but it never worked, it was like talking to the stars. Now I do want to talk to the stars. But I also want us to talk, you and me, with our heads close together, going for the deepest, essential questions —the way I thought you sat and talked to the boys when they were young and they had done something and Mummy would say, 'Well, Jacob, there's Dad, by himself in the garden. Go tell him. Now!' And I would peek through the glass curtains of my bedroom to watch you both, almost sinful in my anticipation of his being taken to the woodshed, and then you would make him sit down opposite you instead and you two would talk and talk, heads close together, and I would be overcome by a terrible jealousy.

What is it like, Dad? What do you feel, what do you think about when you know you are on your last run and— But maybe I should not write this stuff. I love you, and I worry about you, and I am terrified of losing you, and I want us to have time, lots of time, and then I look out the window at the gray winter sky and feel so sad, so sad—

I found myself, again, overcome by the awareness she expressed: of the passing of time, of crucial moments wasted. I should be going to bed, but went to my desk, switched on the lamp, took a sheet of ship's stationery from the drawer and wrote,

My beloved Helen!

Your letter moved me deeply, as did the one I received in the Cape Verdes. Yet I responded to that one in the usual bland and superficially affectionate manner—habit, probably, or maybe I have reached an age where one no longer wants to be tested, one wants to be comfortable. For us to start, after so many years—in your case a lifetime—on a new kind of relationship is not a comfortable thing. I can't just respond by reeling out the usual platitudes, I either say, 'I loved your letter, keep it up; we'll talk when I get home,' or sit down, as I have done now, and set about responding in kind. I feel—(sorry! Louis just jumped onto the paper!) I feel that if you and I want to go after answers to the real questions, we must first establish what those questions are. I think I am in the process of doing that myself, ever since I had my blood pressure crisis in mid-Atlantic—

Suddenly I felt insecure. I hadn't told Sylvia about that. And was I ready for all this? To open Pandora's box?

I started on a new sheet.

My dear Helen.

I loved your letter, as I did the one I received in the Cape Verdes. Keep them up! We'll talk when I get home . . .

2

The next morning, when I was about to go ashore and already had my greatcoat on, there was a knock on the door. I shouted, "Come in!" and there was Mr. Chung: radiating bonhomie, eyes twinkling with good humor.

"Good morning, Commodore! How have you been? How was the trip from Rio?"

He caught me unawares; I certainly hadn't expected him to turn up wreathed in smiles.

"Good morning, Mr. Chung. Good to see you." I continued

[235]

recklessly, "I caught a glimpse of you last night at the hotel with Captain Cho. Fransen and I were having dinner there with the owner of the yacht."

"Ah," he said, "I wish you had made your presence known! We could have settled it last night, with Captain Cho present."

"Settled what, sir?"

"May I sit down?" He moved to the couch.

"Of course, please do. How about a drink?"

"Not now, Commodore. I won't be long, but there is something we should discuss here and now."

"I see." Well, here it came. I took off my coat and sat down to face him.

He smiled. "Commodore, how would you like to stay on as mentor to Captain Cho? Well, let's be precise: remain in your role of convoy commander *de facto* after Talcahuano?"

I gazed at him for what must have been several seconds. "Stay on to where?"

"Taiwan. After delivering the dry dock, this ship is to pick up a new tow for Kao Hsiung: a forty-thousand-ton liner that has been used as a prison by the Chilean Navy and sold to my company for scrap."

"Forty thousand tons?"

"She's big, but no problem for this ship. I presented the situation to Captain Cho, who does not feel qualified to take on an object of that size. Especially not since we're in mid-hurricane season in Polynesia. You'd be sailing with Pago Pago as your next oiling station."

He said it without a hint of guile, his eyes were like a baby's.

"I'll have to think that over, Mr. Chung."

"Of course. You have ten days before Talcahuano, plenty of time to think it over. There are a few details that may help you reach a decision. First, I'll pay you the same salary for the rest of the voyage, with a ten-percent bonus on arrival. And if it would amuse Mrs. Harinxma, she'll be welcome to sail part of the way with you—say, from Samoa to Taiwan. We'd pay for her air fare, of course, both ways." He smiled and rose. "Think it over, Commodore. Let me or Captain Fransen know your decision in Talcahuano. I have to leave for Santiago on the one-o'clock plane and go on to Brussels from there. By the way, let's keep this confidential until you have made up your mind. *Bon voyage.*"

I had hardly had a chance to take it in. "But what about

Captain Cho?" I asked as I followed him to the door. "Shouldn't he be replaced?"

He turned and for once did not smile. "Captain Cho, Commodore, will serve only to conform with the legal requirements. When it comes to sailing the ship, he will be a figurehead. He is happy with that arrangement, and so am I. Good day, Commodore."

"Good day, sir."

He slipped out, leaving me staring at the door.

3

When we left, early the next morning, it was strange to see the dry dock behind us without the yacht. *Agnes'* silhouette was different too. Two aluminum trailers had been welded to the top of the starboard wall, one for the runners and one for Harakiri; they looked flimsy on the ramparts of the old citadel.

As the convoy slowly made its way west, snow-capped mountains began to crowd in on us. The farther we proceeded, the narrower the channel became and the higher the rocky shores. It was a grim, desolate landscape with a strange beauty of its own. At nightfall we anchored in a chilly fjord that was already dark while the main channel was still lit by the setting sun.

The Chilean pilot lingered on the bridge; his cigarette glowed in the darkness as he stood staring through the for'ard window at the stage set of the dramatically lit narrows. We talked about Magellan and his handful of men who first made this passage in 1520. To sail through this icy bleakness was eerie now; doing so for the first time in the superstition-haunted sixteenth century must have been terrifying. He told me of strange experiences he had had in the Strait: visions of fifteenth-century galleons that emerged from the mist, men waving at him from the beach of a desolate little island, only to vanish when he put out a boat to pick them up. The Western Strait was an ideal location for ghost stories; I had a few of my own to tell.

Our last day was a voyage through the Ice Age. Glaciers descended to the blue-green water, a hazy sun occasionally appeared from behind the clouds. The tidal current was fierce;

whirling gusts came spiraling down into the canyons. When we entered the channel north of Isla Desolación, the wind howled, night was falling and the incoming tide nearly brought us to a standstill; by the time we reached Cape Pilar, it was pitch dark and the weather stormy. I had my hands full keeping ship and dock headed into wind and tide. I was too preoccupied for a gracious goodbye to the pilot, who was picked up by a launch which vanished amidst whorls of lashing rain, instantly swallowed up by the primeval darkness.

As soon as we came out of the lee of the cape, we met the Pacific graybeards: foam-mottled black waves, awesome in size. The slowly rising hills of water lifted the three-thousand-ton ship effortlessly to where the wind whistled and the rain streaked green and red through the beams of the navigation lights; they held her there for a moment, then sent her tobogganing down into the valley, where there was no wind, only the sound of rushing water, before lifting her to the crest of the next hill. Despite its size, the dry dock's lights disappeared in the valleys; I lengthened the hawser to a full mile to lessen the stress.

Once the *Isabel* was settled on her course, I handed the bridge to Number One. There had been no sign of Captain Cho since Punta Arenas; I had had to send Whittier down to get the master's signature on the pilot's chit. Normally, I would have sent for him, but after Chung's offer I had decided to forget the moody young man in his cabin altogether. Whether or not I decided to go on to Taiwan, I was through with Captain Cho.

When I entered my dayroom, I found Pete huddled on a perch in his swinging cage. Louis did not jump onto my shoulder from the Bowditch, but watched me apprehensively as I staggered about the cabin with the swell, from handhold to handhold, like a drunk. I lay down on my bed fully dressed, ready to return to the bridge if called.

The swell seemed to strain the entire body of the ship. The wainscoting creaked, the water in the cistern of the toilet sloshed, the door to the dayroom rattled as the propellers accelerated each time a giant wave lifted the stern to the surface. Sleep was out of the question; I lay there listening, waiting for the call from the bridge, until I was wakened by the bosun putting down a tray on the bedside table and saying, "Breakfast, Ome."

When I came back to the wheelhouse, day was breaking behind the immense and somber range of the Andes. We were passing the outer island of the Evangelistas; I could hear the waves moan in the caves on the ebbline with mournful gasps, like the breathy hooting of an Indian flute. The lonely lighthouse high up on the cliff slashed its last signal of the night and went out when the sun rose over the mountains, just as we wallowed past, rising and falling with the massive swell. The first rays of the sun were reflected by the aluminum trailers on the wall of the dry dock when it rose momentarily to the top of a wave a mile behind us. To the west, bright patches of early sunlight raced across the stormy sea, chased by slanting squalls of rain. The sight was breathtaking; Number One and I gazed at it with awe. We were not alone. The bosun, who came to take over the wheel, was stopped in his tracks. B.B. entered the wheelhouse in his anorak; he too was silenced by the spectacle.

After a while he took me aside. "Say, this wave action is perfect for our final testing! I'm ready when you are."

I explained to him why there would be no testing until the swell had subsided somewhat, sure that even he would have to agree.

But he didn't. He behaved like a petulant child and swept off the bridge, or tried to; he was lucky he didn't end up scalded by Hopla's coffee when they collided in the doorway.

"Ting tong, coffee time," Hopla said cheerfully. "Much wave, much experience. Let me tell you about time me butler in earthquake in Mah-Iot Hotel."

"Where's the sugar, Rin-tin-tin?" the bosun inquired.

"I will tell you, big mouth—"

"Gentlemen!" I said. "This is supposed to be the Pacific Ocean. Let's try to start this lap of our voyage in a spirit of peace."

Maybe I was a headmaster at heart.

4

B.B. got his way in the end. I thought the swell was too steep and dangerous to dare it with this sick ship, but as it was essential that the Isabel's deadly secret be ferreted out or there would be no sister ship, I decided not to be overcautious, as was my nature.

Even so, while trying to induce Isabel's suicidal rolling cycle among the graybeards of the South Pacific, I very nearly turned her over because of relentless urging by B.B., who egged me on, toggle switch in hand. During a few endlessly protracted seconds I was certain she was in the process of capsizing; she seemed to lie flat on her side while tobogganing down a slope that, in my worm's-eye view, looked like the Matterhorn. As proof that it was not all in the mind, as soon as she righted herself a bug-eyed Carleton came streaking up to the bridge, yelling something which Hopla translated with even buggier eyes as "Ma Chang stove walking in the kitchen!" I went to have a look and, indeed, the three-ton range in the galley had broken loose from its foundations and was setting fire to the plastic wall-covering with a smell like a gas attack. The blaze was put out, but everyone on board was sleepwalking with shock after that little episode. B.B., proving that genius was closely related to lunacy, chortled with glee as he sat ciphering on his stool lashed to the console, oblivious of the yawning jaws of death outside lusting after his spindly legs. I had a lot to answer for from the other three, who separately told me that they had never been so frightened in their lives; B.B. diverted their ire by crying at the end of his calculations, like Archimedes in his bath, "*Eureka!* She *will* capsize!"

"He has to do *sums* to find that out?" the bosun asked, incredulous.

"Go ping ping?" Whittier suggested.

"Yes, Whittier," I said, "four twins," holding up eight fingers. He went to the pinger and struck the bells, the highlight of his watch.

An hour later, when I was about to lie down for a nap before my watch came up, B.B. and Porks burst into the dayroom in a state of euphoria.

"Martinus! Listen to this! It's—it's *elegant!*"

"Got any paper I can draw on, Skipper?" Porks asked. "We should have brought some blank pages."

I went to my desk and handed him a legal pad and a pencil, at the sight of which Louis rolled onto his back on the coffee table.

"Let's start with the general subject of stability," B.B. began.

"If you want to draw, you'll have to scratch his stomach first," I said.

"Excuse me?"

"Scratch the rat's stomach with your pencil, the eraser end," explained Porks, "or we'll never get him off the coffee table."

B.B. scratched Louis' belly none too gently, causing him to make off to the security of my shoulder. Then he started, "Stability is determined by the distance between center of gravity and metacenter. Show him, Porks."

Porks drew a cross-section of a ship with a mast in the center. On the mast he made a cross and marked it 'M,' in the body of the ship he drew a cross marked 'G.'

"The distance between these two is known as MG," B.B. continued. "The smaller the MG, the less stable the ship; when the center of gravity coincides with the metacenter, the ship turns turtle. In the case of this ship, in seas coming in at a specific angle of attack, height, speed and wave train, a rapid diminution of MG takes place, which will be catastrophic if not instantly corrected. Draw it for him, Porks."

An engineering student would have grasped it; I soon lost my way among the alpha factor, the lambda factor, the H factor, the effective wave length, the F factor and "wind gusts affecting the superstructure." Porks drew them all, with arrows and graphs, curves and wave patterns.

"See?" B.B. commented. "In our case, one specific combination of all these factors causes the fatal cycle. Alpha, lambda, H and F can be calculated in our drawing office, but the basic design fault could only be discovered in the model basin or at sea. We did today."

Porks elaborated. "The danger zone is very confined: this narrow sector of incoming seas, over both starboard and port bow. If we hit this precise angle, together with the critical combination of the other factors he mentioned, she'll start the cycle."

"And if you allow her to continue on that cycle for more than a few minutes," B.B. added, "she'll capsize."

"Who would?"

"Excuse me?"

"Who would leave her on that cycle? The moment the officer of the watch realizes she's cycling, he'll correct it with the thrusters, the way I've been doing all along. I don't particularly like it, but I see no reason to get in a panic about it. I've come to know the ship by now, and I'm sure any tug-driver who knows his job can handle her under any circumstances."

"You realize that on a course to Taiwan she'll be crossing the hurricane belt?" Porks asked ominously. "And that it's the height of the hurricane season?"

"I do."

He and B.B. exchanged a look. "In that case, now that we know that she may actually turn over," B.B. said, "we feel morally obliged to prevent that happening under any circumstances."

"I don't understand."

"Suppose the ship is on automatic and the angle of attack changes imperceptibly until she starts the deadly rolling cycle while the officer of the watch happens to be incapacitated. In that case, she would go down with all hands within minutes."

"What are you driving at?" I asked, bemused. "There are never less than two people on the bridge, the helmsman and the officer of the watch. Not only the Chinese mates but the helmsmen know the procedure, so the one who isn't incapacitated would take her off automatic and throw her head off course with the bow thruster."

"Suppose *both* are incapacitated," Porks persisted. "Suppose toxic fumes or food poisoning—"

"But what exactly are you two proposing?"

They exchanged another look; then B.B. replied, "We would take down the Paradise tree in Talcahuano before she sails."

"That would make her safe under any and all conditions," Porks added.

I had difficulty keeping my face straight. "Gentlemen," I said earnestly, "I see your point and I appreciate your concern. But I'm afraid we can't do that without specific instructions from Mr. Chung."

"Come on, Skip!" Porks cried. "You know as well as we do that if we do it at all, we just have to do it, without his consent. Hell, we've been testing the guts out of the ship without him knowing about it! We can take it down so Chief Liu can put it back up without much of a problem once she's through the hurricane zone."

"Sorry," I said, "the answer is no. Take it up with Captain Fransen."

"Fransen?" B.B. scoffed. "We might as well ask old Kwel!"

"And he wouldn't agree, I take it?"

"Are you kidding? It would amount to— Oh, the hell with it. Let's go, Porks."

Porks stared at me, then said cryptically, "None so blind as those who will not see." He gathered up his drawings, and they left in a huff.

After they were gone, I mulled over what they had said. Their very premise was abstract boffin-nonsense; I could not realistically envisage a situation in which both men on watch on the bridge would be incapacitated while the ship, on automatic, sneaked onto her deadly course. Even so, it had now been established that the ship's 'FF,' which had gradually become a sort of joke, was indeed a mortal danger to the inexperienced or the amateur. Captain Cho might be either or both; in any case, the West Pacific during the hurricane season was an unhealthy place for a man like him. If I still doubted whether or not I should accept Mr. Chung's offer, this should settle it for me: it was no longer merely a question of my wanting to take the ship to Taiwan, it was—well, my sacred duty.

So—if there was no choice, my inward battle, for whatever it had been worth, had ended. I had pledged myself in Rio de Janeiro to the well-being of ship and crew; this was merely the follow-up.

I renewed my pledge to the souls under my care with a visit to the icebox. 'Pop,' a faint voice intoned from the distant past, 'like most other heroes of Holland's Glory, you're a lush.'

Well, if that was what it took to get this parcel of goods through the hurricane zone to Pago Pago, so be it. The last thing a man could afford on board this ship was self-delusion. Take down the Paradise tree? Over my dead body.

Chapter Ten

1

A week later the tow arrived off Concepción Bay in a thick, warm fog. We were in full summer by now, and the colossal glass hills of the Pacific Forties were a memory seemingly unrelated to our life, like a dream.

We lay becalmed in the featureless void of the fog with *Agnes* on the short hawser; even so, she was out of sight, as visibility was less than one hundred feet. We were in radio contact with the pilot station ashore; as soon as the weather cleared, the pilot would board us a third of a mile southeast of the head of Talcahuano breakwater. I was all set to wait it out offshore when, suddenly, the local naval authorities twittering on the VHF insisted we move inside to the quarantine anchorage for fear that local traffic might pass between tug and dry dock and get fouled in our hawser.

As this operation was against my better judgment, I decided I needed to be legally covered, so I sent Whittier down with my compliments to Captain Cho requesting his presence on the bridge as we were entering port. When he did not turn up, I went myself—alas, not as the father figure I aspired to be. Again I found him in his dressing gown, lying on his bunk, smoking his stinker, reading the quotations from Chairman Mao.

"Cho," I said breezily, "get yourself to the bridge on the double; we have to enter Concepción Bay in a pea-souper and your presence is legally required." As I left, I added, "You might also *learn* something," and managed not to slam the door.

Five infuriating minutes later he turned up and headed straight for his corner. I stopped him in his tracks by saying, "Captain, the Chilean Navy requests that we enter port despite weather conditions. Do you give your approval and wish me to execute the maneuver for your instruction?" He nodded imperceptibly. Then I added, with the best of intentions, "Would you also be so good as to man the radar, Captain? Both mates are with the lookouts on deck. We need an extra pair of eyes."

He glared at me and said in a toneless voice, "I wish you to execute the maneuver, Commodore."

I really did need the extra pair of eyes, so I said in a reasonable tone of voice, "Captain Cho, I'm going to pull rank on you. Get yourself to that radar screen on the double!"

Too late, too late. Not only had I made him lose face, I had decapitated him in front of Whittier and Hopla, who had appeared on the bridge with tea. Deeply offended, Cho slowly paced toward his corner, where he turned around to face me and took root.

Regrettably, I said, "All right. I'll report this to the owner." The regrettable part was that I said it in front of Hopla, to whom the whole scene was an undiluted delight. "You *sodemieter op,* you little creep," I shouted at him, in an infantile relapse into gutter Dutch, "or I'll turn you into a box of spare parts and mail it to your mother!"

He beamed with appreciation and said, "*Velly* good, Co'dore! I like that one," before disappearing.

The bosun, who had turned up to find out what the noise was about, was instantly recruited. "You take the scanner, Bosun," I said. "Sing out the mileage. I'm rounding an island over starboard." I flicked the switch of the automatic repeat on the foghorn; braying like a brontosaurian ass, the *Isabel* barged into the fog full speed, which meant from zero to one and a half knots until *Agnes* had gathered momentum, when I would scale her down to half-speed.

This being a fairly standard operation, I ventured into the cloud without any undue surge of gastric juices; then, suddenly, the bosun sang out, "Small echo approaching at twelve o'clock, one mile, Ome!"

I went to take a look.

For a few moments I thought it was a local fisherman without radar, but the echo approached so fast on a collision course that I flicked on the bullhorn mounted on the Paradise tree and bellowed in a cosmic voice loud enough to raise the dead, "You are heading into a tow! You are heading into a tow! Change course to starboard! Change course to starboard!"

The little vessel turned out to be manned not only by the blind but also the deaf; I was waiting for it to pile up on the *Isabel's* icebreaker bow with fatalistic equanimity when it appeared in the cloud half a ship's length away, three times its size because of the distortion caused by fog. It blared through a bullhorn of its

[245]

own, in Dutch, "Keep your shirt on, Harinxma, this is the Navy!" It was Fransen.

"Good morning," I blared back. "Park your glockenspiel over starboard, please!"

"Will do."

"Let's give Captain Fransen something to climb up on, Bosun," I said, and slowed down to half-speed.

The launch swung alongside; moments later Fransen turned up in fedora and skimpy raincoat, looking exactly as he had when we first met in Rotterdam. He was accompanied by a number of important-looking uniformed gentlemen wreathed in gold braid.

"How are you, Harinxma?" he said without taking the cigarette out of his mouth, and gave me a perfunctory handshake. "This is Rear Admiral Whatsis, in command of repair and docking, this is Captain Whatchamacallem, his aide-de-camp, and this is Captain Gonzáles, the pilot. Commodore Harinxma, gentlemen." There was a flurry of saluting and handshaking; I should have introduced Captain Cho, but he had delighted me enough that morning.

"The admiral would like to take over command of the convoy," Fransen said, deadpan.

"It will be my pleasure," I said, equally deadpan. "But as I am only the advisor to the captain, may I present to you Captain Cho?" I strode toward the corner where frozen Cho was awaiting defrosting in the twenty-first century. "Captain Cho, the admiral requests permission to take over command of the tow. What are your wishes?"

He gave my jugular a look of mute contemplation, then he nodded.

I said, "Thank you," turned on my heels and announced, "Captain Cho gives his consent."

Fransen looked at me through narrowed eyes, dropped his cigarette into the ashtray on the chart desk and asked, in Dutch, "What are you trying to do, Harinxma? Toss a cigar into the gunpowder?"

"Sorry," I said, "he got my goat this morning. Can these people handle it?"

He shrugged his shoulders. "It's their dock," he said.

"But it's my boat," I retorted.

"I see," he said. "You've decided to accept Chung's offer?"

The time had come to stop playing games. "Yes," I said.

"In that case, take a look at this at your leisure." He pulled from the pocket of his Columbo raincoat an envelope with the company logo. The address was handwritten.

"Again?" I asked.

He smiled, but his soul wasn't in it. "Seems you're piling up quite a private correspondence with the old man."

"Commodore? Are we ready to proceed?"

It was the admiral, short on patience.

"Absolutely, sir," I replied, stuffing the envelope into my pocket. "What are your orders, sir?"

"I want Captain Gonzáles to take over. He is the pilot."

"At your service," I said, smiling. "There's the wheel, Pilot, and out in the fog is a thirty-five-thousand-ton dry dock. We're running half-speed on the short hawser; you can read off its length on television screen number one up there. You'll see the stretcher on television screen number two. The manipulators are on the small console over here. And here's your water-speed indicator. Depth scanner over there. She's all yours."

The pilot looked at me like a prisoner during an interrogation.

"All right, Captain Gonzáles," the admiral said, godlike now. "Proceed."

I took pity on the poor man and asked, "Would you want me to go back to full speed ahead, Pilot? We barely have steerage now."

"Okay," he said, careful not to show his relief.

"The radar is over there, if you'd care to have a look yourself."

"Okay."

I continued to feed him hints in the form of questions, which he eagerly snapped up. Between the two of us, we managed to nudge the convoy past Quiriguina Island, between the breakwater and the bell buoy of Belén Shoal, to the quarantine anchorage in the southwest corner of the bay. All this purely by radar, with a visibility of less than a hundred feet. It was an exercise for fatalists, or believers of childlike faith, which was roughly the division between myself and the pilot on the one hand and the brass of the Chilean Navy on the other.

Then, just as I was wondering how to convey to the gentlemen that we couldn't just stop and anchor with old *Agnes* behind us, an irresistible mass in motion, the fog suddenly thinned and high up in the roseate cloud flashed a glint of sunlight reflected

[247]

by one of the aluminum trailers on top of the dock. A breath of a wind blew the haze away in a whirl of white spirals and revealed deep blue bay, a green shore, the white tumble of a city, the massive mountain range of the Andes. We turned out to be surrounded by a reception committee of harbor tugs, launches, gigs and, obscurely, landing craft, all waiting to put *Agnes* to bed.

The harbor tugs got hold of her; we reeled in the hawser and the stretcher; then the admiral and his entourage were taken off by landing craft and the pilot begged me to stop whispering and to take over. I collected the bridle, waved at Harakiri and the runners and headed for the second Customs wharf at the northern end of the town, while Captain Cho stood in his corner staring straight ahead.

After Customs had come and gone, I collapsed on the couch in my dayroom and Fransen made for the icebox. "Before you zonk out, old buddy, you'd better read the letter from the old man."

"While you're at it, pour me one too, will you?"

"I thought you were on the wagon."

"I step off occasionally." I pulled the envelope out of my pocket and tore it open.

"The Chinese captain looks about ready to slit your throat," Fransen said as he handed me my glass.

"Don't worry, that's the way he is. He's been like that since the beginning." I started reading the letter.

Dear Harinxma,

I was alarmed and distressed to learn of Mr. Chung's surprising and highly suspect request that you stay on in your present capacity after Talcahuano, which was conveyed to me in the same letter in which he lodged a formal complaint about our abusing his ship by stress-testing her for our own purposes. In my opinion—this, of course, is to be strictly confidential—you would be toying with what is potentially an extremely dangerous situation.

I do not refer to the ship, which, despite her flaw, will present no problem to you. I am referring to the fact that although you were not the instigator, you were the main agent in what to Mr. Chung cannot but appear as a callous violation of his prerogative as owner. Without his foreknowledge and against his wishes, you and the architect submitted the ship to a series of brutal tests on the way to Talcahuano.

In my long and active life I have had several opportunities to acquaint myself with the traditions and customs of Asian cultures; especially in the case of the Chinese, a gross if not to say contemptuous manipulation like this one cannot but evoke bitter and vengeful resentment. Through circumstances not of your own making, you would be the only perpetrator of his loss of face available to him.

Harinxma, I do not wish to sound unduly alarmist, but I must urge you with all the power of conviction I possess to leave the ship together with the others in Talcahuano. I have no idea what form Mr. Chung's reaction might take, but of this you can be sure: he would exact retribution, or his honor and self-esteem would suffer. I fully appreciate that by now you, as master, have identified completely with both ship and crew. But as there must come a moment when you will have to separate yourself from the small community you are now leading, it might as well be now. You have done a sterling job, you have fulfilled the expectations I had of you when I invited you to take on this assignment; now, at the height of your achievement, the time has come to withdraw.

I cannot tell you, dear Harinxma, how seriously I view the situation. I otherwise would not go to the length of writing you this letter. I ask you to burn it without delay.

Harinxma, I look forward to seeing you on your return and assuring you in person of my sympathy and appreciation. Miss Bastiaans joins me in sending you our most friendly greetings.

I looked up and found Fransen observing me through the crinkling smoke of his cigarette with an odd mixture of curiosity and concern. What was he concerned about? I was ready to be seduced by old Kwel all over again, but it would be ludicrous to ascribe the same sentiments to his hatchet man.

"Well, that's very interesting," I said, folding the letter, planning to burn it later.

"Did he write what I think he did?"

"I suppose so."

He sighed and shook his head. "Mind if I pour myself another shot?"

"Help yourself."

At the icebox, pouring, he said, "Don't do it, Harinxma. Don't stick your head in a noose. Chung sure as hell doesn't want

[249]

someone on the bridge capable of keeping her upright in force-twelve weather."

"For God's sake, Fransen! If Chung is planning to scuttle the ship, why should he hire me to keep her afloat? His offer is perfectly straightforward. Cho couldn't handle a forty-thousand-ton tow in a hurricane."

He gave me one of his appraiser's looks. "Harinxma, old buddy, if you ask me, Captain Cho is perfectly capable of towing anything, on condition he hasn't got *you* breathing down his neck."

"Don't be ridiculous! The man's totally incompetent."

"Listen to me for a moment, will you? You think of yourself as a genial, reasonable, self-effacing man, don't you? A bit on the delicate side because of your age? Even fragile, maybe?"

"Well? What's wrong with that?"

He smiled. "I have news for you, friend: you're as genial, self-effacing and fragile as a Sherman tank."

"Come on, Fransen!"

"Maybe you weren't born a tank, but after thirty-five years as an ocean-going tug-driver you're as close to it as a man can get without growing caterpillar tracks. Old Kwel knew that, given the chance, you'd take this ship from any pipsqueak of a captain and install yourself in his place. Why do you think he dressed you like a goldfinch, if it wasn't to intimidate the new captain? When Cho came aboard and was intimidated by the wheelhouse, his goose was cooked. You locked him up and pocketed the key. From that moment on, he was allowed to appear on the bridge only when his presence was legally required, but it was made plain to him that the rest of the time he could get lost. Man, you ate that poor bastard alive."

I couldn't believe my ears. "How can you say that? I gave the man every chance—"

"Come on now! Even you must realize, when you stop to think about it, that the guy was never given a chance. How would *you* have reacted, at the age of—what is he? Twenty-five? Twenty-six?—if you were yanked off, say, the old *Anna* onto this pig? And while you were gawking at her bridge like the control room of an atomic plant, Ome Tinus advanced on you, decked out in glitter like Liberace, and said, "Hello there! I'm your advisor!" It's the kind of nightmare that makes children wake up screaming."

[250]

"Very funny, Fransen, but balls! You haven't seen the man operate—"

"Have *you?*"

"Don't be ridiculous! He couldn't—"

"Seriously: when have you seen him do his job? When has he had a chance to act as master? One squeak out of him and slam—back in the pokey! That's how I read it. That's how old Kwel read it all along. He knew Chung's captain would be no Beast Rufus, and that you'd plow him under and tuck the *Isabel* under your arm for the duration."

"What the hell are you talking about? How could Kwel know about Cho?"

"What do you expect him to do in his eternal darkness? He thinks. That's all he does: think, except for an occasional grope at the Bastiaans woman. Well, as I read it, he thought: 'Why should Chung buy this ship, at that price, no questions asked, if it wasn't because he picked up via the grapevine that she is unstable?' If Chung had in mind what old Kwel thought he had in mind, his captain would be carefully selected as the man least likely to keep her upright in the Forties. The little blind mind took it from there and started to shop around for a retired master to act as that captain's advisor. A tough, knowledgeable old bird who would instantly take advantage of the situation: a ship under foreign flag, a figurehead for a captain—snap! He'd be in command, and no gale, no Chung, no snow, sleet or atomic explosion would make that old bird hand over control of the ship. Well, he found what he was looking for: you. But now it's your turn to do some thinking before you run afoul of the knife-sharpening Chung and Cho. I think I'll get me a third."

While he helped himself at the icebox again, I sat there, stunned by the revelation of the mirror he had held up to me. Was he right? Had I not given Cho a chance to take control of the ship? Nonsense! I had, several times, but he hadn't taken it. On the other hand, as recently as an hour ago I had treated him as an apprentice and told him I would report him to the owner . . .

"But he *is* incompetent!" I cried. "Goddammit, he lost a destroyer by tripping his tow!"

"Who told you that?"

"You know it! I told you in Mindello!"

"Who told you that, Harinxma? Think, now: where did you get that from?"

I tried to remember. "Number One? No . . . Slobkous told me, after hearing it from one of the Chinese officers."

"Ah," he said, coming back from the icebox, "Slobkous. Let's talk about him for a moment. To start with, he was under orders to stress the incompetence of the Chinese captain to you. There *was* no tripped tow. Cho is probably as capable as the next twenty-five-year-old pram-pusher. Slobbo made it up out of whole cloth with whatever was left of his creative mind."

This was becoming grotesque. "Sorry, Fransen, you're getting too operatic for me. I may have shoehorned myself into command of this vessel; okay, I accept that, with some modifications. Old Kwel appointed me because he wanted me to do just that—I'll accept it, I've been manipulated by him before. But that he instructed a drunk to discredit Cho for my benefit—"

"He didn't. *I* did." When I stared at him, he grinned. "I'm allowed to do some creative thinking of my own once in a while, no?"

This brought me up short. "Do you mean to tell me that Cho did *not* trip that tow? That it was all your invention?"

He grinned amiably.

"Why, you conniving, manipulating bastard! What the hell do you think you're playing at? The man's reputation, his whole professional life—"

"Come on, Harinxma! Don't turn into a sky-pilot now—"

"And you have the nerve to tell me that I'm riding roughshod over the poor bugger! Not giving him a chance to sail the ship! I don't know what your game is, buddy, but I think you're a despicable shit!"

It rolled off him like water off a duck, or so I thought; but suddenly he turned on me. Not in anger; it was as if a mask dropped and I was suddenly faced with the real man: weary, shrewd, but with an unexpected concern for me as a person. "Harinxma," he said, "I hate to do this to you, but let me tell you what the old man's *real* worry is. He's afraid he conditioned you too thoroughly, that now you're smitten with the pig and your gooks to the point where he can no longer control you and order you off the ship."

"What in Christ's name are you talking about?"

"Listen to me, I'm serious. I'm not going to tell you this twice. If you stayed on and kept this ship upright in the hurricane zone the way you did in the Forties, you'd be lousing up Kwel's end game."

"His what? For God's sake, Fransen, stop talking in riddles!"

"Now that the old man has the information he needs for building the sister ship, he wants Chung to execute his little scheme and let this pig scuttle herself under the command of the Chinese captain. Cho may not be as much of a bungler as you made him out to be, but he's young and inexperienced and this ship is a killer of the young and inexperienced. As from this moment, Chung's and old Kwel's interests converge: they both want her dead and gone. Chung because he wants the insurance jackpot, Kwel because he doesn't want the gooks to start competing with KITCO in the Far East with one of our own capital ships. It's as simple as that. And now forget I ever told you." He knocked back the rest of his drink, put down the glass and pulled another envelope from his pocket.

I stared at him in disbelief. "You mean to say: if I stay on, old Kwel wants me dead?"

"Ssh! Don't make a drama of it. He doesn't want you dead, he wants God to do His work and punish the reckless and the incompetent. You're standing in God's way. So—" he tossed the envelope onto the coffee table—"here are the airline tickets for your bosun, Porks, Harlingen, Harakiri, B.B. and yourself. Departure time twenty-two hundred hours tonight, by LAN Chile to Santiago. In Santiago . . ." He took out his notebook and leafed through it. "All six of you are booked in at the Sheraton Cristóbal. You'll find a hotel bus at the airport to take you there. Tomorrow you all leave for Amsterdam by KLM. You'll find the times on your tickets." He produced another envelope. "Here's one thousand bucks, in hundreds; you'll have to pay the hotel in cash." He put it on the coffee table with the tickets. "Don't let this fall into the hands of that pickpocket steward of yours, or leave it to your rat for shredding." He gave me another of those looks. "Don't be a fool, Harinxma. I don't know what Chung's game is, inviting you to stay on. It doesn't make sense to me, but then I don't have a Chinese mind. God knows what he's up to. Cho may be in league with him, after the buddy-buddy way we saw them talking together in the hotel in Punta. Maybe they were plotting to push you over the edge, who knows? But of one thing you can be damn sure: the old man is right. There's something in the wind. So, be wise and scram before Chung pulls the latch and you find your-self dangling from a rope, trussed up and ready for the pan." He lit another cigarette and rose. "You're an ornery old bastard, but we'd like to have you around for a little while longer." He went to the door. "Oh, wait a minute: your mail." He produced a handful of letters from a pocket of his raincoat. "This little parcel is pills, I had to sign for them at Customs. Well, I'll go and see the others. I want everybody off the ship and on board that ten-o'clock plane for Santiago." At the door he added, "Take my advice, Harinxma. Don't mess up other people's crap game. Not when the stake is twenty million dollars."

Before I could respond, he stepped into the corridor and closed the door behind him.

2

He was barely gone when the bosun turned up, looking shell-shocked. "Is it true?" he asked. "Are you staying on?" The grape-vine had lost none of its efficiency. "If you are, so am I!"

"Let's talk about it when I get back, Bosun." I pried Louis off my shoulder, put him on the Bowditch and took my cap off the hook.

"But, Ome—!"

"Later, Bosun. I won't be long." I pocketed the envelope with the money, but left the tickets with my mail.

"Ome, you don't understand! For me to stay on, you have to talk to Captain Fransen!"

"Back in an hour." I had to get off the ship; I had to think this through before I found myself in an airport bus.

At the top of the companionway to the deck I was waylaid by Porks. "What's this I hear, Skipper? You're carrying on to Taiwan?"

"It's been suggested," I said, brushing past.

It was a relief to get off the damn ship and past the gate.

Right opposite was a square, very Spanish, shaded by stunted trees with in its center a statue white with pigeon droppings. There was a terrace outside a café with little iron tables, parasols and ornate little chairs; a white-aproned waiter appeared and I ordered a glass of Pisco Sour to help me think. I had plenty to think about.

I would have fallen for old Kwel's concern about my becoming the butt of Mr. Chung's ire if Fransen hadn't revealed that, from here on in, Kwel's and Chung's interests converged—if Chung was indeed bent on scuttling the *Isabel* for the insurance money, which I still thought was nonsense. But both Kwel and Fransen seemed to think so, and that made it painfully obvious to me that Fransen was right: old Kwel's real concern was that if I were to remain on board, the ship was likely to arrive at her destination and might start to compete with KITCO in the Far Eastern market.

It was high time I disentangled myself from the old man's manipulations. He had taken me up the garden path and three times around the mulberry bush. Unlike his inexperienced grandson, he had started by not mentioning Talcahuano, but eased me into it by making it Rio and no farther. He had waited for the bonding to take place between myself, the crew and the ship, then slipped me a patriotic appeal in a handwritten letter after I was good and hooked. Now he was whistling me back. What depressed me was my own predictability; to him, I was as predictable as a dog to his trainer. Which brought me to poor Captain Cho. Old Kwel had known in advance I would usurp the boy's place without my being aware of doing so. Now what? If Fransen's reading of him was right and Cho was indeed capable of taking the tow through the hurricane zone, shouldn't I have the decency to withdraw? But Chung himself had made it plain to me in Punta Arenas that he didn't think Cho could hack it and that Cho himself didn't think so either. Now old Kwel and Fransen came out with the conspiratorial theory that Chung had invited me to stay on only so as to have me in his clutches as an object for his revenge and that Cho might be his accomplice! The whole concept was too ludicrous for words. What was it that lured normally sane, rational people into these sudden bouts of irrational paranoia? I had no illusions about Mr. Chung's being a candidate for sanctification, I was prepared to admit that it would break neither his heart nor his piggy-bank if the ship were lost, but I thought Kwel's assessment was far more realistic: sly, ambitious Chung was planning to give KITCO some hefty competition in the China Sea and environs. And as for Chung wanting my scalp because I had despoiled his honor? Paranoid nonsense, if old Kwel really had meant that seriously; to my mind, he had used it as a device to stop my staying on. And, as usual, all this plotting and scheming on his part and Fransen's had the opposite effect of what they had intended: I was more determined than ever now to see the ship to Taiwan.

"Commodore?"

I looked up and, talk of the devil, there stood Captain Cho, frail and challenging, with a Mussolini jaw, his eyes full of problems. He looked totally out of place in this setting of pigeons and little iron tables in the colored shade of parasols.

"Captain! Sit down. Can I buy you a drink?"

He looked at my empty glass, the dish of peanuts, the frivolous little chair I pulled out for him, and sat down without a word, as if he had received an instruction over a miniature earphone, like a TV reporter.

"Well," I said, "what'll you have? If you like peach brandy, I can recommend the local cocktail."

He shook his head, then said as if in response to a radioed command, "Commodore, I honor you."

"Well—er—look, Cho—"

The waiter came, harvested the empties, leaving the peanuts, and flicked the table with his napkin. "Sí?"

"One Pisco Sour and one mango juice, *per favor.*"

The waiter flicked the table again and walked off, swinging his napkin.

"I honor you," the strange youth repeated. "We do not always see eyes to eyes, but you are an honorable older person of a different race, a great commodore distinguished in wars. I can submit—subject to you without losing face."

"Cho, I'm glad you brought that up. I just sat here, thinking—"

"But if you go and new captain comes, I will have no future. I will be disgraced. You say, 'Captain Cho cannot sail tow across the Pacific, someone else must be sent to take his place.' If that happens, I am dishonored. I cannot continue in this profession. I cannot continue, evermore. I will have to leave the sea." He fixed me with a baleful stare that, for some reason, gave me a chill of discomfort. "Please—" He was interrupted by a wild flutter of wings; a pigeon alighted on our table, attracted by the peanuts. The waiter dive-bombed it with his napkin before putting two glasses in front of us.

[256]

Cho stared at his glass. There was something forlorn about him, something lost. I realized a reaction was expected of me. "Don't take it so hard," I said, "there's no cause. I'm sorry I told Mr. Chung that you were—er—expendable. I suggest that from now on you make yourself known whenever you feel in need of instruction or enlightenment. Any time you wish to consult me or—er—confide in me, that sort of thing, just holler." It wasn't much of a fatherly speech, but it was the best I could come up with. He really had touched a chord, the troubled boy. I was determined to make up for lost time. I polished off my glass and tried to catch the waiter's eye. He caught mine; he wasn't where I had thought he was.

"*Sí?*"

"*Encora, per favor. Doublo.*"

It might not be perfect Spanish, but he got the message, snitched my glass, flicked his napkin at a pigeon on peanut patrol and sauntered off.

The boy said abruptly, "Mr. Chung sends greetings."

"Ah? Thank you."

"He asked me to tell you he had to catch a plane."

I was about to say, 'Fancy that,' but, dammit, that would be driving him into the deck again. "Thank you."

We sat in uncomfortable silence, waiting for the waiter. He came back with a glass fit for a man. Or, rather, madman: the stuff was as potent as Slobbo's 100% proof vodka, despite its ladylike looks and its taste of Bulgarian jam. After that glass I would be fit to be fired from a cannon. "Why don't you start by joining Happy Hour?" I suggested jovially. "You know: join in, get to know us, be one of the boys. We're a friendly bunch—I mean, you're welcome any time."

He looked at me without replying. His face seemed to take on a fleeting expression of melancholy, defeat. For a moment, with the pigeons hovering and the waiter waiting to defend the peanuts with his napkin, it was as if a door were opened briefly, a sudden perception revealed; then it passed.

"I must go," he said, rising. "Thank you for the drink."

I said, "My pleasure."

He bowed slightly and walked away, an alien figure among the pigeons.

When he was gone and I sat sipping my drink, I realized I was facing a new situation. How could I refuse the appeal of a youth I

[257]

had wronged however unintentionally by driving across him on caterpillar tracks? I could see his point, it was as plain as a pikestaff: if I turned down Chung's offer, he would fly in another Chinese captain and Cho would lose face beyond hope of recovery, whereas Ome Tinus harrumphing on the bridge, doing his commodore bit, would just be an act of God. I owed it to the poor boy to stay on.

"No, *señor*," the waiter warned, napkin at the ready, "pigeon no allowed on tables!"

I raised my glass to him. "Have a heart," I said, "live and let live." I placed a coin on the table; he snapped it up as fast as the pigeons, who, I discovered, also snatched peanuts out of the air if I shot them high enough with finger and thumb.

Before ingesting the last of my drink, I raised my glass to them, the sky, the sun, all the good things in life. "All right, Polynesian hurricanes," I said happily, "let's dance."

Of such is the Kingdom of Heaven.

3

I placed the call to Sylvia from a small hotel behind the plaza, chatting with the pretty young receptionist while waiting for the call to come through. The telephone in the booth rang after a surprisingly short time.

When I picked up the handset, Sylvia was on the line. "Martinus?" she asked.

"Yes, love. I'm calling you from Talcahuano, as you probably know."

"No, they didn't say. All they said was Chile. When are you coming home?"

"Well, love, that's what this call is about. Mr. Chung has asked me to stay on board as acting convoy commander as far as Taiwan. I think I should accept. He suggests you join me in Pago Pago for the trip to Kao Hsiung."

There was a long silence.

"Sylvia? Are you there?"

"Yes." Even across all those miles of ocean I could hear her shock and distress. "I think this is terrible, Martinus, terrible. How could you?" She sounded almost in tears.

"Dear love, it's necessary. The captain is a total incompetent, as you know; the crew and the runners are innocents. If I don't stay on, they'll never make it."

"But why you? Can't they replace the Chinese captain? If they need an advisor on board, can't Kwel appoint someone else?"

"It's too late for all that, Syl. To find a replacement for the Chinese captain would take forever. Mr. Chung told me in the beginning that the present one was the best he had. And for Kwel to start shopping around for another retired captain—"

"But why Taiwan, love? I can understand you wanting to stay on as far as Pago Pago to see them across the Pacific, but after that? Why do they need you? From there on it's all plain sailing, isn't it? And with the loose boat, no tow to worry about? Surely the captain, however incompetent he may be, can take a loose boat through Polynesia at this time of year?"

"There's going to be another tow, love. A forty-thousand-ton derelict liner to Kao Hsiung for scrap. He won't be able to handle that, not in the hurricane season."

"But, for God's sake, Marty, you're not well! You're seventy years old, you have hypertension, you had one gale already in the South Atlantic! And now the hurricane season! They *must* bring in someone else! It's madness for you to even consider doing this, you *know* it is! They're not going to risk that ship and its tow by giving it to incompetent people—it's just not possible. Can't you see that?" She sounded desperate.

"Syl, you must understand—"

"I understand all too well!" she cried. "Call Dr. Hébert! Do it now. Call him at home, ask his advice—"

"Love, Dr. Hébert hasn't seen me in months . . ."

"Then go and see a doctor in Talcahuano! *Please*, Marty, that's the least you owe me, for God's sake! Go and see a specialist, a cardiologist, tell him what you're planning, ask him whether he thinks you're in a fit shape to do this. I can't stop you having a last fling at sea, heaven knows, but I can't allow you to commit suicide!"

"All right, love. If you insist, I'll be happy to do that."

"Oh, please do it, do it now and tell him to call me, collect.

Promise me. It doesn't matter what time, day or night, let him call me!"

"All right, love, I will. I—er—I do want to talk to you, but let's wait till I call you back. All right?"

"Listen, Marty, don't procrastinate. Don't give up if he can't see you right away. Find someone else. Ask the Navy!"

"Don't worry, love, I'll see somebody. Bye now."

I put the receiver back and stared at the instrument for a while before I pushed open the door of the booth. I went to the desk to pay for the call and asked the receptionist about doctors. She was very helpful and started to telephone around for an appointment for me. It seemed that no cardiologist, either in Talcahuano or Concepción, could see me for several days, but she persisted; in the end she found someone who was prepared to see me at once: an American neurologist who lived in the outskirts of the city. It was not quite what I had in mind, but it would have to do. The girl called a taxi for me. It meant cutting it fine, for the ship was due at the fuel dock within the next few hours; but Sylvia was right, I owed her this. God knew it was little enough.

4

It was a charming little villa in a rioting summer garden full of alien flowers. Inside I heard the shrill yapping of a little dog; when the door was opened, a snarling powder puff went for my ankles.

"Czara! *Per aquí!*"

He was an ageless man, dressed in emerald-green slacks embroidered with little silver golf clubs and a navy-blue short-sleeved shirt with a little crocodile. He had enormous bushy eyebrows and tufts sprouting from his ears and nose; he had hair on his arms, his neck, his chest, everywhere except on his head. The impression he gave was that of a circus clown off duty.

He picked up the powder puff, which barked so hysterically that it lost its voice and began to sound like a seagull. "Come in, Commodore," he said. "Don't mind my dog. He may not sound like it, but you're making his day. This way, please."

He took me to a consulting room, gestured me to a chair and

stood leaning against the examining table with the little dog in his arms. "Well? What seems to be the trouble?" He had knowing eyes.

I told him that my wife was worried about my continuing the voyage to Taiwan as convoy commander.

"Convoy?"

I explained to him about the forty-thousand-ton liner waiting for us, about the *Isabel*, the Chinese crew, the inexperienced captain, the hurricane season.

He listened carefully, the little dog, mewling hoarsely, struggling in his arms. Then he put it down and asked, "Before we start: if I were to tell you that you'd drop dead halfway, would you turn around here and go home?"

It was an odd question, but he was obviously serious. "I hope you won't," I answered, "but if that was your verdict, I would have to think about it."

"In other words: No."

"I find it hard to answer a hypothetical question, Doctor. Why don't you find out if that is indeed the verdict?"

"All right. Any symptoms? Complaints?"

I told him about the blood-pressure crisis in the Atlantic. He was fascinated by Ma Chang's therapy and went on pressing me for details. He asked me for any other changes I might have noticed, however minor; I told him about the ringing in my ears and the fact that nowadays everyone seemed to mumble. Finally, I told him about my early-morning tremors. That interested him; he prompted me to define the sensation as fully as I could, and I came up with "Not so much a trembling as a quiver deep inside the muscles of my arms and hands, particularly on waking in the morning." I told him that a physician in Rotterdam had diagnosed it as booze. "But, as I've drunk very little since I started Ma Chang's cure and the quiver persists, becoming more pronounced on occasion, it couldn't be that, could it?"

"Let's find out." He moved away from the table. "Please get undressed, put a gown on from that pile in the corner. I'll be right back."

I obeyed. As I lay on the examining table, I could hear the claws of the little dog scrabbling on the linoleum. It had stopped barking.

He proceeded to give me the most thorough checkup I had had since the war. Compared to what he put me through, the

[261]

examination by the doctor in Rotterdam had been slapdash. As he went on and on, probing and poking and listening and taking cardiograms and peering into my eyes and my ears, I worried about the ship and the fuel dock, but there was little I could do, as he ignored my hint that I had to get back on board because of our schedule. He was particularly interested in the shaking of my hands; he brought out instruments I had never seen before, even a tuning fork. Finally, he said, "You can get dressed."

When I sat facing him again he said, "Now then. You realize that you're seventy-some years old. However vigorous you may be, there are certain aspects of aging you can't avoid. We're all mortal, and mortality is not an axe that falls; in the nature of things, it's a process. Slow and insidious at first, then more and more evident, ultimately fairly precipitous in most cases. I'm telling you all this, even though you probably know it yourself, because I want to make clear that you're not the ideal person, physically speaking, to take a convoy of that size across the Pacific in the hurricane season."

"It's not physical prowess that's needed in case of a hurricane."

"Then what *is* needed, in your opinion?"

"Experience. Foresight, which is the same thing really. The ability to read the signs of sea and sky and work your way around the fringe of the cyclone."

He smiled. "All that to be done from your bed?"

"From a deck chair on the bridge."

He gave me a pensive look. "I should tell you at this point that I'm an ex-Navy man who served in the Pacific. Another physician might be taken in by your version of a master's function in a hurricane. *I* know it's a fantasy. More precisely, a dangerous self-delusion. If a hurricane strikes, you'll be under enormous stress, on your feet for up to three days and nights, leaping around like a goat most of the time. So the real question is the one I asked you to begin with: why do it? There's a better than even chance that you'll crack under the strain, emotionally as well as physically, for the simple reason that in order to remain emotionally stable under maximum stress you need the physical resources to back you up. Why risk a serious incident and, possibly, serious danger to ship and crew, given your stage in life?"

"I told you: the captain—"

"Commodore, stop kidding yourself. If you report to the

owners that the captain isn't up to the job, they'll send someone else to take over. I repeat my question: why?"

It was a dilemma. I could tell him about Fransen's and old Kwel's suspicions as to Chung's motives; but then, I didn't believe in them myself. If I wanted a serious evaluation by a man who obviously knew his job, I had better come clean, especially as he had been a sailor himself and therefore might well understand. "I have a ship with a problem. A marvelous ship: strong, nimble, willing, tremendously powerful—the best ship I ever had. But she has a flaw; under certain circumstances, she has a tendency to get into a suicidal rolling cycle and, if unchecked, may capsize. She won't do it while I'm in command, but I can't see any Chinese relief captain keeping her upright in hurricane seas. And she has a complement of forty-five souls."

He nodded. "Very convincing, Commodore. I don't think a layman would be able to pick holes in that. But you know and I know that it's hogwash. You're not the only expert tugboat master alive. For you, say, twenty others. If pressured, any owner, however reluctant, would appoint one of those."

He looked at me shrewdly but kindly while I cast about for a more convincing argument: my special relationship with the Chinese crew, my emotional ties with the ship herself. "How about the love for a ship with a terminal weakness?" I asked finally, almost flippantly.

To my surprise, he took it seriously. "Tell me about that. Tell me about your *feelings,* not the technical facts."

Talcahuano, Chile, was not a place I was likely to return to. He was a kind man whom I would probably never see again. I might as well do as he asked, if only for my own enlightenment. If I was a mental case, I might as well know it and deal with reality on that basis; but it did not come easily.

"All right. She's known as 'the pig.' She'd be the last ship an old hand like myself would be expected to fall for. She's not a thing of beauty, quite the reverse. When I left the sea, tugboats were at their esthetically most pleasing; the best and the biggest looked like yachts. I sailed one that made the captain of a passing windjammer signal, 'Beautiful ship you have there, Captain.' It was like an accolade from the *Flying Cloud.* Yet that beautiful ship meant nothing to me. It only happened to me once before, when I was a young man. She was my first full command. Curiously, she too was called *Isabel Kwel.*"

"What happened to her?"

"I lost her during the war. On the run to Murmansk."

"How many men were lost?"

"Seventeen."

"Go on."

"Well, there's not much else to say. It seems ridiculous to talk in these emotional terms about a ship. When all is said and done, she really is only a mechanical contraption."

"You don't mean that."

"What I mean is I know damn well that whatever I may be smitten with is self-induced. An interpretation, a symbol, a concept—I don't know. Rationally, a man cannot love a machine. Certainly not an ugly, squat, bull-necked stink-belcher like that one."

"The first *Isabel,* was she a thing of beauty?"

"God, no! She was just about as ugly as this one. But she was the most powerful, mechanically advanced tugboat of her time, flagship of the fleet. Like this one, in fact."

"In sum: this one is the ship of your youth in a new guise?"

"In a sense, yes."

"With a terminal weakness, as you call it?"

"But unimportant as long as I'm around."

"Are you familiar with the phenomenon known as transference?"

"You mean I identify with the ship specifically because of my own 'terminal weakness'?"

"Let me say: anything that's done to the ship, you react to as if it were being done to you. But it's only part of the picture."

Suddenly I had had enough. "Doctor, I'm sorry, but I see I've run out of time. I'm sure all this is very valid and I would love to go into it more deeply—"

"Come, come, Commodore," he interrupted with a smile. "Admit frankly you don't want to. Be honest with yourself."

"Ibsen wrote a play about it and showed that, driven to extremes, honesty with yourself can be disastrous."

He smiled. "Very well, let's see what we've got. Physically, you're in no condition to undertake this voyage, however carefully you husband your resources. I've lived through hurricanes in the West Pacific myself, I know what I'm talking about. But over the years I've acquired great respect for the human mind and its power over the physical body. Chances are that if you're determined to see that ship safely to Taiwan, you'll do it even if under normal circumstances you'd collapse under the strain. But there is an element of risk here. The question to ask yourself is, 'Is this fair to the other people? The forty-five souls I have on board?' Only you can answer that question. Would it help if you tried to answer it now?"

Like hell it would. "I don't think so, Doctor. Let's get back to the reason why I'm here: my wife's worries. She requested that I see a specialist before sailing and that he call her, collect, to put her mind at ease. Would you be prepared to do so?"

He thought that over. "If I hadn't been a sailor myself, I probably would say no. As it is—"

"Come on, Doctor! So I'm a seventy-year-old man with controlled hypertension. Otherwise, I gather, I'm in reasonable shape. I have a professional staff who will execute my orders without my leaping around like a goat on the bridge. I'm the only master available who's familiar with the ship's quirk and able to cope with it. Under the circumstances, I'd say I'm the best the crew can hope for. If you nix me, the owner is going to put on an inexperienced Chinese unfamiliar with the ship. He may be able to do the goat stuff on the bridge, but when it comes to sensing what the little devil is up to—"

"Which devil?"

"The ship! She's a little—well, 'little'—she's a devil. I know her, I see her coming with my eyes closed and my head under a pillow. Anyone new, and I don't care how able he is, she'd sneak up on and dunk him before he knew what was happening. I've put her through every imaginable test in both the Atlantic and Pacific Forties; it didn't involve any leaping around on the bridge. It involved insight, foresight, horse sense—knowledge of the ship herself, really. Caring about her. Feeling protective not only of the men under my command, but of the ship."

"A good definition of love," he said, smiling.

I sighed. "All right, Doc. Will you call her?"

"Certainly."

"And what are you going to say?"

"That in my opinion you are capable of accompanying the convoy to Taiwan as advisor to the captain, on condition you pace yourself sensibly. That it obviously is important to your peace of mind and your acceptance of your own mortality to find out the truth about yourself at sea. That you're involved in an emotional catharsis, the repression of which would be more destructive, psychologically, and maybe even spiritually, than the physical risk you are running, which is only a conjectural one. That's what I'll tell her. Now, what do I tell *you?*"

"Why? Is it different?"

He gave me a look which was extraordinarily benevolent, then said with a smile, "Not where it matters."

He wrote out his bill and prescriptions for more blood-pressure pills and a medication that might help if the tremor should get worse; I gave him my home telephone number and he ordered a taxi for me.

I went back to the hotel and placed a call to Sylvia with the pretty receptionist. We chatted as I waited for the connection; the number was busy for nearly twenty minutes. Finally I got through and heard that she had been talking to the doctor. It appeared he had reassured her somewhat, but she sounded more resigned than satisfied. There wasn't much else to say; she didn't know if she'd be able to join me in Pago Pago, she thought probably not; Ella and Tim needed her with the new baby, which was doing poorly and needed a lot of TLC. She made the dog bark into the telephone, which was always the last resort; then we said goodbye until Pago Pago and she wished me Godspeed and happy sailing. It was a sad conversation, really; it left me depressed.

I walked back to the ship; as I crossed the square with the parasols and the pigeons, I wondered what the doctor had meant when he said, 'Not where it matters.' But I pushed the thought aside. I had a ship to sail.

5

When I reached the dockside, I had the shock of my life: the ship was gone! She must be at the fuel dock; Captain Cho, the cocky snotnose, had taken her there without me, and without my permission!

I called a taxi and raced to the fuel dock on squealing tires; it was a long way away at the other end of the city. When we arrived, I saw the *Isabel* approaching from the bay, half a mile offshore.

I paid the driver and waited, arms akimbo, for the ship's arrival. When she swung around to back into her mooring, I recognized young Cho peeking from the bridge. It was all very well, my decision to encourage him to gain self-confidence, but this was reckless to a degree: the silly ass had no experience of actually handling the ship, chances were she would eat him alive.

I had to admit that he moored her deftly, but that was as far as it went. I leaped on board, found him on the companionway from bridge to forecastle deck, gave him my honest opinion of his rash behavior and told him in a fatherly fashion how extraordinarily lucky he had been. I also told most of Talcahuano, and then some; even the gulls on the bollards ashore seemed interested. I left his emotional and spiritual remains on the boat deck, where our discussion—walking slowly, he mostly backward—had taken us, and went to my dayroom.

As I entered, I received the second shock of the day: lounging on the couch, glass in hand like the madam of a brothel, lay Fransen. He gave me a broad grin and said, "Well, well. How to make friends and influence people. That was a vintage performance, old cock."

"What the hell are *you* doing here? Didn't you notice that the Chinese was taking the ship out?"

"Of course. I told him to."

"*You* told him?"

"I thought it would be an educational experience to see it demonstrated that he can actually sail this ship. I thought it might help change your mind."

I could have strangled him with my bare hands. "Now, you listen to me, old cock!" I said, with some volume. "You may be the shore captain, but you stay off my goddam bridge and stop giving orders to my staff! What's more, there's one hell of a difference between taking this ship from one side of town to the other on a windless bay and sailing her across the West Pacific hurricane zone with a tow of forty thousand tons!"

"Harinxma," he said amiably, "you're the orneriest old shite-hawk of the fleet. You should give the poor little bugger *some* room to breathe. You're going on to Taiwan, I gather."

"I sure as hell am."

"In that case, may I have my thousand bucks back?"

I pulled the envelope from my pocket and tossed it onto his stomach.

"And the airplane tickets?"

I went to fetch them from my desk and tossed them onto his chest.

"Okay," he said, "as you're going to tow the damn thing, let me tell you about the hulk." He pulled himself up to a sitting position and produced his dog-eared notebook. "You may have known her in her heyday. She was built in '33 as the *Princess of Orange*."

It suddenly deflated my anger. "What? The *Princess*—how did she get here?"

"Let me see." He flicked the pages. "Present name, *Alfonso Mendozo*, Navy brig stationed in Talca since '65. Ex *Sun Queen*. Ex *Helios*. Ex *Principessa Antonia* . . ."

While he reeled off the stages of the great ship's decline, I saw her as I had seen her as a young man before the war, when I had served briefly as skipper of a harbor-tour boat for the Amsterdam Chamber of Commerce. The departure of the *Princess of Orange* had been one of the most romantic sights in the busy port; the flagship of the Netherlands Steamship Company, she ran a six-weekly service between Amsterdam and Tandjoeng Priok in Indonesia, then the Dutch East Indies. She was the most graceful and luxurious passenger liner under Dutch flag; to see her leave, her decks lined with waving passengers festooned with paper streamers, sounding her mighty horn that made windows rattle as far away as the financial district, had never ceased to thrill me. My dream had been to serve on her, if only as third or fourth mate, but a new regulation inspired by old Kwel's father had stopped his captains from deserting him for the great steamship companies. His lobby had rammed through Parliament the law that time served on board ocean-going tugboats would no longer be valid for a mate's ticket in the merchant marine. The sight of the *Princess of Orange* in her romantic glory had made me hate the Kwels even more, a hatred that had only been dissipated under the pressure of my wartime service, when old Kwel and I had buried the hatchet to set about salvaging what was left of Holland's Glory.

". . . before ferrying Dutch refugees from Australia to Holland, she served as a troopship. You must have known her during the war?"

"Yes. I saw her ghost by on the horizon occasionally. What condition is she in?"

He shrugged his shoulders. "What do you expect, after twenty years as a Navy brig? For one thing, she must be stuck on a shoal of kidney beans of her own making; you may have to help the harbor tugs by giving her a heave tomorrow."

"Tomorrow?"

"Yessir, time is money. Tomorrow twenty hundred hours is cast-off time. In the morning you and I will go and have a look at her nipples."

"Excuse me?"

"Two nipples, one in each flank, six feet above the waterline, covered with a watertight hatch bolted from the outside. All of her oil tanks and three of her four water tanks are being filled right now with fuel for you to use under way, whenever the need arises. All you do is wait for a calm day in mid-Pacific, or anchor in the shelter of some atoll once you get to Oceania, put out a boat towing the female end of a two-hundred-foot fuel hose with floats, take off a hatch, marry the hose to the nipple and slurp. Your hose has to be hitched to one of your own pumps, of course. The hulk has no power of her own, not even a generator. The runners will have to work by candlelight."

"Harakiri isn't going to like that."

"Harakiri is going home, like everyone else, so you'll have to start talking Chinese into your walkie-talkie."

"Who's taking over?"

"I don't know yet, I suppose his mandur. Now—the stores to be brought on board here: fruit and Chinese cat food from the chandlers, the new charts from the Institute . . ."

Hawsers, provisions, tackle—it all seemed nebulous compared to my taking the *Princess of Orange*, dream ship of my youth, to her grave in a knackers' yard in Taiwan. I found I was almost afraid to see her; with her history, she must be a wreck by now.

Outside, in the corridor, the intercom started the speeded-up version of 'Bouncing Balls,' interrupting Fransen's summing up of our preparations. "Jesus! How can you stand it, Harinxma? That's not music, that's a cat fight!"

[269]

"I happen to like it."

"Boy, you're really gone native. You know what you remind me of? Hoagy Carmichael's 'Honky Tonk Blues.' That's going to be you, brother, down to the caterwauling chorus."

"All right, what else?"

"That's it," he said, putting his notebook away. He hoisted himself to his feet. "Are you seeing them off at the airport tonight?"

"I think we'll probably have a farewell dinner. Do you know of a good place?"

"Yes. Come with me to the fuel office here and book a table. Give yourself plenty of time, though. I won't be able to ride herd on them, I have an appointment in town." He grinned. "Small perks of big job." He slapped my shoulder in a sudden excess of chumminess. "See you tomorrow, six hundred hours, for a visit to the hulk. I'll have a taxi." He went to open the door. "And take it easy on the poor little sod, old friend, or out in the Pacific, when you're all by yourselves, he may go berserk and nail you to the old rugged cross."

With that, he opened the door to a wave of honky-tonk blues.

6

When I came back from the fuel office, I found, to my surprise, B.B. and Porks at work in my dayroom. They had moved the desk, which was covered with tools and coils of electric wire, and were in the process of putting back a wall panel above it.

"What the devil are you doing?"

They hadn't heard me come in and looked like small boys caught red-handed. "Er—we have to talk to you, Martinus," B.B. said solemnly. "Just let us put this panel back. You lift your end first, Porks, and I'll slip this side in."

"But what are you doing?"

"Hold it, Porks! All I need is just one more millimeter . . . Yes! That's it."

The panel was back in place; in the center of it I saw the red pustule of a push-button that hadn't been there before, and underneath it a notice screaming FIRE!

"What the hell is *that* for? The ship's lousy with fire alarms!"

"Sit down, Martinus," B.B. said, keeping his voice low. "It has to remain a secret."

"A secret? That fire button?"

"It's not a fire button, Skipper." Porks took my arm and guided me away from the desk. "It's a panic button."

"Who's supposed to do the panicking? Me?"

"Hush!" B.B. whispered. "We don't want this to make the rounds of the ship!"

"I can't wait," I said.

"Remember those stores I brought on board in Rio de Janeiro?" B.B. started.

"What about them?"

"You must have asked yourself what they were for."

Porks contributed helpfully, "*I* certainly did!"

"B.B.," I said, exerting patience, "I dealt with boffins during the war, and one thing I learned: never ask what anything is for. They either lie the daylights out of you, or they actually tell you, which usually is worse. I take it you lied."

"Well—yes." He tried to charm me with a smile. "They were meant to repair the superstructure temporarily, in case I was forced to pull the emergency brake."

"You've lost me."

"The purpose of my joining you in Rio was to test the ship's stability to the limit, right? We needed that information desperately for the building of—"

"I know all that."

"So we—that's to say, me and the other architects—agreed that 'testing to the limit' meant just that: under the right creative circumstances I would have to push the ship to the point where she would start to capsize."

"I like the word 'creative.'"

"Skip," Porks admonished, "let him talk. This is important."

"The trouble was," B.B. continued, "that no one could say exactly when that point would be reached. Yet I had to push her that far to find the answer we needed. So we decided to make certain provisions in case—"

"In case you turned the goddam ship over?"

"Well—not quite."

"Skip," Porks urged, "it's important for *you!* Listen, just *listen* for a moment, will you?"

[271]

"Briefly," B.B. continued, obviously in a hurry now to get it over with, "it was decided that I would take the ship's chief engineer into my confidence and, together with him, install a dynamite charge at the foot of the Paradise tree, to be detonated if I pushed the ship to the point of no return. The explosion should be strong enough to hurl the Paradise tree well away from the hull and thereby restore the MG to positive. But as it was likely to cause some damage to the flying bridge and the wheelhouse—"

"God almighty! You *are* insane! Destroy another man's ship for the sake of some lousy information? Was *that* the toggle switch you were clutching every time? The trigger to blow up the ship?"

He looked smaller. "Well, yes."

"So, any idiot bumping into you, any rogue wave that made you lose your balance would have resulted in your turning this ship into a cigar?"

"We *had* to prepare for it, Skip, even though we knew it would never come to that! It was our moral duty!"

I was rendered speechless. Moral duty! This took the prize.

"We were planning to dismantle the charge here in Talca before leaving," Porks continued. "But then we heard—"

"I should goddam well hope so!" I didn't know what infuriated me more: their insane unworldliness or the outrage they had planned for my ship. "When I get home, I'm going to have a word about you two with Mr. Kwel! Do you realize that if Chung made a case of this you'd end up in jail, both of you?"

"Skipper," Porks said appeasingly, "we knew you'd be mad, we know how you feel about the ship, but even you must realize now that she's a menace that can turn on you in a flash when you're not looking. When we heard that you'd decided to stay on to Taiwan all by yourself—"

"What do you mean, all by myself? Who do you think you are, the world's only engineer? Chief Liu makes you look like a goddam amateur! And as to *you*, dear Baron, the sooner you get your goddam ass out of here, the better I'll like it!"

They took it well. Their earnestness kept me in check; if I had had my emotional druthers, I would have kicked them both off the ship then and there.

"We've been through a few gales with you, Martinus," B.B. said with the voice of sweet reason, "and not once have we seen you leave the bridge to Number One or Number Two, let alone to Captain Cho. The moment there was a hint of an upcoming blow, you'd be on the bridge in your deck chair. You'll have to keep that up for days on end, maybe for weeks, in the hurricane zone."

"We want you to get sufficient rest, keep up your strength and your wits," Porks continued, "and the only way of achieving that is by leaving the dynamite charge in place. The moment the ship starts to cycle, if you're down here in your quarters, even if you're asleep in your bunk, all you'll have to do is press that button, trigger the charge and: bang! Off flies the Paradise tree, the ship rights herself, the cycle is broken and you'll have plenty of time to dress and go to the bridge."

"Let me see if I get this right. To give me peace of mind and sufficient bed rest, you propose to leave a dynamite charge at the foot of the Paradise tree, so that if the ship should start to cycle while I'm in bed, I can say, 'Oh, well, let me blow the top off before I put my pants on and go to have a look'?"

"Well, yes."

"I appreciate your concern, and I'm sure it's very ingenious, but, as far as I'm concerned, if you don't mind my being frank, it's an idea for a Laurel-and-Hardy movie."

Porks took over the sales pitch. "It's no joking matter, Skipper! We know it's far-fetched, but there *is* a chance that the ship could start to cycle when there's no one on the bridge to take action. That's not likely, but it's a theoretical possibility. What we're leaving you is an emergency brake."

"I appreciate the thought—"

"At least look at the drawing," B.B. pleaded. "See for yourself —here . . ." He unrolled the blueprint on the coffee table; it was a detailed plan of the ship's electrical wiring, with a circuit from the dayroom via the wheelhouse to the Paradise tree in green.

"It's only a small charge," Porks said in a reassuring tone. "Look—the damage would be minor."

At the foot of the Paradise tree a fuse box was drawn. From it radiated red lines representing the direction of the blast and the area of destruction. It was not minor at all; the flying bridge would be destroyed, the aft section of the wheelhouse and the stacks severely damaged.

"If having the button on the wall bothers you," Porks said, "we can put it on the desk."

I visualized the red button on the desk and Louis, with his insatiable curiosity, demolishing half the ship.

"And Mr. Chung?" I asked. "How do you think he'll react

[273]

when I deliver his ship in Taiwan and he discovers there's a dynamite charge at the foot of his Paradise tree?''

"Mr. Chung need never know," Porks replied. "I'm leaving a letter for Chief Liu with full instructions on how to dismantle it. Give it to him once you're approaching Taiwan, then he can toss the whole caboodle overboard."

"We could put up a picture to cover that button," B.B. mused. "No one need ever know."

"All it is," Porks urged, "is extra security. You'll probably never need it, but what's wrong with that? Honest, now?"

"Oh, for Pete's sake," I said, worn down by their persistence, "you're both as crazy as coots, but—okay."

"Anyhow," B.B. said happily, "everything's in place and ready to go. Only, if you do put a picture over it, do it gently. Ha-ha!"

"Thanks for the tip," I said.

They gathered their tools and their coils of wire, rolled up the blueprint and headed for the door; then a thought struck me. "Tell me: does Mr. Kwel know about this? Or Captain Fransen?"

Their reaction was so horrified that I knew B.B. was speaking the truth when he cried, "No—no, for Pete's sake! My colleagues and I planned this off our own bat, in the office!"

Porks added, "Do me a favor, Skipper: don't mention it to Captain Fransen. I'm in enough trouble with the company as it is. So, better put that picture up before he comes back. Would you do that for me?"

"Okay. By the way: I appreciate the thought."

"Any day, Skip," Porks said, opening the door.

After they had left, I went to have a look at the ghoulish button on my virgin white wall. I could foresee Fransen's reaction; he would want to know what it was for and wouldn't let up before he had ferreted it out. So, for Porks' sake, I took the picture of the old *Isabel* from the wall of the dayroom, drove in a nail—gently! —above the button and put up the picture. It looked odd, higher than the others, but not odd enough to raise questions.

Come to think of it, we had all had a narrow escape; I suddenly remembered B.B. scootering the length of the wheelhouse on his stool when the first wave of that Atlantic gale hit us, and Harakiri casually picking up the toggle switch. But I knew boffins, and although they irritated the hell out of me with their almost criminal unworldliness, I had a tender spot for them; there had

[274]

been one or two occasions during the war when one of their Rube Goldberg contraptions had saved my life. It was a comfort to know that while the breed might be hibernating, it hadn't died out. But you had to watch them like a hawk, or they would blow your world to smithereens.

I went to feed Pete. Stuffing himself, he shook his head furiously and spilled most of his seed on the floor. This was usually the signal for Louis to stir on my shoulder so I would put him down underneath the cage, but this time he wasn't there. He wasn't on the Bowditch either. Suddenly a thought hit me—nervously I checked to see if he was already exploring the mystery of the button behind the picture. It really was crazy of B.B. to leave that button active—just as crazy as clutching the trigger of a landmine had been while tossed about by gale seas. My thoughts were interrupted by a knock on the door.

"Come in!"

It was the bosun. "Can I have a word with you, Ome?"

"What's up?"

"You're not going to believe this," he said in his foghorn voice. "I told Captain Fransen I wanted to stay on, without pay. Do you know what he said? That I would be fired! That I would be out of a job! That KITCO would never hire me again! What's going on?"

I was so touched by his offer that, on impulse, I said, "I know, Bosun, it must seem strange to you, but the ship belongs to a Chinese owner now and he doesn't want any other Dutchmen to stay on. Captain Fransen must have told you that more forcefully than he intended."

"That's ball—balderdash, Ome! The Chink would certainly let me stay on without pay! Why isn't anybody allowed to stay on to help you? You're an old man! You need somebody to look after you!"

"Thank you, Bosun, but that's the way it is. I would have loved to keep you, that goes without saying. Now Hopla will have to make out as best he can."

"Rin-tin-tin? You might as well have a chimpanzee! That man isn't going to look after you properly! That man isn't going to bring you your nightcap every night! That man isn't going to see to it that you put on the proper clothes, or that you get a haircut! You need a haircut right now! Look at you! You look like a scarecrow!"

"I'll get a haircut tomorrow, Bosun. Now you go and pack

your bag and I'll come to the airport with you all. We'll have a farewell meal together and booze it up and talk about the good times we had. Okay?"

He looked at me, hurt, bewildered. I could see he was trying to think of something, an overriding reason for him to stay on even if it cost him his job. All he could come up with was "And who's going to look after the canary?"

"I will, Bosun. I've been doing so, off and on, for a while now. Come, pack your bag. Let's have a blast at the airport."

"By the looks of this town, there ain't no airport to have a blast in," he said somberly, heading for the door.

"I booked us in a restaurant nearby. Trust me. We'll have a proper farewell party."

"But I want to stay on!" he bellowed, outraged, anguished.

"I know. I'd like you to. But that's the way it is."

He left. I took a perfunctory look around for Louis, then shrugged my shoulders and sat down in my chair. He must have found a new place to hole up in, probably a slipper or something. He would show up when he was hungry.

I had barely started to open my mail when, knock knock, there came Harlingen, to say goodbye and ask, casually, if his work had been satisfactory. I remembered that they all had volunteered under duress, so I put my mail aside, went to my desk and wrote glowing testimonials for them all, to be handed to them at the farewell meal that evening.

Halfway through my eulogy on the bosun—*trustworthy, expert, a man of great integrity*—there was another knock on my door, a bang this time.

"Yes!"

Harakiri stuck his head in. "Harinxma?"

"Here! At the desk."

"Listen, I just popped in to tell you I'm staying on to Taiwan. I thought you'd like to know."

"But didn't Captain Fransen tell you to go home? He has a ticket to Amsterdam for you."

"I told him to stick it up his asshole. My Chinks have kind of taken to me; when Fransen turned up and told me to get off, the mandur blew snot at his feet. You should have seen him! He took off like a bat out of hell. Those jokers don't piss around, if you know what I mean. So, I'm on. We won't see much of each other, but let's keep the daily chinwag going. Have to run now."

"Hold it! Have you seen the new tow?" He nodded. "What's she like?"

"Oh, just another old rustbucket. Seen one, seen 'em all. Ta-ta."

"We're having a farewell meal tonight! Join us!"

"Sure thing." And he was gone.

Sighing, I went back to the *man of great integrity*. It was going to be lonely without the bosun and the others; but, at least, Fransen had met his match in Harakiri. For some reason, it made me feel a lot better.

7

The six of us—Porks, Harlingen, the bosun, B.B., Harakiri and myself—had dinner that night in a Chilean version of an American diner, which, surprisingly, was filled with people in evening dress: women with tiaras and flowing gowns of the kind that seem to change color, men in tuxedoes and high-ranking officers in uniforms compared to which my Russian admiral's outfit was that of the doorman of a cheap hotel. We looked like a bunch of hoboes; only Fransen, once he'd shown he was wearing a tie under his shabby raincoat, looked presentable.

Because this was our last meal together, I ordered a bottle of champagne. The cork popped like a gunshot and the glasses foamed; I rose for a toast. "To the *Isabel Kwel*, God bless her soul. She has carried us halfway around the world, which was a bit of a miracle if one believes the rumors, and we owe it in large part to the four of you now about to leave. So: B.B., Porks, Marco, Bosun —thank you, God bless you, hope to see you again soon." We did not clink glasses, as each glass that rings means a sailor who drowns.

The bosun responded before anyone else had been able to get in first. Standing up to make a speech, he spoke as if he had to make himself heard over a gale. The clientele in the diner fell silent; they had no choice.

"Men! Brothers!" he bellowed. "We are gathered together to say farewell to Ome Tinus—"

"Hell, Bosun," Porks interrupted, "this isn't a funeral! Keep it light, man."

"Ome," the bosun continued in a major key, "the time has come for us to say farewell but not goodbye. We've had a good trip together, with a few ups and downs—"

"You can say that again," Harlingen said.

The bosun was not to be sidetracked. "Even so, on the whole, we had a good time. We ate good. We got on good. We—"

"We slept good," Porks contributed.

Harakiri said, "Let him talk, wise guy."

"We had a good time," the bosun concluded. "Now let's drink to Ome and wish him and Hari Godspeed and happy sailing."

"Godspeed and happy sailing," the others chimed in, raising their glasses.

"Ome," the bosun bellowed, "here's looking at you!" He sat down to loud applause from the diners at the tables, which must have been from sheer relief, as they couldn't have understood a word he was saying. I ordered another bottle of champagne.

After the farewell at the airport and the long taxi ride back to the ship, during which Harakiri gave an evocative play-by-play description of his sister's hemorrhoid operation, I was in a depressed state as I made my way down the corridor to my dayroom. Beast Rufus' accelerated tape was caterwauling over the intercom; with the others gone, the ship had become a floating Chinatown. I was now the only white man left on board.

I went to put some decent music on the hi-fi to drown out the intercom in the corridor, but discovered that Hopla, in a dramatic access of tidiness, had gathered all loose objects in the cabin and stacked them on my desk: boxes of booze sealed by Customs, a pair of open-toed sandals, a pile of official documents; I had to dig like a terrier before I found the tapes under a box of oranges delivered by the chandlers. I put on Handel's 'Water Music' and settled down on the couch to read my letters at last. Louis was not on my shoulder. I looked at the Bowditch again, he was not there either. I made kissing noises, called, "Louis!" Where could he be?

I looked for him everywhere—dayroom, bedroom, bathroom —groped behind the books on the shelf, opened the drawers of my desk, my wardrobe. Finally I called Hopla.

"Hopla, have you see Louis?"

"No, Co'dore. He gone?"

"He must have gotten out. Did you leave the door open while you were cleaning in here?"

"Who, me? No, no, Co'dore! No, no, never. I always close door very careful."

"Well, he'll turn up, I suppose. Take a look around the ship for him, will you? Tell the others. Well, good night. See you in the morning."

I went back to the couch and tried to read my letters, but couldn't concentrate. If he had indeed slipped outside, where would he have gone? The galley seemed most likely. I got up and went to look.

There was little traffic in the corridors; either everyone had gone to bed or they were ashore. To my relief, I found Ma Chang, as always both tidy and disheveled, setting out the dishes for tomorrow's breakfast on the long counter opposite the range.

"Have you seen Louis?" I asked.

As she frowned and gazed at me with a look of incomprehension, I remembered that, of course, she didn't understand what I was saying, so I tried to imitate a rat by saying 'Peep! Peep!' and making pointed ears with my fingers. When that seemed to break her up, I went back to the door and called down the corridor, "Hopla! Hopla, come here! I'm in the galley!"

He turned up at once; he must have been keeping track of me. "Hopla, ask Ma Chang about Louis. Find out if she's seen him around the galley."

Hopla translated. She nodded, and gazed at me.

"Have you any idea where he can be?"

Hopla translated. She said something in her bird language.

"She say: no idea. She say: him ashore looking for a bride."

Ashore . . . the idea didn't bear thinking about.

"Well, thank you, Ma Chang. Keep looking, will you? If you see him, I'd like him back, please. Good night."

As I turned to leave, Hopla called, "She say: wait!"

I waited while she rummaged in the pockets of her smock and produced her pendulum. She made it oscillate back and forth, the way she had done when she checked me over after the magical cure in mid-Atlantic. Her face took on a faraway expression, as if she were concentrating on something unseen yet real to her. Then she grinned as the pendulum started to swing in a circle, uttered a few twittering sounds and pocketed it with a giggle.

"What was that, Hopla?"

"She say: him on—on—I do not know word. Pinge? Him visit wine shops. Him will turn up drunk. She think very funny."

"But where *is* he?"

He translated my question; she shrugged her shoulders and then twittered something, giggling.

"She say: she do not know. She say: never look in sailorman bed."

I left, feeling very alien. I no longer believed in her hocus-pocus, for if Louis had indeed slipped ashore, how could he—tame pet, pampered all his life—ever manage to find his way back? And if he couldn't . . .

I suddenly felt certain that my little friend and I would never see each other again.

8

The next morning, after I had everybody search the ship for Louis once more, I was picked up by Fransen and taken to the break-water beyond the Navy repair basin and the two dug-out dry docks. Inside the mole a huge old liner was moored. The moment I saw her silhouette looming over the sheds, I recognized the *Princess of Orange;* as the taxi rattled down the railroad-track-rutted quayside, I stared at her wordlessly.

I accompanied Fransen on board. It was a grim and depressing experience for me, having known the ship in her days of glory. I am not a sentimental man, but I refused to go beyond the entrance hall with its peeling gilt, toothless chandeliers and ratty carpet, still faintly showing the outline of the coat of arms of the late Dutch Empire. What got to me was the stench, a mixture of disinfectant and decay reminiscent of a morgue. But I stayed long enough to hear that Harakiri and the runners were happy; they had already installed themselves in first-class staterooms, Hari appropriating the captain's quarters. When I turned away to leave, he grabbed my arm and said, "You've got to see the rest, Harinxma! It's like the set of a horror movie. Do you know what they did to the first-class dining room?"

"Sorry, Hari," I said, "I don't have the time. We should take a look now at the foredeck, to decide how we're going to attach the bridle; after that I have to take a look at the fueling arrangements." The sight of the ship affected me deeply; it was like looking in a mirror at the age of twenty-five and seeing a man of seventy.

Harakiri and I walked the length of the main deck to the forecastle, where we inspected the huge anchor winches and chains. After some discussion we decided to have the anchors tipped and detached and use the terminal links of both chains to attach the shackles of the bridle. The ship had no power of her own and it would have been impossible for her to weigh anchor anyhow. This way Hari could give some chain in case the critical links were worn by chafing against the bow if she started to sheer in bad weather.

Fransen joined us, and we discussed how to take her out of the tight corner where she was moored. Then a Navy launch with eight ratings took Fransen and myself to take a look at the watertight hatches in the flanks of the ship, secured by removable bolts, with inside them the capped fuel pipes to which the hose would be coupled. The hose, Fransen said, would be delivered that afternoon, to be coiled in the *Isabel*'s storage hold.

The moment I returned on board, I checked to see if Louis had returned; he hadn't. Pete sat quietly in his cage; even he seemed to miss him. There could no longer be any doubt: Louis had slipped ashore under the cover of darkness and got lost among the sheds and the containers and the stacks of cargo. It seemed final, for what chance had he among the tribes of vicious wharf rats? How could he fend for himself, find food, escape marauding cats, stray dogs, little boys with slingshots or air guns haunting the docks? He didn't have a hope; he was probably dead already.

I was surprised by my own reaction. I had had no idea how emotionally attached I had become to my little companion. It all added to the depression which darkened the rest of that day.

At sunset three harbor tugs tried to dislodge the *Princess of Orange* from her bed of kidney beans; the fact that in the meantime her tanks had been filled from fuel barges did not help. The *Isabel* was called upon; it took her full moon-rocket power to tear the old hulk from the mud with a gigantic sucking sound, an overwhelming stench of tropical marshes and a cloud of mosquitoes that swarmed like bees and headed straight for the tugboat. On the aft deck the Chinese sailors started to dance around, slapping themselves as the vicious insects zeroed in on them.

[281]

By the time we had swung the *Princess* around in the bay and were set to leave, darkness had fallen. Our departure was an unexpectedly solemn occasion. The *Isabel*, with the aid of the three harbor tugs, slowly moved the old liner out into the Pacific. Two naval vessels escorted us and squealed bleeps of farewell that echoed in the night; the *Isabel* responded with the deep 'broon' of her horn. The black silhouette of the liner, outlined against the stars and the glow of the city across the bay, was majestic even in death. At a given moment the lights of Concepción, diffused by night haze, seemed to surround the dead hulk with a halo. It briefly gave her a magical life; as I gazed at her from the bridge, I saw what Turner must have seen before he painted *The Fighting Téméraire*.

I gazed at the sight until darkness engulfed us, and mourned for Louis, little speck of evanescent life lost among the stars.

9

By the time I had set the ship on her course and started the slow paying out of the hawser, it was too late for our traditional departure Happy Hour; it would be two hours before the hawser reached its full length, and I wanted to be there when it did. It was hardly worth undressing for two hours' sleep; I left the bridge feeling bereft and lonely.

Of course, it was all in the mind. Porks would have been in his engine room, Harlingen in his cubicle, the bosun on the aft deck or below at the winches, B.B. asleep in the hospital. Practically speaking, they might all have been still on board. Yet I missed them with a hollow feeling in the pit of my stomach that I hadn't experienced since the war.

When I entered the dayroom, welcomed by Pete, the absence of the familiar thump of Louis jumping me from the Bowditch brought about such an acute feeling of loss that I went to get myself a drink. But when I opened the freezer, I found that Fransen had polished off the crock of gin; all unopened bottles were in the cardboard box on my desk, sealed by Customs. If the bosun had still been on board, they would have been unpacked and stowed away by now; Hopla was probably in bed, or gambling with his cronies in the corridor of the crew's quarters. My desk looked such a dreary, desolate mess that I couldn't be bothered to start opening boxes, so I undressed and went to bed feeling sorry for myself.

As I lay staring at the ceiling, reluctant to turn off the light even though I was dead tired, I realized I was waiting for the bosun to appear with my nightcap. And for Louis to settle, after turning around three times, on the blanket between my feet. I was overcome by an intense, rather childish feeling of loneliness. Or maybe it was just the underlying awareness of the vastness of the Pacific Ocean we were now set to cross: five thousand four hundred miles of loneliness between here and Samoa, and no landfall before Pago Pago. Fifty-four days before Fransen would come sauntering onto the bridge again. Eight weeks of exile in Chinatown. Two months of honky-tonk blues.

I couldn't understand it: I loved my Chinese, they were my friends; why this sudden sense of isolation, of being lost in some alien country, friendless and alone? Louis, of course. I really missed the little bugger. The feel of his warm, furry body in my hands. The little wet snout exploring my ear while I was asleep, making me waken with a yodel. Well, there was always good old Pete, so I got up and went to feed him.

But for some reason, without Louis, Pete looked and behaved like any dumb bird in a cage. I realized now that his spunky reactions and cocky strutting as I fed him and talked baby language had been his response to Louis' presence on my shoulder. Now, baby language sounded what it was: a lonely old man talking doobie-doobie-doo to a dumb bird that watched him, unmoved, with a glass eye.

I was so dejected, so depressed, so haunted by the dawning realization—as yet unacknowledged—that I had committed a fatal folly by continuing the voyage, that I went back to the bedroom, opened the drawer with the socks and the pajamas and pulled out the Ouija board and the planchette.

HELP ME HELP ME HELP ME WHERE AM I BOYS WHERE AM I . . .

Crazy to toy with it, certainly at this particular moment; I knew what the damn thing could do once it tore loose.

BULLFROG BULLFROG THIS IS BULLY WHERE AM I BOYS PLEASE GOD-DAMMIT HELP ME WHERE AM I— But I simply wanted to find out where Louis was.

I put the board on the coffee table and opened it. It looked

[283]

even more fraudulent than when I had peeked at it earlier: a soothsayer's tool. Yet, I was going to give it a shot. I tried out the planchette, just to get the hang of it. It rolled smoothly on its caster, ready for its little spook driver.

How did one address a Ouija board? I tried to remember. 'Spirit, are you there?' was what the mate of the *Amalia* had intoned in Shadwell Basin in June '44, before dead Bully began to spoil the fun. But I didn't want to contact any ghosts. I just wanted to know where my rat was.

So I said, "Board? Er—could you by any chance—er—are you prepared to tell me where Louis is?"

Nothing happened. Maybe I should put my hand with the planchette at the starting point, which presumably was at the bottom, in the center, on the D of GOODBYE.

"Er—hello there. Excuse me, but could you . . ." I felt like a fool. Imagine the bosun coming in! The bosun was not going to, not ever again. No more 'Ome, here's your nightcap. Now, have you done your teeth?' Suddenly I was close to tears. Everyone was gone, every single one of my countrymen, even Louis, damn him.

"Board," I said. "Please tell me—" And then it happened.

Suddenly, startlingly, the planchette moved. It was not I who moved it; it was some impulse independent of my will, separate from my very identity, as if an invisible hand had got hold of mine and pushed the pointer from letter to letter, unerringly, going for the word it wanted to spell: B E W A R E. A pause; then again: B E W A R E. And again: B E W A R E. B E W A R E. B E W A— I literally had to tear my hand free from the force that propelled it.

I felt shocked, scared, fascinated—it exerted the irresistible attraction of a street accident, which you know will be gory and horrible, sullying you with the foulness of a gawking ghoul.

"Who's telling me this?" I asked. "Who are you?" I put my hand on the planchette again.

It whizzed at once from letter to letter, spelling T J A L L I N G. Then it went limp.

Tjalling? What the hell was tjalling? A name? Ah—yes: an old Friesian first name. Or was it Groningian? One of the northern Dutch provinces. Hadn't heard it for years, not since I was a boy. Even then I hadn't known anyone called Tjalling. I never had. The whole thing was a hoax.

I became so disgusted with myself and the whole brazen

[284]

hoodwinkery of the thing that I flung it aside, hoisted myself out of my chair and headed for the box with the bottles.

But halfway there I thought, 'No, dammit! I'm not going to sit here and drink myself to a standstill in maudlin self-pity! Go back to bed! If you must put something in your damn mouth, get a sandwich!' But it was too late to ring for Hopla, and I didn't feel like traipsing all the way down to the pantry, it wasn't worth it. So: to bed, to bed, old lush.

On my way to the bedroom I spotted the untidy stack of junk the good-for-nothing Chinese had left on my desk. It should all have been stowed away: the booze in the icebox, the sandals in my wardrobe, the box of oranges in the pantry . . . Wait a minute: an orange! How healthy, how sane: tired old master partakes of an orange at dead of night before going to rest up for the midnight watch. I removed the sandals, the ship's documents from Customs, the booze sealed by Customs, opened the box and—"*Whaaaow!!*" Instead of the smooth, round globes of MOUTH-WATERING NAVELS FROM ISRAEL, I felt a soft, furry—

Furry?

I tore open the box and—my God!—there he lay: on his back, white belly exposed, paws spread, eyes closed, snoring—surrounded by the hollowed-out ghosts of oranges as empty as eggshells. Ma Chang, God bless her, had been right! He *was* drunk—on orange juice fermenting in his stomach—and snoring it off surrounded by empties.

I lifted him out of his fruit rat's heaven; he was as floppy as a doll. Dead? Like hell he was. He was blotto, a corpse with a heartbeat.

I carried him to the bedroom and put him on the bed, then went to pick up the Ouija board and its planchette and stuffed them back where they belonged: out of sight, out of mind. All that time he lay there on his back, eyes closed, spread-eagled, the Rodent Flasher out for the count.

I went to bed, put him on my chest and turned off the light. The ship lived, secretively, in the stillness. The bathroom door rattled softly. The lamp tinkled like a little Christmas bell. There was a slow, lazy, protracted creaking as she heeled, slowly, in the long, lazy swell of the Pacific.

[285]

═══[*Chapter Eleven*]═══

1

After twenty-four hours at sea, the spell of the Pacific began to take hold of us.

Up to Talcahuano we had followed the coast; the eastern horizon had been dominated by the jagged ramparts of the Andes, their icy peaks, white with eternal snow, turning the color of coral when the sun went down and glowing with a ghostly sheen by night. They had balanced the emptiness of the infinite ocean to the west; now we were alone under the stars, a black beetle guiding a blind mole, for once we were out of sight of land, the old liner seemed not dead but blind. It was the first intimation of the spell of the Pacific.

The old *Princess* lumbered behind us a mile away, continuously changing aspect with the shifting witchery of the light, from massive pyramid on the horizon to fragile toy in infinity. During the decades she had spent in that backwater she had grown a forest of algae and crustaceans under her waterline which, according to Fransen, would have been more expensive to clean off than taking an extra week to tow her to her pauper's grave. The maximum water speed we could make, with the *Isabel*'s engines churning at their most economical number of revolutions, was only four knots. Inevitably, this deepened the spell of the vastness through which we were crawling by day and apparently lying still under the dome of blazing stars that overwhelmed us by night. I thought I had never seen a sky like this before in all my years at sea, but it was the eye of the beholder that cast the spell of our being lost in another dimension.

The succession of identical days in the timeless void brought about a new intimacy with the staff, especially Chief Liu. I had always liked him, not just because he was an articulate, occasionally funny man but because he was the oldest of them by far. I found it difficult to judge the age of a Chinese, but he told me himself, during one of his impromptu visits to the bridge when I was on watch, that he was fifty-three. He was a family man who carried an accordion of pictures in a special wallet, whole flocks of grandchildren, all the spitting image of Mr. Chung. Sylvia had furnished me with a set of my own, which I was happy to bring out in a reciprocal gesture; I wondered who mine looked like in his eyes; the bosun, probably. We talked philosophy, Chinese art and, ultimately, war. He was reticent about it, so was I; I wasn't even sure which war he was talking about. But it somehow brought us closer: two old bores among the twittering young.

Happy Hour became a lot livelier, now that the Chinese staff was no longer inhibited by the presence of Porks, Harlingen and B.B. They swapped stories, told jokes, frequently slipping into Chinese. But Chief Liu quickly brought them back to our private brand of English, and Harakiri kept up his daily chat with a vengeance. He now took twenty minutes instead of ten telling lies on the walkie-talkie, long, involved stories about safes he had discovered that must certainly be full of foreign currency, about rivalries between the runners which ended in shrieks and gurgling at dead of night so that he felt compelled to count them in the morning. After a few days his stories became rather hackneyed, as if the Pacific sapped his creative powers, but the Chinese loved them and rewarded him with gratifying laughter, which I transmitted by pressing the TALK button.

The only one who didn't share in the general amusement was Captain Cho. A week after my bawling him out in Talcahuano, which had led to his total disappearance, he decided to take up his watch on the bridge again. I had no idea why; maybe he had become bored in his cabin, maybe the laughter from the dayroom became too strong a lure. I was not unhappy that he took on his share; it had never been the idea that I stand watches at all, let alone regular ones. But even though he was back in circulation, I rarely set eyes on him. He still had his meals served in his cabin, and whenever I turned up on the bridge during his watch he was so conspicuously uncomfortable with my presence that I left him to it. At times I felt rather than saw him looking down on us from a window of the wheelhouse as Bryn Mawr and I checked the hawser for chafing. When I looked up, he would turn away. I couldn't interpret the expression in his eyes when he saw me there, hobnobbing with his bosun. Occasionally, from my dayroom, I could hear his high, cantankerous voice yell at someone during his watch, but I had the impression that everyone ignored him.

After eighteen days at sea I decided to bunker from the old *Princess*. We still had plenty of oil in our tanks, but the wind had died down overnight and the sea was exceptionally peaceable that morning. In the clean, young day the hawser was slowly reeled in, bearded with algae, bringing with it the childhood smell of summer beaches; every foot of it had to be scrubbed. When finally we reached the stretcher, I swung the *Isabel* alongside the *Princess* and went by workboat to have a look at the fuel hatch. As it turned out, I was not the only one tempted to break the monotony with a boat ride; loaded to the gills with free riders and towing the white fuel hose with the bright blue floats, the launch made its way across the lazy sea. When we came to the hatch in the liner's flank, Harakiri shouted greetings from the promenade deck, ten stories above. The Chinese runners, lined up at the railing, glared down at my pregnant dogs without responding to my wave. Chief Liu and the second engineer removed the hatch and connected the hose coupling to the nipple, then Chief Liu told his Number One by walkie-talkie to start the *Isabel*'s pump. The hose acquired a sudden life of its own, writhed and filled out until it was hard and firm; I could feel the fuel oil pulsing through it under my hand. After a few minutes Harakiri lowered the Jacob's ladder and invited me to climb it; after a look at the height of the perpendicular cliff, I begged off, so he came down and was taken on board the *Isabel* together with the other passengers. The workboat took him back again hours later when the fueling was completed; in the meantime he had regaled me with stories about glassed-in verandas with deck chairs where the Chinese runners drank beer from cans and crapped in a corner. I took his Hogarthian picture with a grain of salt.

2

The next morning, waking early from one of those dreams that are instantly forgotten, I dressed and went out on deck. The wind had not picked up; the weather was hot, still and muggy. There was a haze in the sky; the sun had a convalescent look, its strength sapped by mist. After wishing Number Two good morning and patting Whittier's shoulder, I checked the barometer. It was lower than the night before. I heard Hopla curse behind my back because he had lost his footing and spilled a mug of tea on the deck of the wheelhouse; only then did it penetrate to me that the *Isabel* was rolling heavily. The sea looked torpid and oily; the swell, long and fast, slid by, glinting in the misty light. I checked the night's log. Just after midnight the swell had started to increase sufficiently for Number One to make a note of it.

Although there was no mention of any hurricanes in the official weather report, I decided to take no chances. I raised Harakiri on the walkie-talkie. He took a long time responding; when he did, he sounded as if I had roused him after an all-night party.

"Yeah?"

"*Princess*, this is *Isabel*. Good morning. Do you read me?"

"Where's the fire, Harinxma?"

"We're running into the fringe of some bad weather. I'm heading into the swell. Tell your men to stand by, over."

"When did all this happen, hey? I don't hear any wind. Over."

"There isn't any wind, but the swell is getting higher and the barometer is falling. You'd better get out of bed and check your bridle, over."

"Jesus, man, can't that wait a little? Everybody here is asleep except the lookout, over."

"No, sorry. And carry your walkie-talkie with you so we can check on each other when it starts to blow, over."

"Are you sure about this?"

"Yes. At this latitude, depressions build up very fast. I'll try to work my way around it, but I don't want to be caught with my pants down when it starts to blow. Over."

"All right, Harinxma. You're the boss. Over and out."

An hour later the swell had become faster and white mares' tails had swept into the sky from the distant horizon. But there still was no wind, which made it impossible to locate the center of the disturbance. I called the radio room; Marco Two said no weather station had reported a hurricane threat. No wonder, we were in the largest no-man's-land on the globe; cyclones could be spawned here, rage and die without anyone being any the wiser.

I went through the ship to make sure that everything was stowed seafast. Ma Chang took her pots and pans off the range and secured the contents of her shelves. Carleton and Bryn Mawr put up hand lines on the aft deck. The ventilator cowls were reversed by Chief Liu and Tulane. The boat covers were taken off

[289]

and the decks cleared of loose objects by Wellesley, Haverford and Yale. After that, all I could do was wait for developments.

An hour or so later a distant mountain range of cumuli appeared on the horizon. The mares' tails in the sky became a gray overcast, obscuring the sun. There was still no wind. I gave the order that everyone now on deck should get some rest while they still had the chance; I myself went below after arranging with Number One that he would call me when the going got rough. Then I went to see Captain Cho.

To my surprise, he was not reclining on his bed this time with the thoughts of Chairman Mao. He was sitting at his little desk in his number-one uniform, counting money. The Mysterious East indeed.

"Captain," I said, "we're in for bad weather, maybe a hurricane. I'll try to skirt it, but for the time being there's no wind and the center is hard to locate. I sent everyone to their bunks to rest, but as you're up and about—"

"Very well," he said with an eagerness he hadn't shown before, "I will take Number One's place. Who has the wheel?"

"Whittier."

"You want him to rest too?"

He sounded ready to take the bridge singlehanded. I was relieved by this sudden spurt of enthusiasm, but I had to go and lie down myself; the idea of his being alone at the helm wouldn't make for healthy sleep. "No need to, thank you, Captain. Whittier will have time to catch up after his watch."

"Very well," he repeated, keen as mustard. "I will go at once. Just one moment, please."

"No need to break your neck, Captain. There's no emergency yet. Thanks all the same."

"My pleasure," he said, with the first smile he had given me since Rotterdam.

On my way to my quarters I reflected how odd it felt to thank the master of a ship for going to the bridge when bad weather threatened; but at least he had joined the human race. Who knows, after the hurricane—if we were in for one—he might even join Happy Hour.

As I entered the dayroom, headed for my bunk, I expected to feel the thud of Louis on my shoulder, but it didn't come. I looked for him and saw his intelligent little eyes peeping at me over the Bowditch. Obviously, he sensed something was coming and had found himself a secure place. Pete didn't seem to be alarmed; he hopped from perch to perch and practiced his mating call, apparently unaware that the cage was swinging wildly with the laboring of the ship. I took it down and lashed it to the radiator; that alarmed him to the point where I had to cover the cage with the towel.

I called the engine room from my bunk. "Chief, tell everybody in your department that they should get some sleep. Once it starts, it may keep us up for a while."

"Hokay. I thought she was taking up skirt for dance." He loved risqué metaphors.

"My guess is we have an hour, maybe two, before it hits. Make the best of it."

"Hokay! Have good dream!"

I called the bridge to tell Number One he was about to be relieved, but Captain Cho answered. He reported that every man had turned in; he was alone in the wheelhouse with the helmsman, there was no one left on deck. I put back the receiver, closed my eyes and made myself slide into sleep.

3

I had a dream. I was lying helpless as a baby in my bunk, only it was not a bunk but an outsized cradle being rocked by a woman who made soothing noises. I knew the woman and yet I didn't. I got worried when the rocking became stronger; in the end it became so violent that I had to grasp the edges of the cradle so as not to be thrown out—the woman was being very rough. Then I recognized the smiling face looking down on me: it was Chung, wearing a wig, and suddenly it became terrifying. His smile turned into a grin, his face took on an evil expression, he rocked the cradle more and more violently. I was about to be thrown out when suddenly my head hit the side and I was wide awake, holding on to the sides of my bunk. The ship was rolling crazily, my bunk soared up and down; all around me things were sliding, crashing to the floor. The *Isabel* was in her deadly cycle!

I swung myself out of my bunk, was picked up bodily and hurled against the wall. The ship swept over onto her other side and hurled me back against the bunk. My arm went numb, the ship's rolling was such that I couldn't keep my footing; yet I managed to pull myself into the dayroom and made a dash for the door to the corridor. The ship picked me up and flung me against the room divider. My head exploded in pain; I felt sickness rise to my throat and lay there for a moment, disoriented, paralyzed by terror. I knew this was it, we were going, going! I heard a voice shriek. I didn't know where it came from or who it was, but it brought me to my senses. The deck rose in a sickening surge as the ship rolled onto her other side; I tried to crawl to the door and was thrown down the length of the room again. Somehow I managed to direct my fall toward the desk and grabbed it; it was bolted to the deck. The ship heeled over onto her other side: everything loose in the room tumbled past me and crashed against the wall. It was too late, I would never make it to the bridge in time. Where the hell was Cho? Why didn't he use the thrusters? The ship was totally out of control. There was nothing for it: I must get to the panic button. The ship hovered for a second before sweeping onto her other side; I managed to throw myself across the desk and held on for dear life as it heaved. Every muscle in my body screamed to let go, my arms were being torn out of their sockets, but I was able to hang on and waited for the moment she would hover before starting to swing back. The moment came, but she didn't swing back. I realized with horror that she was lying on her side; she wasn't going to swing back, but would go on turning over and capsize. With a despairing lunge I hauled myself across the desk, pushed aside the picture and pressed the red button on the wall.

What followed was not an explosion but a convulsion of the entire body of the ship, as if a shell had struck and slammed through two decks before it exploded with a sound of splintering wood and a shower of glass. I had a last, wordless thought of Sylvia, followed by a terrible sense of sorrow for my men about to go down with the ship while I was locked in the dayroom. I waited for water to engulf me; I was as ready to go as a man could be. Then the strain on my hands clutching the edge of the desk seemed to lessen. With a slow, tormented sigh, the *Isabel* began to right herself. There was a sound of sliding wood and slithering glass in the corridor, a tumult of slamming, tearing; then it ceased. A hill slid under her, lifted her martyred body, passed under her, and she started the deadly cycle of her rolling again. The thrusters! Why was there no one at the thrusters?

I staggered to the door and tore it open; the corridor was a chaos of glass and splintered wood. When I headed for the companionway, glass crunched under my feet like thin ice. I heard a feeble cry for help somewhere near, but what passed through my head with unnatural clarity was B.B. saying, "Unless it's been hurled well away from the ship, the fall of the Paradise tree will only give you a few minutes' respite. Get yourself to the thrusters as soon as you can!" I clawed my way up the companionway.

When I reached the top, I stood still, at a loss, facing a tangle of metal, gigantic shards of bulkheads, bits of rail angled crazily at the sky. There was no door, no way into the wheelhouse; above me, hanging across a section of rail, wearing a life jacket, a man looked down on me, motionless. I saw something move in the tangle of steel that barred my way: a glint, a turning movement. The steering wheel! The ship was on automatic!

My confusion cleared. I clambered across the shards of metal, unaware of cuts and scratches. I reached the wheel, flicked the switch and turned off the automatic pilot. Now for the thrusters. I waited for the next heave of her wallowing hulk to pass, crawled across the pile of wreckage, grabbed the handle of the forward thruster and gave full starboard power to the bow, praying that the lines that transmitted the signal hadn't been severed. They hadn't; with a mighty surge, her bow was swept off course. The fight was over. She was safe. Only then did I become aware of blood trickling down my forehead into my eyes.

It had been a supreme effort; as I felt myself collapsing, a voice cried, "Commodore! Commodore!" from the direction of the companionway. I saw Number One emerge and clamber toward me across the debris.

"Commodore! What happened?!"

"No idea," I heard myself say. "Seems the bridge was unattended while the ship was on automatic."

"What happened to Captain Cho? Why is he dead?"

I stared at him. "Dead?"

"Yes! Half—half of him is hanging in the rail up there, look!"

As in a dream, I heard a small, metallic voice call, "*Isabel! Isabel!* Do you read?" It was the walkie-talkie, somewhere in the rubble. *"Isabel! Isabel Kwel!* This is *Princess!* Do you read? Harinxma, do you read?"

I groped for the walkie-talkie under the pile of wreckage and managed to put my hand on it, but I couldn't pull it free.

"Isabel! Isabel! Do you read? Do you read?"

I found the talk switch, pressed it and shouted, *"Princess,* this is *Isabel! Princess,* this is *Isabel!* Harinxma here! Over!"

"Harinxma, what happened? Was that your engine? Was that your engine that exploded?"

"No, Harakiri, no! It was an explosive charge at the foot of the Paradise tree! We nearly capsized!"

"What? I do not read! Harinxma, what were you saying? I do not read!"

"Never mind, Harakiri! I'll explain later!"

"Do you need assistance? Harinxma, do you need assistance?"

"I don't know, Harakiri! I'll contact you again in ten minutes, over."

"Jesus! From here it looked as if your whole top came off! What exploded?"

"Over and out." I turned off the walkie-talkie and again tried to free it from the rubble.

"Omi! Omi!" Bryn Mawr loomed over me, distorted by the blood running into my eyes. "All right, Omi? All right?"

"Take the wheel, keep her headed into the seas. Mate Number One is there."

I scrambled to my feet, made my way across the wreckage to the back of the wheelhouse and clambered across the jagged barrier of glass and metal to where I could see Cho. He was where I had last seen him: leaning over a slanting section of rail which must have been part of the flying bridge. Now I realized he was not leaning over the rail, but buried in it, stuck there like a smashed fly, his torso in a life jacket, his legs gone. His face was half gone too.

I gazed up at him, sickened by the sight. How could he have ended up there? He should have been inside the wheelhouse. Yet, judging from his position, the explosion must have flung him against the rail of the flying bridge with such force that his legs were sheared off.

"Commodore!"

The voice seemed to come from overboard. There was wind now; the swell was ruffled with fierce little waves; the cumuli had conquered the sky. On the horizon was the silhouette of the *Princess.*

"Commodore! My God . . ."

I looked down. Marco Number One was standing at the foot of the remains of the companionway, gazing up at what was left of Captain Cho. I looked around me and saw what the explosion had wreaked. Not only was the Paradise tree gone, the stacks had been blown sideways and now hung at a crazy angle. The whole of the flying bridge, the entire walkway on which the Paradise tree had rested were gone. The wreckage had a strange, haunting aspect, as in a dream.

"What happened?"

I found Chief Liu was standing beside me. I had no idea how he had made it up here—probably the same way I had. "There's been an explosion. The Paradise tree was hurled overboard. If it hadn't been, we would have capsized."

"But how? What exploded? Who did it?"

"I did." I still had that dreamlike feeling. "Are the engines okay?"

"Hokay! Hokay! But what—"

A voice called from below, "Commodore! The radio is dead! I lost all communication!"

I looked down again at the anxious young marco standing among the wreckage, and suddenly I knew that the dream was a memory: Sparks of my old *Isabel,* after the shell had turned him into a mangled mess of flesh and bone and cloth, with one boot sticking out, back to front. For a hallucinating moment the two disasters melted into one: Cho's mutilated torso was that of a member of my crew decimated forty years ago on the Murmansk run. Then the time warp ceased and I was back in the present.

I said, "There's been an explosion. The Paradise tree is gone and all your equipment with it. Forget about the radio. Help me down and let's check out the rest of the ship."

The distance I had to lower myself in order to reach the remains of the companionway scared me, I couldn't understand how I had made it up there to start with. I turned away and called to Number One, "Steady as you go, while I have a look below! I'll only be a few minutes!"

"Don't worry, Commodore!" he shouted, small against the wild black sky where the wall of the wheelhouse should have been. "I look after ship, you look after men!"

"I must call a detail to take care of the body," I said to the marco still waiting below me. "Here I come."

He caught me in his arms as I made the jump.

4

The voice that had feebly called for help in the corridor was Hopla's—a crumpled white form, covered with debris, at the far end. For a sick moment I thought he was dead too; when we got to him, he stirred and moaned, "My leg! I think it broken!"

We cautiously removed the tangled mass of wood and glass; his right leg lay half under him at an unnatural angle. I sent the marco to the hospital to get splints, bandages, scissors; when he came back, I cut Hopla's pants to free the leg. It was indeed broken. I put on provisional splints with a bandage; then, before leaving to get help to carry him to the hospital, I put on a Band-Aid to stop the blood running into my eyes.

The first man I saw as I left the hospital was little Whittier, who should have been at the wheel. His eyes had a glazed expression; he was carrying a plate with a sandwich. "Captain Cho," he said. "For Captain Cho."

"Did Captain Cho ask for that?"

He shook his head vigorously: Cho had.

Mate Number Two came running, visibly shaken. "Bad news, Number Two," I said. "Captain Cho has been killed. Take Whittier with you to the bridge and collect his body. Put him in his cabin."

"Yes, Commodore . . ." They hurried off.

The main deck was a shambles; the crew's corridor looked as if the shell had exploded in it. The doors must have been open; everything loose in the cabins had been thrown into the corridor by the wild gyrations of the ship. The men were dazed, some of them had blood on their faces. I went from one to another, checking that they were all right; the injuries were minor, mostly cuts and bruises, but the men were scared and shaken and totally bewildered. Wellesley, who had bellowed, "Woo, Omi!" at the slightest provocation, threw his arms around me in a bear hug. I sent him, together with Carleton, to take Hopla to the hospital.

Ma Chang, when I got to her in the chaos of the galley, was

profuse in her welcome. She hugged me and gazed into my eyes with a look that made it clear she knew how narrow the margin of our survival had been. I said, "Hopla—ouch! Leg! Broken!" and tried to act it out for her; she caught the meaning at once and hurried after the two men.

In the engine room I checked on the Chinese engineers, who proved to be remarkably calm. They assured me that all was well and the engines were running normally; then the telephone rang. It was Number One on the bridge. "Commodore, please come up! Boat is coming from liner!"

I reached the bridge with difficulty, even though Chief Liu and his men had replaced the broken companionway with a ladder. The wind had freshened, the sea looked angry; white-maned rollers came foaming past; a rain squall swept the ship. The silhouette of the *Princess* was partially hidden by one of those; out of it came, pitching and rolling, propelled by spidery oars, a white lifeboat. As it drew closer, I recognized Harakiri at the rudder; four runners were rowing. I sent Bryn Mawr down to catch their line and haul the boat alongside; Number One took over the wheel; I rang the engine down to half-speed, which virtually brought the tow to a standstill.

When the boat was within hailing distance, Harakiri yelled, "The raft! Have you seen the raft?"

"What raft?"

"Orange inflatable raft! Over there!" He pointed.

I went to the broken starboard window, looked at the angry sea and spotted an orange speck as it was lifted by the swell, swept along by the wind.

The main switch panel on the port side was still in place; its door swung back and forth with the swell. Hoping it was still operative, I pulled the switch for the alarm bell; bells started to ring all over the ship: MAN OVERBOARD!

"Number One, I'll take the wheel. You go and have the men swing out the motor launch. Tell the runner captain to go after the raft. We can't overtake it, and they'd never make it in a rowboat."

He hurried off. In response to the alarm bells, the rest of the crew appeared on deck; I could see the raft clearly now, each time a wave lifted it. The wind rampaged in the wreckage of the wheelhouse; clouds of dust spiraled from the debris. The motor launch, with Harakiri at the wheel, reached the raft sooner than I had expected. I saw the mandur grab hold of it and pull it on board.

"Empty!" cried Number One, lowering his binoculars. I hadn't noticed he was back.

"Okay," I said as the launch headed back to the ship, "you take the wheel. Keep her headed into the seas. Don't let her roll more than you can help. No course. Steady as she goes."

I went to the temporary ladder to the boat deck, but had to wait for Number Two and Whittier, who were putting Cho's remains in a sheet. There were no legs; they must have been blown into the sea by the explosion.

After the two men had left with their gruesome burden, I made my way down to the boat deck. The launch was just being hauled up; Chief Liu was there, the back of his boiler suit bulging in the wind.

"How did raft get into sea?" he asked. "What happened?"

"It must have been blown overboard by the explosion and inflated itself in the process."

"But what *happened?* What was explosion?"

"The moment Harakiri is on board, let's go to the dayroom and I'll tell you."

The launch was swung on board; Harakiri and his four runners peered down at us. "What the hell happened, Harinxma?" Harakiri shouted.

"Come down and I'll tell you."

The launch was lowered and settled into the blocks by Bryn Mawr and two sailors; when the mandur and his companions climbed down, they stood facing each other for a moment. 'Oh, my God,' I thought, 'no snot-blowing *now!*'

But it seemed that under the pressure of the emergency a truce had come about; the three runners started to help Bryn Mawr and the sailors cover the launch with its tarpaulin. The mandur followed us as Harakiri, Chief Liu and I set out for the dayroom; to prevent his losing face, I signaled Bryn Mawr to join us. But first I should have a look at Hopla and see if Ma Chang needed any assistance. I let them into the dayroom, excused myself and went to the hospital.

I found Hopla enthroned on the high bed, attended by Ma Chang, Tulane and Wellesley. The moment he saw me, he went into high gear, moaning, rolling his eyes, shrieking, "Ayee!" When I bent over to look at his leg, he squealed; Ma Chang said,

"Shoo!" The effect was as if the sound had been turned off in a television set; he went on writhing and rolling his eyes, trying to make up for the loss in pantomime. Poor beggar, it must hurt like the devil. I gave him a shot of morphine, under the wary eye of Ma Chang. The leg had been expertly set; she had found everything she needed. I couldn't better it, but even so I would have liked to have a look at the fracture before it was covered up. Reading my thoughts, Ma Chang touched a spot on the shin of his other leg, causing another dramatic convulsion in the patient. I understood the meaning: 'fracture of the tibia, six inches below the knee.' The fibula apparently was unbroken. He was a lucky boy; we had all been lucky. Except Captain Cho.

I bowed to Ma Chang, patted Hopla on the shoulder, making him shriek and collapse, eyes upturned; Ma Chang showed the gap in her teeth as she grinned. Whatever had happened to him, he would survive.

In the dayroom the four men were waiting for me, Harakiri and Chief Liu each in a club chair among the debris, the bosun and the mandur side by side on the couch, staring straight ahead with impassive faces.

"Jesus, Harinxma," Harakiri said when I came in, "what a mess! What in hell happened?"

I told them about the ship's cycling and the dynamite charge, showed them the panic button and told them that there had been no one on the bridge.

"But what possessed those boys to put in a charge that big?" Harakiri asked. "It damn near destroyed half the ship!"

"As I understand it, it was essential to blow the Paradise tree well away from the ship."

"But how were they going to trigger it during those test runs? This button is half an hour's walk from the bridge!"

"The architect had a toggle switch, as you may remember."

He gazed at me. "You mean to say . . ."

"Yes. He dropped it at your feet, and you picked it up."

"Christ almighty . . . ! I half wanted to press it just to see which one of all those gadgets of his was connected with it!"

"Good thing you didn't. Now, what do we do? The last I saw, the barometer was dropping. It's building up to quite a blow out there."

"I gather the Chinese captain is dead?"

"Smashed into the rail of the flying bridge by the explosion,

[299]

losing the lower half of his body. The top half was protected by a life jacket."

"My God—he must have been right next to it—"

"What was he doing up on walkway?" Chief Liu asked.

"I don't know."

"Harinxma," Harakiri said, "if we're in for a blow, you've got a problem. You've lost most of your wheelhouse, your stacks, your flying bridge— Is your steering gear still operational?"

"Yes. But we've lost the automatic."

"And your wheelhouse is open to the weather. You need help."

"What kind?"

"I'm leaving my mandur with you. I would stay myself, but I can't leave the old girl—and I have to go now or I may not be able to get back on board."

"How are you going to haul up your lifeboat?"

"Oh, I'll let it ride, I've got thirty of 'em. Give the mandur any job you like, he's terrific. And you can do no wrong as far as those jokers are concerned. They may be part of the Chinese Mafia, but you're the one who risked an arm and a leg to try and get them to run for cover; I don't think any fool ever did that for them before. So don't be shy: he may not look it, but he's your man."

I glanced at the mandur. He stared at me as if he were about to wring my neck. "Well," I said, "I'll have to ask my bosun here—"

"Don't ask, Harinxma, you're too damn nice. Let 'em work it out themselves. Now I'd better be going."

"Captain Cho was on watch, yes?" the chief asked, from his own world.

"Yes."

"Who was at wheel?"

"Whittier. But I met him in the corridor afterward carrying a plate with a sandwich to the bridge."

"Captain was alone on bridge?"

"He must have been."

"And wearing life jacket?"

"Well, folks," Harakiri said, rising, "I hate to break this up, but I don't want to get my ass wet. Have baby clear the wreckage on your bridge and dig out your walkie-talkie." He nodded at the mandur. "He's good at that. Well—Godspeed and happy sailing. And if you can, keep my snoot in the breeze. She can't take hurricane seas broadside anymore."

"I'll do my best."

He gave me an odd look. "I know you will. I knew that the first time I set eyes on you. I wouldn't have stayed otherwise. Well, let's keep praying. Toodle-oo. Have fun with baby."

He let himself out; baby stared at my adam's apple.

"Life rafts not inflate alone," the chief mused, in his private world. "Must be triggered on purpose." He slowly turned his head and gave me a smiling look. "How come life jacket? How come life raft inflate? How come ship on automatic on bad course? Questions will be asked, Commodore. Questions will have to be answered."

"Not now, Chief. A hurricane may be barreling down on us, we have to get cracking. Would you take charge of clearing the wheelhouse? There's so much debris, the helmsman can barely stand at the wheel."

"If hurricane, who will stand at wheel, please?" he asked politely.

"I suppose I will."

"Well," he said, rising, "in that case we better look for seat for you. Maybe long hurricane. Come, Mandur."

The mandur hesitated, as if he hated to lose sight of me. Then he followed the chief into the corridor, while I set out on a search for an oilskin suit.

5

I discovered long ago that the way to handle a crisis is to be as laid back as possible. This time it wasn't easy.

While rummaging in the oilskin-airing cupboard for a suit and sou'wester, I was shaking in my boots; the delayed shock of what had happened to us, how close we all had been to death, caught up with me. Suddenly, what I wanted more than anything else, what both my body and my mind seemed to be crying out for, was to go to bed, take a Valium and hide my head in the pillow. Well, that was not an option; I had to hang in there, however tired or shell-shocked I might be.

The thing was not to take myself too seriously; if I could find a convincing reason for laughing at myself, the tension would let up, the taut muscles slacken, the whole desperate situation be reduced to its proper proportions. But I could find little to laugh about in a seventy-year-old man looking for an oilskin suit in which to face a hurricane on the open bridge of a crippled ship. It was only after I had suited up in my bedroom and looked at myself in the long mirror inside the wardrobe door that I cracked a smile. I didn't look like a folk hero about to battle the elements, I looked like an ad for a fish restaurant.

The wind had picked up during my absence. The sea was angry now, full of white horses mottled by curling wavelets on their flanks. The ship was working heavily; I had a problem hoisting myself up the temporary ladder to the wheelhouse in my stiff, unyielding outfit. When my eyes were level with the bridge deck and I saw the interior of the wheelhouse, my heart sank. It had been cleared, but there was nothing left: no aft telegraph on either starboard or port side, no bank of controls for the winches, let alone television screens to show their workings. Of the radar scanner only the pedestal was left; the navigating desk with its charts, pilots and log had disappeared altogether. There was only a vast empty space, like a stage, with the jagged remains of the for'ard bulkhead for a backdrop, its windows, miraculously, still intact. So was the connection between the master gyro compass below and its daughter in the wheelhouse; the computer numbers of the course flicked back and forth above the wheel. All the rest of the navigational wizardry connected with the Paradise tree had been wiped out; no Decca, no Loran, no satellite navigation—we were back in the days of sextant and chronometer. Number One was at the wheel; beside him two space-age creatures in helmets were welding something to the steel dividers between the planking of the deck. As I approached, I saw what they were marrying to the ship. I could hardly believe my eyes: it was half a bicycle. It took a moment before I recognized the rear end of the exercise bike from the recreation room.

"My God!" I said. "Whose idea was this?"

The space man on the port side stopped welding and lifted his mask; it was Chief Liu. "Solid as rock!" he cried, beaming. "Now you need seatbelt!"

"Chief," I said, relieved from stress, tension and old man's terror by a sudden sense of comedy, "I don't think I'll actually need a seatbelt."

"Oh, but you do!" he persisted. "You may be blown away, if big hurricane!"

"By the time that happens, Chief, a lot of other things are going to be blown away."

"Try it," he said, scrambling to his feet. "See if comfortable. I have blocked pedals."

'Thank God for small mercies,' I said.

The other space man stopped sparking away and flipped up the front of his helmet; I saw to my surprise that it was the mandur. The chief spoke to him in Chinese; he rose, gave me a mortifying look and pointed at the saddle. I climbed onto it, put my feet on the pedals and took the wheel, a child in a toy car.

"Yes?" Chief Liu asked expectantly.

"Excellent," I said with feeling.

"Is all right?"

"Steady as a rock. Thank you very much. Now everybody should get back to their posts; we may have more wind than we bargained for."

It was an understatement. The sky to starboard looked as black as night. The rain would soon be upon us. This being the southern hemisphere, cyclones whirled clockwise; if we were lucky, we would find ourselves in the left quadrant. I had been making light of the possibility of our being hit by a hurricane, saying that I would skirt it; but at a speed of four knots, towing a forty-thousand-ton liner, I couldn't do any skirting, only head into the seas and hope for the best. If the eye passed to the north of us, it would give us a hard time but not be life-threatening, on condition we frequently checked the hawser for chafing. Harakiri would do the same on board the *Princess* where her anchor chains were concerned. Had the wheelhouse been watertight and all navigational aids intact, my only worry would have been that the drag of the tow would put the *Isabel* at a critical angle to the incoming seas. With her topload gone, that worry no longer existed; instead, I worried about the limits of my endurance. Even under the best of circumstances, this was going to be a trial of strength lasting between eight and sixteen hours, depending on the size and the forward speed of the cyclone.

"Number One," I called.

"Yes, Commodore?"

"You'd better suit up and tell Number Two to do the same. I

want you to take turns on the aft deck, keeping an eye on chafing, but I need one of you on the bridge at all times to man the thrusters. Now, before you do anything else, do me a favor. Go to my dayroom. On the desk in my office you'll see a cardboard box sealed by Customs. Inside, you'll find a number of earthenware crocks. Bring one of those up for me, will you? I won't need a glass."

"Yes, Commodore," he said almost reverently, like an acolyte hurrying for the consecrated wine.

The mandur came back accompanied by Bryn Mawr; together they strapped me down in the saddle. I felt secure; if the baling wire that held me together held out, and if the eye of the hurricane passed to the north of us instead of barreling down upon the two pieces of jetsam in its path, I would have plenty of time to ponder on the questions Chief Liu had posed, to which answers had to be found.

It was not a happy prospect.

6

As it turned out, there were not going to be any pondering thoughts. The moment I took control of the *Isabel* and headed her into the seas, the total identification with the ship took place to the exclusion of all else. I was no longer an old man teetering in a saddle, feeble and faintly silly; I became the eyes, the ears, the will and the spirit of the ship. It was an instant transformation: one moment I was an ad for a restaurant, the next the nerve center of the huge, lumbering body of the blinded ship. The two of us became one.

I had geared for battle, but found it wasn't a battle at all. Now that my eyes and ears had replaced the ones she had lost and I had fused with her into one living being, she took the seas with the same curious elation that had struck me the first time I handled her in the gale seas off Flushing. Even with her Paradise tree and her flying bridge gone, her stacks truncated and a roofless wheelhouse, she seemed to face what was coming with anticipation, as if this were what she had been created for: to be turned by mountainous waves from a wallowing pontoon into a thing of grace and beauty.

That was what she became as the first gale winds hit and the spray and spindrift started to fly. The swell came in fast, huge, precipitous; the parasite waves on its back grew in size and fury. The wind whisked the foam off their crests into horizontal sheets of water, lashing the windows of the wheelhouse, now no more than a windshield, in blinding torrents. All water became one: rain, spray, spindrift. The wind, in increasing gusts of tremendous sustained force, occasionally stopped her dead in her tracks. But she never wavered. She no longer showed the unnerving hesitancy which preceded her rolling out of control; at last she had become the glorious sea ship I had always felt her to be. By some miracle, the clearview disks were still whirling; so, despite the fact that there was a lot of flying water inside the wheelhouse, I never lost contact with reality outside. While it was still possible, Number One had hoisted a storm pennant on the foremast; in the confusion of whirling water I could keep the head of the tow into the wind by watching the whipping pennant, hoping it would survive the beating it took.

The hawser was my main concern. As the bridge controls of the winches had gone, Number One and, after his watch, Number Two had to pass the order to give a few fathoms of slack to a sailor on the boat deck below, who then passed it on to Chief Liu or his relief in the winch room. The procedure involved hazardous shiftings of the stoppers and the reparceling of the hawser on the tow bars; I could no longer watch it on the screen, but knew that under Bryn Mawr, and possibly the mandur, the operation would be executed expertly.

With the increase of the wind, the sheering of the *Princess* became a problem. Despite the *Isabel*'s massive power, occasionally the gale won out. The old liner's head veered away, her windage acted as a sail and gave her forward momentum as well as broaching her. Number One or Two stood by at the thrusters, watching me; whenever I felt the ship's stern yanked aside, brutalizing the hawser, I gave the signal to throw in one of the thrusters to compensate for the skid. It worked; the thrusters were indeed the greatest invention of the century for tugboat masters. Instantly the ship lined up, her powerful forward thrust no longer diminished by the angle; in short order the huge, wallowing mass behind us would heave to again, until another major gust came to blow her off course once more.

As night fell, I ordered that a floodlight be directed at the pennant. Sailing the ship now became entirely a matter of following the shifting direction of that tattered rag. The wind seemed at its worst, the waves monstrous, their size and fury enhanced by the dark. The ship labored heavily, but she never seemed to lose that curious sense of elation, of relishing the battle with the violence out there. I had occasional contact with Harakiri via the walkie-talkie; his crackly voice became almost inaudible, and I had to press the speaker of the instrument to my ear. Everything seemed to be all right aboard the liner so far; he too was regularly giving slack to the anchor chains carrying the bridle to counteract the chafing of the shackles. His refrain was, "We're okay, Harinxma, but, for God's sake, keep my snoot in the wind!"

During the night, as I continued to keep the tow headed into the gale, there was a steady change in course; it looked as though the eye of the hurricane was sweeping by at a fair distance to the north. At a given moment we were at right angles to what our course had been when we first headed toward the growing fury. The change occurred gradually but fairly fast; the cyclone must be compact and relatively small for it to move at such a speed. But it gave us a hard time despite its size; there were moments when I felt as though I were standing in a wind tunnel.

My problem was not tiredness; on the contrary, I seemed to be as exhilarated by the challenge as the ship was. What got to me was the cold. As the hours went by, I gradually became colder despite frequent swigs from the earthenware crock. The cold, or maybe the swigs, brought about a strange lucidity, almost a disembodiment. Occasionally I saw myself, as if from above: sitting on the ridiculous bicycle, hanging on to the tiny wheel. Oddly enough, only in those moments of dissociation did I become conscious of the presence of someone beside me. One time it was Bryn Mawr; the next, the mandur. I knew that Number One or Number Two was around because I gave them orders, but I hadn't been conscious of someone right next to me. Whenever the ship, hit by a sudden roll, swept me off balance, I was pressed against the body of whoever it was who kept me from toppling sideways. It was very touching; I smiled down on the two of us from above in those odd moments of out-of-body observation.

[306]

There was a strange peace about the scene, a feeling of security, a wonderful stillness at the center of my being. It might be the gin, but I was as lucid as I had ever been and aware at all times of what was happening to the ship, my lovely, gallant, trusting *Isabel:* alive, lithe, obedient, colossal. I felt like a *kornak,* one of those little Indian boys who guide an elephant by tweaking its ears. I felt like singing. I did; it seemed to give my young Chinese mates, cowed and shivering like drenched kittens, a curious re-assurance. The Old Man was singing; Death, where is thy stingalingaling?

When dawn broke over the first day of creation, we had changed course a hundred and thirty-six degrees. The hurricane, though at its height the wind was over seventy-five knots, had been a minor one on the scale of the monsters that sweep the region at this season. Harakiri's small, crackling voice in my ear sounded relieved when it shouted, mouse-like, "Well, the worst seems to be over! Good show, Harinxma! You can start thinking about bed!"

But, though chilled to the bone, I didn't feel tired at all. I felt I could keep this up for another twelve hours and maybe freeze to death, but not die of exhaustion. I patted the console of the little wheel and muttered, "Well done, old girl. Terrific. Terrific." Somebody patted my shoulder as if to convey the same. I looked up and saw it was Bryn Mawr.

"Woo, Bryn," I said.

"Woo, Omi!" he replied, grinning.

Number Two came skating toward us from handhold to handhold as the ship continued to pitch violently. "More slack, Commodore?"

"Ask Number One on the aft deck, or isn't he there?"

"Not at the moment, Commodore, but the mandur is."

"All right, ask the mandur."

Mentioning the mandur made me pat Bryn Mawr's back again to reassure him that, although the ship had been invaded by pregnant dogs, there was no change of loyalty.

The sun was beginning to break through the cloud cover of the hurricane's tail when Chief Liu appeared on the bridge to find out how things were. The moment had come for me to hand over the watch to Number One. The rain had stopped, the wind had died down, spray no longer lashed the windows. The clearview disk spun idly; the tattered remains of the pennant flapped limply.

"All right," I said, "Number One, time for you to take over. Would someone please help me out of this harness?"

Chief Liu started by taking the crock off my lap and tossing it overboard. He unstrapped me, which turned out to be less easy than strapping me down had been; twelve hours of sustained drenching had made the straps swell and in the end they had to be cut. When helped to my feet, I discovered that all that was left of me was my brain. My legs simply gave way; I had no feeling in my feet. Bryn Mawr and Chief Liu supported me as I staggered toward the ladder; Number One called anxiously after me, "Commodore! What's the course?"

A good question. Where the hell were we? Satellites were coursing overhead, but we could no longer receive their signals telling us our position. Not that it mattered; there certainly was plenty of room; if we drifted for days, no one would be any the wiser. But organized shipboard life had to go on; to remind me of it, Whittier's head appeared above the deck as he climbed the ladder. He looked about him with stunned amazement, gazed at me and asked, "No ping ping?" He must have been shell-shocked, as there had been no "ping ping" for twenty-four hours.

"No ship's bell left, Whittier, I'm afraid," I said. "But I'm sure Chief Liu will rig one up for you. Won't you, Chief?"

"Yes indeed," the chief replied reassuringly, like a doctor to a patient. "I will do many things. You and me should talk, Omi, much talk. But first, to sleep."

"First to sleep," I repeated, feeling dazed. "Whittier, take the wheel. Number One, come down with me to my quarters and I'll give you my sextant. You'll have to sight the sun the old-fashioned way, my friend."

The prospect appeared to depress him.

7

I cannot remember going to bed, but I found myself there in my pajamas with the lights on. Chief Liu was standing beside my bunk.

"Sorry," he said, "I think you should see this." He held out his hand and showed me a small black object.

Half asleep, I groped for my spectacles, picked it up and looked at it. "Part of a telephone?" I asked.

"A microphone. Mandur found it among wreckage on bridge."

I couldn't understand what it was all about; I was still partly in a dream about Héloïse chasing a seagull. I glanced at the clock; I had been asleep for only two and a half hours. "So?" I asked wearily.

He pulled something out of the pocket of his boiler suit and held it out to me: another small black object like part of a telephone.

"I found this in captain's cabin. In bunk."

"What is it?"

"Speaker. Sister to other one. You speak on bridge, he listen. He hear every word."

I wondered why I had to be called out of the depths of sleep after only two and a half hours for this. So, Captain Cho had had a listening device that enabled him to follow what was being said on the bridge. Maybe my potential for excitement had been depleted; all I wanted was to sleep—I felt sick with exhaustion.

"I been thinking," the chief persisted, impervious to my condition. "I have answers to many questions."

"Good for you. Would it be all right if we discussed this later? I need more sleep before I can function again."

But he pressed on. "You must get up. Number One mate cannot use sextant. We must bury captain's body before he stink. You dress. Everybody lined up on aft deck."

"For what?"

"Burial. We do not know what service. Do you have service? Maybe he was Christian. But he must be buried quick."

"I see," I said. "Okay. I'll be right up."

"While you dress, we must talk. I found answers to questions. Very important."

"Chief," I pleaded, "let's talk later. It can wait." As I sat up, I felt a wave of giddiness; I closed my eyes.

"Captain Cho did it," the hectoring voice hammered on. "Captain Cho tried to scuttle ship."

I opened my eyes and looked at him: a small, wizened man with bright black eyes, obsessed by—what? Hatred? Anger? He was not his usual witty self, but in the throes of some over-whelming emotion.

"Remember: decks and corridors empty. Captain alone on bridge, with helmsman. He send helmsman to galley for sand-wich, then put on life jacket. Why? Tell me: why life jacket?"

"God, Chief, I don't know. Maybe he was in a panic because the ship started her cycle."

"No panic. No cycle. Alone on bridge. Puts on life jacket. In-flates life raft. Then puts ship on bad course, on automatic. Runs out of wheelhouse, tosses raft overboard, holding on to line, climbs onto walkway between the stacks."

"Why the walkway?"

"I think a long time for that: with ship lying on side, walkway farthest you can get from body of vessel when she turn over. Less chance to be pulled down with ship when she sink."

Suddenly I realized I had known all along that Cho was the culprit. Under the pressure of the emergency, I had suppressed that knowledge; now, here it was.

"But why?" I asked. "What drove him to do such a thing?"

Chief Liu looked at the door, then whispered, "Mr. Chung! Insurance."

My heart sank. Another Fransen. I knew in my gut, my very soul, it wasn't so, that there was another reason.

He continued, "If Captain know about dynamite charge, he would have done different thing. But he did not know, and ship very lucky."

"Er—yes indeed. Look, Chief, we should talk more about this, but not now. You say everyone's waiting for me?"

"You must write report!" he cried, bent on retribution. "You must report on Captain Cho death! Reveal dynamite charge! In-clude ship's log, take testimony from me, from all members of staff, then combine into one big document and give to authorities. Mr. Chung must have no more chance to kill people for money."

I could understand his rage: Chung, the bastard, the bloody murderer, should be dragged in front of a judge and condemned to hang for murder. Yet I knew in my bones it was all part of Fransen's conspiratorial world, a nightmare web of plots and counterplots. Greedy Chung might be, but I couldn't see him callously engineering the death of forty people.

But I would have to think about it all later; now I had to get up, oversee the burial, sight the ship's position, put the tow back on course, determine, together with Chief Liu, the extent of the damage and what to do about it, make the rounds of the ship to see if everyone was all right, visit Hopla in the hospital. I sat up and swung my legs out of bed; it felt like swooping upward on a seesaw. "Okay, Chief, you go ahead and let me get dressed. I'll join you in a minute."

He left, reluctantly. I tottered to the wardrobe and took out my number-one blues, which seemed to weigh a ton. I put them on the bed and slowly took off my pajamas; while doing so, I had the feeling of being observed. I discovered Louis on the shelf, staring at me with bright little eyes, fascinated. I remembered a comedian on television asking, "Have you ever undressed in front of a dog?" I turned my back on him as I put on my underpants.

8

When I came out on the aft deck, I indeed found everyone lined up for the burial. Maybe because I was physically exhausted and emotionally drained, the scene seemed to have a haunting clarity: the clean, new sky, the silent ranks of the crew, the wind flapping the Taiwanese flag which covered a small bundle on a bier, the foot of which rested on the rail. The head was supported by the two junior engineers; Chief Liu joined them.

The sea swished past in foaming waves; the deck heaved slowly with the swell. In the far distance the last of the cumuli, white and harmless, were still massed above the horizon.

I had brought along a Bible and a Book of Common Prayer, but the standard hymn, 'Father, in Thy Gracious Keeping Leave We Now Thy Servant Sleeping,' seemed inappropriate. Instead, I read a few passages from Ecclesiastes which appeared universal.

"Remember now thy creator in the days of thy youth, while the evil days come not, nor the years draw nigh when thou shalt say, I have no pleasure in them; while the sun, or the light, or the moon, or the stars, be not darkened, nor the clouds return after the rain . . ."

The wind stirred the flag on the bier. In my state of lucidity it seemed as if all the young men I had buried at sea during my life as master were present among us.

[311]

"And the doors shall be shut in the streets when the sound of the grinding is low, and he shall rise up at the voice of the bird, and all the daughters of music shall be brought low . . ."

I was no longer sure for whom I was reading this: the mutilated body we were about to commit to the deep, myself standing here at the end of my life, or those who had gone before, now waiting on that distant shore beyond the horizon. How young we had been, how young . . .

"Fears shall be in the way, and the almond tree shall flourish, and the grasshopper shall be a burden, and desire shall fail, because man goeth to his long home, and the mourners go about the streets."

It occurred to me that this must be totally meaningless to the crew lined up in their clean T-shirts; they didn't even understand the language. So I ended with, *"Then shall the dust return to the earth as it was, and the spirit shall return unto God who gave it."*

I nodded at Chief Liu, who signaled his companions to start lifting the bier. According to tradition, I should now have read the Lord's Prayer; instead, I said, "Farewell, Captain Cho. Rest in peace."

The small bundle slid down the bier with gathering momentum and dropped over the side. We all stood for a moment motionless, in silence, while the flag flapped on the empty bier. Then I put my cap back on and turned away.

There was only the foremast left on which to hoist a flag halfway.

9

The moment the ceremony was over, Chief Liu sought me out. I managed to shake him by saying, "Chief, first I have to go to the bridge and get the tow moving, then there are a few other things I must do. Let's you and I get together later today. I'll let you know the moment I'm free."

I went up the companionway to the boat deck and climbed the ladder to the wheelhouse. The bridge was empty but for the helmsman; to my surprise, I saw it was the mandur. It seemed surprisingly tactful that he should have enabled the helmsman on watch to join the ceremony.

Number One had followed me onto the bridge and he started an embarrassed apology about being out of practice working the sextant. Of course, he had learned how to use it in Naval College, but he had done mainly coastal work so far, and—

"Don't worry," I said. "I'll run through it with you now, and afterward I have just the book for you, the best refresher course in celestial navigation money can buy. It's Bowditch's *American Practical Navigator.* My rat sleeps on it, but he'll have to rough it until you can give it back to him."

He thanked me profusely. I proceeded to shoot the sun. The horizon was beautifully clear, as always after a hurricane, and the sun was at an easy angle in the cloudless sky. I had taken the stopwatch with me and handed it to him; when I had the sun lined up, I gave the word and he pressed the button. Together we went to my dayroom and computed the exact moment of my observation by deducting the minutes and seconds on the stop-watch from the time on the chronometer. I had to reintroduce him to the tables and the almanac; he obviously needed the Bow-ditch. I gave it to him to take to his cabin.

In the hospital I found Hopla sitting upright, his leg in plaster. The morphine must have worn off, for the moment he set eyes on me, he cried, "Co'dore! I have much, much pain! I cannot move! I cannot serve you! I am desolated! Are pregnant dogs still on board?"

"Hopla," I said, "the time of pregnant dogs is past. If I catch you starting that all over again, you'll be in trouble."

"But who is replace me?" he wailed, nimbly changing the subject. "Who is to look after co'dore? Who will give you break-fast, drinks, wash clothes, make bed?"

"Don't worry about that. I'll ask Ma Chang to appoint a tempo-rary replacement. In the meantime, keep quiet, get well. How are you feeling?"

"Much pain, Co'dore! I desolated! I look at you, you look like—like vagabond. You not look like co'dore at funeral, no? You must have haircut. Is very bad your hair."

"I'll have a haircut before we get to Pago Pago. Now, is there anything I can do for you? Anything you'd like?"

"I would like leg back!" he cried dramatically. "I would like hobble-hobble on crutches, serve co'dore!"

"I appreciate the thought, but that leg will need a couple of weeks at least before you can move around."

"I move around *now!*" he cried. "I hobble-hobble to

bathroom! I not use *that!* He pointed at a bedpan beside him on the chair. "I am not like *them!*" he said, a Pharisee pointing at the door. "I butler from Mah-Iot hotel!"

After a few more minutes of bedside chat, I left him to his woes and the cigarette he must have hidden in the pot cupboard when he heard me coming, the smell of which permeated the atmosphere in the small, aseptic room. It was reminiscent of the sickly-sweet smell of Captain Cho's tobacco; maybe it was this memory that made me decide to have a look at Cho's cabin before his possessions were stowed away or divided among the crew.

I stepped inside, closed the door behind me and found myself in an arid little world; it felt like a cell on Death Row after the execution. I went through his wardrobe, his desk, his chest of drawers; what struck me was that there was nothing there of his own culture. Everything was Western: clothes, shoes, a few pornographic paperbacks and the little red book he had been reading each time I went to see him. I picked it up and discovered to my surprise that it was not The Thoughts of Chairman Mao but a secondhand copy of *The Rubáiyát of Omar Khayyám* in English. On its flyleaf was written, *For Gloria from her loving Dennis on our special day: December 3rd 1898.* That had been crossed out; underneath was written in a child's hand, *Marjorie Eleanor Farley from Ginger (cat) for Xmas Anno Domini 1923 in Bristol, Gloucestershire, England, Great Britain, Europe.*

I leafed through the little red book and saw a stanza marked by pencil in the margin.

> *Come, fill the Cup, and in the fire of Spring*
> *Your Winter-garment of Repentance fling:*
> *The Bird of Time has but a little way*
> *To flutter—and the Bird is on the Wing.*

What had attracted the troubled youth from Taiwan to these elegiac Victorian poems, so utterly British? What had made him read them over and over again, to the point that each time I entered his cabin I found him with this book in his hand? Had it been a sham? Had he, hearing a knock on his door, quickly hidden the earphone and picked up this book? No, that belonged to Fransen's conspiratorial world. If Chief Liu was right, as I suspected he was, and Captain Cho had planned the whole operation in detail over a long period of time, he must have been clinically insane. Part of his madness had been his efficiency, his ingenious plotting down to the minutest detail, patiently waiting for the opportunity to execute his plan. I remembered the eagerness with which he had offered to take the watch while everyone else on board rested up before the hurricane. After he got rid of Whittier by sending him down for a sandwich, the whole operation must have gone as planned, ending with his climbing the ladder to the walkway, intending to paddle to the liner in the raft, after the ship had gone down, as the sole survivor of the disaster. But for the dynamite charge, he would have succeeded.

But why? I looked around the cabin in search of a clue. A calendar on the wall, headed *Charlie Chung Enterprises, with Compliments*, showing the current month, each past day crossed out. On the desk his pipe, a box of Chilean tobacco, a portable radio, an imitation-leather nail-trimming set, a ballpoint pen with the legend *Halcyon Hotel, Punta Arenas*.

During the war, after one of my men had died in action, I had sat in his cabin like this, looking around, wondering what to write to his next of kin, other than the standard letter furnished by the Admiralty. What could I write to Cho's mother, girlfriend, brother? 'Dear Mrs. Cho, It is my sad duty to inform you that your son perished during an unsuccessful attempt to scuttle the ship and drown forty people'? There was no clue to the reason for it all, only FitzGerald's daydream of a desert poet remembering lost loves. I leafed through the book and found another stanza marked in the margin.

> *There was the Door to which I found no Key;*
> *There was the Veil through which I might not see;*
> *Some little talk awhile of ME and THEE*
> *There was—and then no more of THEE and ME.*

I wondered who 'thee' had been, if it was Cho who had made those markings. It could not have been the child from Bristol; it might have been Dennis or his Gloria, eighty-five years ago.

Could Chung be the culprit after all? Could he be at the bottom of this sad boy's madness in a different way? Cho must have known that the ship was overinsured; had he been motivated by the desire to be successful in the eyes of Chung, his master, at last? Had he fantasized about turning up in front of Chung's desk to say: 'I did it for *you*'? No one would ever know.

I put the little red book back on the desk and left, closing the door softly behind me.

[315]

10

Chief Liu was waiting for me in the corridor. "Come with me to bridge," he said. "We must discuss what to do. There is dangerous damage."

He was right; the results of the bomb blast were dangerous to the watch on the bridge. The remnants of the walls and the aft bulkhead had sharp, jagged edges; what was left of the roof covered only the for'ard third of the wheelhouse; two thirds were exposed to the sun, which would become fiercer as we moved closer to the Equator. The mangled bridge was a sorry sight.

Chief Liu and I decided that he and his staff would cut the jagged wheelhouse walls and aft bulkhead down to railing height and weld lengths of two-inch pipe on top for safety. The roof would be cut at the point where it could be done in a straight line; then B.B.'s eight-foot lengths of galvanized pipe would be used to form a cage meant to support an awning made from B.B.'s rolls of tarpaulin. The truncated stacks, at present spewing noxious fumes onto the bridge in the following wind, would be restored to their original height by using B.B.'s stovepipe. Chief Liu suggested that he "embellish" the top of those pipes to make the ship look less like a derelict.

This was not all. The explosion had caused massive secondary damage; everything relating to the Space Age was gone. Radar, Decca, Loran, Plath, radio, Telex, weather-chart machines—even the foghorn was gone, as were the aft floodlights. The *Isabel* had suffered a throwback to the time when I was a junior mate; only the tremendous power was left of the Ship of the Future.

Before turning in, I arranged for the mandur to be taken back to the *Princess,* now a mouse lost in the blue infinity of the ocean under a vast, empty sky. I said farewell to him with a feeling of gratitude, but he stared at me exactly as he had when we first set eyes on each other on the quayside in Rotterdam. I watched the launch leave, intending to wait until it had safely returned; but someone behind me asked, "Commodore? Could I speak to you for a moment?" It was Number One, holding the Bowditch. "Very sorry," he said apologetically, "but something happened to this book."

"What do you mean, happened?"

He opened the Bowditch for me to see. The center of the body of the book had been cut out, leaving only the margins. It was, in effect, a box filled with what looked like airmail letters; Haversma must have used it as a private safe.

"Good heavens! Sorry about that," I said. "Well, I'll have to teach you myself. Say, tomorrow morning, first watch?"

"Yes, Commodore."

"Now let's go down and see what we can find in the way of charts. All the charts we had up here are gone?"

"Yes, Commodore."

"Well, at least we'd just started a new log. The new one's gone too, I take it?"

"Yes," he said. Something in his voice made me aware that his eyes were full of tears. Well, it had been a tough twenty-four hours for the young mate of a coastal tug.

"Let's go and see," I said, "and have a look at the icebox in passing."

"Yes, Commodore."

He sounded about to come apart; to cheer him up, I said, "Well, now Captain Cho's gone, you're the acting master of the *Isabel*."

It didn't cheer him up. He stared at me with eyes of horror and said, "Oh, God. Dear God." His English was much improved from when he first came on board five months ago.

Only later did the thought occur to me that his horror might not have been at being burdened with the responsibility, but at the realization that he was next in line to benefit from the help and support of Ome Tinus, advisor to the captain.

11

Down in my dayroom, all we could find was a general chart of Oceania. We entered our position on it; the hurricane had swept us farther off course than I had expected, below the Tubuaï archipelago and the Cook Islands. In the space of twelve hours we had lost three days. We plotted a new course north of Rapa and Marotiri Island for Samoa.

After Number One had gone back to the bridge, I opened the Bowditch. Inside was a tight wad of thin sheets of airmail paper that I at first took to be letters. They turned out to be essays written in the form of a dialogue between two partners, 'T' and 'H.'

> *Sunday, October 27, 5:30 A.M.*
> *T: The usual sick worry—about mouth cancer this time. The white papilloma on my lower jaw does look different from previous ones, and has a fairly alarming aspect. Did not wear my lower denture yesterday and the swelling of the gland has diminished, but the eruption itself is unchanged—if anything, it is more prominent. I am scared sick, Henry. Is there anything you can say to help?*

> *H: Dear, dear friend: we have been here so often! I wish I could truly convince you this time that there is no question of cancer. I know this does not convince you, just lessens the panic temporarily, but do try to have some faith in my reassurance. Have it looked at when you get home; in the meantime, stop agonizing. I have no other counsel to give you than this: contact me frequently, whenever the need arises. Short communications like this are helpful—and you know that I am instantly available at all times. Don't worry! It is benign, totally, and will disappear without a trace in a short while. Bless you, dear friend—and calm down! All is well. We're here, I'm here; you are not alone.*

It sounded like the verbatim record of a telephone conversation with a radio doctor or the physician of another ship. As I leafed through page upon page of small copperplate handwriting, I found that most of the communications concerned the inquirer's health: mysterious pains under the rib cage, blinding headaches that led to giddiness, black spots on the inside of the man's cheeks—the kind of complaints any master is familiar with; among most crews there is a hypochondriac who takes Vitamin C after talking on the telephone to someone with a cold. But there were more puzzling communications.

> *Wednesday, Nov. 16th, 5 A.M.*
> *H: Dear friend, I am somewhat reluctant to bring this up again, but once more I have been asked, with considerable urgency this time, if you would be prepared to pass on certain messages from discarnate entities to people (relatives and friends) still in earth life. I know you have turned this down*

several times, and I am loath to put it to you again; but in this particular case the applicant is of some importance and the message is said to be crucial to the recipient's well-being. Would you, for this once, be prepared to act as a conduit?

T: I am sorry, but the answer must be no. I cannot and will not act as a medium. You are my personal guide; I can accept our relationship as it is without feeling that my feet have left the ground; but I know in my bones that the moment I start passing on messages to and from others, the credibility of our communication would suffer disastrously. Surely there are plenty of mediums ashore who would be happy to act as go-betweens? And how would I pass on the messages? Via my radio room? Do you know that my marco has to keep a record of every word he transmits? How would it look to the company to find in the ship's radio log, 'Please tell Aunt Agatha's lawyer that her will is under the mattress in the guestroom'?

H: I understand your reluctance but not your spirit of levity. These are messages of utmost importance to the people concerned. And you would not be 'a medium.' They would be passed on to you by me.

T: Sorry, Henry, the answer is NO. *I feel shaky enough about our communication as it is; I am not going to jeopardize a dialogue which is vital to me by acting as a post office. Let this be the last we say on the subject.*

So that's what they were: somebody's communications with a discarnate entity. I was fascinated and repelled at the same time; anything pertaining to ghost-mongering filled me with instinctive resistance. But these communications were different from the ones I had occasionally come across in books or stories: this ghost—as I presumed 'Henry' to be—did not speak or write in the usual solemn and mystical vein. His dialogue with 'T' was crisp and casual, and 'T' gave as good as he got; a ghost who was told to shut up and change the subject was new to me. But who was 'T'?

I leafed through the stack of flimsy sheets in search of a clue, fascinated despite myself; at the bottom of the stack I came upon a small newspaper cutting.

TUESDAY, MAY 3RD, *Jeanette Haversma, née van Dalen, at the age of 63. Mrs. Haversma is survived by her husband, Capt. Tjalling Haversma, now at sea. No flowers, please; contributions*

[319]

*may be made to the SPCA in the name of the Jeanette Ha-
versma Memorial Fund.*

I stared at the name with an eerie feeling, as of a presence
behind my back. The Tjalling who had warned me to 'Beware'
the first night out of Talcahuano had been Spooks Haversma. Or
so it would appear.

12

As I came out into the open, I was startled by the almost blinding
brilliance of the starry sky. The atmosphere had been swept clean
by the hurricane and the air must be as dry as that of a desert, a
rarity at sea; as a result, there seemed to be twice as many stars in
the sky as usual; the Milky Way was a stark-white luminous wake
across the sky from horizon to horizon, a solid furrow of light.
Even though there was no moon, it was bright enough to read a
newspaper. As I stood staring at that awesome world of billions of
stars, planets, galaxies, I discerned a curious noise over the familiar sound of throbbing stacks and swishing bow wave—a hooting
and booming which seemed to come from the direction of the
stern. I went to investigate.

When I reached the end of the boat deck and looked down, I
discovered that the aft deck was full of slowly moving shadowy
figures. Underneath the world-large conflagration of the starry
sky, lanterns wobbled and smoking torches waved; they were
carried by what seemed to be a procession led by a small figure in
a robe. The figure proceeded to the aft rail, where it stood still,
silhouetted against the fiery brilliance of the phosphorescent
wake. Suddenly there sounded the sharp reports of firecrackers,
the baleful lowing of a Chinese flute. The robed figure clashed
two huge cymbals together against the backdrop of the luminous
wake; they made a dry, dull sound; I realized they must be the
lids of trash cans. Could the figure be Ma Chang?

Then the crowd started to shout—a confused cackling of individual voices yelling what sounded like curses or insults. Objects
were passed down the ranks until they reached the robed figure,
who took them and hurled them, one by one, into the sea; they hit
the phosphorescent water with splashes like fire. The volume of

the shouting swelled, a cacophony of angry curses frightening in its hostility. Then the robed figure took another object passed down the line and hurled it aloft—a fluttering, tumbling thing: a small book. I saw a faint flash of red in the torchlight and realized that it was Cho's *Omar Khayyám.* Only then did I understand what was going on down there: the crew, led by Ma Chang, was exorcising Captain Cho's spirit by trying to frighten him away from the ship, throwing all his belongings after him.

While I watched, hypnotized, everything went: clothes, shoes, his portable radio, his cap—until the crowd cheered, the flute hooted, the cymbals clashed tunelessly. The robed figure turned around and slowly, solemnly, walked back to the midships, followed by the torches, the lanterns, the shadowy, chanting crowd.

It was a night of ghosts, all right.

Chapter Twelve

1

During the days that followed I managed to rationalize my way out of the maze of superstition into which I had been lured by the discovery that Haversma's name had been Tjalling.

They were glorious days of sunlight and blue skies; the ship was full of life and the sounds of activity. Chief Liu and his crew were busy reconstructing the bridge and the wheelhouse, erecting a sort of veranda shading the deck with a billowing awning of tarpaulin which made soft slapping noises on its cage in the quiet of throbbing stacks and whispering waves. A spirit of renewal, of a new spring, pervaded the ship, even though with the destruction of her electronic wizardry the *Isabel* had been thrown back in time to the state of her great-grandmother, the lumbering *Isabel Kwel* of my wartime days.

Without computers, calculators, satellites and hourly weather charts, the Chinese mates were virtually helpless, or pretended to be. As a result, I found myself, despite my state of bone weariness, not only standing watches but making frequent visits to the bridge during my periods of rest to help them shoot a star, enter the tables and calculate our position. I also found myself caught up in long technical planning sessions with Chief Liu, who was capable, inventive, but liked to protect his behind by getting my approval for even the most picayune modifications.

My periods of rest were no great shakes. As a result of the destruction of the stacks, the air-conditioning units had been damaged beyond repair; the fans went on turning, but the air they produced was no longer refrigerated, so we were back in the good old days when all we had to relieve the heat of the tropics below decks were fans and air scuppers protruding from open portholes. I had opened all my windows, but the bedroom was an oven; I spent my off-watch hours stark naked on top of my bunk, tepidly bathed in warm air from a little fan the chief had dug up from the flea market of his storeroom, trying to shoo away Louis, who persistently curled up on my stomach, generating heat like a little furnace. I could not shut him out without shutting out whatever fresh air the fan could draw from the dayroom, so my periods of rest were troubled by his sneaky return to the mysterious attraction of my solar plexus.

Because of the open windows, the sounds of the ship came closer, invading my private world: singing and laughing on deck, hammering and drilling on the bridge overhead. One evening I was wakened by the sound of applause; I pulled on my shorts and flip-flopped to the bridge in my sandals. It turned out the applause was for Chief Liu: he had embellished the stark stovepipes that had now replaced the stacks with two crowns, cut out of sheet-iron in an elaborate pattern, like doilies, gilded to boot. They were indeed worthy of applause; Chief Liu stood beaming with satisfaction; as for myself, I found them rather frivolous. What was more, our aft navigation lights and floods had been replaced by lanterns strung the length of the aft deck; in the evening, combined with the fancy stacks lit from below, they gave the growling, bull-chested vessel the incongruous aspect of a floating cathouse.

It depressed me that I couldn't share in the general spirit of cheerfulness and camaraderie that had taken hold of the ship after our miraculous escape from destruction. Not only did I have a problem getting over the explosion, followed by the exertion of my hurricane watch at the wheel, but I could not shake the memory of the sad, neurotic youth who had come to such a tragic end. In retrospect, I felt I was to blame for the desperate isolation in which he had lived and which had finally driven him to his act of sheer insanity. I think it was the little red book turning out to have been the *Omar Khayyám* that did it. The error of judgment on my part had been typical of our entire relationship. I had taken his ship away from him, stomped on him until he locked himself in his cabin to nurse his powerless hatred and dream of revenge —Fransen had been right when he had warned me to take it easy on the boy or, out in the Pacific, when we were by ourselves, he might go berserk and nail me to 'the old rugged cross.' It was me Cho had wanted to destroy in his madness, not the ship and the forty souls who would have gone down with her.

Weariness made me lie down on my couch and doze at odd hours of the day. The fact that Hopla wasn't there to act as my steward passed unnoticed, as different members of the crew started to visit me, bringing tea and Ma Chang's concoctions. They wandered around inspecting the pictures, the glass statue,

[323]

my office, the bedroom, to wander off again after having touched my arm and said, "Omi." I only discovered later that in the process they had made my bed. More and more frequently someone opened the door of my dayroom, came in, whistled and cooed at Pete, squealed when Louis jumped them from the Bowditch, put him on my shoulder after scratching him, touched my arm, said, "Omi" and wandered off again. As a younger man, I might have told them to come only at a specific time, to protect my privacy; now I began to look forward to their visits. Every single member of the crew turned up at some time or another; even the oilers, whom I hardly knew. They looked at my books, stroked the nude, wandered into my bedroom, the bathroom, flushed the toilet, made the bed; occasionally one would fiddle with my alarm clock and I would hear the bell go off. After a few days I barely noticed them coming in and out. I just sat at my desk writing my report, or went on reading on the couch.

From time to time Ma Chang turned up in person to check me over with her pendulum, pat my cheek and give me a gap-toothed grin. Louis would leap onto her shoulder and rub his head in her neck, having discovered that she was the keeper of the goodies. She would always produce some snack for him from the voluminous pockets of her smock, and had to disengage him forcibly before leaving.

The only one who seemed not to share in the general atmosphere of goodwill and equality was Number One; the fact that after Captain Cho's death he was now, administratively at least, the ship's acting master had gone somewhat to his head. The other members of the staff started to check on me too; but instead of making kissing noises at the canary, scratching the rat and wandering through my quarters, they sat down on the couch and started to talk, a bizarre, debonair interchange in fractured English, expressing their growing acceptance of me as a sort of father figure who needed some tender loving care. Out came impromptu biographies, descriptions of their families, monologues on Mr. Chung. Nobody stated directly that Mr. Chung might have been planning to scuttle the ship for the insurance money; but their eulogies on the man who governed their lives acquired a bitter edge. Being Chinese, they dealt in shadings rather than primary colors. Their suspicion was never explicit, their bitterness not expressed in so many words. Before the explosion they had occasionally gone so far as to sing his praises;

now, details about his various enterprises began to surface. It seemed that he owned not only the largest demolition yard in East Asia, but bus companies, banks, groceries and—with a sly smile—a chain of brothels called Singing Flowers. Some of their stories sounded more outlandish than Harakiri's fantasies on the walkie-talkie, but I was convinced that every word was true and that much remained unsaid. They contrived, while praising the master of their fate, to depict him as a thoroughly ruthless, rather sinister individual.

My most frequent visitor was the big oiler called Tulane. I still called them by their collegiate T-shirts, even though most of those had been replaced with new ones depicting lurid sunset scenes and motor boats pulling water skiers, which they had bought in Talcahuano. Tulane would turn up daily, immediately after his watch, sit down on the floor and browse through my books. He could not read them, but they seemed to have a fascination for him that for some reason was deeply moving. He repeatedly leafed through *Human Personality and Its Survival of Bodily Death,* looking at the graphs and the chapter headings as if they contained the key to another dimension, a world in which some inarticulate potential, some shackled creativity would break out of its cocoon of ignorance, spread its wings and fly to join birds of dawning like Chief Liu and the two engineers. I tried to communicate with him verbally, but it was impossible. He was so backward, so prehistoric, that he didn't even speak Chinese. After he had thumbed through the books and put them carefully back on the shelf, he would sit there with such dejection that it was as if his questing mind were facing a blank wall. One day, on the spur of the moment, I produced a travel chess set I had found in a drawer of my desk; it had probably belonged to Haversma. When I showed it to Tulane, he hooted with glee; I set up a game and invited him to play. As I might have expected, his game of chess was different from the one I knew—more like Halma or Mah-Jongg, with dice. The moment we started to play, others turned up, began to explain; soon I found myself sitting in a crowd of excited sailors and oilers, being taught their form of gambling chess.

It was a mother hen's daydream; not only were all the chicks accounted for, they turned up continuously, in ones, twos, droves, for a few moments under the wings before wandering off again, whistling, as if some solace had been received. I began to feel a lot better; it took me days before I realized I was drawing vitality from them, the way the *Isabel* drew fuel from the old *Princess.*

2

Finally I was charged up sufficiently to start writing my report in earnest. I tore up what I had written so far and started afresh, beginning with an analysis of the *Isabel*'s history. It was like writing in a Chinese marketplace; what was more, under the influence of all those people milling about, Louis was overcome by an excess of playfulness which made him chase my pen as I wrote, making it impossible for me to go in for any bathos. It was just as well; in the unemotional language of a traffic ticket, the chain of cause and effect that had led to Cho's death and the ship's near-destruction became chillingly clear. KITCO had deliberately put the lives of a foreign crew at risk by selling a flawed ship to Chung without informing him of the deadly danger. At least, that was how the case presented itself; if they had informed Chung, then he had callously disregarded the information by having her tow a dry dock through the Atlantic and Pacific storm belts. Which of the two was the primary culprit was for the authorities to decide; from the looks of it, they might even have been in on it together.

To point the finger was not, however, the object of the report. My intention was to see to it that, after receipt of my dossier, the authorities who ruled over the certification of ships would ensure that the *Isabel Kwel* would never be restored to the lethal threat she had been. As she was now, she was as safe as any ship could be. Without Paradise tree, flying bridge and wheelhouse, it was impossible to induce her rolling cycle. I tried to, while taking on fuel from the *Princess* again; even though the seas were moderate, I could tell from the feel of her that her suicidal tendency was a thing of the past.

The stifling heat in the corridors below forced the crew to shift their permanent floating crap game into the open. They had discovered the bridge was the coolest part of the ship and were no respecters of persons; after dark, in the soft golden light of the lanterns that had replaced the floods, it acquired the atmosphere of a Chinese gambling den. By one of those twists of fate that preserve glass bowls with goldfish during bombardments, leaving them to glitter playfully among the ruins, the lifebelt locker on the bridge deck, pathetically flimsy compared to the stacks and the wheelhouse, had been spared unscathed; it provided a perfect gaming table for the crew. I did not understand the game, but occasionally I joined them for a go at Mah-Jongg mainly to cure Number One of his imperious disapproval of the noisy plebs invading the officers' domain. From time to time I seemed to win a game, for they would cheer and slap my shoulder; most of the time I was trounced. All of this was observed with amusement by Chief Liu, who often came up to watch.

During the nighttime hours I occasionally woke up in my bunk to hear through the open window the chattering and laughter and the rolling of dice on the bridge deck. One night, as I half woke up and heard those by now familiar sounds, I found myself caught up in a fantasy, as occasionally happens before you are fully awake. I was struck by the thought that all this was a dream, a posthumous one. That instead of my reaching the panic button in time, the ship had capsized and we were all dead, and that the ghost of the *Isabel* was sailing beyond the horizon toward that distant shore, on which a small crowd was waiting and someone cried, 'Here she comes!'

3

As I worked my way, slowly and in painstaking detail, through my report of the chain of events which ended with Captain Cho's demise, a decision formed in the back of my mind. When finally I had handed my report and the ship's log to the authorities in Pago Pago, I would have attained my objective of protecting my crew from harm. We had passed the hurricane zone of the southern hemisphere; after Samoa, any tug-driver of reasonable experience could sail the ship and the *Princess* to Taiwan. I would go home from Pago Pago.

When the cloud-shrouded mountain ridge of Tutuila Island was sighted, Hopla *redivivus* emerged on the bridge, after throwing his crutches onto it first. He had been getting restless as the days went by; the fact that virtually the entire crew was now taking care of me instead of he alone was driving him slowly rabid with fury. Suddenly he turned up, a tiny angel of retribution on spider legs, crying, "Disgrace! Co'dore look disgrace! There is harbor coming up, and co'dore look like vagabond! You need haircut!" It was a symbolic statement, more in response to his personal agony than out of a real need, but I agreed.

I expected him to do it himself, but he arranged for a professional to perform the operation: Ma Chang. Ma Chang could do everything, she cut everybody's hair. So, ten minutes later I found myself sitting on a stool on the aft deck under the fascinated eyes of a small crowd lined up at the rail of the boat deck. Ma Chang draped a sheet around my neck and placed on my head a small copper wok she had brought with her. She had also brought a galley knife that glittered in the sun; when the wok was in place, the knife started to scrape audibly while tugging at my hair. I worried about my ears, but told myself not to be childish. As the process continued, I gained confidence; finally the wok was removed, she whisked the sheet away like a matador, the spectators on the boat deck applauded and Wellesley bellowed, "Woo, Omi!" I bowed to her, she bowed in return; but a twinkle in her eye made me hasten to the privacy of my bathroom to take a look at myself in the mirror. The creature that gazed at me seemed to have nothing to do with the man I had known for seventy years. It was no longer Martinus Harinxma, or even Ome Tinus; it was one of the old Chinese drunks I remembered from years ago staggering out of Shanghai wine shops. I opened the wardrobe door and looked at myself in the long mirror through, say, Sylvia's eyes: a skinny old Chinese with a wino haircut, sweat-drenched shirt, flaring shorts like a tutu, thin, hairy legs and open-toed sandals. There was a thud; the apparition was completed by a rat on his shoulder. When I thought of myself coming down the steps from an airplane, seen through tears of emotion, the chance that Sylvia would flee, screaming, was a real one. And I would be carrying a cage with a canary as well.

Fransen in a tropical outfit came on board the battered *Isabel* with the pilot off Pago Pago. He looked shell-shocked. "For Chrissakes, Harinxma, what in God's name happened to the ship?"

Conscious of the pilot's presence, I thought it wiser not to go

[328]

into dramatic details at that point. I said vaguely, "We passed through a hurricane and, as you see, sustained some damage. Otherwise, all is well." Addressing the pilot, I asked, "Where are you going to put us?"

"Pardon?" He was a short, stocky Samoan. They are known for their composure, but he too looked nonplussed. "Er—what's your tonnage, Captain?"

"You mean the liner? Forty thousand."

"And she draws?"

"Thirty-six feet, give or take a foot."

"In that case, I'll anchor her in midstream off the main dock in twenty-five fathoms, mud and sand."

"Sorry, we can't anchor her. She has no power, it'll have to be either buoys or quayside."

He looked peeved. "We should have had all this information radioed in twenty-four hours ago, Captain!"

"Sorry about that. I thought Captain Fransen would have prepared you."

During all this Fransen had been looking around openmouthed, not believing his eyes. "What in the name of Christ *happened* to this ship?"

"How long are you staying in port?" the pilot asked.

"Twenty-four hours, thirty-six at the most."

"We can make room for you at the Station Wharf, but you'll have to be out in twenty-four hours. We're expecting one container and two Ro-Ro vessels tomorrow." He started to mutter into his walkie-talkie.

In the meantime two small harbor tugs had got hold of the *Princess*, all the port had to offer; the *Isabel* would have to do most of the mooring herself.

"And why is Captain Cho not on the bridge?" Fransen inquired, angry with perplexity.

"I'll tell you the whole story after we've put the *Princess* to bed," I replied. "Let's have dinner somewhere."

"All right, Captain," the pilot said. "Your tow has a temporary berth at the Station Wharf, but nobody is allowed off the liner until she has been cleared. The tug will have to go to the Customs Pier. You realize that all this is highly irregular?"

"Thank you, Pilot," I said. "We went through some irregular circumstances ourselves."

4

Three hours later, when darkness had fallen and it had started to rain, Fransen and I shared a meal in a dark little restaurant smelling of tropical decay, in the village of Fagatogo, west of the government administration buildings. There was a splendid hotel complex called the Rainmaker in Pago Pago, but he had judged it too public for the story I obviously had to tell.

The heat was oppressive; the evening rain cascaded off the awning of the terrace on which we were having a drink; it was like dining behind a waterfall. The whole island seemed to be full of waterfalls; a distant drumbeat throbbed in the air saturated with moisture.

He polished off a tumbler of neat whiskey, lit a cigarette, blew a plume of smoke at the waterfall and said, "Well, let's have it. What happened to the ship? And to Cho?"

I told him the bare facts, starting with Cho's unexpected offer to take the watch while everybody else rested up before the hurricane. Even so, it was a long story. Meanwhile we were served by an overweight woman in a sarong who was followed around by a plaintively yowling cat.

He listened without comment, and apparently without emotion. However, he chain-smoked continuously and did not touch his food. When I was through, he gazed at the cascade of water splashing off the awning, then ground out the cigarette he had just lit in the steak he had ordered. I expected him to start asking questions, probe for details; but his reaction was typical: his primary interest was not in what had happened, but in how it would affect the company. "All right," he said. "Now what?"

"Now I hand you the ship's log and my report, for you to give to the authorities. Let them decide what should be done with the ship."

He looked at me with incredulous amazement. "You mean— you're planning to report everything? Explosive charge and all?"

"Of course," I replied, equally amazed. "What else? That's the crucial part, isn't it?"

"Do you realize what that would mean, man? If you report that the architect put an explosive charge on the walkway, and why, it means the ship was unseaworthy to start with! That KITCO sold Chung a ship they knew was unstable!"

[330]

"We have no choice, Fransen. As acting master, I have to report the events as they happened."

"You're not the acting master, dammit! Your first mate is!"

I took a deep breath. God, he could be insufferable. "Officially, maybe," I said evenly. "The fact remains that whoever is the master has to report the facts and hand over the log to the proper authority. That's the law."

He lit another cigarette and heaved a smoky sigh. "Harinxma, let me spell it out for you. If we hand in that report, the first thing they'll do is chain the ship to the quay for months while they investigate. That over, she'd have to be modified or she'd lose her certificate, which would mean that Chung couldn't sell her except for scrap. Apart from that, because the damage is self-inflicted, the insurance company would reject any claim. So what Chung would do is take KITCO and the architects to court, the kind of international litigation that can go on for years—"

"Fransen, all I'm concerned about is the safety of my crew and future crews of this ship. If she's rebuilt the way she was before the explosion—"

"All right, I'll tell you what we're going to do. We'll submit another report, stating that the damage to the ship was caused by a rogue wave during a hurricane, one of those tsunamis that wipe out whole villages. The wheelhouse was smashed, the Paradise tree toppled, the captain washed overboard; in short, the effect of the explosion. You've compromised the evidence by slicing off the wheelhouse walls and welding on rails, but we'll say that was done because of the potential danger the jagged edges presented to the officers on the bridge."

"And the ship's log?"

"We'll state that was washed away with the chart desk when the wave smashed the wheelhouse."

It was vintage Fransen: unscrupulous, shameless, brazen; but I had, reluctantly, to admire his ingenuity.

"Who in hell would believe that? Not one wave in a century would rip off the Paradise tree, the flying bridge—"

"Don't worry, everybody will accept it. Who'd look for a hidden motive? Why would anyone blow up half a ship? For profit? The insurance will pay only for the damage done, if it's an act of God. So, prepare an itemized list of the damage tonight, we'll shoot it off to Chung tomorrow and get the tow out of town. We don't want it to hang around waiting for the insurance company to send an agent. After Chung has filed his claim, with itemized list of damages, all they'll do is a *post hoc* inspection after you arrive. It's cutting it fine, but, believe me, it's foolproof." He looked at his plate, the steak with the crushed cigarette, and said, "God! Even a dog would puke," but started to carve the meat anyway.

"Sorry, Fransen," I said calmly. "It's no deal."

"Huh?" He stared at me with a mouthful of steak.

"You didn't get my point at all, did you? I want to protect my crew. They're illiterate fishermen, a century behind the times. No union will stand up for them. No politician is going to champion their cause. If we do what you suggest and report that the damage was done by the hurricane, what is to stop Chung from rebuilding the ship into the death trap she was? I want to force him to keep her as she is now, and only a court ruling will do that. I demand that you hand in my report and the ship's log to the authorities. And that's final."

He gave me a look I couldn't interpret; it was like that of a doctor trying to evaluate the state of my arteries by appraising my eyes. Then he raised his hands in mock surrender. "Okay," he said. "On your head be it." He pushed away his plate.

The tired woman came back, the plate was given to the cat and an insipid dessert placed in front of us. We sat listening to the downpour for a while; then he said, "All right, let me try this on you for size. When I get to Kao Hsiung, twenty-four hours from now, I'll go straight to Chung. I'll show him the log and your report and tell him to have the architects design a safe profile for the ship along the lines of what you have now. If he refuses, the report and the log go to the authorities, in which case he'll be put through the mangle of an international court case with KITCO while his ship is chained to the quay. If you ask me, he'll play."

"Suppose he does, what kind of report are you going to file in the meantime?"

"None. I'll wait until I've talked to him. Let him decide, it's his baby."

"I don't know if I'll go along with that."

He stared at me for a moment through narrowed eyes, then said pleasantly, "Harinxma, old boy, sorry to be blunt, but you don't figure in this at all. Nobody will call you as a witness. You're not an officer but an advisor, an outsider whose opinion interests nobody, and tomorrow you go home. When the captain was killed, the first mate took over command; he'll take the ship and the tow to Taiwan. This will be the last you'll ever hear of it, I promise you. And don't give me any problems; I'm the one who'll be taking the heat, not you. Now—is this all we're getting in the way of a lousy dessert? Yuck!"

He called for coffee. The tired woman came slouching out of the rain again with two cups and took our plates away. After she had left, I said, "Fransen, if I find out that you haven't handed the report and the log to the authorities—"

"For Christ's sake, what do you take me for? I'm prepared to do minor fiddles for the company, but I can't suppress legal evidence! You know that as well as I do. All I want is to go and see Chung first. It's his ship, goddammit. KITCO won't like it, but, hell, they've only got themselves to blame. Now please let me have my coffee in peace. Have a heart, man!"

When ten minutes later we stepped out into the street, we found ourselves in a downpour and had to put our jackets over our heads while crossing the road to the taxi.

"I need the log and your report," Fransen said once we were seated inside. "I'll take you to the ship and pick 'em up."

"Why? We'll be passing the Rainmaker on the way. Get out there. He'll take me to the ship. Tomorrow morning I'm going to call my wife from the hotel. I'll bring the documents along and leave them for you at the desk."

"Okay, thanks. Boy, I'm beat. It's the heat, you know; that and the moisture. Takes the stuffing out of you." After a few moments he asked casually, "You want to pick up your plane ticket at the same time?"

"I don't think so."

"You changed your mind?"

"Yes."

"Mind telling me why?"

"I want to make sure the ship stays as she is. I want to be there when she arrives, talk to Chung myself."

"Also, your Number One isn't up to the job. Right?"

"Right."

He sighed. "The mate you're waiting for, Harinxma, is Admiral Drake."

There was a silence while the dilapidated taxi bounced and splashed through potholes, its headlights sweeping shuttered bungalows that looked like a stage set for a movie about sin in the tropics. Then he said musingly, in the tone of reminiscence I remembered with wariness, "You know, in all the years I've worked for the old man in my present function I've known him to make only one mistake. One miscalculation in seven years. Pretty good scoring."

I said nothing.

"I don't want to blow my own trumpet," he continued in a mellow mood, "but I warned him he was wrong."

"About what?"

"He knew you would take root once he put you on that ship —that was the idea. But he was confident that you'd get off in Talca when he whistled you home. I told him you wouldn't. I told him you'd never leave the goddam ship until somebody shot you."

"Fancy that."

"Well, who knows?" he continued warmly. "This time somebody may. Chung's not going to clap hands and sing when he finds out his little stooge messed up the operation."

"Captain Cho was after *me*, not a share of the insurance money."

He sighed and said, "Okay. Have it your way."

We drove the rest of the way in silence.

5

Before leaving the documents with the hall porter of the Rainmaker for Captain Fransen, the next morning, I had them photocopied by a helpful young lady at the reception. She gave me two medium envelopes and one large one; the originals went into one of the medium envelopes, addressed to Captain Fransen, the photocopies into the other. I wrote on it TO BE PLACED IN SAFE DEPOSIT BOX and inserted it into the large envelope, addressed to Sylvia, together with a letter.

> *Dear Love, the sealed envelope is to be put in the safety-deposit box at the bank. It contains legal papers concerning the ship and should be carefully stashed away. Should they be needed, I will telephone you or cable instructions as to what to do with the contents. For the time being, the mere fact that they*

are in your possession is enough. Sorry that this is such a short note, but you know almost everything from my letters written during the crossing which go by same mail. We have to be out of here by nightfall because the Princess' moorings are spoken for after midnight. Thanks for your letters (four!) which Fransen handed me, and please thank Helen for hers! Must hurry now: much love, M.

In my letters I hadn't told her about Captain Cho's attempt to turn over the ship, just that during the hurricane it became necessary to activate the emergency dynamite charge, making it sound as casual as possible. I handed in my mail, together with the large envelope which I sent registered, to the post office in the lobby, and wrote out a telegram: SORRY UNABLE TO TELEPHONE LONG DELAY IN CONNECTION SHIP MUST VACATE BERTH WITHIN TWELVE HOURS LONG LETTERS IN MAIL LOVE MARTINUS.

The rest of the day was hectic; we had to do in twelve hours what would normally have taken twenty-four. The run to Kao Hsiung was about five thousand miles without passing a grocery; we put plenty of fuel in the old *Princess* to get us there, but drinking water might become a problem if we weren't careful.

Just before we were due to sail, Fransen turned up with some documents for Number One to sign as acting master and he came into the dayroom for a quick final drink.

"Sorry, Harinxma," he said, "My plane leaves at twenty-one hundred and I don't want to shave it too close. Well, cheers, Godspeed and happy sailing. See you in Kao Hsiung."

"Before you go," I said, "I think I should tell you that I had photocopies made of the log and my report."

He carefully put down his empty glass on the coffee table. "Let me see if I understand you rightly," he said. "Unless everybody does exactly what you want them to do with this ship, you're going to resort to blackmail. Is that it?"

"I want to be sure that this whole business is handled according to the law, that's all."

He sighed and went back to the icebox. "Harinxma, I'm worried about you. When I first knew you, you were a genial, chubby old boy the crew instantly called 'Uncle.' Now look at you. You eat catfood, you're as thin as a rail, you've turned into some sort of a religious fanatic with a crazy haircut and nipped-in waist—"

"Dammit, Fransen," I exploded, "I was nearly killed by this

[335]

ship! Together with forty others! What the hell do you want? A genial old boy who says, 'Oh, well . . .'?"

"Don't go for *me*, Harinxma," he said amiably, "I'm just the middleman." He knocked back his drink. "Don't worry, your precious Chinks will be safe. Now I've got to be going or I'll miss the damn plane." With that, he put his glass on the table and left.

Two hours later I took the *Isabel* and the old *Princess* out of Pago Pago harbor into the most gory picture-postcard sunset any tourist could wish for. When our course was set and Number Two had taken over the watch, the rest of the staff and I gathered in the dayroom for Happy Hour.

"Well," Chief Liu said, raising his glass, "here's looking at us."

Louis got his cocktail nibbles and Pete his drop of Kirschwasser in his drinking water. Hopla hobbled around on his crutches dramatically, in death-defying devotion to his duty.

6

Dear Dad,

Last night I had a dream about you. I went to see you on board ship just before leaving, as I used to do as a little girl when everything seemed so enormous. The ship in my dream was huge, but somehow dented, or twisted. The walls were at an odd angle, the door to your cabin would not close. You were there in your pajamas and you said, "Well, this time I'll send you the longest letter I ever wrote." In the dream I said, "No, you won't. The longest was the one you wrote to Mart and he never read it, not all of it. I did." You said, "You'll see! I'll ask my rat to make footnotes." We both laughed until we cried, and I woke up crying. Sorry to sound soppy, but there it is. Nobody knows, really, how soppy I feel sometimes. By nobody I mean the kids, the neighbors, or Harry, who came yesterday to ask if it was all right if he sorted out the books and took away the ones that were his. I told him to help himself, I had an errand to do. I went to the supermarket and suddenly thought, No! I'm not going to wheel this shopping cart around trying not to bawl; I'm going to the movies! And so I took myself off to see some god-awful movie for teenage creeps about murders by chain-

saw, but had to leave halfway anyhow as the kids were due home from school. It's okay during the day, but at night, when everybody's been put to bed, it gets almost unbearable some-times; tonight was very bad. So I thought I'd write you a letter. I know that writing you a letter is like sticking it in a bottle and letting it float out with the tide, but it doesn't matter, it will get to you one day.

Mother was upset after talking to the doctor in Chile. He was very patient with her and understanding, but she had the im-pression that the two of you were in cahoots, that instead of going to see a cardiologist as you had promised, you had dug up an ex-ship's doctor whom you'd seduced into reassuring the little woman that all was well, that your first duty was to the crew and the ship, and that she should not worry. In other words, 'Men must work and women must weep, though the harbor bar be moaning,' or whatever the poem says. She was especially suspicious because of something he said like 'Your husband is on a pilgrimage toward the truth.' When she asked, 'What truth?' he answered, 'About himself, life, death—a final voyage of exploration.' I agreed with her that it sounded as if the two of you had decided that would do it; but secretly I was fascinated. Is it true? Are you on that 'final voyage of explora-tion'? Will you come back with answers about life and death? Will you keep a diary? If you think that's self-indulgent or some-thing, can't you do it in the form of a letter? To me?

Sorry again. I'm just thinking aloud. It's late, and the house is so still. Even the cat is asleep in her basket. I never knew what true loneliness was. Come home, Dad. Wherever you go, what-ever you see, experience, discover, come home, come home soon, to tell me about it.

I love you.   Helen.

Chapter Thirteen

1

In retrospect, the happiest day of my voyage with the *Isabel* came a week later.

After Pago Pago we had been sailing through the most romantic part of the world: one idyllic island after another, fringed with palms, surrounded by surf breaking white on coral reefs. The scent of tropical flowers was wafted by the warm evening breeze across a deep blue sea; exotic birds came clattering out of Paradise to alight briefly on Ma Chang's laundry line; we were traversing the world that had bewitched Gauguin and Melville.

After a week the tow anchored off the tip of one of those magic islands, a wooded, wedge-shaped atoll surrounded by a coral reef. As the sun rose, haloed by an orange morning haze, its light revealed a dreamlike vision of palms and a sandy beach beyond the surf breaking on the reef. Two cone-shaped beacons, one faded blue and the other a sun-bleached pink, marked the narrow pass through the reef for small boats only.

Our oil line was connected to the *Princess* and fuel began to pulse to the *Isabel* from the liner's tanks; then I saw one of her old lifeboats being lowered and heading our way. Inside were the ten runners and Harakiri with a rolled-up towel under his arm. "Hi there, Harinxma!" he hailed as the boat was rowed past. "Coming for a swim?"

"Where?"

"Off yonder beach! Come on, man!"

My first impulse was to refuse. I was too old, I had no swim trunks, my aged white body would look ridiculous among all those yellow athletes doing the Chinese crawl. But the beach looked as romantic and inviting as the beaches of my childhood. Then the two marcos asked if it was all right if they went along. Chief Liu, who had come out on deck to have a look, called, "Hold on! I coming too!" and hurried off to get a towel. Then Tulane turned up with a towel for me. Ma Chang grinned like a permissive mother, then cried something which Hopla somberly translated as "She say: wait. She say: take food. For everybody." Suddenly, midsummer madness got me and I shouted at Harakiri, between cupped hands, "Wait! I'm coming! Ma Chang is making up a picnic!"

"Okay!" he shouted back. "We've got the beer!"

At that magic word, understood by all, everybody wanted to go. Ten minutes later Ma Chang reappeared on deck with two cook's mates lugging a huge basket of goodies; the entire crew was crammed into the waiting boat, loading it to the gunnels. When we pushed off, the *Isabel* was left, with a feeling of recklessness on my part, to Number One, engineer Number Two, Ma Chang and a morose Hopla, whose leg was still in a cast. The runners rowed the boat through the gap in the reef into the blue-and-green lagoon and beached it with a crunch on the most beautiful, blinding-white sandy beach I had ever seen. Everybody splashed overboard with gusto, leaving me and the picnic basket inside, and pulled the boat high up the sandy slope. A mass of waving hands helped me climb out; the sand I jumped onto was warm and magical: with one arthritic leap I landed back in my childhood.

But then, so did we all. Everybody threw off their clothes and splashed and frolicked naked in the blue lagoon like children. The only one who kept on his undershorts was Harakiri, chalk-white among the yellow Chinese, saying that we all would have our manhood assaulted by jellyfish and rise screaming. It didn't stop him from diving and trumpeting as loudly as the rest.

I was the first to leave the water; despite my energetic rowing session in the gym every day, I was soon out of breath. Tulane, who had been keeping an eye on me, helped me up the steep beach and spread out a towel for me to sit on, before loping back to join the others.

I sat there drying in the warm sun, watching them splashing, paddling, chasing one another, listening to the childhood sounds of happy shouts and laughter. The ancient hatred between the tribes of the two islands was forgotten, or maybe, in this magical world of sand, sun and sea, blowing snot at pregnant dogs was a ludicrous aberration, a form of lunacy. Watching the happy group gambol in the lagoon, children in Paradise, filled me with a sense of gratitude. I had brought a sick ship full of enemies through five months of danger and disaster to where they were now: laughing and splashing in a blue lagoon, all enmity forgotten, with in the background the long, low profile of what was now a safe, strong, even handsome tugboat. Apart from the

[339]

spindly stacks topped with Chief Liu's doilies, she was massive, yet elegant. How little it would take to turn her into a truly beautiful ship! It would be the crown on my life as a sailor to see her as she finally could be: the most beautiful ocean-going tugboat in the world.

At a given moment, as if driven by a sudden communal urge, they all came trooping out of the water and up the slope of the beach, headed for the honey pot of the picnic basket. Ma Chang had managed to prepare a feast; Harakiri and his rogues had brought along enough beer to gladden us all. It was an idyllic meal, a sailors' *déjeuner sur l'herbe;* it seemed to symbolize the ultimate escape from Fransen's demonic world. As I sat there, white mother hen going pink in the sun surrounded by my yellow chicks feasting, I tasted happiness.

Maybe it was the beer, but as I lay back, eyes closed, sunbaked, about to drift into sleep, a chill, a darkness surreptitiously closed in. Maybe it was not a foreboding, just the superstition, common to us all in moments of bliss, that it cannot last, that darkness and evil are the permanent realities underlying our lives.

2

At daybreak three days later, toward the end of my watch, I saw in the growing light of the dawn a bizarre edifice emerge from the night still hovering on the horizon. It looked like a stack of native houses on stilts.

It took me a while to make out what it was: a floating hotel structure, towed by one large tugboat. As I stood looking through my binoculars, trying to get a glimpse of the flag that hung limp from the mainmast in the windless morning, the telephone rang.

"Bridge. Harinxma."

"Commodore," the voice of Marco Two said, "Netherland tugboat *Piano* make contact. The captain—Prong?—ask will you visit?"

"Prong?"

"Sorry about name. Marco there not good Morse."

"Bron! You mean the *Fiona?* "

"Oh? Oh, yes, see now. What shall I signal, Commodore?"

"Say 'Yes.' Tell him I'll come over as soon as we're alongside."

"Very good, Commodore. Bye-bye."

How about that: Beast Rufus! I remembered his telling me in Flushing that he would be pushing and pulling in Indonesia, waiting for a hotel structure that was to be towed to the Marquesas; but this was like two needles meeting in a haystack.

An hour later I was on my way to the *Fiona,* a beautiful tug of the doomed old class, as elegant and feminine as a yacht. As I approached her in the workboat, a flutter of wind stirred her flag; I realized it was flying at half-mast. One of the crew must have died.

It wasn't Beast Rufus himself; he stood waiting for me at the rail. I had never seen him in his tropical working outfit; he looked like the butcher of a small town, complete with apron and straw boater. "Hey!" he yelled as we drew within range. "What have you done to my pig, Ome Tinus?" So my nickname was common coinage now on the fleet.

I waved by way of answer. When we drew alongside, he reached down to haul me up like a sack of flour, plonked me on my feet on deck and yelled "Hello there!" He emitted a powerful musky smell, like a large male animal in the wild. "How have you been, Ome Tinus?"

He was wearing a muumuu, half nightshirt, half hospital gown, which I presumed was the garb best suited for the job in this climate, on condition you didn't give a damn what you looked like. "Come to my dayroom," he said, slapping my shoulder. "Let's pour some Morning Glory into you. What the hell happened to your ship?"

"I'll tell you. How about us just meeting like this?"

"Nuts," he said, "my marco's been tracing you since you left Samoa. I changed course twice to hit you on the button. Why didn't your marco reply to our calls? Or do they only speak Chinese?"

"We lost our electronic gear," I explained. "We're back to Morse, ten minutes twice a day."

"How about that?" he said. His Arabian slippers flopped on the deck as he led the way to his dayroom; seen from the back, he looked like a patient about to be X-rayed, except for the boater. His crew, a motley crowd of not demonstratively happy men, none of whom I recognized, stared at me with what looked like amaze-

[341]

ment. Obviously, I had no justification for feeling sartorially superior; there was little to choose between a small-town butcher in a
muumuu and a scarecrow with a coolie haircut in a tutu.

The *Fiona*'s dayroom was smaller and scruffier than I had
expected; I had forgotten how tugboat captains used to be
housed, even in the recent past. There was no couch, no room
divider separating lounge and office; there was no office, only
two club chairs the worse for wear, a small built-in desk between
two wardrobes and a refrigerator large enough for a morgue
which took up most of the space. "Let's start with a snort," my
host said, opening the door of the icebox and letting out a blast of
polar air. "Sit down. The far one is the best."

When I sat down in the twanging club chair, I stifled a cry. A
repulsive creature, half monkey, half tomcat, with huge amber
eyes and obscenely male, leaped onto my lap.

"How about that?" its master cried, kicking the door of the
freezer shut. "He never does that to strangers, only to me!"

"Fancy that," I said. The unprepossessing animal proceeded
to sniff all over me, like a dog, standing on its hind legs on my lap
to check the shoulder where Louis always perched. "What—er
—what *is* it?"

"A lemur," he said, tossing his boater onto the desk like a
Frisbee. "Here, take a bite out of this." He handed me a glass so
cold that my hands almost froze to it. "I won him in a poker game,
back in Singapore. He brings in the newspaper."

"Terrific," I said.

He shot me a glance of his extraordinarily small, mean eyes.
Maybe they weren't mean, just those of a different species. With
his wild red beard and matted hair, he looked like the Missing
Link.

"I gather you ran into trouble with the pig," he said.

"An explosion."

"No kidding. What of?"

I began to tell him the story, uncomfortably conscious of the
lemur exploring my pelvic region.

"Clout him one," he said. "If you don't, he'll unzip your fly.
He has real little hands, you know, fingers and all."

I tried to prise the animal off my lap; its fur was unpleasant to
the touch. With one hand it clung to my belt with surprising force
while the other hunted for Jack the Zipper. Not the beast but I
gave a startled cry as, out of the blue, it was whacked across the

rump with a rolled-up newspaper. It leaped onto its master's lap; he dropped the newspaper. It was the *Singapore Times.*

"All right—then what?"

I told him how, nineteen days into the Pacific, we would have capsized but for the dynamite charge.

"Capsized?" He peered at me as if I had made a shameful confession. "*You* let the pig sneak up on you?"

I told him how it had come about. He was fascinated; the activity of the lemur underneath his hospital gown went unnoticed. His house brand, meanwhile, froze the sweat on my brow while burning a hole in my stomach.

After I had told of Captain Cho's insane plot to punish me for making him lose face, he asked, "You aren't serious, are you? Come on, Harinxma! Who are you kidding? That was a set-up job! He was in league with that smooth little creep in Taiwan, of course."

I told him why I didn't think so; he looked at me with an odd expression. "Is that what happens when you get old?" he asked.

"What?"

"That you want to believe only the best of people?"

I had no answer to that.

He rose and picked up my glass; the lemur dropped out of his gown, he threw it out of the door into the corridor on his way to the freezer.

"No more for me," I said.

"You've got to be kidding. Here—" He handed me my glass; smoke rose from it, as in a laboratory test. "So what *did* you report? That your Chink captain ran amok and tried to turn over the ship in a fit of madness?"

"Just about. But that isn't the critical part."

"Then what is?"

"Why the dynamite charge was installed in the first place."

His eyes widened. "You reported *that?*"

"Of course, I had to. Wouldn't you?"

"Like hell I would! Have myself blackballed as a tug-driver for life, worldwide? Thanks very much!" Then he added, "But, of course, that's not your problem. All you have to worry about is your pension. Who did you file your report with? The Yanks in Pago Pago or the consul?"

"I left that to Fransen."

His face was a study. "To *Fransen?*"

His astonishment was so genuine that I felt a twinge of doubt. "Why not?"

"Didn't you know that when you talk to Fransen you talk to KITCO? What do you think they'd want him to do with that report? You played right into their hands, Harinxma—you practically asked them to sweep it under the rug! He must have ditched the lot."

" I don't think so." I said it with sturdy self-confidence, but the doubt was real now. Had I gone wrong somewhere? Was there something I'd overlooked? "They can't suppress legal evidence."

"Oh, no?" He snorted derisively. "Jim Kwel would suppress his own mother if he saw money in it. You're crazy, Harinxma, you know that? You had one chance in a million to yank the fangs out of the pig, and you buggered it up."

"I'm not as crazy as you think," I protested. "Before giving it all to Fransen, I had photocopies made."

"So you have photocopies! By now they aren't worth the paper they're printed on."

"I don't understand . . ."

"You gave them all they needed, brother: time. How long is it going to take you, towing that hulk with its underwater garden from Pago Pago to Kao Hsiung? Fifty days?"

"Just about."

"There you go. By the time you get to Taiwan, the whole thing will be over and done with. They'll have filed a fraudulent claim without mentioning any explosion. The insurance company will have accepted it and paid up. All maritime reports will have been dutifully filed. The dead captain's next of kin will have received a nice letter and a little pension so they won't make trouble. The case will be closed, and you, with your story about dynamite charges and captains running amok and trying to scuttle the ship, will be a crazy old man jumping out of a closet yelling 'Murder!' You'll be a threat to everybody, even the civil servants involved, and if you don't beat it, you'll end up in a Taiwanese nut farm."

His dramatization was so exaggerated that I felt relieved. He was just another Fransen, seeing plots and assassins under every bed. Either that, or he was getting drunk.

"You don't believe me?"

"Frankly, no."

The look he gave me was one of commiseration. "No, I guess you don't." He took a swig from his glass. "Okay, I'll spell it out for you. Mind you, I'll just have a shot at it, but I've dealt with those jokers long enough to have a pretty good idea how their minds work. You told Fransen when?"

"Oh, I don't know. During a meal, after I came in."

"Same night?"

"Same night."

"You told him you were going to report the whole story exactly the way it happened? Dynamite charge and all?"

"Yes."

"He asked you not to be hasty? To think it over first? To report it in some other way?"

"He suggested reporting it as hurricane damage."

"And you said no?"

"I said—well, never mind. We ended by agreeing that he would go straight to see Chung, show him the log and my report, get him to agree not to rebuild the ship the way she was originally, but to have the architects design a lower profile along the lines she has now—"

"And if Mr. Chung didn't agree, he'd hand your report and the log to the authorities. Right?"

"Yes."

He finished his drink and rose to get himself a third. "Okay," he said, pouring, "I'll tell you what happened." He came back with his drink and put it on the table cautiously, as if it might explode. "The same night he talked to you, Fransen called The Hague and warned them that they had a loose cannon on deck: you. That he'd stalled you for the moment, but what should he do next?"

I shifted uneasily. "So?"

"So they told him, 'Hang in there. We'll call you back.' They did, probably in the middle of the night. 'Okay,' they said, 'here's what you do: play the old man along. Agree to whatever he says, as long as you get that convoy out of there on the double. But before you do, have the acting master sign a report stating that the damage was caused by a hurricane.' And that's exactly what he must have done."

I remembered Fransen coming on board with a sheaf of documents for Number One to sign. My heart sank. "But he couldn't! The boy knew I'd written a full report, that I had the log—"

"Harinxma, who are you kidding? You sincerely believe that Fransen, the wiliest hyena in the business, couldn't make a Chinese babe-in-the-woods sign a bunch of papers saying it was a hurricane? That the captain was killed by a rogue wave, or a falling spar, or what have you? I can hear him say it: 'Captain'— he's sure to have called the poor bugger 'Captain'—'it's been decided by Mr. Chung that we should report that the damage was caused by the hurricane.' He'll have told him some so-called inside stuff, very hush-hush, about insurance, corporate responsibility—hell, you could write his sales pitch yourself. How long do you think a boy giddy with self-importance because of his new position as master could hold out against that wily bastard? The kid would have signed his own death warrant within three minutes.''

"But what difference would that make? I have photocopies of everything! My report, the log—''

"You told Fransen that?''

"Of course!''

"Did he faint dead away? Or did he wag his finger at you and tell you how naughty you were to try and blackmail people like Mr. Chung?''

I was quite cold now. "But it *will* work!'' I cried. "If Chung doesn't agree to keep the ship's profile as it is now, I'll telephone my wife and she'll hand the documents to the authorities!''

"Your wife has them?'' He shook his head. "Harinxma, you may be a great sailor, but 007 you ain't.'' He bent over and slurped the top off his drink before picking up the glass.

It gave me time to rally. "Look here, Bron, they're not going to risk having it all brought out into the open. Fransen wasn't at all pleased about those photocopies, I can tell you. He took straight off for Kao Hsiung to give Chung the log and my report and to warn him I had copies.''

He gave me another look of commiseration. "Harinxma, why didn't you spend some time in front of the mirror before you came up with that plan to blackmail the big, bad wolf?''

"I don't know what the hell you mean.''

"Fransen and KITCO know you better than you know yourself, man. You'll never do it, and they know you won't. All you've done is bellow 'Boo!' as far as blackmail is concerned. *Their* blackmail is going to work because it's real. Understand? Those boys deal in millions; they deal in realities, not fancies, or they wouldn't last a day. They have you over a barrel, friend. You'll never do it because you can't.''

[346]

"You're dead wrong, I tell you! Boy, even if I end up in prison—"

"You in prison? No, Harinxma, not you. The little Chink. That gullible snotnose, the 'acting master' who must have signed the fraudulent declaration. If you bring out your report and the log, every page of which he initialed at the end of his watch, they can have him up for perjury. What do you think they'll do to him? Not only will his career be shot, *he'll* end up in prison, not you. Jim Kwel knows, Fransen knows and I bet you Chung knows you'll never do it, because your hands are tied. Because you're a captain and he's part of your crew and to your generation that mattered. So, forget it, Harinxma. Chung is going to rebuild the pig the way she was, to have another shot at picking up the insurance money. And this time you can bet your life he's not going to put another old salt on board who could sail the world in a bathtub, and who fights for his crew like a tiger. He'll have a wide choice of shits, like your Captain Cho. Your generation has as good as died out; soon the sea'll be alive with eager beavers of the 'me generation' who don't even *know* that their souls are for sale."

My God, I had forgotten Number One. He was right. I could never do that. But then maybe it wasn't so. He was just like Fransen; they both shared the same conspiratorial view of the world. Now, old Kwel might be a tough, hard-nosed old bastard, but always, when the chips were down, he had proved to be an ultimately decent man. I said, more to myself than to Beast Rufus, "I'll talk to old Kwel."

He fixed me with a strange, unfocused stare. He had to be sitting there in precarious equilibrium, with half a gallon of high explosives in his gut. Then he asked, "You don't know?"

"What?"

"Of course—all you had left was Morse."

"Why? What happened?"

"Haven't you seen my flag? All ships of the fleet are under orders to observe one week of mourning, ha-ha. If I'd had the pennants, I'd have dressed her overall."

"But who—"

"That's who," he said. "The old bastard. May his soul roast in hell." He raised his glass. "Here's to Arnold Bleeding Kwel, hiss hiss."

"My God . . ."

"Don't tell me you're planning to radio flowers?"

[347]

I suddenly wanted to get out of there. "I have to be going," I said, putting down my glass.

"Why?" he asked, hurt. "You just got here!"

I rose. "I must get back before our tows start drifting apart."

"No tow is drifting anywhere unless I tell it to," he said truculently. "If that Indonesian whorehouse behind me starts a life of its own, I'll sink it."

I went to the door. "So long, Bron. Godspeed and happy sailing."

"And nuts to you," he said. "You didn't even finish your drink!"

When I opened the door, the lemur, which I had forgotten, leaped up at the front of my shorts and clung, refusing to let go. I turned back, trying to pluck it off; Bron hoisted himself to his feet, grabbed the newspaper and socked it on the head. It let go with a yelp.

"Want him?" he asked. "You're an animal lover, and you'll be going home soon. He brings in the newspaper."

"No thanks."

I went out on deck and looked up at the flag, now flying free in the freshening wind, at half-mast.

Old Kwel was dead.

3

I couldn't understand why the news affected me as it did. I was stunned, numb with shock. The sunlit world had suddenly darkened, transforming everything. On my way back in the workboat I gazed at the *Isabel* and the *Princess*. The derelict liner, her hull streaked with rust, her stacks peeling and her torn boat covers flapping in the wind, looked like an outsize piece of junk. The *Isabel* with her cropped profile looked equally derelict; the nearer I drew, the more depressing the sight of her became. The crew had done their laundry; a line of disreputable-looking underwear, including a row of petticoats, fluttered on the aft deck.

The moment I was back on board, while the boat was still

being hoisted into the davits, the *Isabel* churned ahead. There was an exchange of greetings: ear-shattering blasts from the *Fiona*, goatlike bleats from the *Isabel*'s hand-operated horn. On the hotel structure, runners waved to us. It was only when I was alone in my cabin that the full realization hit me. On an impulse, I went to the desk, sat down and took a sheet of paper out of the drawer.

Dear Miss Bastiaans,

I have just received the news of Arnold Kwel's passing. My immediate response is to write to you. As you know, he and I knew each other for a long time, over fifty years in fact, and I find myself deeply affected by his death. But you probably knew him better than I did; the few times I saw you together, I was struck by your dedication to him and your concern for his well-being. It was largely thanks to you that he was able to concentrate on the world of the mind, in which he was forever young.

He put his indelible stamp on the ocean towage business. That may not sound like much, compared to the movers of empires and the shakers of men, but he will be remembered as long as there are long-distance tugboats sailing the seas.

Miss Bastiaans, I'm far away, in Polynesia, after five months at sea. I wish I could stand with you at his grave, to bid farewell to the Old Man.

I feel as if I had lost part of my life, and thereby of myself.

> *Yours, in sympathy and mourning,*
> *Martinus Harinxma.*

4

Although there was nothing I could do about it, not for weeks, I had to know the truth.

That evening, after supper, I invited Number One to my day-room. He accepted with alacrity. I sat him down on the couch; Hopla, groaning and limping demonstratively, served coffee and cookies. When we were alone, I asked, "Number One, before we left Pago Pago, did Captain Fransen ask you to sign any documents concerning the damage to the ship?"

I expected a shifty look, or one of bewildered innocence; instead, he beamed at me. "Don't worry, Commodore. It has all been taken care of."

"Captain Fransen did give you a report to sign?"

"Of course, I acting master."

"So it's hurricane wave damage now, officially?"

"Yes. Very good solution, okay."

He picked up a cookie and started to munch it. Then he took another.

I sat listening to his crunching for a moment, then I asked, "And the log?"

"Shh," he said. "Gone."

"How was it done? Did he tell you?"

"He said he deep-six it." Suddenly a doubt crossed his mind. "That mean what I think it mean, no?"

"It means 'to destroy.' "

He looked relieved. "I told you," he said smugly, "everything taken care of. Don't worry."

I could no longer contain myself. "You stupid idiot!" I cried, struck by the awful realization that Bron had been right after all. "What possessed you to sign a fraudulent report? Don't you see what you've done? You've screwed up the only chance I had to stop this ship from being turned back into the death trap she was!"

He looked as if he had been hit by a bucket of water; then he stammered, "What, Commodore? Wha-what do you mean?"

"I mean Captain Fransen talked you into signing a fraudulent declaration, that declaration has now gone to the insurance company and Mr. Chung will get the money to rebuild her the way she was! I could have stopped him, because I have photocopies of the original log and my report, but now, goddam it, if I do that, you'll end up in jail and you can forget about any future as a ship's officer! You ass! You pompous, arrogant pipsqueak!"

He rushed out of the dayroom with Louis on his shoulder. I went after him and yelled down the corridor, "Come back, goddammit! You've got my *rat!*"

For some reason, as he stood there, swallowing, while I plucked the little animal off his shirt, I realized I had been yelling at Fransen, Jim Kwel, myself, not the poor, hoodwinked youth. "Get out of my sight," I said, "I'll talk to you later," and slammed the door.

5

Alone in my dayroom, pacing like a caged bear, I began to see that the whole scene had been emotional, gratuitous. I had known it from the beginning: Fransen himself had told me quite calmly, as if it were the most normal thing in the world, in that restaurant in the rain; but somehow I had suppressed the knowledge. I must have—or else I had not taken in the full portent of that shameless solution. Whatever the answer, I had failed to realize that in order to give Chung a choice, a report other than mine had to be presented to him, and the one to sign that was the acting master. How could I have failed to make that connection? I had been so proud of my photocopies, of having for once in my life outwitted the man-traders, that I had overlooked the obvious. Beast Rufus was right: I might be a good sailor, I was a lousy plotter. I had been an easy mark: a seventy-year-old man with hypertension who had been out of the running for nine years, and who had never involved himself with the shenanigans and subterfuges of the owners whose ships he sailed.

But no, it had nothing to do with age; it had to do with my lack of insight when it came to dealing with Fransen's demonic world. I had turned my back on it; I had, as Beast Rufus said, firmly believed the best of people. Was it up to me to change now? No, goddammit, I was not going to get caught in that cold, cynical hell of dog eat dog, stick it to 'em, charity begins at home, no pity for suckers, it's a man's world, blow 'em up, rob 'em blind, let them jump out the window, they've only got themselves to blame.

It was a noble decision, but a hollow one. I had painted myself into a corner. There was no way out of the dilemma: either go along with them, cover up for Number One and save his life, or throw him to the wolves and protect the lives of the rest of the crew, of all future crews that might sail on the reconstructed *Isabel*, the killer ship. There simply was no other alternative: I was utterly stymied. No matter what other plan I might come up with, by the time I reached Kao Hsiung, Bron's prophecy would have been fulfilled. I couldn't reach Sylvia to discuss with her the possibility of bringing out the photocopies, and I couldn't radio her to release them without knowing what Chung's final decision was. They had me over a barrel. Or was there something else I could do . . . ? No idea. Total confusion, frustration—well, who knows? I had time. Plenty of time. Fifty days. Forty, now. Plenty of time to work something out.

But I knew I would never work something out. Not by myself. It needed a mind like old Kwel's. If only I could have picked his brains! If only I could have appealed to those fifty-odd years of our self-conscious relationship of father and son! Where was he now? Was he still around, as Harmsen's mate had been? BULLFROG BULLFROG THIS IS BULLY WHERE AM I— That night in Shadwell Basin we had tossed the Ouija board aside and gone back to Monopoly. Because it was nonsense? Because we didn't believe it? The reverse: we had turned away because we *did* believe it was Bully, lost in limbo. We hadn't wanted to face reality, our future, death. We had resumed rolling the dice for Park Place, a hotel, three houses. We hadn't been mature enough, secure enough within ourselves, to keep the contact, maybe help him.

Was that the answer? To contact the world beyond the veil?

It was a measure of my desperation that I went to the bedroom, opened the drawer, took out the planchette and the Ouija board. But when I had taken them to the coffee table and opened the board—GOOD BYE, YES, NO, the smiling sun, the pouting moon —everything that was sane, adult, rational in me made me close it up again. I might be in a God-awful fix, but I wasn't going to get caught in the world of shadows and mirrors in which Spooks Haversma and Slobbo had lost themselves. Yet the few pages I had read of Spooks' record of his communications had been sane, adult, rational . . .

It seemed an acceptable compromise: don't rush into this, read up on it first. Read the pilot, study the chart, before venturing into unknown waters; then proceed slowly, cautiously, prepared for reefs, currents, whirlwinds, the song of the sirens. Let's listen to the sirens and take their bearings.

I lifted Louis off the Bowditch, put him on my shoulder and took the book off the shelf.

6

I read for hours, lost to the world. I was vaguely aware of the usual crowd wandering in and out, making kissing noises at Pete, tickling the rat, flushing the toilet, touching my arm and saying "Omi." They drove Hopla to chittering like a monkey trying to re-establish lost territory; in the end I had to shoo the lot of them out and lock the door. The silence and the peace came as a relief; I resumed reading, engrossed, captivated by this eerie dialogue between a lonely captain and a voice from beyond the veil.

Either Spooks Haversma had been a schizophrenic, split into two personalities like Dr. Jekyll and Mr. Hyde, or the communications he had received via the Ouija board had originated outside the confines of his own personality. It could not be his own subconscious, not even a contact with the collective unconscious, let alone himself in a state of self-induced hypnosis. He came out of these pages with extraordinary vividness as an intelligent, thoughtful man, one of those captains—I had known a few—who on closer acquaintance seemed more like philosophers seeking isolation than sailors. To a cynical observer like Fransen he must have been an amusing eccentric; some lonely captains, in the privacy of their dayrooms, got their kicks from pornographic magazines, Spooks Haversma gazed bug-eyed at a Ouija board. But to me, as I read on and on, his incorruptible objectivity and intellectual honesty in his dialogues with 'Henry,' his alter ego, guru or guide, were impressive.

He was in good company. Among the books on his shelves, I had found one by Carl Jung, the Swiss psychiatrist, who had communicated for years with a similar guide outside the confines of his own personality called Philemon. Jung wrote about meeting an Indian philosopher who, when asked who his guru was, had given the name of a Hindu sage, dead eight hundred years. When Jung asked how that was possible, the Indian had answered, 'Some of us have living gurus, others have spirit ones.'

However intelligent and objective Spooks Haversma might have been, it seemed impossible that his personal subconscious could have harbored this erudite alter ego, full of wit and superior insight, Henry, who had such fascinating things to say about life, death, the afterlife, the spirit world. Henry seemed to have an

intelligence different from that of Haversma, who had been Prot-
estant, almost puritanical, defending inch by inch his crumbling
fortress of rational materialism. Henry gave a fascinating description of the process of dying, the actual transition from life into
death, almost a duplicate of the process of birth: a dark passage,
easy for some, difficult for others, with at the other end—

The telephone on my desk rang shrilly. Sighing, I put the
stack of rice-paper sheets on the coffee table and went to answer
it.

"Dayroom, Harinxma."

"Oh, Commodore, excuse me, a light show in far distance, not
on chart, could you come identify, please?"

"Who is this? Number Two?"

"No, Co'dore, this is Number One. I am sorry for disturb you,
but light flashes dot dot dot dash dot dot, not on chart, not in
Pilot."

"Have you taken our position recently?"

"Yes, Commodore. I shot Arcturus and Battle-goose—"

"And what are your findings?"

"We are exactly where we suppose to be, Commodore . . ."

"In that case, stand on your own feet. What would you do if
you were the captain of this ship, without me on tap? Call the
marco on duty, ask if he's received any notices to mariners for
this area. If not, let him contact Rabaul or Truk and find out."

"Yes, Commodore . . ."

I went back to the couch, chased Louis, who had profited
from my absence by burrowing among the flimsy sheets of paper,
and continued to read:

> *. . . at the other end an idealization of our earthly existence,
> with as its focus our spiritual ambition. A doctor, if his earth life
> was centered on his patients, will go on helping people; an
> actress might find herself in some ethereal greenroom, gossip-
> ing with old friends and colleagues; an industrialist might be
> playing golf in a summer land with men of his own class and
> professional interests; some women will roam the streets of
> cities with erstwhile lovers, other—*

> Spooks would not sit still for it: *Come, on, Henry, this
> concept of the hereafter as a world of eternal light, in which
> there are only benevolent spirits and old friends, has to be
> hogwash! Where on that golf course or in that greenroom or in*

the streets of the lovers' cities are the victims of famines in Africa? The people who died in agony during torture in prisons in the Third World? The muggers gunned down in the street?

Henry replied: *At this initial stage the afterlife is closely related to the reality of the individual's earth life. No victims of famine will roam the golf course or invade the greenroom, no muggers haunt the lovers' streets. The only ones who might meet these would be the doctor whose life has been centered on human suffering, or the missionary who worked among them. Those are the ones who will be drawn to people crying for help, blind and terrified, in this limbo.*

Spooks: *So what you are in effect saying is that each of us creates his own afterlife?*

Henry: *Only in the early stages, according to your needs. You might go for long walks through sunlit landscapes with a dog—*

Spooks: *Which dog?*

Henry: *A dog you particularly liked.*

Spooks: *That would be the one that jumped in through the porthole in New Orleans twenty years ago. The one I called Cat. She was a ship's dog, she couldn't stand long walks.*

Henry: *How would you like to find yourself on the bridge of a ship? Blue sea, seagulls, old engineers and mates who went before . . .*

Spooks: *Friend, I have been sailing ships for a living all my adult life, and during that time met very few mates or engineers that I would care to see again. Frankly, the one I'd like to be welcomed by is you.*

Henry: *If that is what you want, you will.*

Who would I like to be welcomed by? My mother? Not really. Captain Bosman, guru of my young years at sea? Not particularly. I wasn't really all that interested in the afterlife; my problem, the insurmountable problem, was right now, right here. The one I would like to talk to at this moment was old Kwel. ('Sir, what do I do to have my cake and eat it? Protect that young idiot Number One, as well as my own and other crews that will sail the *Isabel* in years to come?')

The planchette and the Ouija board were still lying on the

coffee table. I opened the board and, again, was turned off by its gypsy-caravan aspect. Frankly, the whole thing was ludicrous. A man my age, after all these years, fooling with the same device that had once, in Shadwell Basin, produced—

I picked up the planchette with a feeling of defiance. I was my own master and a mature man without any inner insecurity. I was not going to bury my head in the sand. If the thing was real, I wanted to face it. After all, Haversma had told me via this sooth-sayer's tool to 'beware' and been proven right. Even so—

Somebody banged on the door. My first impulse was to shout 'Go away!' but it would be less of an interruption if I went to find out what the devil was the matter this time. I unlocked the door, opened it, and there stood Hopla, bright-eyed, toothy-smiled, carrying a tray. "Co'dore like tea?"

I did not know what the time was; it certainly wasn't a time at which he normally would ply me with tea. "All right, put it on the table."

"Yes, Co'dore . . ." He limped to the coffee table, put down the mug, stood there taking it all in: the board, the planchette, the open Bowditch, the scattered pages.

"Come on," I snapped irritably, "get a move on."

"Oh, yes, Co'dore!" He tiptoed out, looking saintly and servile, but forgetting to limp. Well, no harm done; he probably hadn't the faintest idea what it was all about, and even if he had, no one else on board would be even remotely interested.

But the interruption had for some reason unnerved me. It took quite a while to crank myself up again to the same momen-tum of determination, or the same degree of folly, with which I had picked up the planchette. Really, all I wanted to know was if old Kwel was still around, or anyone like Henry who might have an intelligent answer to my problem. So, almost casually, I put my hand on the planchette and, on the childish impulse to give this some intellectual respectability, asked, "Just as a matter of inter-est: do I have a Henry of my own?"

I don't know what I had expected—a classy answer, a witty phrase—but with alarming force the invisible hand got hold of my wrist and guided the planchette as it whizzed, at frenzied speed, from letter to letter: JESUS HARINXMA THIS IS A MESS I CAN'T GET THE HELL OFF THIS SHIP AND I WANT TO WALK WITH MY CAT BUT ALL THIS DARKNESS AND THIS WATER I CAN HEAR THEM YELLING ALL AROUND ME

WHAT THE HELL HAPPENED WHO ARE THESE PEOPLE TELL ME TELL ME—
The force let go of my hand.

My God, this was Bullfrog all over again! None of Henry's seductive descriptions of the afterlife had come true; Spooks Haversma was somehow tied to this ship, or a ship, lost in the fog on a dark sea just as Bully had been, crying out to me for help. Or was it myself, my subconscious heavy with suppressed memories that had grabbed hold of my hand? I was about to take up the planchette again when the door was opened and Ma Chang came in.

If it had been anyone else, I would have made short shrift of him, but she was the one person whom I had to treat with circumspection. She stood, a black apparition in her shapeless smock, staring at me, at the board, at the planchette, and then, with an odd, unfocused gaze, at something behind me. I turned around to see what, but there was nothing.

When I turned back, I saw her coming toward me. I wondered what it was she wanted; she picked up the mug, with a whiff of a smell of cats, and turned to leave. But she found her way barred by Number One, standing in the doorway, his face sick with fear. "You must come!" he yelled in a high-pitched, querulous voice. "I can't handle it alone! I can't!"

In a flash of recognition, I knew this had happened once before, exactly like this, but when? Where? In a dream? I couldn't remember, but a sudden sense of urgency made me say, "I'm coming."

I went to the door, took my cap off the hook and set out for the bridge at a run.

7

When, out of breath, prepared for the worst, I arrived on the bridge, I found it strangely quiet. There were plenty of people about, but they were all standing still, gazing ahead into the night. The sky was full of stars.

I joined them and looked through the for'ard windows; on the horizon, right across our course, a row of lights was strung out, each of them flashing in groups of dots and dashes. I breathed easier; there was no emergency, they were at least five or six miles away. But what could they be? Fishermen? A convoy? No wonder Number One had got into a panic.

I called the radio room and a chipper, jolly voice answered.

"Who is this, Marco One or Two?"

"Two, Commodore. Yes, please?"

"Did you pick up any notices to mariners recently?"

The voice said cheerfully, "Moment, please!" I heard a rustling of papers. "I tell him already: about erections of Australian Navy flashers."

It took a moment to get out of him what the message had actually said; it turned out to be an official warning to local traffic that the Australian Navy would start night bombing practice at 0:00 hours in an area delineated by pontoons, each showing a different sequence of flashing lights. I had come up just in time, or we might have been dive-bombed by the latest version of World War II Stukas.

I changed course; the tow headed north into the open, we were safe. Even so, I felt I should stay on the bridge until we were far enough away from the danger zone for the faint-hearted to breathe easier.

Half an hour later, while studying the chart, I was startled by the booming of the first bombs; but they seemed to explode astern of us instead of to the west. Were we inside the danger zone after all? Then I heard a hooting sound, as of an Indian flute, and realized that the sounds were not those of exploding bombs. They were drumbeats on the aft deck.

I went to the aft rail of the bridge, looked down, and there, indeed, were the smoking torches, the wobbling lanterns, the solemn procession of shadowy people, led by the small, robed figure. What in the world were they doing at this hour? Was it another ceremony, one that I hadn't seen before?

The drum banged, the flute hooted. The robed figure at the aft coaming, silhouetted against the phosphorescent wake, clashed the lids of trash cans like cymbals. The crowd started to boo, curse, shriek threats, insults; so it *was* another ghost to be exorcised. Was it possible that one of the crew had died without my knowing about it?

The crowd, booing and shrieking, started to pass objects down the line to the robed figure in the stern. To an orgy of

[358]

shouts, bangs, hoots and curses from the crowd, she began to throw them overboard. Suddenly I recognized a black box, opening as it tumbled and showering the wake with fluttering white leaves. The Bowditch! The other objects had been the Ouija board and the planchette. It was Haversma's ghost they were exorcising.

I stared at the spectacle, open-mouthed. How dare they! Ma Chang must have snitched those things from my dayroom while my back was turned. By God, I would teach her! I was halfway down the companionway to the aft deck when a deep, growling rumble, like thunder in the distance, stopped me in my tracks.

This time the sound was unmistakable; these were indeed bombs. Now I recognized the memory that had brushed me when Number One shouted, 'I can't handle it alone! I can't!'

Shaken, I went to my dayroom instead.

8

When I entered, I saw that indeed everything was gone; the coffee table was empty. I felt a return of anger, but the memory of what had happened forty-two years ago had taken the sting out of it. That time, on our second run to Murmansk, I had fled to the chartroom when the bombs started, to write a frantic, passionate letter to Mary, the girl with whom I had spent only one night between the two convoys. An endless, anesthetizing letter to make me forget the hell outside which I could no longer face, a letter full of tender descriptions of the life we would lead once I came back and we were married. A fantasy world of conjugal bliss, passionate nights, tender awakenings to the sound of bacon sizzling in the pan and the smell of coffee from the kitchen. It had reduced to insignificance the sounds of approaching bombers, of the convoy being attacked by U-boats, Stukas, Dorniers throwing strings of mines chained together. I had continued writing about summer mornings, babies chortling, diapers drying on the line; then, at the height of the fury, the mate, his face sick with fear, had shouted, 'Jesus Christ! I can't handle it alone! I can't!' and it had penetrated to me what I had done: by withdrawing into a world of my own, I had deserted my crew and thrown the fear of death into them. So I had taken up the burden of being Master

[359]

After God again, all-knowing, all-powerful, cool, collected, in control. Freighters had been sunk, tankers had exploded; then the shouts in the night had started, the cries for help, the screams of horror from the drowning, black with oil, their mouths gaping pink holes in black masks, the bleeding, burned, brutalized, shell-shocked refuse of war. The memory brought back the revulsion, the sense of insanity that human beings could do this to one another merely by pressing a button in a cold lunacy that destroyed both friend and foe.

Suddenly I felt a sense of relief at what Ma Chang had done; but I couldn't let this incident pass without response. Nobody, not even the crew's den mother, whom I respected and even admired, must be allowed to grab things off my table and fling them overboard, whatever the motivation. I might be prepared to let it ride as far as I personally was concerned; in public I couldn't let Ma Chang get away with it.

I went to the door; Louis jumped me from the gap in the row of books where the Bowditch had been. With him on my shoulder and my cap at the angle of attack, I set out for the galley.

Dawn was breaking, the morning watch about to change. The corridor outside the galley was full of squatting men, yawning, grinning up at me as I strode past them. I knew I would find her at the range; breakfast was about to be served, the men in the corridor were the mess boys waiting to carry the trays to the messroom. There would be a capacity audience, and that was how it should be. No private, courteous showdown; she had thrown my private possessions overboard with the whole crew banging drums and blowing hooters and she herself clashing trash-can lids together, shrieking like a banshee. Well, I could match that production all on my own. She was in for a surprise.

When I came in, I found the galley full of people. The breakfast dishes were lined up on the shelf opposite the range; Ma Chang, looking harassed and untidy, was skating about, ladling noodles, pouring sauce, slamming bowls onto trays. When she saw me, she froze.

Everybody froze. It became silent. The noodles bubbled on the range. On my shoulder Louis scratched his ear close to mine, loud in the silence.

She uttered a raw shout, so primitive in its anger that I felt it in the nape of my neck. Then I realized it had not been directed at me but at the jug-eared audience standing there open-mouthed, waiting for the curtain to go up. They all scurried like cats; I had never seen a space the size of the galley emptied so fast of all human habitation. Then she shrieked another command, and in came—limping, geared for drama—little Hopla, eager to function as interpreter, proud to be the sole spectator of the theatrical treat about to unfold.

She barked commandingly. He forgot to limp as he dashed to close the door.

"Ma Chang—"

She silenced me with a gesture that could only belong to a society where a matriarch ruled the world. Then she spoke. Hopla, in a whisper, trying to be small and unobtrusive, translated. "She say: you her friend."

She spoke again with the same intimidating authority.

"She say: you help her and our people, she help you."

"Balls," I said. "What she did was impermissible."

He translated; she answered without the intimidating authority. She no longer needed it.

"She say," Hopla whispered, "you were in danger from ghost."

"What ghost?"

"She say: ghost not good. Ghost want company, because ghost fried."

"What the hell are you talking about?"

He whispered to her reverently; she replied, staring at me. "She say: ghost no real bad. No ghosts real bad. Ghosts fried to cross bridge, wait for company. Must be made to go, or they try to live life other peoples. She say: you were in danger. You were—how say?—foolish." He eyed me warily.

"Foolish? Goddammit, who does she think she is? Nobody chases any ghosts off this ship without my permission! And that stuff she threw overboard was private papers!"

God knew what happened to all that when Hopla was done with it; it was pretty fatuous before he started. He translated humbly, ingratiatingly, obviously trying to make it sound less contentious, but she wasn't fooled. I was losing this battle of wills, or whatever it was. She looked me straight in the eye, then said something that sounded pretty aggressive to me.

Hopla frowned in bewilderment, then he gave it a try. "She say: you must not cross bridge before time."

I asked, "What bridge?"

He put the question to her; she answered with one word. He did not translate it; he rolled up his eyes, his mouth sagged open, tongue lolling, his head dropped sideways in his gross imitation of death.

She spoke again, a sharp series of barks. He bowed abjectly, trying to make himself smaller, unobtrusive, little mouse in the kitchen that hoped to escape unnoticed. "She say," he whispered, eyes downcast, head bent, "you be glad it is bridge, not— how you call? Big gap in ground, very dangerous, ploof?" He hazarded a dramatic gesture in miniature. "If fall in, you be killed."

"Precipice?"

"That it!" he cried, delighted. "You see! Me speak the English. Me butler in Mah-Iot—"

This time her bark made him flee. When he was gone and had closed the door behind me, she beckoned me and pointed at a stool. Deflated, I sat down at the table. She went to the stove, slopped a bowl full of noodles from a small pan at the back, dashed on a spoonful of sauce, grabbed a pair of chopsticks and slammed them in front of me.

"Woo poos," she said, daring me.

"Meow," I replied, daring her.

Then we both burst out laughing, she with the high, whinnying shrieks that had startled me so when I first heard them in mid-Atlantic. There was a sound of scurrying feet outside.

As I sat spooning the noodles, which were awful, a Chinese version of slung hash, it occurred to me that she might have saved me a second time, in a way more subtle than the first.

Chapter Fourteen

1

I dismissed the idea of Ma Chang having saved me as soon as the spell of the exotic episode receded. She had done nothing of the sort. By starting to fool with the Ouija board, I had been sucked into the mythical part of her primitive culture and, for a few hours, lived under its spell. The whole business about Haversma's ghost communicating with me was obscurantist nonsense. At a moment of vulnerability, I had, through the symbolic device of the Ouija board, given the suppressed memory of the Arctic convoys the opportunity to invade my consciousness: the oil-black faces of the drowning, the dead, the wounded, whose bodies we had dragged into the boats and hauled onto the deck of the old *Isabel.* Now, having buried the memory once more, I found myself back where I started, facing the insoluble dilemma of how to save Number One's silly neck without endangering the lives of the present and future crews of the ship. Again I realized that I couldn't find the answer on my own; I decided I would discuss it with Chief Liu. He was intelligent, experienced and as involved in the fate of the *Isabel* as I was; as a matter of fact, he was the one who had raised all the questions in the first place. I invited him for a drink.

He came up to the dayroom at once in response to my invitation. But the moment he realized what I wanted to talk about, the jolly, mischievous man I knew changed back into an inscrutable member of an alien race. He refused a drink, sat opposite me in a stiff, angular position as if expecting an interrogation and listened, eyes averted, tense, without a word, to the summary of my conversation with Beast Rufus. When finally he spoke, I knew that my idea of our finding an answer together had been an illusion.

"I am older man with large family," he said carefully. "I have children in school, in university. Two daughters needing dowry. I am no slave, but I—what you call?—behold to Mr. Chung. If Mr. Chung say, 'It was hurricane,' I say, 'Down in engine room there is much noise. Suddenly, "Bang!" upstairs. I rush up, find wheelhouse gone, stacks gone, captain killed. No idea what happen, none. No knowledge of anything.' "

"You mean to say that's the story you're going to tell if there is an inquiry?"

This time he looked me straight in the eye. "As I told Captain Fransen, I in no position to contradict Captain Hu's report."

"Who in hell is Captain Hu?"

"The one you call Number One," he replied, smiling.

I should have known. While I had been worrying about stores and drinking water and new rope for the stoppers that last day in Pago Pago, Fransen had got not only to Number One but to Chief Liu as well, and probably all other members of the staff. Beast Rufus was right: the report had been filed by now, the claim made, the testimonies of captain and staff registered, the insurance compensation paid. The case was closed.

"Thank you, Chief," I said. "How about a drink?"

"I would be ravished, thank you," he said.

While we sat there chatting pleasantly, I couldn't help thinking how his opposite number, Porks, would have taken this. He would have cursed, fumed, damned the tyrants to hell, told me I was a champion of the poor and the downtrodden. In the end, he might have come to the same conclusion as Chief Liu—that for him to become involved would be professional suicide—but his reaction would have been less ruthless, more emotionally satisfying.

My Chinese friend was telling me, in effect, that Don Quixotes must tilt at their windmills alone.

2

A sense of total loneliness, after my conversation with Chief Liu, made me decide to start a letter to Helen. I had neglected her shamefully out of sheer ineptitude; I had not known how to handle a daughter who suddenly made me her confidant; now I decided to make her mine. I needed desperately to see the whole situation in a new perspective. The fact that this too would be a letter stuck in a bottle to float out with the tide didn't matter. Really, of course, I should be writing to Sylvia, we always talked things over together. But there had been so much dissimulation on my part in the recent past that to spell it all out for her in detail would be the reverse of comforting. So, the next morning on the bridge, in a deck chair with a clipboard on my lap, I started a letter.

Dear Helen,

I have been woefully inadequate in my responses to your moving letters. I did not know where to begin. Your suggestion that I keep a diary of my voyage of exploration in the form of a letter to you made me decide to give it a try. For you to under-stand what it is all about, I will have to start at the beginning. It may indeed become, as you dreamed, the longest letter you ever received; all I can say is: you asked for it. Here goes.

My voyage started a few days before last Christmas, with a telephone call. I was decorating the kitchen with holly and angel's hair, the radio was bellowing carols, your mother had sausage rolls and mince pies in the oven and looked apple-cheeked like a Russian doll . . .

3

I continued my letter as the days went by, sunny, somnolent days of solitude which I spent on the bridge in my deck chair in the cool shade of the awning, writing, while the tow slowly coursed across blue-and-green seas, past islands large and small, some mountainous, others a mere fringe of palms on the horizon, all of them asleep in the tropical sun.

I had told the story of the *Isabel Kwel* in my report, but that had been a factual, unemotional summing up of events, ad-dressed to a faceless tribunal. Now, telling it to a lonely mother of three who would read it in the still of the evening after everyone had been put to bed, I found myself arriving at a number of surprising conclusions.

To start with, Beast Rufus' categorical statement that by the time I arrived everything would be cut-and-dried was wrong. Chung might have filed Number One's fraudulent report claiming that the damage had been caused by a hurricane wave, but what was he going to do with the ship after she arrived? Looking back, I became confident that, despite the time lapse, the existence of photocopies of my report and the ship's log would be sufficient to make Chung agree to repair the *Isabel* along the lines of her present safe profile and not reconstruct her to her original design. He couldn't afford to turn down that demand; the documents in my possession were highly damaging not only to KITCO, who had sold a ship which they knew to be unseaworthy to an unsuspecting buyer; Chung himself was heavily implicated too. To buy a tugboat of this complexity, put in command an incompetent captain with only a one-thousand-ton license, a crew of fishermen from a remote island who had never seen a tugboat in their lives, and then to send her through the worst storm belt of the world with a thirty-thousand-ton dry dock in tow might result in no more than raised eyebrows among the judiciary; the fact that the captain had deliberately tried to scuttle the ship with himself as the only survivor would be interpreted the way Fransen had: Captain Cho and Mr. Chung had been conspiring to collect the insurance money. In my official report I hadn't mentioned that I personally believed Cho had acted out of a lust for revenge which ultimately had turned into insanity; I had enumerated the facts, leaving it to the authorities to draw their own conclusions.

My real problem, I discovered, was not whether Chung would accept my conditions, but how to stop him from weaseling out of our agreement after I had left the scene. Once back in my retirement village in France, I would be no more than a retiree of modest means; how could I keep track of what Chung was doing with the ship? He could have her rebuilt in some distant yard into the killer ship she had been and put her into service without me being the wiser. There certainly would be no judicial ruling to stop him from doing so. What I needed would be a representative, someone on the spot to keep close tabs on what happened to her. But who? The Dutch consul? I could hardly take him into my confidence . . .

It was only at this point that it became clear to me, belatedly, that for me to allow Charlie Chung to cash in a fraudulent insurance claim after he had bought my silence with a gentlemen's agreement would make me his co-conspirator. I would be party to the suppression of legal evidence, a felony.

The noble words I had spoken to old Kwel in the limousine on the dock in Rotterdam came back to haunt me. He had tried to make me join the conspiracy of silence regarding the *Isabel*'s FF. My reaction had been, 'Sorry, sir, I cannot be a party to that.' He had peered at me with his blind eyes in amazement. 'What makes you feel responsible, may I ask?' I had answered, paragon of virtue, 'The fact that I know the truth.' He had sighed and replied, 'If knowing the truth made people responsible, Harinxma, history would look very different.' I had said, with what now looked like insufferable smugness, 'Sorry, sir.'

According to that standard, my course of action was clear. I should forget about Number One. The moment we arrived in Kao Hsiung, I should file my report and the ship's log with the authorities and with Lloyd's in London and let the pieces fall where they may. As a result, the *Isabel*'s certificate would be suspended, the ship herself chained to the quay to lie there and rot for months, maybe years, while the litigation between KITCO and Chung dragged on; chances were she would never sail again. Number One would be brought to trial for perjury, end up in the clink for a couple of years and lose his license. But I must do my civic duty. Either that, or join the tarnished herd.

I didn't have to think it over. I couldn't throw Number One to the wolves, not even to preserve my so far spotless record as a law-abiding citizen. He was a member of my crew, and I had to stand by him even though I didn't like him, even though he had behaved like an idiot, to say the least, and put his future and his freedom in jeopardy by his own action. The mother hen's compulsion to protect even the ugliest among her brood might be purely a conditioned reflex, like Pavlov's dogs salivating at the sound of the dinner bell, but I was stuck with it. Bron's theory was that Chung knew this and therefore wouldn't believe me capable of going through with it; but I doubted that. How could he be absolutely certain I wouldn't sacrifice Number One? A stand like that on his part left no margin for error. In my opinion, he would try to throw me off balance, but in the end agree to my conditions for keeping silent.

So, once I had joined the tarnished herd, what would be the next item on my agenda? In chronological order: first, blackmail Chung into accepting, then appoint someone to keep track of what happened to the ship after I left, someone in a position to get wind of any monkeyshines the moment they occurred. Again I was faced with the question: who? If not the Dutch consul, how about a lawyer in Kao Hsiung? But would I find anyone I could trust on Mr. Chung's home turf? I thought of a number of other possibilities and ended up with our son Martinus, the bachelor pilot. He would be delighted to check on the ship at regular intervals, after wangling out of KLM a transfer from the Amsterdam–New York line to the one to Taiwan. He would probably succeed in doing so; he was a charming boy, everybody loved him. That was part of the problem; he thought of himself as a walking phallus and had a tendency to fall for the type of girl that went with his low-slung sports car, one of those that growl and throw gravel on take-off. He would be a happy-go-lucky bunny hopping into Tiger Chung's lair; Charlie would have no trouble corrupting him with free hotel suites, cabin cruisers for skinny-dipping parties, even—God help us—free access to any branch of Singing Flowers on the island. Chung would hang on the boy's lips, catch any pearls dropping from them in his little notebook for his secretary to type out; it would be child's play for him to convince good-natured Martinus after proper preparation that his father was a dear old man with a bee in his bonnet, hopelessly behind the times. And when it came to the seaworthiness of the ship in her original form, well! He would produce architects' drawings, surveyors' certificates, anything needed to convince his young friend that the *Isabel* was perfectly safe and always had been until Papa pressed the panic button.

Finally I hit upon the solution: ask Ma Chang and the mandur to be the watchdogs. After all, it was their ship, their own lives were at stake. With bright-eyed spies like Hopla and the mandur's cub scouts on the job, Chung would have a hard time doing anything without my knowing it within twenty-four hours.

I was so pleased with this obvious solution that I couldn't wait for our next anchorage, where I would organize a meeting between Ma Chang, the mandur and myself with Hopla and Hara-kiri as interpreters. We would talk the whole thing through, consider all angles and come up with a workable plan of action.

From that moment onward, my letter to Helen hummed with optimism and self-confidence.

4

Merir Island, our last fueling stop, two weeks short of Kao Hsiung, turned out to be a long, low hill in the infinity of the ocean. The Coastal Pilot listed it as uninhabited; but the moment we dropped anchor, a launch set out from the beach with in it two ruddy-faced young Americans in need of a shave, who, after they had been hauled on board, told me ecstatically that they were from the local marine weather station and all by their lone selves on this here island, Cap.

I invited them to join me in the dayroom to meet the Chinese staff and Harakiri, who came over for the occasion. The two young men became happily flushed at meeting so many fellow human beings all at once; their only contact with the world was a mail plane that came once a month; it was due in two days' time, so if we had any mail to go, they would be delighted to take it. I had Hopla broadcast a mail call into the void; the only one who responded was myself. I entrusted to their Hornet on skis the letter to Miss Bastiaans, two to Sylvia and the first installment of the one to Helen.

Before leaving, they rifled my bookcase, parched for reading matter. I allowed them to make off with a couple of paperbacks and Haversma's *Kinship with All Life*, after they told me they had only a turtle, a myna bird and a cat for company. The cat had been washed ashore clinging to a crate, blind and skeletal with exhaustion; they had called it Farrah Fawcett and nursed it back to health. In the face of such dedication, I felt they should have a book by a man who had befriended a fly called Freddy. They put-putted back to the shore, waving the book in farewell.

After the others had left, I told Harakiri about my plan and why I wanted to arrange a meeting with Ma Chang and the mandur with himself and Hopla as interpreters.

He listened without comment. When I was through, he remained silent for a while, then asked, "What gave you that crazy idea, Harinxma?"

"What's crazy about asking them to keep an eye on their own ship, to make sure she won't be turned back into a death trap?"

"Harinxma, I don't know what's the matter with you, but can't you look at this thing through a normal person's eyes? What you're proposing is to blackmail a Chinese. Do you know what that means, man? Haven't you sailed with them long enough to realize that if you do that, you put your life in danger?"

"Don't be silly."

"Silly? Well, let me tell you, friend, that if you try to blackmail that Chink millionaire, he's going to have you rubbed out."

"Nonsense. If anything happens to me, my wife will take the documents out of the safe-deposit box—"

"Either that, or you'll end up in front of a judge. You're the one who pressed the button. The judge is sure to be in Chung's pocket. He's going to rule that the explosion was caused by you, a mad old sea captain going berserk, and unless you have enough money to pay for a crackerjack lawyer, you'll be locked up. And for what? For a bunch of weirdos who don't need any help. They can look after themselves, believe you me."

"Hari, look: you know as well as I do that this ship is going to be unseaworthy again if—"

"You've seen them at work, with your own eyes! You've seen them sail that yacht in the gale off Argentina, for Chrissakes! Those people have sailed nothing but unseaworthy ships all their lives, Harinxma. Metacenter height? Rolling cycle? They wouldn't know what the hell you're talking about. If they feel sometime in the future that the ship is a threat to them, they'll do something about it. Don't you go and get mixed up in it, you'll get hurt."

"But my crew is different from your runners! They—"

"Don't fool yourself, Harinxma. They're exactly the same. The only difference is that mine belong to a Triad."

That gave me an idea. I asked eagerly, "You mean the Chinese Mafia?"

He frowned. "Why?"

"Look here, if that's the case, maybe your runners could put a bit of pressure on Mr. Chung to make him keep his promise. In that case, I may not need any observers on the spot."

He gave me an odd look. "Now let me see if I've got this right. You want my runners to go and see Mr. Chung and tell him that he's got to leave the ship as she is, or else?"

"Well, it's just an idea—"

"That unless he leaves the ship as she is, they'll rape his daughters, castrate his sons—"

"For God's sake, all I—"

"Murder his wife, burn down his house and, after he's had a good look at that, ram a stick of dynamite up his ass and blow him to Kwan Yin? Is that the general idea?"

"Of course not! I wasn't thinking in those terms!"

He shook his head. "Are you sure you've been all right since that explosion, Harinxma? It would have knocked me off my rocker, and I'm only forty-three."

I stared at him. For a moment I saw myself through his eyes: a confused old man, struck by an obsession from which he could no longer disentangle himself.

"Hari," I said, "let's stop arguing. I want that meeting. I'm calling it now. I'll see to it that Ma Chang is here. You go get your mandur, and I'd appreciate it if you could interpret for me."

"Harinxma, be rational, man! You—"

I refused to listen to him anymore.

5

Half an hour later Ma Chang and Hopla were installed in the dayroom. A few minutes later Harakiri and the mandur, who looked fierce and suspicious, entered and sat down. I opened the proceedings with a brief introduction. Hopla translated, Harakiri did his best.

It became a long introduction. I went into the history of the ship. Hopla was so fascinated that I suspected he left out the telling details. At a given moment, Harakiri threw up his hands; it couldn't be helped. I hoped the mandur would pick up the essence of what I was saying. Ma Chang listened intently; for some reason she looked worried.

After I had taken care of the background and explained the rolling cycle, I came to the reason for the meeting. "The ship is safe now, having shed her topload, but Mr. Chung may want to restore her the way she was and send her back to sea. I want him to promise me that he'll keep her as she is. But how can we make sure he'll keep his promise? I'd like to know what ideas you have on this. Would you be able to watch the ship while she's in the yard?"

I sat waiting for their response. The silence lay heavy in the room. Nobody stirred, not even Harakiri. The cast-iron mandur stared at me with a vacant expression. Ma Chang sat gazing into space; impossible to read in her face what she was thinking.

The silence lasted. Nobody stirred. I was about to speak when the mandur put a question to Harakiri; at least, that was what it sounded like. Harakiri seemed to have difficulty understanding it; after some muttering back and forth between them, he finally said to me, "As far as I can make out, he wants to know what's in this for *you*."

"My God! If he hasn't understood that, what *has* he understood?"

"Take it easy, Harinxma, don't get emotional just when the guy shows some interest. Answer his question, but don't make a speech."

"I want to safeguard their goddam lives!"

He shook his head. "That's not going to buy him, he can take care of that himself. Think of something else."

"But there *is* nothing else! Sailors have to look out for each other! Translate that for me."

Harakiri scratched his head. "Boy," he said, "I don't even know the word for 'sailors,' " but he tried. He pointed at me, at the mandur, at himself, at the deck. "Sea," he said. "Person." The mandur watched his mouth. There was some muttering. "Okay," Harakiri said finally, "I've done my best. The rest is up to Buddha."

I rose. "Well, that about wraps it up. Thank you for your attention." I went to the door; as I passed the mandur, he put out a hand and stopped me.

"Person," he said. "Sea. Person." He gave me a startling grin of stainless-steel teeth.

"Yes . . . That's right." I managed to usher them out and closed the door on them, shaken. Louis jumped me from the gap on the shelf; in a conditioned reflex, I went to feed Pete. There was a knock on the door, Harakiri came in.

"Well, Harinxma, I hope this cures you of your fancy ideas. My mandur seems to think you're a sea person. That's all."

I filled Pete's little dish.

"Of course, I don't know about your woman cook, but if I was you—"

"Hari, I've said what I have to say, I'll do what I have to do. Drink?"

He gave me a searching look. "Do you *know* that you're crazy, Harinxma? Or don't people know that when it hits them?"

"Don't worry. I'm okay."

"But what are you going to *do*, man? You're not going to go through with this in some other crazy way, are you?"

"Hari, thank you very much for your help, but now—"

"I mean it, Harinxma. I like you. You're a nice old guy, I hate to see you do something to yourself that I can't understand. All I want you to do is make me understand. Why?"

"Why what?"

"Why you won't just let it go! The people don't give a damn, you've seen that. Chung will send a bunch of contract killers after you, you know that. Why don't you just go home, get those documents out of the safe and send them to whoever can put a stop to this thing? Stop it, Harinxma! All you have to do is open your goddam safe and send the log and your report to a judge or something. Why don't you? Tell me. I want to understand."

I looked at him. He was all of the breed personified: leathery, tough, eyes as blue as the morning sky, as straight as they come. His life was made up of simple things and colossal objects which he handled with mastery, even in the worst of weather, even with a crew of people from the Stone Age. Also, once he gave his friendship, he was the truest friend a man could wish for.

"All right," I said, more to be rid of him than in the hope that he would finally understand. "If I do that, my Number One will go to jail and lose his license for reporting the damage to the ship as hurricane damage. Fransen made him do it."

Slowly, some sort of dawn spread on his face. He heaved a sigh of relief—at least, that's what it sounded like. Then he slapped me on the shoulder and said, "Goddammit, man, why didn't you tell me that right away? What's the matter with you? Can't you talk *straight* to a person?"

"Sorry," I said. "So, that's where I am. *We* are."

"All right, all right," he said, sounding vastly relieved. "Now at last I know what this is all about. What are you going to do, do you know?"

"You don't think these two and their tribes can keep an eye on the thing for me?"

"Of course they can, but what the heck are they going to *do* about it? They can't read, they can't write, they've never seen a telephone. So they see that something is happening to the ship that isn't kosher. What do you expect them to do? Go to the post office? Ask for a telegram form, send you a cable? Man, forget it. They'll do anything for you, these runners of mine think you're a little pal, but don't ask them to do something that's a hundred years ahead of their time."

"All right. In that case, there's only one thing I can do, apart from throwing the little bastard into the meat grinder."

"Don't talk shit. What can you do?"

"Keep an eye on the ship myself. Rent a room on the waterfront in Kao Hsiung and make a daily round past the yard."

He looked at me through narrowed eyes, thinking. "Do you know the Kao Hsiung waterfront?"

"Yes."

"How long is it since you were there?"

"Not recently."

"Let me tell you, it's not a healthy place, Harinxma. Not a place for a white man your age, or any age. It's a jungle, friend. I wouldn't want my worst enemy to shack up there."

"Well? Any other ideas?"

Again he looked at me with those slits of eyes as if I were a distant horizon on which he was trying to locate a ship. Then he said, "All right. I'll tell my runners that you're planning to take a room in hell town, and that a gentleman called Chung is likely to send some nasty people after you, who may try to knife you, shoot you, poison you, garrote you or put snakes in your bed."

"Come on, Hari—"

"They'll love that," he continued. "You'll be living the life of Omi Looney under the protection of the Triad. That's all I can do for you at this point."

"You're a friend," I said.

He slapped me on the shoulder again, hitched up his pants, said obscurely, "Jesus! Some people . . ." and left me alone with my animals.

A few minutes later Hopla came scurrying in, bright-eyed and ready for a long, long talk. "Good," he said, "very, very good. She like you very good."

"Apart from that, what ideas does she have?"

"Idea?"

"About stopping Mr. Chung rebuilding the ship."

"Re— Huh?"

"Oh, my God," I said. "Get out of here."

"Ah! But she *like* you! She say: very good, but you need haircut before you see Mr. Chung."

"Hopla," I said, "if you don't bugger off now, I'll give *you* a haircut."

He squealed with glee, but vanished.

I ended up alone on the couch, my head in my hands. So that seemed to be it, for the duration: old white man with China haircut, tame rat and canary in hell town, under protection of the Chinese Mafia.

Well, I had lived under worse circumstances. Through worse things. The thing to do was look at the bright side. It would give me time to finish my letter to Helen. To stretch my legs. Have a glass with the hell-town boys.

Tickle the ivories, Hoagy Carmichael! Honky Tonk Blues, here I come.

⟦ *Chapter Fifteen* ⟧

1

In the early-morning hours of the one hundred ninety-first day of our voyage we passed Liu-Chiu-Yü island, entering Kao Hsiung approaches. The weather was stormy with low, racing clouds and an angry, slate-coloured sea. The awning over the open bridge flopped and thundered in the breeze. To the north I could see the barren peak of Shou Shan mountain, half obscured by rain, a mile and a half from the entrance to Kao Hsiung harbor.

I was quite calm, surprisingly so. Ever since Merir Island, I had resigned myself to the prospect of having to live on the Kao Hsiung waterfront until the *Isabel* had acquired her permanent low profile. I had not finished my letter to Helen yet, but I would have plenty of time to do so in my room or garret overlooking the harbor of the large industrial port now profiled, a jumble of building blocks, against the somber black background of the rain-shrouded mountains. In a moment of wishful thinking I had toyed with the idea of Sylvia joining me, together with Héloïse if need be; not only would it be very expensive to fly them over, Héloïse was sure to end up in the cooking pot of some gourmet restaurant on the harbor. I even considered the possibility of Helen joining me; but it would be a matter of a few months at least, and she couldn't leave her small children that long without risking the loss of custody; also, to have them run wild on the Kao Hsiung waterfront under the protection of the Chinese Mafia was not a realistic proposition. So I was feeling resigned, even serene, when we approached the quarantine area outside the breakwater and the pilot launch came out, snorting and sneezing with a bone in its teeth. When the launch swung alongside, I expected to see Fransen wearing his Columbo raincoat, but he was nowhere to be seen.

He didn't turn up until we were well inside the pierheads. In the meantime a bevy of harbor tugs had come plunging and wallowing out of the shelter of the breakwater, headed for the liner; before they sucked onto her like leeches, there were excited shouts and waving from their bridges at my Chinese staff, who stood on the lifebelt locker waving back and yelling excited responses. I suddenly felt alone.

But as we were swinging the *Princess* in the second harbor's turning basin, with to southward a forest of cranes and the skeletons of ships, giant black ribs in the yellow sky, Fransen finally climbed on board from a bumboat. A minute later he appeared on the bridge, holding on to his fedora, sparks flying off his cigarette, his raincoat billowing in the wind. I was extraordinarily moved to see him; if the bridge hadn't been full of excited Chinese officers pointing at the shore and slapping one another's shoulders in the excitement of homecoming, I would have embraced him.

He was not in that mood; as he came toward me, his face bore an ominous expression.

"Hello there," I said, wondering what was the matter.

He took the cigarette out of his mouth, shook his head and said, "Well, boy, while you were frolicking on the waves, the china cupboard fell on its face at home. Jesus! Your missus is something else."

My heart skipped a beat.

"Sylvia?! What happened, what's the matter?"

"I'm not going to tell you, Harinxma," he said, "I'm going to leave that to someone bigger than you and me. Don't worry, she's okay, but you'd better put on your helmet and your breastplate, as the Good Book says, before you meet Mr. Chung." He shook his head again; the expression on his face changed to commiseration. "You think that when you pressed that button out in the Pacific you made a big bang? Wait till you—"

"Captain?" the pilot called sharply. "Would you mind joining me for this maneuver?"

"I'm not the captain," I said, "*he* is." I pointed at Number One.

But the young Chinese ducked it; he was not about to blot his copybook at this late stage. So I had to assist the pilot in taking the old *Princess* to her graveyard, a pier with a forest of cranes and a huge shed saying in man-size letters: CHARLIE S. CHUNG, KAO HSIUNG STEELWORKS. What could be the matter with Sylvia? What had happened?

I tried to get more out of Fransen, but he wasn't in a gossiping mood. "Wait till Mr. Chung tells you," he said, "and hold on to your seat." Then, relenting or maybe unable to keep up the strain of restraint, he glanced around to see if anyone was listening; no one was—they had other things to do, like cheering and waving at a small crowd waiting on shore. Then he muttered, "For openers, after the old man died, who do you think inherited his half of the business? One guess."

"Look, Fransen, all I want to know is—"

"The Bastiaans woman! So, whatever you do, buddy boy, watch your step. Between you and me, I think we've been barking up the wrong tree all this time. These last years, the old man may well have been no more than a ventriloquist's dummy on her lap."

"Goddammit, Fransen, what about my wife? I'm not interested in goddam gossip, tell me what happened!"

He gave me a crooked smile. "I told you, Harinxma, she's as sound, healthy and happy as President Truman must have been when he received the telegram, 'It's a boy!' "

"What in God's name—"

"That was the code telling him he had successfully blown up Hiroshima."

I was ready to explode when he said, "Well, here's your mail." He pulled a small stack of letters from the pocket of his raincoat. "Most of them are from Mrs. Harinxma; let her tell you in her own words."

Now what was in store for me? I felt myself sliding into a panic of worry, speculation, confusion; I was about to start tearing open envelopes when I heard Fransen say, "O-oh! There he comes . . ."

I looked up and saw a stretch limousine slowly approaching down the quayside in front of the giant warehouse. As I stood staring at it, I suddenly became aware that the ship had fallen silent, as when old Kwel's limousine had stopped at the foot of the gangway in Rotterdam.

2

The ship was moored, the gangway lowered. I pulled the engine telegraph back and forth, signaling, 'Finished with Engines.' All vibration ceased. The ship was as silent as the grave. There were no sounds from the scrapyard either; it was Sunday. "Thank you, Pilot," I said, "it was a pleasure."

"Likewise, Captain," the unsmiling Taiwanese replied.

As I passed him on my way down, Fransen whispered, "If you need me, I'll be in the hospital, preparing bandages." I didn't respond, but hurried to my dayroom, hoping to have a chance to read Sylvia's letters before Chung turned up.

As I opened the door and stepped inside, Louis leaped from the bookshelf onto my shoulder. Pete squeaked and rummaged in his cage. I didn't sit down; I tore open the first envelope, hands shaking, and pulled out the letter.

My dear Martinus,

After all these months of subterfuge and dissimulation, how did you expect me to put a sealed envelope containing legal papers concerning the ship unopened into the safe deposit box? I was sick with worry, especially after my conversation with the doctor in Chile. I could get no sense out of anyone at the head office when I called, everybody was shifty and elusive. So I did what any wife would do who is worried sick. I opened the envelope and read what was inside. I need not tell you what it did to me. At last, at long last, I was told the truth! There it was, from the beginning, from the very first time you—

The door opened and there, smiling, eyes twinkling, stood Mr. Chung.

"Welcome to Taiwan, Commodore! Mind if I come in?"

"Of course—hello—good afternoon, sir . . ."

We shook hands, he didn't bat an eyelid at the sight of the rat on my shoulder. "May I sit down?" he asked pleasantly. "You and I should have a talk."

I gestured at the couch; he sat down. His small, dark eyes, as enigmatic as a baby's, stared at me without expression.

"The ship is quite a sight."

"Yes," I said.

"Captain Fransen gave me a report describing the damage sustained, but I could not quite visualize it from the description."

"Indeed, that must have been difficult."

"I'm distressed about Captain Cho," he continued. "What a sad occurrence. Well, we were lucky to have you on the team, Commodore. You did a sterling job. Thank you very much."

Trying to sound casual, I asked, "Did Captain Fransen inform you of the cause of the damage? I may have a different report for you from the one you received."

[379]

"Ah?" He said it lightly. His smile didn't waver. The enigmatic eyes observed me, unmoved.

"I must tell you, sir, that I am determined this ship shall never sail again, either on salvage duty or long-distance, unless her present profile is maintained. She was a death trap. She would be again if you restored—"

"Commodore, you are worrying unduly." He gave me a look that suddenly was unnervingly kind. "Tomorrow morning at six o'clock we start breaking up the ship for scrap."

I stared at him, thunderstruck.

"The operation should take little time; a month from now, at the latest, all her components will have been stacked ashore and sorted out. At that time I will mail you a certified surveyor's statement of demolition, with photographs, for your records."

"But, sir, *why*—?" I felt stunned. I couldn't believe this. It wasn't possible!

"In exchange, I expect you to mail to me by return mail all photocopies of the ship's log and of your report that you have in your possession. I wish to include those when we close her file. Now—" He put his hand in an inside pocket and brought out an envelope. "Here is a check for what we owe you."

I accepted the envelope mechanically.

"You'll also find in there your flight ticket to France. You leave on China Airlines tomorrow for Taipei, where you change planes. I want everybody off this ship by six o'clock tomorrow morning." He rose; I was too stunned to follow his example. I just sat there, staring at him in disbelief.

"Well," he said cheerfully, "I think that takes care of every-thing. Thank you very much, Commodore, and have a good flight. No, no! Don't get up, I know the way out."

After he had left, I didn't know what to do—finish reading Sylvia's letter, rush to the hospital to see Fransen? It *could* not be true!

I ran to the hospital.

3

The air in the hospital was blue with cigarette smoke. On the bedside table stood a bottle and a tumbler. Fransen was lying on the high bed in his shirt sleeves, fanning his face with his fedora. "Jesus," he said, "this ship is like a furnace without the air-conditioning. Well, how did it go?"

"Fransen, what the hell is going on? I mean, who—"

"Sit down, Harinxma. Calm down, make yourself at home. Want a snort? I smuggled it through Customs under my maternity dress."

"Fransen, listen to me! Chung has just told me the ship's going to be broken up! Did you know that?"

He peered at me through the smoke of the cigarette dangling from his mouth. "I told you that your missus had dropped the atom bomb. Didn't she tell you why in her letters?"

"I haven't read them yet! Tell me what happened! For God's sake, Fransen, it can't be true, they cannot break up this ship! She's the best tugboat I ever sailed, she's—"

"Harinxma," he said with an authority he had never used on me before, "take it easy, man! You're as tight as a drum. Here, have a swig. Either that, or grab a fistful of Valium from your medicine cupboard."

"Why, for God's sake?" I cried. "The ship is perfectly all right the way she is now! Why break her up? Why?"

"Because," he said, handing me the glass, "no one has any use for a barge with thirty thousand horsepower. It doesn't make sense, Harinxma. All the guy could use her for, the way she is now, would be pushing and pulling outside the harbor here, maybe do some tootling to Japan and back with a piece of junk. That's not an economical proposition. He'd be crazy to do it, and you were crazy to think he would. Go on, drink up."

Shaking, I took a swig and handed the glass back to him, tears in my eyes, suddenly overcome by grief. This hadn't been my intention at all, I had never thought in terms of killing her! My God, what had I done? "Fransen, please," I said, "explain it to me. Why—"

"Harinxma, I know," he interrupted kindly. "I don't blame you. I would have reacted the same way if she'd been mine. You can't sail a ship this far and go through what you went through with her without thinking she's the greatest bucket ever built. But you know as well as I do, if you look at it soberly: she's a killer, a monster, an abortion. Everybody, including yourself, will be better off when she's put down. So don't stand there as if you'd murdered your own mother. You did a good job, but the job is over, and you and everybody else were lucky to get here in one piece." He finished the glass, filled it up again and held it out to me. "Here, take a belt, cry your heart out and start packing. You had better be off this ship tomorrow morning by six hundred hours, boy. These men mean business."

"But when was it decided? What happened? What brought it about?"

"You'd better read her letters."

"The hell with her letters! Tell me!"

"Okay. It's simple, really. Your missus got that envelope with the log and your report and she opened it. Once she had read everything you had told her, she took the first plane to Holland, turned up at the head office in a taxi, marched straight into Jim Kwel's office despite those harpies in the anteroom, slammed your little contribution on his desk and accused him of trying to murder her husband and his crew, and threatened to publish your report in the newspapers. At least, that's what they say she said; I wasn't there. You know how it is, people like dolling things up a little to keep your attention. It seems Jim Kwel wanted to take the stuff away from her, but—so goes the fairytale—she hit him with her reticule, stuffed it all back inside and marched out. And there, in the corridor, who did she run into? One guess: our new director, little Miss Bastiaans. They took off to have lunch together, leaving little Jim going berserk in his office, steam screaming from his navel. At least, that's how the secretaries like to tell it."

I asked incredulously, "Don't tell me it was *she* who decided—? Not Miss Bastiaans!"

He lifted one hand in a gesture of blessing, raising his glass with the other. "I told you I warned the old man you'd never leave the ship unless somebody shot you. Well, leave it to a woman. As no one seemed prepared to shoot you, she shot the ship."

"But how—why—where did she get that power?! What possessed the old man to leave it all to her?"

"Ah, that's what happens to little boys who kick their grand-pappy out of his office and put him in a cupboard in the attic, behind a desk with a cracked top."

"But how could she decide all by herself—"

"Not she alone, of course. She and Jim and the architects, with a couple of whiz kids from our legal department. They decided that, things having gone this far, what with Mrs. Harinxma on the loose ready to pull the pin of the hand grenade, it would be best if somebody went to see Mr. Chung to remind him over a glass of

Alka-Seltzer that he too was up to his neck in this, that his little stooge had tried to scuttle the ship with forty people inside for the insurance money, and that nobody would look too good if this ever came out in the open. So, as far as I can see—mind you, I'm just a flunkey—it's a good bet that KITCO paid him some compensation, just to save his face, and that he decided to take the honest man's way out and destroy the evidence."

"But this is crazy! This must cost them—"

"Harinxma," he said soothingly, "let me give you a fact of life: when you're in their league, you know when to cut your losses. What they lose on the swings, they gain on the roundabouts. Chung has his fingers in many pies, that's what separates the men from the boys. Now, would you like to hear what little Bastiaans is planning to do?"

"Fransen, I think I—I would— I'll see you later."

"Don't take it too hard," he said as I headed for the door. "Remember, tomorrow, six hundred hours. If you can't sleep, I'm staying at a little hotel in town called Singing Flowers, one of a chain Chung owns. Feel free to call me there."

I opened the door and was about to go down the corridor when he said behind me, "Harinxma, once more: watch your step. Little Bastiaans is fresh out of the woodwork, but already, compared to her, Mr. Chung is a pussycat. I thought I'd warn you."

"Why? What is it to me?"

"You never can tell. The lady is in town."

4

I desperately needed some time alone. I was still in a state of shock. It hadn't penetrated to me fully yet, but I knew that once I confronted the truth that with all my plotting and scheming I had contrived to kill my ship— I opened the door and found Number One waiting for me in the dayroom.

I was about to tell him to come back later; then I saw the expression on his face. He was in some sort of agony—had he been fired? Was Chung going to get his pound of flesh out of this defenseless young fool?

"And?" he asked, standing very still.

It took me a moment before I realized what he was asking me. "Don't worry, Number One, you've been saved by the bell. Things look better for you than you could have dared to hope, my friend. Tomorrow morning they're starting to break up this ship. All photocopies of the log and my report will be destroyed. You'll be able to start with a clean slate."

He stared at me, not believing. "But you spoke to Mr. Chung—"

"It's all over and done with, I tell you. Your fraudulent report will never be challenged, it's already forgotten. As Queen Elizabeth said to the nobleman banned from court after breaking wind in her presence, 'You may come back now, sir, your fart has been forgot.' "

He seemed about to burst into tears, and small wonder. All these weeks since I took him to the cleaners, he had been certain his life as a sailor was at an end. To my shame, I had omitted to tell him that I would never let that happen, that as mother hen I would defend to the death even the ugliest of my brood.

As I caught myself thinking that smug little phrase once again, I suddenly knew it wasn't the whole truth. I hadn't done what I had done, and not done, to save him alone. I had wanted to save my ship, keep her from being chained to the quay for years, rotting away, maybe never to sail again. That was why I had been so shattered by the news.

The poor sod did burst into tears. I put an arm around his shoulders and said, "Okay, okay now. Pull yourself together. But let it be a lesson. Never sign anything that distorts the facts, stick to the truth." I was a fine one to talk. I shooed him out.

"Will we—will we have Happy Hour . . . ?" He asked it as if it were a sacrament. Maybe it was.

"Of course we will." I closed the door on his anxious face.

Finally alone, I felt so tired that all I could do was drag myself to the bedroom, climb into my bunk and pass out.

At least, that's what I thought. Once I lay on my bed, my back to the room, I became aware of a small, familiar vibration. I put my hand on the wall beside me and felt what I felt the very first night on board, in Rotterdam: the vibration of the main generator deep down in the ship, the one of which Porks had been so proud when he showed it to me on my tour of inspection. I remembered lying like this, my mind a blank, my hand pressed against the wall, feeling that faint vibration, the living body of the ship, and this time I knew what the elusive memory had been that I had tried to recapture in vain at the time, just before drifting off into sleep. I looked at the hand on the wall, wrinkled, veined, marked by age spots, and saw it change into another hand, smooth, firm, young, pressed against the wall of the captain's bunk on my first *Isabel,* my first command, when for the first time I had knowingly touched a ship with a feeling of intimacy. I remembered the sounds: the lock of the communicating door rattling softly with the throbbing of the engine; the wardrobe creaking with the rolling of the ship; water sloshing in the cistern over the toilet. Overhead on the bridge, the steps of the mate coming and going. Down below, iron had clanked in the engine room; somewhere in the ship a man had been singing. How totally absurd it had seemed, that summer afternoon in 1942, that this world, this vibrant, living reality, should be in danger of being annihilated. She had seemed as immortal in her youth, her joyous life, as I was myself. I had tried to conjure up in my mind scenes of fire and death and destruction, the horrors of the Murmansk run I had been warned about; but they had had an unreality that made my awareness wander back to the sounds, the smells, the vibrancy of life, to the animal enjoyment of the warmth, the sun-drenched somnolence, the sensuous contentment of being part of a summer's day, a ship. For the first time I had felt as if I were part of her, as if we formed one body of which I was the center of awareness; all nerves and tendons and veins and viscera, reaching into the remotest corners, were concentrated in me. Without realizing it, that afternoon long ago, I had experienced for the first time in my life the never known and never suspected physical union between captain and ship, that most ancient mystical relationship between man and matter. Now, in the winter of my life, here I lay again. The hand was old, the ship was doomed. Without knowing it, we had shared the last voyage of our lives, the long voyage home.

And the grasshopper shall be a burden, and desire shall fail, because man goeth to his long home, and the mourners go about the streets.

Mourning for us both, our brief, star-crossed lives, I fell asleep.

[385]

5

"Commodore?"

I was dreaming of the *Isabel* leaving. I had just come to the bridge and looked at the sea ahead of us, a hazy expanse of still, gray water. I turned to see who had called me: it had been a woman's voice. There was no one on the bridge; I walked over to the wing and looked back at the quay we had just left behind. A small crowd of well-wishers stood there, waving; there were some handkerchiefs, there always were.

"Commodore!"

The voice sounded more urgent now. Then I saw Sparks come to the bridge; he said, "My wife just brought something I forgot. Can we stop, please? Please?" It was a ridiculous request, but this was going to be a long voyage. So I moved over to the engine telegraph; as I put my hand on it, I saw someone standing in the doorway from the bridge to the bedroom. I was lying on my bunk. I stared at the figure; in the last vestige of the dream, I thought, 'Death is not going to be a man standing in the doorway. It's going to be a beautiful young woman.'

"Sorry to wake you," the beautiful young woman said, "but my plane leaves in a few hours and you and I have things to discuss. Don't hurry, I'll be waiting for you in the lounge." She gave me a smile that lit up the room; only then did I realize who it was.

I got up, washed my face, wet my hair, combed it, straightened my crumpled short-sleeved shirt and my tutu shorts and went to face the beautiful young woman who Fransen had said was worse than Chung. Another phantasm from his demonic universe.

When I came in, she was sitting on the couch in the dayroom, scratching Louis' belly. Pete trumpeted and strutted in his cage, noisy with jealousy.

"He's charming," she said, looking up. "Where did you get him?"

"In Antwerp. He was brought on board in a basket of fruit."

"A basket of fruit?"

"A farewell gift from Mr. Chung. The grocer, or whatever he was, had two little girls, Louis must have been their pet. By the time I discovered him, it was too late to send him home. I suppose they've forgotten him by now. I hope so."

"You're going to take him with you?" She seemed totally relaxed, as if she had all the time in the world and I was her uncle and we were having tea at the Ritz.

"Can I offer you something?" I asked, heading for the icebox.

"Whatever you are having, Commodore."

"I'm afraid all I have is Dutch gin. But it's from the freezer."

"Thank you, that'll be fine." Well, she certainly knew her way around tugboats. I only would have to tell her that 'the lounge' was called 'dayroom' and she could be one of the boys.

I poured us each a dainty one and carried them carefully to the coffee table, trying not to splash; my hands were bad right now.

"You may have a problem importing him into Europe," she said, driving Louis to ecstasies with her delicate, persistent scratching. Soon I would have to cover Pete's cage with a towel; he began to sound like a burglar alarm. "You would have no problem in Curaçao."

Again she gave me the smile that had beguiled me when first we met in the hall of the head office in The Hague. I lifted my glass and said, "Cheers, Miss Bastiaans." We each took a nip and put our glasses down. I said, "All right, tell me."

She looked at me with an expression that I could only define as soulful, then said, "I must thank you for your very kind letter on the occasion of Mr. Arnold's passing. You were the only one who spoke from the heart."

"Well," I said uncomfortably, "I had known him for a long time. I just felt—well, I thought you would understand."

"It was quite mutual, Commodore. I appreciated what you said."

It all sounded sincere and spontaneous, yet there was something I couldn't put my finger on. But why should I? I might as well lean back and enjoy it. She looked ravishing, a beautiful hothouse flower which made the dayroom seem drab. "Tell me about Curaçao," I said.

She smiled. "I don't know how much Captain Fransen has told you, but after Mr. Arnold's death I was put in charge of a new branch of the company to be based in Willemstad. Mr. Jim will stay in The Hague, he'll have the more powerful and modern

[387]

ships; I have been asked to take charge of a small fleet of older ones, very modest, which would be put on station in the Caribbean and the Gulf during the hurricane season. There will also be some oil work to do, not as pressured as in the North Sea, so we can use the older boats despite the fact that they are less mobile and need a larger crew. The company will be called KITCO N.A., for Netherlands Antilles. Its headquarters will be in Willemstad, and I would like you to take charge as head of operations." Again she gave me one of those smiles that would melt a heart of ice.

"If you'll forgive me for being frank, Miss Bastiaans, I think that's a crazy idea."

"Your wife didn't think so."

This was getting serious. "You mean you discussed this with my wife?"

"Oh, yes, we had lunch that day in The Hague, you know. I mentioned this idea to her, just casually, and she said that if that was what you wanted, she wouldn't stand in your way. As a matter of fact, I think she rather liked the idea of a house with plenty of servants in the outskirts of that beautiful old city, lots of interesting people in town, plenty of social activity. And, of course, as any woman would, I think she'd enjoy seeing you realize your full potential, put to good use your experience of a lifetime with crews and ships." She smiled. "And owners."

I was wide awake now, and very much on my guard. "I can tell you here and now, Miss Bastiaans, that there's no question of my accepting. But why choose me?"

"Because," she said, "KITCO N.A. will be different from the parent company insofar as all ships will be manned by Chinese or Indonesian crews. It seems you have a particular affinity with the Chinese, especially with this crew, and your runners. So I went ahead and hired them all." She said it as if she had just bought herself a new handbag.

"You mean, you talked to them?"

"No, no, Mr. Chung will do that. He, by the way, has a small share in the company."

"Was that the price KITCO had to pay for his cooperation?"

She frowned. "I beg your pardon?"

"I'm sorry, it's none of my business. Well, I appreciate your confidence in me, but I'm through with the sea. For good, this time. I'm going home to spend the years that are left to me with my wife."

"But you would do so in Curaçao! I told you, I discussed it with her. She seemed very willing—"

"Miss Bastiaans, head of operations is the most exhausting job in the business. You don't want a man in his seventies for that."

"Mr. Arnold was ninety when he died. He told you, in my presence, that the seventies were the best years of a man's life." She sounded more like herself now, tough, determined and very ambitious. I remembered her curt gesture to the chauffeur after she had seen me into the limousine, outside the head office that first day. It had stuck in my memory because of its contrast with the charm for which I had fallen during the preceding hour.

"To be quite frank, Miss Bastiaans," I said, testing her, "I'm afraid I may be showing the first signs of Parkinson's Disease." I had been sitting with my hands clasped during our conversation; now I held them out.

Her blue eyes remained unmoved. She picked up her glass. "Mr. Arnold went blind and remained ahead of the competition for seven more years." But I knew that at that moment she gave me up as a lost cause. She finished her drink and put the glass back on the table. "Well, we have to be going." She rose. "I would have liked to have had lunch with you, but there won't be time. Instead, what I'm going to do is take you to a tailor and put you in some decent clothes. You cannot travel in what you are wearing now, your wife would never forgive me. You've lost a lot of weight, haven't you? Your dress uniform must be much too large."

"But I have a tailor on board, an oiler who—"

"Commodore, you're re-entering the real world and you're about to meet your wife. Mr. Chung called the man for me. I was promised it could be done before you leave for Taipei, where I gather you'll be spending the night. Let's go." She opened the door.

"Miss Bastiaans," I said, with a feeling of tenderness at all this dazzling efficiency, "I'm sorry I can't join you in your new venture, but I wish you luck."

"What has that got to do with traveling in acceptable clothes, Commodore? I want your wife to recognize you when you come out of the airplane."

"With a rat in my flight bag and a canary in a cage."

That got her. "No!" she cried, showing true emotion for the first time. "You're not going to lock that poor animal in a *flight bag?!* That'll kill him!"

"Miss Bastiaans, he survived being locked up in a fruit basket for a night, and after that in a box of oranges for more than twenty-four hours. He'll survive. And I'm grateful for your kind offer, but I cannot go to see a tailor. I have too much to do on board this ship before we leave."

"But the ship is about to be broken up! What is there for you to do, except pack?"

It was comforting to know that owners remained owners, whatever their gender. "There are people on board, Miss Bastiaans. I cannot walk out on them just like that. We've just spent six and a half months together."

Suddenly she gave me a quick, fleeting view of her insecurity, deep down, behind those hard blue eyes. "It isn't just for your know-how that I need you, Commodore. I've always been guided and protected by the wisdom of someone much older than myself."

Pity it hadn't been a fleeting view of her secret insecurity. It had been manipulation worthy of old Kwel. She was a chip off the old block. "There's not much wisdom I have to give you, Miss Bastiaans," I said, "except, maybe, don't try to become one of the boys. When the jokes start, go and play Chopin. In memory of Arnold Kwel and me."

"That was a pompous remark, Commodore," she said. "But you are forgiven."

"Thank you," I said.

6

Dear Dad,

you must have heard the news by now. Mother was terrific; for the first time I could believe that during the war she had been a Leading Wren. She rang me very late, I was already in bed, and told me to park the kids for the day, meet the KLM plane from Nice the next morning and go with her to The

Hague. I asked what had happened, what was going on; she said, 'They're trying to kill your father and I'm going to put a stop to it. Now go back to sleep.' You can imagine! I sat there worrying my head off. What on earth could be the matter? I didn't sleep much the rest of the night, I can tell you. The next morning I went to meet her at the airport; Francine, my neighbor, took care of the kids. Mother came through Customs with a briefcase and a small carry-all, looking determined. We had breakfast at the airport and she told me she had your report and the log, with full descriptions of an explosion on board the Isabel and the hurricane, and how both Kwel and the Chinese wanted the ship to be lost. I sat there, gaping at her, feeling we were helpless in the face of a monolith of power that would not even be aware of our presence; but she said, 'And now we go to The Hague!' She took a taxi, something I've never known her to do for such a long distance. During the drive we said nothing. I did not know what to say, I was just worried sick. But there was about her something so convincing, so certain of her own power, that all I could do was tag along. I wanted to go with her into the office when we arrived, but she told me to wait; so I sat in the hall looking at shipping magazines for nearly two hours. In the end I was going frantic, I thought they had done something to her—kidnapped her, I don't know. I was just about to take the elevator to find out where she was when she came rattling down in that little iron cage with a middle-aged woman who looked like a doctor: very nice, but professionally so. 'Come, Helen,' Mother said, 'join us for lunch. This is Miss Bastiaans, one of the directors.'

And so we went and had lunch. I could hardly eat a thing, I just sat there sneaking looks at this Miss Bastiaans, wondering what had happened in the office; then the woman started to talk about a new branch of the company in the Caribbean for which they needed an experienced tugboat captain as head of operations, someone who had had the total confidence of the late Mr. Arnold. How would Mother like to move to Willemstad, Curaçao?

My mouth fell open, but Mother took it in her stride. 'How interesting,' she said. 'Tell me more.' So the woman told her about a free house with lots of servants, car, lovely climate, a great fulfillment for her husband in his later years. Mother said,

'I think it's a lovely idea. If that is what my husband wants, I'll be the last one to stop him.'

I didn't know if she meant it, she wouldn't tell me afterward. She said she did, but I have a feeling that she absolutely despises the idea. Oh, Daddy, you're not going to move to Curaçao, are you? I don't want to stop you if that is what you'd like to do, but I had so hoped we would have some time together now. I have believed in my own letters, I'm afraid. You must forgive me if I used, not you, but the ideal of you to help me through some dark, sad times. You did, you know, you really did.

I have to go now, here come the kids.

Love, love, love—Helen

7

Dear Martinus,

As I told you, I went to see Jim Kwel and the Bastiaans girl, who now seems to be one of the directors. There was a confrontation; in the end they said they would try to work out things to my satisfaction, could I give them twenty-four hours before going public with the log and the report? I said I would, but that I was staying with my daughter and would be back at the same time next day to discuss whatever they might be planning. Young Kwel was rather offensive at times; the girl as cool as a cucumber. It is obvious that, whatever may happen to the company, Jim Kwel is going to be eaten alive. I wondered what her hold on the old man had been, other than the obvious one; for a ninety-three-year-old stone-hearted cardsharp like him to leave all his shares to his secretary could not be just senile infatuation. Maybe it was revenge; if so, it would be the old rascal's last grand slam.

We were taken out to lunch, Helen and I, by this young lady. Over a sole meunière and a bottle of Spätlese, she told me about a new branch of the company in Curaçao and how she would love to have you join her there. I was noncommittal, but if you want to know my instant reaction: don't you dare!

I've had forty years of that, Martinus. Surely the time has come for you to at last be old. Accept it, love. There are so

*many things we can do if we want to; but all I really want is to
spend those years with you in peace and intimacy, not rushing
about. No more pressures, no more telephone calls from ra-
pacious owners, no more antacids at midnight, no more secret
boozing to calm your nerves, no more folly, folly! I'd go with
you, of course I would, if you insisted; but I think it would be a
terrible waste of something essential, some soul we shared
which to me was of unutterable sweetness. I love you, you
stubborn, devious old bastard! I want you home. Héloïse sends
barks.*

Love,
Sylvia

8

Charlie S. Chung Enterprises,
Brussels and Taipei
Dear Commodore Harinxma:
*Please find enclosed your flight ticket and the bill for per-
sonal telephone calls made by you from the* Isabel Kwel *between Antwerp and the Cape Verde Islands. All calls are listed
in detail; the sum total amounts to 786.50 US$. We look for-
ward to your remittance.*

Yours sincerely,
Unreadable, Secretary to Mr. Chung

*P.S. As Mr. Chung may have told you in person, you are
expected to vacate the ship by 6 A.M. tomorrow morning, when demolition will commence.*

9

Happy Hour that afternoon would have been a strained affair but
for Harakiri. Marco One's and Mate Number Two's wives were on
board and were invited to join us; Chief Liu's three daughters and
four sons also turned up, locking out the clamor of children as

they shut the door. I gathered there were grandchildren, and that Mrs. Liu had been detailed to look after them.

Harakiri had had the foresight to bribe someone ashore and harvest six packs of Taiwanese beer called Kwak; maybe the mandur and his colleagues had lifted them from some warehouse. Anyhow, we all drank beer; even the ladies sipped delicately, little fingers in the air. Harakiri handed around more cans, saying, "Let's polish 'em off, folks, plenty more where these came from. Well, here's mud in your eye: Chief, Mate, Mate, Marco, Marco, Chief One, Chief Two, Ome Tinus! Ladies, here's to no more snot on the carpet. Brotherhood and equality to all!" He must have been drinking before he arrived, because there was no stopping him. He told his audience about the yacht, about life in two aluminum trailers on top of a dock, the murals on board the liner, which I had not seen, but which I could imagine when he said that his crew had spruced them up in their spare time during the crossing. He also told about the diaries he had found on board the *Queen of Persia,* about the oval bed, the mirrors in the ceiling, and how the only thing overlooked by whoever had picked the ship clean was a tiny book he had found in a bedside drawer called *Squirrel Nutkin* with lovely illustrations. "So you see, life is full of surprises. You never know about people, do you? Here you had a bed built for sin, nudes complete down to the pink, mirrors reflecting six times what went on in that bed, and what did I find? That somebody had been lying there reading a tiny book called *Squirrel Nutkin* by a woman called Potter."

I thought the time had come to break this up—not an easy thing to do with Harakiri going full blast. Luckily, fate came to my aid in the person of a roly-poly Chinese gentleman who entered with beaming apologies, produced a note pad and rolled-up tape measure and asked, "Excuse. Who of you be Condor Eczema?" Harakiri pointed at me and said, "Who do you think, bozo? There's only one of us dripping with gold."

The gentleman bowed and handed me a little note which read, *Allow me this for old times' sake, Eleanor B.* "Please be upstanding," he said, bowing; he must have been looking at *Rumpole of the Bailey* on Taiwanese TV.

I complied; he began to measure my neck, my chest, the length of my arms from the pits, hips—the audience became restless. When he proceeded to the in-seam, the ladies rose and bowed and I bowed in return, while the gentleman, on his knees, measured my underwater part. In no time at all, everyone was gone; then the gentleman left too, after saying, "Will be at plane tomorrow, Condor."

Harakiri asked, "Now that there's just the two of us, how about cracking another six-pack? And do you mind if I sleep on your couch here tonight? I'm sick at heart, leaving the captain's suite on the old girl. I sort of want it to sneak up on me, if you see what I mean."

I thought of telling him that the hospital was available, but gave in. "You're welcome," I said. "You'll have to excuse me, I have some packing to do. But go ahead and help yourself to anything you need."

I went to the bedroom to pack my suitcase and hold-all. Harakiri took me at my word and helped himself; I heard the icebox open and close several times. When I came back to the dayroom, I was surprised to find he was still upstanding. He joined me for the evening meal; together we went down the empty corridor of the officers' quarters, from which everyone seemed to have vanished, leaving the doors open with views of unmade beds. The desolation of a ship arriving, everybody eager to shake her dust, was getting to me until I saw the messroom. Not only was it as full as always, but more so. There was no watch on deck, and the runners with their mandur had joined us, not mingling with the rest but at a separate table, scowling. Harakiri put a stop to that with the insouciance of inebriation, saying, "Come on, boys, no shit. Join the crowd. Bring the beer."

The mandur rose, his crew followed suit, and they joined the main table after Ma Chang's tribe had shuffled down the benches to make room for them. The mandur produced more six-packs from somewhere, as did other members of his Mafia family; when everyone had an opened can in hand, Harakiri tried to lead us in song by bursting into raucous bawling, pounding time with his fist on the table, setting bowls and chopsticks jumping. The mandur and two of the runners, who obviously had seen him like this before, picked him up and carried him off, singing, conducting with his beer can.

There were no speeches at the end of the meal, but lots of grins, and no toasts except for "Woo, Omi!" from Wellesley, followed by his own manic laughter. It seemed a comfort of sorts to realize that even among prehistoric tribes on remote little Chinese islands there was sure to be one crashing bore.

When finally I got back to my dayroom, Harakiri was snoring on the couch. Louis jumped me, and Pete drew his beak back and forth across the bars of his cage with a harplike sound. I fed him, covered the cage with a towel, went to my bedroom and found that I had packed my pajamas. But it was stiflingly hot in the small, closed-in space, so I lay down on top of my bunk in my shorts, realized I should have called Sylvia, and fell asleep.

10

At dead of night I suddenly found myself wide awake, staring at the ceiling, feeling tearful. I fled into the dayroom. Harakiri lay sprawled on the couch, open-mouthed, snoring like Cheyne-Stokes breathing, so I opened the door to the corridor.

The ship was silent. It felt as if there were not a soul left on board: a feeling of finality and desolation. Well, I might as well face it, I could either make my farewell rounds or go back to bed and take a sleeping pill. Someone had to say goodbye to her, it might as well be me. So I went to the bedroom, put on my short-sleeved shirt with shoulder tabs, shorts, sandals and cap, and started my farewell tour.

I walked down the empty corridor, past dark cabins with half-open doors, down the companionway to the boat deck, the one to the main deck, the one to the 'tween deck, finally the one to the tank top, exactly as I had done that first night in Rotterdam when everything had been new. Starting with the winch room, I walked past storerooms, cabins, recreation room, gym, saying goodbye to it all without undue emotion other than occasionally patting a handrail or touching a bulkhead. Goodbye, old girl. Goodbye.

I came apart in the most unlikely place: the shower room with its row of toilets. Here I and my crew had jostled each other stark naked under the rainstorm of the shower while yellow squatters sang 'I gave you ring, you gave me finger' to a tune from ancient China.

I had no idea why this spot made me suddenly turn around, run down the corridor, up the companionway to the next deck, as if Death were at my heels.

[396]

As I came stumbling up the steps, I saw right opposite me the entrance to the galley; at the table inside sat a motionless figure —Ma Chang. She and I must be the only ones awake on board. She beckoned me without a word; I stepped inside.

The breakfast dishes had been lined up on the shelf, her early-morning concoctions were sputtering and gurgling in pots on the range. Yet the place had a barren look; the spices that had dangled from the ceiling were gone, the baskets of mushrooms like severed ears were gone; she must have been sitting there, alone in the emptiness, listening to the silence, a teacup in front of her.

She pointed at a stool; I sat down at the table. Then she reached up and took another teacup from the shelf, reached down and produced a curiously shaped bottle without label from under the table. With little glugs, loud in the silence, she filled both cups, pushed one across to me, raised hers and stared at me without a smile.

I followed her example, raised my teacup; when she drank, I drank. It nearly blasted me off my stool. Never before in my life had I drunk anything remotely like it. With most of it still in my mouth, I gazed at her, wide-eyed with disbelief, and watched her swallow the poison. She put the empty cup in front of her, smacking her lips.

I could hardly spit it out, so I swallowed it. I cannot describe the sensation; it was as if my soul and body were separated. She and I were sitting opposite one another in some other dimension beyond space, she solemnly trying to blow us up. For she went on pouring the stuff, sipping it, and lifting her cup without a smile, forcing me to do the same. There came a moment when it all flowed together: gratitude, sorrow, friendship, wordless understanding, the incredible richness of life. I was overcome by a feeling of gratitude, and suddenly wanted to give her something, a token, however small, that would somehow embody it all. But I had nothing on me, and I knew that if I were to rise and leave in search of something, I might never make it back. Then, on an impulse, I took one shoulder tab with commodore's gold off my shirt and held it out to her.

Without looking at it, she picked it up, put it in a pocket of her smock and stared at me. I had the feeling my gesture had been misunderstood, that I had failed to express the emotion that inspired it. I took off the other shoulder tab and put it on the table too. Again, she didn't even look at it, but picked it up, put it in her pocket and stared at me again. Then her hand went into the other pocket and brought out a small object which she put in front of me. It was her pendulum.

I looked up, not believing. She stared at me without a smile, then shook her head: yes, that was her present to me. I looked at it again; it was just a bead on a bit of string, but it was her symbol of power. Well, so were my shoulder tabs. I picked it up, put it in the breast pocket of my shirt and matched her, stare for stare.

She filled the cups once more; I knew this was the zero in the count-down, but it seemed unthinkable for me to refuse it. She drank hers in small, sensuous slurpings, I downed mine in one go. Nothing happened. When I opened my eyes, we were still sitting at our table, alone in the universe, staring at each other with total understanding. Or misunderstanding; it no longer seemed to matter.

She bowed. I bowed. I rose slowly to my feet and floated back to bed.

11

I was awakened by a voice calling, "Harinxma! Harinxma, wake up, man!"

Groaning, I opened my eyes and saw it was Fransen, fully dressed. "Get up!" he urged, shaking me. "You have to be off this ship in ten minutes! The wrecking crew is here, the funeral service is already in progress on the dockside. Hurry up!"

"Funeral service?" My tongue felt as if it had grown hair overnight.

"Come on, come on! Here's your shorts."

"Where's Harakiri?" I asked, closing my eyes because of transparent worms wriggling in front of them.

"He's out there already. Everybody's lined up for the funeral service. Come on, man! What's the matter with you?"

I dressed, unstable on my feet as if the ship were rolling, put on my short-sleeved shirt, wondered what had happened to the shoulder tabs, then I remembered. My God, what had the woman been drinking? Was this what the Chinese did to themselves when they wanted a lift? I went to the dayroom.

Fransen stared at me. "No!" he cried, as if I were a cat bringing in a dead bird. "You can't go out like that! For Chrissakes, man, you're the commodore! You look like—" Words failed him. "Don't you give a damn that you're leaving your ship for good? That she's going to be broken up? There's a Chinese religious service going on outside, goddammit! Put on your number-one uniform!"

"You handed me the shorts yourself," I said, wondering what the worms were.

"Get changed!"

"Where's Louis?"

"Oh, God," he moaned, slumping down on the couch. "Not that."

"What?"

"You're drunk."

"Don't talk nonsense. I took a sleeping pill last night, that's all."

But I went back to the bedroom wondering if he was right. When I caught sight of myself in the mirror, I looked ten years older, but perfectly sober. A stubborn, devious old bastard seen through a glassful of worms darkly. I wondered if my friend Ma Chang had intended her potion to do this to me: I knew I was leaving my ship forever, I knew she was about to be broken up, and I didn't give a damn.

I should go and find Louis, but I didn't want to run into Fransen's buzz saw again, so I dressed in my number-one uniform. It looked ludicrous, and it was going to be too hot later in the day. The jacket hung around me in folds, the sleeves seemed longer than when I had last seen them, the ribbons commemorating forgotten sea battles added a final touch of drollery.

I found Louis hiding behind the books on the shelf; it took some persuasion before he would let himself be zipped into the flight bag, despite the apples and the piece of bread soaked in Kirschwasser I put in there.

"Let's have a look at you," Fransen said.

I modeled for him.

"All right, it'll do, let's go."

"Don't be ridiculous," I said.

"Harinxma!" he pleaded. This time I ignored him. I covered Pete's cage with a towel and took it off the hook. I fetched my suitcase and my hold-all from the bedroom.

"Is that it?" Fransen asked. "What can I carry? You *must* hurry, man!"

"You take my carry-all and my suitcase. I'll take the animals. Lead on, Macduff."

"Jesus," he said and opened the door.

When we came out on deck, I saw that the yard was bright with floodlights and the blinding pinpoints of welding. The giant skeletons across the basin were silhouetted against a skyline yellow with the dawn. At the foot of the gangway the staff, the crew and Harakiri and his runners were lined up, watching a Chinese priest dressed in unfamiliar robes make sweeping gestures with an incense burner over the gangway, intoning a chant. He stood aside to let us pass; after we had stepped off the gangway, he put lighted candles on it and began to swing his incense burner again. Fransen and I joined the staff and watched the ceremony. To one side, a group of workmen in blue coveralls and welding helmets were waiting, ready for action. I wondered why I was so unmoved. The whole thing had an unearthly quality; maybe I was just dreaming this and Ma Chang and I were still sitting opposite one another at the table, alone in the universe.

Fransen nudged me and whispered, "Okay, that's that. Now say goodbye to them. Go on! Go down the line, Harinxma!"

I put the cage down, but held on to the flight bag, as I could feel Louis wriggling inside it. The Kirschwasser had not yet taken effect; until it did and he calmed down, I was not going to let the bag out of my sight. I started with the staff, and shook hands with the officers that were left: Number One, Chief Liu, Engineer Number Two, Marco One; then Bryn Mawr, little Whittier, Yale, Loyola, Nebraska, Swarthmore, Notre Dame—all those who had wandered into my dayroom, flushed the toilet, touched my arm and said 'Omi' before wandering off again. The last in the row was Wellesley, who pumped my hand long and hard and whispered, "Woo . . ."

I went down the line of oilers: Carleton, the donkey man, Purdue, Harvard, Brown, Dartmouth; when I shook Tulane by the hand, I felt something hard being pressed into my palm. I looked at it; it was a brass name plate, like the ones on the doors of the officers' cabins, the galley, the messroom; in the same letters as on the others, this one said, on two lines: KOMM ODOR.

"Him make," a voice whispered beside me. "Him make himself, for *you*." It was Hopla, bright eyes beaming. "He not read, me tell him how to spell: Co'dore. For your door at home, him make. Him and me."

I looked at the little plate and its bizarre legend. It was beautifully made; he must have spent hours on it, filing, scraping, tapping on the workbench . . . For some reason, that did it. Suddenly I could take no more of this.

I shook him by the hand, said, "Thank you, Tulane, thank you very much, I'll use this always," and hurried on down the line of oilers to the runners, where I found myself facing the mandur. He took my hand, bared his stainless-steel teeth and said, "Sea Person."

"Godspeed, Mandur," I said, "happy sailing." Finally, I got to Ma Chang, the last in line. She stared up at me poker-faced; on her shoulders were my commodore's tabs. "Ma Chang," I asked, "when did you sew those on? How did you find the strength after last night?"

"Translate?" Hopla chirped by my side.

"Not necessary," I said, "she understands."

I wondered if I should bring out her pendulum and wear it in my buttonhole, but I didn't have it on me; it was still in the breast pocket of my short-sleeved shirt. I bowed to her, she pulled my head down and kissed me on both cheeks. The only response I could think of was to kiss hers; they were bristly.

"Godspeed, Ma Chang."

"Woo poos," she said.

I went back to where Fransen and Harakiri were waiting and picked up the cage. Harakiri took my luggage.

As I walked away, a whistle sounded behind me; I heard the gangway rumble.

It was a long walk to the gate. Before leaving the quayside, I turned to look back. A crane was swinging something off the ship onto the dock: the lifebelt locker.

"Come on, Harinxma," Fransen said, putting his arm around my shoulders, "let it be."

He took me through the gate to where a taxi was waiting.

12

We were about to pass through Security at Kao Hsiung airport when the Chinese tailor barred my way, bowing, to hand me a large cardboard box; Fransen took it. "Many happy return, Condor," he said, bowing.

I bowed back; then I heard Fransen say, "Come on, Harinxma, give me that rat, you carry the box."

I didn't want to be parted from Louis, so I said, "No, I want to hang on to him."

"Harinxma," Fransen said patiently, "if you send that animal through the X-ray machine, he'll be cooked. And if you hand that bag to the meter maid on the other side for inspection, she'll scream the place down when she opens it. I have a diplomatic passport, I'll take him through without inspection."

So he did; I passed through the metal-detector gate with Pete in his cage; Fransen flashed a piece of paper full of stamps and sauntered past with Louis in the bag.

In Taipei, Harakiri took the KLM plane to Amsterdam that same night. Fransen and I stayed in adjoining rooms in a motel at the airport; the next morning he was to leave for Curaçao and I for France.

That evening, in my room, Fransen lay down on my bed, cracked a bottle of Taiwanese Scotch called Beethoven and watched me feed Pete with Louis on my shoulder. "I'll take your rat through Security again tomorrow morning," he said.

"I didn't know you had a diplomatic passport."

"Passport, hell. Just a sheet of paper saying I'm the Netherlands consul in Harveysville, South Africa."

"Where is that? Never heard of a place called Harveysville."

"Must be where the wallbangers come from. I got it from an understanding person who took pity on me having to stand in line in airports all my life."

Louis, who had been restless from the moment he was let out of the bag, jumped Fransen just as he was taking his first swig from Beethoven's fifth. "Christ!" he yelled, and had a coughing fit. Louis, squealing, leaped to the floor and ran to pick up the seeds tossed out by Pete.

Coughing, Fransen said, "By the way—*cough cough*—don't worry about getting that little creep through—*cough cough*—

through French Customs. I've got a health certificate for him—
cough—and for the bird."

"You did? That was nice of you! Where did you get it? When?"

"From a little Chink who sells stamped documents. Any document, any stamp. Must have been the most innocent document he ever forged, he let me have it for a drink with the singing flowers." He raised the bottle. "Well, here's to the pig. God rest her oinking soul." He took another swig, rubbed the neck of the bottle dry with his hand and asked casually, "Are you going to Curaçao with little Eleanor, or are you going to be a good boy and stay home?"

"What ships has she got so far, do you know?"

"As far as Jim Kwel's concerned, only those that were about to be junked, like the *Fiona,* leaving him all the good ones, especially the pig's little sister on the stocks. What he doesn't realize is that she's taken all the topnotch captains along with them—Beast Rufus for one. But then, Jim doesn't believe in captains, he believes in ships. He's sure that before the decade is over they'll be sailed by robots."

"Who's getting my crew and runners, do you know?"

"Beast Rufus, I gather. Why? Are you worried about them? Don't be, Harinxma. Beast Rufus may not sound like you, or look like you, or think like you, but he's just the same as you are when it comes to his crew. You must stop thinking that after God made you, he broke the mold. If he did, then where's your immortality?"

I stared at him as he lay there, bottle raised, adam's apple bobbing: a skinny, tired, disreputable man; it was the last thing I would have expected him to say.

"What do you mean by that?"

He waved it away. "Oh, just some cheap wisdom out of a bottle. What did that Chinese oiler give you on the dockside? A keepsake?"

I took the brass plaque from my pocket and showed it to him. He took it, turned it over and said, "German, is it? 'KOMM, ODOR.' One guess what door your grandchildren will want you to put it on, back home. They're going to love it."

I thought it was time to work him out of the room; I should call Sylvia, in France it was eight o'clock in the morning. "I'd like to place a call to my wife now, if you don't mind."

"Righto. See you tomorrow, bright and early." He got off the bed. "Aren't you going to try on the new suit Auntie Eleanor got you?"

"Tomorrow morning. Good night."

"Good night, happy dreams." He opened the connecting door. "Here—want this?" He held out the bottle to me.

"No thank you."

"Then be a friend and pour it down the drain for me, will you? A man should know when to stop." Before closing the door behind him, he added, "That goes for you too, old buddy."

"I know," I said.

13

While waiting for my call to France to go through, I lay down on the bed and must have dozed off with the little brass plaque in my hand. I found myself running down a dark alley, beset by a primeval terror. I was myself and yet saw myself—part of me was the terrified runner and part the observer. I couldn't understand why I ran panting, choking with terror, down that long, dark alley. Then I discovered it was not a road but a narrow passage; I could feel rough walls on either side of me. It was getting narrower and narrower. I stumbled and stood still, beset by the desperate urge to turn around and run back; then I discerned a pinpoint of light at the end. I started to run; before I knew it, I ran into a door; the small slot of light was a keyhole. I groped for the knob or the handle, but there was none. A voice said behind me, 'There was a door, but I found no key.' Key! I needed a key. I searched my pockets and found they were empty. The voice behind me said, 'There was the veil through which I might not see.' As I stood there in a panic, wondering what to do next, I heard a soft musical sound that I knew but could not recognize. It sounded like a child tapping on a toy xylophone, three notes close together on the scale, repeated over and over again. I opened my eyes, looked down at my hand and thought, 'There you go, getting into a panic while all the time you had the key in your hand.' Then I recognized the three musical sounds. It was Pete hopping from perch to perch in his cage. What I had in my hand was the brass plate Tulane had made me.

As the dream drew away, I remembered the words the voice had spoken. It was a stanza from Captain Cho's little red book.

Where would Cho be now? Would he be one of those splashing in that dark, misty sea in their lifebelts, like Bullfrog? One of the voices Haversma had heard crying for help in the darkness?

But I had known the real voices. I had heard them from the bridge of the old *Isabel* when she sailed as a rescue ship. 'Help . . . Help . . .' I could hear them now. I could see their mouths, red and open in their oil-black faces. I could see them slapping the sea in a desperate effort to catch our attention. 'Help . . . Help . . .' The vividness of the images, the sounds, was unbearable. It had been a nightmarish experience, to be forgotten at all costs, with prayers for delivery from the evil that man had done to man. I had tried to forget them. I would forget them now.

I closed my eyes, waiting for Sylvia to respond to my call. I drifted off again, not into a dream but a fantasy. With Pete hopping musically from perch to perch in the background, I opened that door with the brass plate and found myself on the bridge of my *Isabel*, not as she had become after the explosion but the way B.B. and his fellow architects had seen her before she was born: a beautiful, majestic ship, the biggest and most powerful rescue ship that had ever been. With her electronic ears and eyes high up in her Paradise tree, all those esoteric dish antennas and reflectors and scanners, she could pick up a cry for help a thousand miles away and pinpoint its position. I walked to the for'ard windows and looked at the sea. We were sailing in a mist; I only caught a glint of the surface through the swirls of fog rising like smoke from the water. There sounded a thin, wailing cry, far away, which we picked up with our Paradise tree and heard magnified from the speaker on the bridge. BULLFROG BULLFROG THIS IS BULLY WHERE AM I BOYS PLEASE GODDAMMIT HELP ME WHERE AM I— The voice of my mate at the radar scanner said, 'Another one, Skipper, at eleven o'clock.'

We found him, lowered the boat and brought him in. Beyond him there were others in lifebelts, rafts, whole lifeboats lost in the mist, calling. And when our decks were crowded with all the men we had been unable to save before, whose young lives were strewn about the icy wastes of the Arctic Ocean in the wake of the convoys to Russia, we headed for home. On the distant shore, people would be waiting: fathers, mothers, friends, brothers, wives, lovers, a crowd on the beach, gazing at the horizon. Then one of them would discern in that thin blue line of haze the first glint of the Paradise tree and cry, 'Here she comes!'

I lay there overcome by an inexpressible feeling of happiness, which made no sense. This was the end of my career, my life; by all standards, I should be steeped in sorrow and hopelessness. But, gazing out at the thin blue line of the horizon now ahead, I was filled with that strange happiness, a sense of fulfillment and anticipation, as if I were heading for the most exciting adventure of my life.

I heard a telephone ring. I must have fallen asleep again, for I reached out, took it off the hook and was about to say, 'Bridge. Harinxma,' when a girl said, *"Ne quittez pas! Je vous donne Cannes."*

Suddenly there was her voice, very close. "Martinus, is that you?"

"Yes, love," I said. "I'm in."

About the Author

JAN DE HARTOG, born in Haarlem, Holland, the second son of a Calvinist minister and a Quaker mother, ran off to sea at the age of ten. At sixteen he entered Amsterdam Naval College, ending up as a junior mate in the Dutch oceangoing tugboat service. When war broke out, in 1940, and Holland was occupied by the Nazis, de Hartog was trapped in his native country. During this time he wrote and published his first major novel, *Holland's Glory*, which became an instant and historic bestseller and a symbol of the Dutch Resistance; the German occupying forces banned the book in 1942, but it went on selling in large quantities in the underground market. When he escaped to London in 1943, he was appointed war correspondent for the Dutch merchant marine. There he gathered the material for his postwar novels *The Distant Shore* and *The Captain*.

In the late sixties de Hartog, himself a Quaker, undertook the ambitious project of a multivolume novel on the history of the Religious Society of Friends. *The Peaceable Kingdom* was the first book, followed by *The Lamb's War*.

De Hartog has written many plays, among which the most famous is *The Fourposter* (later turned into the musical *I Do! I Do!*), and several volumes of essays, the best known being *A Sailor's Life* (memories of life at sea before World War II) and *The Children* (a personal record for the benefit of the adoptive parents of Asian children).

Mr. and Mrs. de Hartog live in New Jersey.